I0653460

Run, Rima!

A novel by

Carol Pechler

Menlo Publishing Company

Menlo Park, California, USA

Cover location: Mt. Tamalpais, Marin County, California, USA. Photo by author.
Cover Runners: Wendy Newman, Suzana Seban, Cara Hanson, Yong Cho Haber

Copyright © 2013 Carol H. Pechler

All rights reserved.

ISBN: 978-0-9896154-0-2

Printed in the United States of America

Menlo Publishing Company

225 McKendry Drive, Menlo Park, California 94025

Menlo Publishing.net

DEDICATION

Runners who show me the way, especially those still
running in their late 70's and 80's, Helen Klein and Harriet
Anderson; Sam Roake and Jim Kauffold. In memory of
Joy Johnson who died at age 86 in her running shoes after
the New York Marathon in November 2013.

ACKNOWLEDGEMENTS

- Our writers' group, essential for our useful deadlines, and especially for supportive criticism: Kat, Lynn, Sandra, Judy, Mel, Stu. Betty Schneider and Ruth Shaffer, both, at 93, powerful models of optimism. Chris Witzel, for invaluable organization, formatting, and editing.

-Avenidas, Palo Alto's Senior Center, especially Judith Taksa Webb, for facilitating our meeting place.

-Editing: Miriam Hutchinson, Paula Jefferis Nilsen, Araceli Placido, Frances Reneau, Janice Rensch, Kt. St. Claire, Janet Werner, and more dear family and friends who shared experiences and time for editing.

-Lee Blevins, for formatting, designing, and first printing.

-DSE Running Club of San Francisco, founded 1964, still adding new members weekly, and supportive of every type of runner.

-Buck's Runners' Wednesday morning group.

-Buck's Restaurant in Woodside, accepting our rowdy group for breakfast every week after our run up in Huddart Park.

-TNT (Team in Training) of the Leukemia and Lymphoma Society of America, who trained me for my first three marathons.

-Dear friends Paula, Denise, and Arlene, who helped me start running; and

-Newer friends Judith, Wendy, Suzana, Carole, Gene, Vince, Jim, Pat, Sam, Bill, Mort (and others) who keep me going.

-My dear Henk, whose loving support includes editing, accompanying me to destination marathons, and who at home has a bathtub of hot water waiting for me as I return from those early morning runs.

PROLOGUE

She thought of the tropics she had left behind a few weeks earlier. *That long, long flight over the Pacific just one month ago. I looked out at the light blinking on the end of the wing, the maraming bituin [many stars] blinking overhead, very clear sky, no moon. Couldn't sleep, just looked out the window. Couldn't see that vast ocean down there, like I can't see the future. Had two big worries for the future, my dear Sofie's grades, and my diabetes. Oh yes, and a small worry, the knee. Doctor said "rest the knee." Other doctor said "change the diet, get exercise." Exercise! For 30 years now I've been just standing in my high school science classroom!*

Note to the reader: See the glossary in the back and the list of characters showing family relationships.

TABLE OF CONTENTS

PART I. WHY RUN?

1.1 America's Greatest Running Carnival
Sunday, May 20, 2007

Why no crowds? Rima wondered, looking around as she and three other shivering women rushed through quiet pre-dawn streets. Alongside their feet scurried a few crumpled papers, blown by a light wind that also pushed the San Francisco fog through their clothes. They saw only a few other people, most of them skimpily clad, all headed in the same direction. But when the four women rounded the corner from Mission Street, they gasped. Spear Street, several blocks long, was completely filled with a multitude of people, all standing quietly.

"You told me that 65,000 runners had registered for this race, but I had no idea! So many, but so quiet that we came upon them suddenly; and look, they pack several blocks!" exclaimed Rima. Her eyes stayed wide open in wonder, but with a shiver she crossed her arms to capture warmth from her somewhat-lumpy body inside her gray sweatshirt.

Having arrived just four weeks earlier from the tropical Philippines, this visiting grandmother knew that her 59-year-old body would take months to acclimate to the Bay Area weather and especially to San Francisco's chilly fog.

And what am I doing here anyway? I'm a newcomer to the country and cold, a newcomer to running. I'm not a runner, anyway. I don't belong here. All these people probably know what they're doing... They look like they're experienced. She retrieved her right hand from her left armpit to pull her sweatshirt hood over her short, nearly black, but graying, hair.

On this Sunday, May 20, 2007, and now with two hours before the start of San Francisco's 96th Bay to Breakers 12K (kilometers), each woman anticipated her big experience ahead—especially the two newcomers to this event, Rima and her 17-year-old granddaughter, Sofie.

Their more experienced friends had invited them, 54-year old Gloria and her 17-year-old daughter Tiffany. The two girls had met in club soccer three years earlier and had become close friends.

Rima's new friend Gloria responded, "If we could see around the corner on Howard Street, it's just as crowded, and the elite runners are up front at the start line. They've got a chance for the purse, and it's big, almost $100,000 in total." Gloria had convinced Rima to share this "major San Francisco experience, something to write home about."

Gloria had started running 10 years earlier "to get toned," and she modeled success. Below her trim, smoothly fitting emerald-green microfiber running shirt and shorts, her muscular legs, with their slightly leathery tan, appeared quite capable of the race ahead. Her fine features and her caramel-colored, chic bob hairstyle, lightly frosted in light champagne, showed that she intended to stay "with it" for a long time. Gloria was one of those older women who, in her younger, glamorous days, had grown accustomed to creating excited tension in social settings. While men wanted to move closer, maybe even hoping to talk with her, young women appeared suspicious that she might lure their men away. In later years, and past her femme fatale appearance, Gloria had successfully turned other women's suspicions into appreciation for her solid work as PTA president. When she took on endurance running at age 44, late for becoming an athlete, she had shown, even in public, that she was willing to do something that she wasn't particularly good at. She had gotten accustomed to no longer being the best-looking woman in the room, and she transferred this concession to her new interest, running. Recently, she had focused her leadership skills on helping other runners, including today's small group. Not that she was universally appreciated for her active care. Her daughter Tiffany grumbled that her mother wanted her to be more like Tiffany's friend Sofie, a faster and more passionate runner.

Gloria saw her new "project," Rima, to be a kindred spirit: a beauty in the past, perhaps inciting jealousy in other woman, and now capable of showing that although she's not in front anymore, she still has plenty of energy.

"Wow," said Sofie, looking around at the multitude, and then up to the tall buildings. "Look, spectators already out on their balconies!" Sofie had lived her whole life on the peninsula of the San Francisco Bay Area, and like her grandmother, this was her first experience of the famed Bay to Breakers race. *Coach Ramirez told me I'm fast; I might even place in my age group, but how'm I ever gonna get through this crowd?*

"Yep, world's largest foot race, and you'll see that San Francisco knows how to make it a moving carnival." Gloria was delighted to lead these two newcomers to this adventure, and besides, she hoped that Sofie, with her potential for serious running, would have a good influence on her own somewhat apathetic daughter.

Rima wondered how so many people could be so quiet. Some waited in long lines before the wall of Porta-Potties that lined the sidewalk, but most people stood, packed tightly in the street, quietly waiting, and occasionally stretching one leg and then the other. Looking up at the sky, Rima said, "That blanket of fog up there and the people down here muffle even the soft talking, like the street is covered in a thick carpet." Sofie followed her gaze upward. "Wow, we're in a canyon between skyscrapers— look at that one under construction," she pointed. "'60 stories,' the sign says."

Tiffany added, "Hey, look! We can see the crowd mirrored in those windows up there. Can you see us in the reflection?"

"No, but why, with two whole hours before the start, are so many here already?" asked Sofie.

Gloria laughed. "Because we wanted to get parking spots, and find our place to wait, and now of course we're all so anxious to start. And, besides, we want to avoid the drunks and the runners with baby strollers; they always show up later, so they'll be behind us."

"Yuck."

Gloria added, "Yeah, by starting early, we'll never have to see them."

"It's so quiet, so packed, but they're playing Frisbee with tortillas!" said Sofie. "Look!"

Hundreds of raw corn tortillas sailed silently over the thousands of heads, forming little arcs. An arm reached above the heads; a tortilla was re-tossed. At the end of the arc, another arm reached up to catch it. And here and there large orange balls painted with the letters "ING" for the sponsoring Dutch bank formed slightly larger arcs; the balls were also kept in the air by the otherwise still people waiting to run.

"You'll want to guard your head from them," Gloria said. She and Tiffany were familiar with this tradition of the Bay to Breakers, though they didn't bring their own package of fresh, uncooked tortillas to "share."

"Smell the ones people didn't catch; they're ground into the asphalt," sniffed Tiffany, looking down. Our four runners shuffled their way into the crowd, and others closed in behind them. They had become part of the multitude.

Looking down in the midst of their tight squeeze, Rima saw running shoes all around, most of them dirty white. Above the shoes, most legs were bare, and above these were running shorts. Looking higher, Rima saw that many of their (now very close) neighbors were bundled up on top. They wore jackets, and she knew from Gloria that most of these jackets would be "donated" to Goodwill. That is, a few minutes after starting the race, runners would toss them over to the sidewalk. Rima also saw that many of those waiting for the start kept warm by wearing black plastic trash bags as capes, having cut out holes for their heads.

"What a teeming humanity," Gloria offered. "Do you notice that we're warmer in the crowd?"

"Yeah, I think 20 degrees warmer," said Tiffany, who reached down to rub some warmth into her thighs while trying not to bump her head into other runners.

"Wow, I'm glad you told us how to dress," said Rima, looking around at the closely packed crowd, many shivering in shorts and tank tops. To stay warm before the start, all four of them wore heavy cotton sweatshirts and sweatpants that Gloria had supplied from Goodwill, over their short shorts and short-sleeved shirts. Tiffany explained that for the best running temperature and clothing, "you're always gonna be cold when you're waiting for the start."

"Yeah, especially with bare arms and legs, like those people," Rima said, motioning with her lips toward a couple nearby.

"But we'll all warm up within five minutes after we start; you'll see," said Gloria.

A half block behind them they heard some shouting, and they looked back to see that the crowd had parted for a few men who were setting up a large slingshot on the asphalt. They shot water balloons, one after another, toward spectators standing on a balcony some 10 floors up. One aim was successful, with happy screams coming from up high.

"So many people are packed together, but no one's pushing," Sofie observed.

"Everyone's so polite," Rima added.

"There's no road rage, maybe because everyone knows the pack will break loose at eight o'clock," said Gloria, "so we all just wait."

"It's so different from cars on the freeway."

"Yeah, I guess because here everyone has the same appointment to meet."

"And we're all in agreement about our goal, and we're all going there together."

"What an experience! You lured me into this, Gloria, but I'm happy you did," said Rima.

Tiffany pointed. "See those large 'Repent' signs? They're here every year. They bob up and down above the heads, but you can't see the observers holding them until you get real close."

"I can't read the smaller words underneath; what do they say?" asked Rima.

Tiffany squinted and then read: "'Greed, lust, fornication, sloth, envy ...' Sins to repent from."

Gloria laughed. "They always tell what to turn away from, not what to turn toward, as if sins are fun words to write."

Rima wondered if **she** could repent from sloth, if her old, overweight body accustomed to tropical warmth would hold up to complete this run. *Can I really do this? It's so far, a 12K for me.* She marveled that the teenage girls were willing to share the experience with these older women. She wondered if she, or Sofie, would be grossed out seeing several naked old men running; she'd heard about them. Gloria was right, this **would** be a major happening, and Rima wondered if it would really help her forget her worries, even if for just a few hours. *Diabetes. Knees. Sofie's in trouble and her mom has no time for her.*

Five minutes before the scheduled start, Tiffany squealed, "I'm so nervous! I always get too scared! So much pain ahead."

Sofie thought, *I'm scared, too. Scared that these women count on me to be a good influence on Tiffany, running. They don't know how bad my grades are and that I'm not ready for tomorrow's midterm.*

Tiffany leaned over to whisper to Sofie. "Did you blaze this morning?" [take marijuana]

"Couldn't. Lola's been around the whole time. Gotta run without it."

Neither Rima nor Gloria noticed the girls turn away from them to continue.

Sofie quietly added, "Haven't seen Raoul since Friday, as you know, my source. Lola's keeping a watch on me. I guess that's why my mom asked her to come. Hard time breathing around here; can't get any privacy."

They turned back toward Rima and Gloria.

Gloria grabbed them all together for a group hug, "Well, ladies, we have another chance to celebrate life!" Then, just before eight o'clock, an announcer started the countdown, and the tremendous crowd thundered, "Ten! Nine! Eight! ... Zero!" and then released a tumultuous roar. But Rima was surprised by what followed: just a quiet and very slow shuffle toward the start line.

Finally crossing the start mat, the crowd ahead had thinned out so that all could walk. For the first mile, along Howard Street, they could only slowly walk. The pace gradually picked up until they could finally run, and then they floated on the aura of the crowd's pent-up energy.

"Wow, you're right about the costumes, Tiffany," called Sofie. It seemed that more men than women wore tutus, and many of those men were partnered with women in tuxedos. The few nudes, most of them gray-haired men, carried shorts, some under their baseball caps—Rima could see the shorts hanging down their necks—or some shorts tied around their ankles above their shoes. A few of the nudes wore small backpacks that surely were filled with clothes.

"They'll put on their clothes in Golden Gate Park just before the finish," Gloria reported. "Some have hidden their clothes in the park's bushes."

Every couple of blocks, bands played peppy tunes.

Just after that level first mile, the four turned onto 9th Street for a block and then left on Hayes Street.

"Oh my God!" Sofie said.

Looking uphill, they could see for several blocks ahead where the runners had become a unit. The runners resembled a viscous liquid like a lava flow, but flowing *up* the hill. The flow leveled out at each cross street, then continued uphill to the next cross street. And the four women were part of it, all headed over the crest, where they would then flow downward toward the Pacific Ocean and the finish line.

But we probably all have individual goals as well, wondered Rima. *My Sofie—maybe she wants to be a serious runner... maybe she's running away from bad influences ... she might even get an athletic scholarship ... college. For me... worries to avoid and forget. But Gloria's right, outside thoughts are fading into the distance while I'm out here running.*

Still on the Hayes Street long uphill, Gloria noticed Rima gasping for breath. "You've got courage, dear; keep it up!"

"But this hill is a walker!"

"It's **okay** to walk the hills, and you can still call it all a run. Come on; we'll walk together."

At the top of the hill, they caught a glimpse of some of the costumed runners, including several-person "centipedes," who pulled over to the official who was judging the best costumes and a local TV crew that was filming it all.

After Mile Three and the teenagers had long ago left the two older women behind, Rima observed, "Hey, Gloria, we'll get a contact high here, from—what do you call it—Mary Jane? Phew!" as the Fulton Street residents called out to the runners, "Wanna hit? Wanna hit?"

Before long the two women reached Golden Gate Park, and they left all buildings behind. Rima slowed to a walk and gasped, "Just go... on ahead. I'll see you at ... the Cliff House ..." But Gloria insisted on staying with her.

On the downhill toward the Pacific Ocean, Rima was able to talk again. "Gloria, I used to love to run; I mean, all little kids love to run, don't they? But my "sitz bones" and my knee —I get sharp pains—I'm becoming an invalid."

"You'll be fine after you finish, honest. And you'll see the finish in five minutes."

"I do love everything here: the carnival, the race, sharing with you and the girls, beautiful San Francisco. That is, everything except, oh, the pain!"

"Yeah, pain's no fun, but most of it will be gone a few minutes after you stop running. You will have soreness, but for just a couple of days."

"So can I overcome the pain?" Rima wondered. *Is it possible*

for me to really run again like when I was a kid? Or is running behind me forever? Maybe I'm too old, after all.

"I'll show you, my dear. Gradual buildup, that's the key."

Past Mile Seven and close to completion, they ran downhill past the Dutch Windmill, the "Queen Wilhelmina," and then picked up their pace to a sprint. They turned left onto the Great Highway and another 200 meters to the finish. Under the balloon arc hung the finish time clock showing … Rima squinted, *was that 1:30:44? It's taken one hour and a half. Is that all? Such a short time … such a long time!* This late in the race, the tight clusters of fast runners had already finished, and the slower runners were more spread out. A volunteer near the finish read many of the bib numbers and quickly looked up the associated names. He then provided names to the announcer who called them out over the loudspeaker. "And here comes Gloria Kent from Atherton and Karima Masuhud Osorio from Redwood City!"

They shuffled behind other finishers, and each stopped at a footstool where a volunteer snipped the straps of the time chips off their shoelaces. Next, another set of volunteers handed each of them a bottled Calistoga water. Pushing through the now-milling throng of finishers, they searched the crowd of faces and discovered their girls waiting and looking for them.

Seeing her granddaughter happily approaching, Rima surprised herself by bursting into tears. She laughed at her foolishness and wiped her eyes. "I don't even know why I'm crying," she whispered through her tears to Gloria, as she hobbled along with the others. They went up to the polo field to collect their goodie bags and finisher shirts, white with an artsy design featuring the Golden Gate Bridge.

"I hadn't realized it would be such a **big** experience. It was so hard, so painful, and … I … I feel so changed."

She paused, and then asked, "So, Gloria, is that why I'm blubbering?"

"Sure, a lot of people cry, especially finishing for the first time. And maybe because you overcame your doubt,"

Gloria offered.

"Maybe that's why… I feel so—*maligaya*—so elated!"

"Oh, I'm delighted for you!"

"I hadn't known about this world. Thousands right here in San Francisco so passionate about running."

"And thousands more came to watch us as well."

I feel like an invalid, Rima thought, *but I know I want to run again.*

1-2. Warm-up
Sunday, May 20, 2007, and Monday, April 30, 2007

What was I thinking? Rima mumbled to herself after the Bay to Breakers as she slowly limped toward a volunteer holding out a water bottle to her ... *that I could do this, at my age, and without any training? And how did I let this new friend talk me into running! And 12 kilometers! Should I have listened to her? I hope there's no permanent damage to this knee.*

Rima recalled how she had first met Gloria, just a week after arriving in California. They were introduced at the sideline of a youth soccer game while watching their girls; that is, Gloria's daughter and Rima's granddaughter. *Watching that first game, I was still confused with jet lag ... the sun rises nine hours earlier here than in Manila. Sus, I met Gloria just three weeks ago ... and* now *look at me, limping!*

"Can you go to the soccer game without me?" just an hour earlier, her daughter, Tess, had begged. "Sofie will show you where to sit, and I'll ask her to introduce you to some moms. Gotta catch up on some stuff."

Tess had immediately, on Rima's arrival, started turning over a lot of her parenting responsibilities. Months earlier, Tess had managed to get her mother on the phone in Manila. "Oh, *Inay*, please come to California right away. Sequoia Hospital is keeping us RNs too busy, and Sofie has been getting into trouble." Now Rima mused, *and I know Tess wants to find more time with that new nobyo, that what's his name, Steve. I hope* he's *a good one."*

Sofie carried a fold-up chair onto the grass for her grandmother and helped Rima get set up on the home side of the field.

"And, oh, this is Gloria Kent, Tiffany's mom. Tiffany's over there, number 32." She pointed to the group of girls slowly congregating with the coaches for their pep talk and warm-up. Then she ran over to join them. Other parents arrived and set up their chairs along the sideline a short distance behind the team. Several greeted Gloria and put their chairs near hers.

Oh, maybe she's the queen bee here. Very classy, she observed, of Gloria's neat, short hairdo, dark blond with highlights. She wore slim blue jeans and a carefully pressed white shirt. *She's calm, appears confident. Everything is in place.*

She saw this woman—*Gloria, didn't Sofie say?* —smile and kindly greet the arrivals.

I wonder how I look to her? Not quite as perfectly tidy, but maybe as confident, not bad for a newcomer. Glad Sofie told me not to wear a skirt. But these slacks ... maybe I'd better get sports pants to wear to Sofie's games.

Today Sofie had told Rima that her team, the Menlo Park Mavericks, would play the strong Palo Alto Predators, their traditional and neighboring rivals. "I'm bummed that Mom isn't here again, but I'm glad **you** can be here, *Lola.*

The coin was tossed; the game started. Rima sat quietly, avidly watching. She didn't know the game well. *I never saw a football game at home ... soccer they call it here.* She wanted to experience it all, including the parents' behaviors. She wondered how active they'd be in rooting for their girls.

She didn't mind being a newcomer. *Understandable, I'm new. I feel fine with myself.* Her mind drifted from the hard-to-follow game. She noticed ethnicities. *Most of these girls and their parents are white, but maybe that couple is Mexican; I can't always tell. Asian couple over there, probably Chinese... So many Asians, even Southeast Asians, in California. Tess says that almost half of the RNs at her hospital are Filipinos, even a few of them men.*

She watched the players run to one end of the field, then back to the other, and wondered why the referee sometimes stopped the play and put the ball on the ground for the other team.

Her attention drifted again. *I wonder if anyone notices I'm a* Pinoy. *But of course, they know Sofie, and maybe Tess. People don't look at me like I'm strange, even the little kids. They've seen plenty of Asians before. They don't even notice. We sure notice Americans in the Philippines!*

Rima noticed that most of the parents on the sideline attentively watched the game, a couple of them with video cameras. The few fathers quietly watched, but some of the mothers chatted, not looking toward the field.

First time, little kid, I saw a white man, came to our small island, couldn't believe my eyes! —Such pink, puffy skin, little spots on it, hairy, and shining with sweat. Eyes so light colored. I remember asking Mom, "How can he see out of those eyes?" Only very old people, blind, had light gray-blue eyes like that. Eyes, nose, mouth crowded up in the center of his face. Looked scary, but seemed friendly, maybe even kind. Talked with the imam of our masjid for a while, together with a Filipino from the big city, and then they waded back to their boat and took off. So tall! Seemed twice as tall as the tallest man on our island.

"Yay, Tiffany!" the woman next to her shouted, and then all the parents jumped up to scream, "Yay, Kristen! Yay, Mavericks!" Rima jumped up with the other spectators to clap as well. The woman next to her—Gloria —shouting and clapping, turned to Rima and said, "Did you **see** my daughter's great assist? That's my Tiffany!"

"Oh, congratulations. She looked very clever to me, kicking the ball just ahead of Number 11, anticipating her fellow player's pace as she ran toward the goal. But I don't know this game very well."

"You're Sofie's grandmother, aren't you? She told us you were coming. I've been **so** looking forward to meeting you; my Tiffany and your Sofie are such good friends."

1-3. Gait Shift
Sunday, May 20, 2007

As soon as they crossed the finish line of the Bay to Breakers, what a downshift of gait! While running the race, everyone had pushed their bodies, and most had tried to sprint across the finish line. But after crossing the finish mat, the throng slowed to a stroll, like shoppers at the mall. Then they meandered up to the polo field for the finish celebration, toward eucalyptus trees lining the rim of the polo field "bowl." Most had found their companions. They chatted; they laughed; some limped. During that 10-minute too-slow, too-crowded climb, Rima overheard bits of conversations, all about their big shared experience.

"Hayes Street was as hard as they say. I had to walk up it."

"Me too."

"Did you get sprayed by the guys with the garden hose sprinklers? I'm still wet!"

"Weren't the nudes gross? —If I … I wouldn't…"

"My right knee gave out."

"Oh my God, did you see the buffalo?"

"Bison."

"Bison, then. I didn't even know about them."

"How can those centipedes—13 runners, right? —run under one costume without tripping?"

"Yeah, I wonder how they can run so fast right behind each other with that costume covering them all? I bet they can't see beyond the ground directly beneath them."

"And I hear that each year the winners of the centipedes are very fast; they finish right behind the Kenyans."

Reaching the rim of the polo field, our four women saw that thousands had finished the race before them. The crowd spread out to the variety of destinations below. From food stands emanated barbecue smoke. To the right, a few runners emerged from the enormous medical tent with ice bags wrapped around their knees. Off to the left, on a tall stage with an amplified rock band, performers jumped around while singing and playing their instruments. Below the stage, some finishers danced in the grass. Many runners had put on their new finisher's shirts, showing on the back, "Always the third Sunday in May." Some lay on the grass with their legs stretched out vertically above them, rubbing their calves, their quads, their feet.

"Now where did they get their finisher's shirts?" Gloria squinted to see a large crowd at the far, eastern end of the polo field. "That must be the shirt booth." The four headed there. They stretched their legs like the others waiting in the lines, and finally a volunteer handed each of them a shirt, as another volunteer marked a line on their bibs, indicating "received shirt." Rima received her size large shirt and held it up to her body. "Yep," she grimaced.

Sofie asked, "Did you read it yet? 'Official Breaker, May 20, 2007.' I can't wait to wear this T-shirt to school tomorrow!"

"Now to the Cliff House," said Gloria, and they turned around to walk through the churned up earth and grass past the booths and the crowds, back up to the eucalyptus trees. From the rim, they headed back down to the Great Highway, where they noticed what they had hardly seen at their own race finish: hundreds of spectators lined up along the sidelines, cheering the even slower finishers, and probably waiting for their own special runners. The four ducked under restraining tapes to make their way out to the far sidewalk closest to the Pacific breaking waves, where they turned right and trudged up the hill to the Cliff House. Gloria's husband and Tiffany's father, Stanley, would be holding down an ocean view table for them.

The girls moved upward purposefully in order to retrieve their dry clothes from Stanley's Lexus LX 570— Tiffany had a spare remote tucked into her shorts pocket— and they'd be relieved to change out of their sweaty and by now chilly running clothes in the clean restroom of the restaurant.

The two older women climbed more slowly. Partway up the hill, they looked over the sea wall and down onto Ocean Beach, a wide expanse of sand stretching to the south for several miles. The sun had finally managed to burn off the morning's fog, and—how quickly, how easily—the ocean's gray colors had turned into deep blues. Long furrows of white-churned water plowed toward the shore, and each took its turn to crash, with an enormous low roar. With each wave's crash, a thousand suns darted through smooth spilling water, a moving brilliance too much for human eyes to manage. Through fingers held up to protect their eyes, Rima and Gloria tried to take in this phenomenon.

"I love your ocean," Rima smiled to Gloria. She closed her eyes, turned to the sun, and inhaled deeply.

"I'm happy to experience it with you," replied Gloria, squeezing Rima's arm.

Rima continued, "Here, the blues are deeper and more gray, less green and aqua than in the Philippines. The breeze is chilly, and the salty air smells ... colder."

"It smells cold?" smiled Gloria, waiting for an explanation.

"Must be different plants and animals inside this water."

On the wide expanse of sand, they saw sunbathers, and at the water's edge, waders and even swimmers. Dogs left their humans to run into the water and back again to shake it out of their coats— then they headed back toward the water. Hundreds of dogs and their people, adults with chairs and ground covers, their little children with shovels and buckets, enjoyed a by now warm, sunny Sunday at the beach, facing the wide Pacific Ocean.

"They don't know, or care, about the big happening right behind them, the finish line," said Gloria.

"They'd sure notice it if they'd just turn around; that is, if they wanted to."

"Well, maybe, their beach experience is a major

happening as well."

They turned back to their trek up to the Cliff House. Rima wondered, *how could they not care or even notice? It's such a big experience for us! ... But... the people across the Pacific, even in my bayan kong Pilipinas, they don't care or even know about it.*

Shortly before reaching the Cliff House, Gloria exclaimed, "Well, Rima, you showed you have what it takes!"

"How?"

"You can run, and you can overcome the difficulties."

"Well, I do hope the pain in my legs will be over soon."

"Probably. I've got ice in an igloo in the car for you."

"Uh ... okay ... thank you ... I'm still astounded; I hadn't **known** about this world, but so many people **do** know: thousands of runners, spectators."

"And don't forget the volunteers—handing out water, guarding the side streets from "bandit" runners... The whole city shut down for this event."

"It's so big! It seems like a world event."

Turning again to the climb, Rima thought back to a new world she had discovered as a child, maybe four years old, when her Uncle Samad whittled *tupara* for her, underwater goggles of wood. He embedded them with window glass from the city of Zamboanga, a half day's outrigger canoe ride away, which he had carefully snipped into size and inserted into grooves he had whittled for the irregular shapes. Then he had tied a short length of plastic fishing line over the bridge of her nose, and a strip of inner tube from a car tire, also from the city, which strapped the goggles onto her head. For the first time, Rima was able to really see under water, the whole new vast, colorful, living world. So quiet—she heard only the distant putt-putt-putt of outboard motors at the sterns of fishing canoes.

The fish! Such variety, such vivid colors. Angelfish, light blue-white; clown fish, bright orange, white, black stripes; blue damosels, triggerfish, with blue, yellow stripes on white. Some swam singly, in contrast to the many, many schools of smaller fish, hundreds together, that darted back and forth in formation. How did they decide to all turn at once? And then again? How did they avoid touching her as she floated through them? So heavily populated, this world, but so quiet. Mainly, she heard only her own breathing through the snorkel her uncle had shown her how to use, and the gentle scratching of sand on the sea floor as the water's sway gently moved the top layer of sand. The sea grasses near the shore swished slowly back and forth, and a little farther out, many kinds of plants floated over the giant coral tables just beyond the low-tide zone. Such a grand vista off her little village of Pasil Manta on Sakol Island—she hadn't known how grand until that wondrous moment when she was four.

Fifteen years later, as a university student 600 miles to the north in the big city of Manila, she recalled reflecting with new perspective on her first glimpse under water.

People on top of the water, in boats, on shore, or going overhead in planes, they can see only the sky's reflection; they can't see below the surface, or at best, they get just a little glimpse of a darting fish. It's a big world under the water, maybe even bigger than the world we've known on land.

Close to their destination and looking forward to their sit-down rest after the race, Rima looked again over the sea wall, down across the beach past the tiny people, faintly hearing their calls and children's laughter. *I guess I can forgive them for not noticing the Bay to Breakers. The world's too big to notice or to know everything.* She turned her eyes out across the white-crested waves, past the wide expanse of darker Pacific water to the southwestern horizon. She imagined she could glimpse, just over the rim, the outer coral reefs of the Philippine Islands.

Gloria opened Stanley's car, the two women took the last two bags of dry clothes from the trunk, and then Rima followed Gloria into the Cliff House.

1-4. Every Finisher is a Winner
Sunday, May 20, 2007

Their waiter, Chris, placed crab omelets topped with avocado slices before them and readily agreed to take a photo. He stood before them at just the right vantage point to include the famous rocks outside the window, waves spilling around them, and he knew which setting – "snow setting" he had said - on Gloria's camera would capture both the people inside and the much brighter ocean and sky outside.

"Wow, what an adventure," Rima exclaimed. "And I'm surprised, the young runners treated me—and you—just like one of them."

"Yeah, imagine the contrast if we tried to join their soccer team."

"So why do they accept us in this race?" Rima looked around the table at Stanley and the other three runners, especially the two 17-year-old girls.

Gloria answered first. "Maybe because they know it's hard, as hard or even harder for the slower ones, and so we're all in this together."

Tiffany added, "And—you're always telling me, Mom—every finisher is a winner, and most do finish."

Sofie entered in. "Oh, you're right, Tiff: that's one reason I like running; we're all winners. Not like on teams, football and soccer, where one whole team loses—half of the players."

Gloria said, "But here, only the non-finishers lose. We—at least we back-of-the-packers—don't really compete against one another; in fact, we encourage each other."

Sofie said softly, "I do like to race at school."

Gloria noticed, and said "hmmm" with a smile. But Sofie didn't respond.

Rima asked, "Do the front runners even notice us?"

"Some of them do, certainly the ones you've known and trained with."

Stanley sat quietly, confidently, somewhat aloof in his quiet, casual elegance. His short, slightly grayed hair was full and neat; his navy blue cashmere pullover and jeans fit loosely over his trim body. Entering the conversation, he leaned forward slightly. "I hear that Sofie here is fast. But for you other three, isn't it kind of hard, entering an event where you know you don't have a chance of winning? At least in my golf game … I'm glad that I'm as good as I was 20 years ago, maybe better."

Gloria looked up to the ceiling, deeply inhaled, exhaled slowly, and then said, "As you know, Stanley, running slowly is not my nature. I'd much rather be fast, and I was fast as a kid. Of course age does matter more in this sport than in golf. But running for me is still fun, even though I'm slower. And I *can* still finish; I can do endurance."

"I've heard you say that you're getting slower." His shoulder shrug was barely noticeable.

Gloria couldn't drop the topic. "In golf you use a handicap so that you can compete with the more skilled and younger players. Runners? We all run the same course, with no handicap."

Stanley exhaled and then shifted his body toward Rima. "How about you, Rima?"

Rima was a little startled by his question, and didn't want to get caught in a marital squabble. But she didn't see a way to avoid responding. "Yes, Stanley, I was fast as a kid. Faster than a lot of the boys."

"Are you jiving me, Rima?" He emitted a friendly laugh.

Hmm, sexist. I'll just ignore that. she thought. "Jiving? Well, we ran barefoot, and our feet were tough enough to withstand the coral sand. Oh, many coral sand grains are bigger than your sand here in San Francisco and in Half Moon Bay. And it's sharp; it's powdered coral. But we were always barefoot so we had tough feet."

Gloria said, "You know, the way I'm able to accept being slow now is that as a child I was the third and youngest, therefore accustomed to being smaller and less capable. Back then, I didn't ever get to be first, but I did learn to perform well enough by age six to be included on the long hikes, the backpack hikes in the mountains."

Tiffany contributed her history. "I've never been as fast as my mom **or** my big brother."

"Oh, you **will** be faster than me, if you keep at it." Gloria patted her daughter's shoulder. Tiffany shuddered very slightly.

"And you, Rima?" persisted Stanley. "Can you handle being slower now than the front runners?"

"I was the eldest; I have two younger sisters. But my dad died, and so I took over his fishing. I went night fishing with my uncle and the other men and the older boys. Something like being a younger sister, maybe." She paused, and then added, "Anyway, after today, nothing more to hide; everyone knows I'm slow!"

Stanley's mouth stretched into a quick smile; his eyes probed without humor.

Rima added, "I'm naturally fast, but actually slow!" She smiled broadly and looked around the table. All, even Stanley, responded with surprised, supportive chuckles.

Sofie had noticed Mr. Kent's ribbing of their sport and performance, and blurted out in defense of her grandmother, "Oh, Lola, you did fine! I'm proud of you, and I can't wait to tell mom you finished."

Rima stayed on the topic of age. "There were so many gray-haired runners— people in this country think it's okay to run when you're old?"

"Lola, you're just like us. We all ran the same course." Tiffany and Gloria nodded vigorously.

Rima carefully placed her knife and fork on the right diagonal of her plate, the American way to show "finished," and gazed out the window at the ocean. The rocks below were covered with seagulls sunning themselves, preening, spreading out their wings, occasionally flapping, and then settling down in the sunshine. Beyond the rocks she could just make out the swells marching toward the shore. As each reached the rocks, it separated and advanced around both sides, then met together in front of the rocks, but at different tempos. She noticed that the trip around one side was longer than the other. Now and then the front pacing coincided. *Can I discover a regular pattern?*

She counted: *Five, six waves...* and the seventh wave converged in front of the rocks.

Number seven next time as well? She counted:

Five, six, seven, eight ... Nope. Ten. Together. This is mesmerizing and hard to predict. Is there a more complex pattern? Hmm. Can I see any hint here for my family? Maybe it's too complex to see into the future? She turned back to the table where her four companions had been eating and chatting.

She brought her thoughts of the future to the others. "Hey, girls, where do you want to be five years from now? And Gloria and Stanley, how about you? Will you still be playing golf"—with a nod to Stanley—"and running?" She nodded to Gloria.

They laughed, but avoided answering.

Tiffany said, "Go for it, guys."

Stanley laughed and said, "Sure, I'll still be playing."

"You women are so quiet! No answer? How about in **one** year?"

Gloria said, "We live in earthquake country, and I've got a song for it." She quietly whisper-sang the refrain of the World War Two song:

> So love me tonight,
> Tomorrow was made for some;
> Tomorrow may never come
> For all we know.

1-5. Use It Or Lose It?
Sunday, May 20, 2007

Back in Gloria's Bimmer, they rode southward along Freeway 280 for the half hour's drive home, with the girls in the back seat already asleep. Stanley had dropped them all off at Gloria's car near the start.

Gloria drove calmly, eyes on the road, hands at nine and three on the wheel, competently steering everyone home. Her expression was as smooth and tidy as her hair; she was satisfied. "We can coast now; we succeeded."

"These dry clothes feel heavenly, don't they? Thank you for having me bring them." Rima closed her eyes against the sun coming in her side window, and smiled, snug in the dark emerald-green après-ski outfit that Gloria had given her.

"I'm super tired and have many pains in these legs… But thank you for the ice pack; it helps this knee."

"Put your feet up on the dashboard, dear, that's fine with me."

Rima's shoes were already off. She carefully lifted her dry-socked feet onto the dashboard.

"For the first couple of miles I felt like I was floating above the pavement."

"Yes, there was so much excitement in the air, so many people— maybe 200,000 including all the spectators."

"Oh, I'm happy you talked me into coming!" She turned to smile at Gloria.

"And I'm delighted you came."

"You know, I'm reminded how I used to love running when I was a kid."

"Me too. Maybe every little kid loves running. But not everyone remembers it."

"Do you think we can ever find that joy again?"

"We can keep trying for it. With spirit and body, both."

"Oh, Gloria, I'm so afraid I'm using up my joints. My pelvis, my knee, the diabetes … I mean, look, I already used up my skin under the sun all these years."

"Well, we can't get good skin back, but we can build up muscles, I promise."

"And I ruined my body eating fried food. When I moved to Manila for college, I started eating "modern" food. And near the university we even got an American Burger King."

"Oh, Lord," grumbled Gloria. "Great American export."

"So our bodies get used up, right? Like machines wear out. And just now I think the Lord is telling me to stop using mine." She rubbed her knees, and they both laughed.

"Well, they tell us our bodies are made to move, and if we don't move, we rust."

"But we do wear out, right? And we are mortal, I remember."

Gloria signaled for her turn into the left lane in order to pass a car. "They tell us we can move longer if we keep moving."

"I mean, I know all little kids want to run. I loved running as a kid. But it wasn't painful; now it is."

"Yes, especially the first day."

"Maybe it's like milk."

"How do you mean?" Gloria glanced at Rima's eyes and quickly returned her eyes to the road ahead.

"God wants babies to drink milk, that is, human mother's milk."

"Yes, and I know what you'll say, that the majority of older children and adults have some trouble with milk later."

"You Americans drink cow's milk when you're adults. Most Filipinos can't handle all that cheese and ice cream. We get bellyaches, at the least. Usually worse."

"Mainly, I agree with you, because as you know, I'm vegan. I don't eat animal flesh or exudations— eggs, milk, even honey. Seems to me, God doesn't want adults to drink milk; save it for the babies, but then, give them only human milk."

"The bottom line for me is: as an old woman, the pain tells me to stop. And is running good for a diabetic?" Or maybe I'm so sore just because I hadn't trained."

"If you had been moving a lot all these years, you'd be less likely to have pain. Rima, I promise you, if you start slowly and increase very gradually, you'll overcome the pain."

"You think so? All of it?"

"Well, the chronic pain. You might get temporary pains, like now, but you'll overcome them. Willing to try?"

"Well…"

"Try this mantra, Rima: 'This pain is temporary. I'll feel much better in two days.'"

"Two days!"

"Show me the painful places again," Gloria said.

"Here, here, and this side as well," Rima pointed.

"Well, that one is probably your IT band—your iliotibial band. It ties your leg to your core and goes from your side above your pelvis bone down the outside of your thigh to just below your knee. I'll show you a stretch when we get out. It's best if you do it three times before you go to bed. Oh, and then ice for 20 minutes after each stretch."

Gloria signaled a right turn, passed to the outermost lane, and then turned into the Highway 92 overpass.

"Ooh, sounds difficult."

"More ice will feel good to you, I promise. Just wrap a soft blue ice in a dishtowel, so your skin won't get burned. Surely Sofie has one in your freezer."

Rima nodded.

Gloria waited a couple of minutes, and then said, "And, I want to send you to my sports masseur for a deep tissue massage."

1-6. Use It, Wear It Out?
Monday, May 21, 2007

Rima helped her daughter, Tess, get off to work and Sofie off to school—breakfast, lunch bags—and then she took a walk to think and loosen up her sore legs from yesterday's big run event. *Back into my warm-up suit. I do have mostly happy memories of yesterday. I need my old brown jacket; it's cold out here.*

She walked in their neighborhood, the "Little Michoacán" immigrant barrio of Redwood City, past neat, modest suburban houses with low fences around small lawns and older cars in the driveways and at the curbs.

Tess says this is a low-income district of Redwood City, but these houses are neat and clean, like out in the provinces in the Philippines. They're not like the Manila slum squalor, makeshift corrugated tin tiny dwellings alongside the railroad tracks—trash and so crowded.

Most workers and school children had already gone for the day, and the cool fog kept remaining residents inside, so Rima had the streets to herself.

Aray! My knee! She limped slightly, but she happily looked into the sky. It's still gray, but it might burn off soon—that's how Tess calls it. It's good to have this fleece jacket. She patted the sleeves.

Tapus na! I did it! And Sofie, and those new friends, Gloria and her daughter Tiffany. She heard birds sing and looked for them in the trees. Little brown birds, sweet chirping, little seed-eating beaks; they must be migrating back to the north. I wonder about their name, their habits…

Felt like an invalid at the finish yesterday, and I'm still sore today. But maybe I'll loosen up.

What a surprise, even thinking of running!

Walking, she tried hard not to limp from the pain in her left knee. *Oooh. I told that doctor in Manila that I was sore after moving books home from my high school classroom. I told him that I was going on extended leave to California. He said to rest the knee, but then yesterday I ran on it.*

She walked quietly. *But I loved the running, especially before the soreness started. Tiny glimpse of what fun I had running when I was a kid.*

The rumble of morning traffic a couple of blocks away along Middlefield Road could be heard in the little neighborhood, and in the distance, Rima could also discern the low roar of freeway traffic approximately one kilometer away. She felt grateful that the residential streets near her daughter's house were spared the morning bustle.

I'm loosening up; good. Before going to school, Sofie said she wasn't very sore. Why not? Is it just youth? Her youth, my age? Or, is it her training on the track at school? Both, I suppose.

Rima kicked a tennis ball over the low fence of the closest yard. *Saw a dog in that yard the other morning; this must be his ball.*

Sofie's troubles…—. It's good that Tess sent for me.

My dear Tess, too busy at work to help her own daughter in trouble. She's changed, like Americans now, Type A. No time for her own daughter, can't stop multi-tasking. And she's so irritable. She loses her keys and gets mad at Sofie and me. And now she makes time for that new boyfriend; she's focusing on her boyfriend instead of Sofie. She has no time to even look into my eyes, the few times we've talked.

I've already been one month here, and Sofie… took her a little while to trust me. Kind of sullen at first. Now very loving to me. Told me her mom had said, "Wait until your lola gets here!" Sofie's not like other American teenagers, insolent to their elders. I'm so grateful we could use that … that Skype … to talk. Heard her coach said last week: "She could run a marathon! For our school and for herself.".… That'd get her back on track in school. Bad boyfriend, too late for a bantay, a chaperone.

Not talking back to her mother, but not minding her either. Tess says she's been staying out all night with him. Not since I've arrived, we sleep in one bed together, so I'd know. I've gotta be super soft, super slow, with any advice.

Rima decided to turn left. *I'll walk a little longer. Brr, California cold.* She pulled her jacket sleeves down over her hands and held them in place with her thumbs. She walked briskly. *I told Gloria that she walks fast; she said it's exercise for fast turnover of the legs when running. I told her that we Filipinos, mmm, saunter, to avoid getting sweaty. This brisk walking is hard. But at least I'm not so sweaty here in the temperates.* She smiled.

She thought of the tropics she had left behind a few

weeks earlier. *That long, long night over the Pacific, just one month ago. Looked out at the light blinking on the end of the wing, maraming bituin [many stars] blinking overhead, very clear sky, no moon. Couldn't sleep, just looked out the window. Couldn't see that vast ocean down there, like I can't see the future. Had two big worries for the future, my dear Sofie's grades and my diabetes. Oh yes, and a small worry, the knee. Doctor said "rest the knee." Other doctor said "change the diet, get exercise." Exercise! For 30 years now I've been just standing in my high school science classroom!*

Ahead of her, Rima saw exhaust coming out of a car's tailpipe, and now she heard the engine. She stopped, waited for the middle-aged man, baseball cap over his thick dark hair, to back out and then turn toward her. She gave a neighborly wave; he waved back and was off to work.

Maybe running isn't the right exercise? Which is better for me, running or resting? I'm so worried; diabetes means over the hill, fragile, and worst of all, vulnerable. Running yesterday, I felt, for a little while, that I still have life ahead of me. Maybe I'm not an easy target, yet, for that sugar disease or for other infirmities or even bait for young hoodlums. I did meet the challenge yesterday; I finished that race. The challenge was good for me... I didn't know I could still run at all!'

Who am I, anyway? Yesterday's experience was causing Rima to wonder.

Came here as a mother and grandmother. Living alone, unusual in the Philippines, hard to help them here from over there. The last many years she'd been complacent, set in her ways.

I've been satisfied to be a veteran teacher, professional, up from peasant life out in the boondocks. They call me a kagalang-galang balo, a venerable widow, because I'm still teaching and still look decent, respectable. Still have some vigor, but losing energy and strength with these old-age ailments, on the long slow decline.

But yesterday, I had a glimpse of my youth! Am I trying to be a kid again? Am I kidding myself? Trying to kid others? Foolishly endangering this old body?

She turned the last corner and saw their house come into view. *And Sofie—Coach said she's so fast, and she has passion to run long; she has great promise. She'll have to bring her grades up to stay in varsity sports, and she'll get strong enough to leave that bad boyfriend behind—maybe even the damo, the marihuwana.*

Rima unzipped her jacket pocket, pulled out the house key, and turned into the driveway. *She's still a little cold to me; doesn't completely trust me. Hey, maybe I could support Sofie's running by running myself. Strengthen the bond between us. And maybe it'd help my body as well... or would it?*

1-7. Running with Sharp Scissors
Monday, May 21, 2007

Sofie had just gotten home from track practice and flopped onto her bed when she heard her new iPhone, a gift from her mother, buzz. Since her grandmother's arrival a month earlier, she shared her bed at night. *No time to myself anymore.* But this afternoon she was alone in her privacy. Reaching down to her backpack on the floor, she retrieved the buzzing phone and saw Tiffany's text: "Can u talk?"

She rolled onto her back, clicked on "recents," and then "call back" for her friend.

"Hey, Tiffany, whatcha doin?"

"Nothing. Too much homework. Got a book report due tomorrow for AP World Literature, and I haven't even started the book."

"So I'm your excuse, hmm?" They both laughed.

"Hey, Sofie, did anyone at school today notice your Bay to Breakers shirt?" Tiffany had poured herself an AriZona Iced Tea before settling down on the chaise lounge on her bedroom balcony in the late afternoon sun.

"Yeah, a few kids in Econ said they wanted to buy it from me."

"Wow, they didn't even run it!"

"No, but three on my track team did. We didn't see them on Sunday, though."

"What did **they** say?"

"'Cool. It was cool.' Oh, and our coach said it was cool, and asked about our finish times—always thinking about our times."

Tiffany moved inside her room, into the shade, and set her tea down on her nightstand. She grabbed the remote and switched on the television as she sank onto her bed. She fluffed the pillows around her head, and then flipped her long blond-highlighted hair off her neck until it rested on top of the pillows.

"Sofie, I thought you said they were dropping you from track."

"Only a warning, so far. They can't drop me until the

grades come in at the end of the quarter."

"So, are you going to be dropped?"

"Oh, God, I've got to get at least **three** *B*'s to have a two point average."

"By June?"

"Yeah."

"Can you do it?"

"Maybe."

"Hey, Sofie, want to use my tutor, Matt? I'm sure my mom would agree..."

"Well, thanks, but... That's why my mom sent for my grandmother again."

"To be your tutor?"

"I guess. But more than that."

"How?"

"Promise you won't tell anybody? To be my chaperone."

"Huh?"

Sofie rose from her bed to look out the door into the hallway; she wanted to make sure her mother had not come home, and that her lola was in the kitchen. Yes, her grandmother was still cutting vegetables for the evening stir-fry while catching the end of the Oprah show: her "American cultural lesson," she called it.

"Well, Filipino girls have chaperones; *bantay*, they call them."

Tiffany propped her head up with one elbow and reached with the other arm for a sip of her iced tea. The sun had followed her into her room and was now lighting up half of her deep-bronze Hotel Collection comforter, so she carefully rolled over, glass in hand, to move her tea to the nightstand on the other side of her bed.

"What do they **do**?"

"Sirens going by ... wait a minute." And Tiffany closed the bedroom door. Laughing, she said, "My lola always says *maraming sasakyan* [plenty of traffic]. It's so noisy here."

"O-o-okay, so what's that?"

"Plenty of traffic."

"Oh, I learn so much from you, girl—my very own 'east of El Camino' friend!"

"Well, we're both slumming, my very own 'Atherton' friend." And they laughed.

"So what, what do the *ban* ... *ban* ... chaperones do?"

"One thing is, they go on dates with the girl."

"No! A threesome?" Tiffany hooted in laughter.

"Yeah, Mom says the poor ones—that is, those out in the boonies. Hey, did you know that *boondocks* is a Filipino word? Anyway, people in most of the country, their sisters or nieces accompany them on dates."

"And your Raoul will go for that?"

"Well, you know my mom hates him."

Yeah, I know, the *ganja* [marijuana], the falling grades."

"And the coach called up my mom."

"Oh, God. Why?"

"He seems to think I show potential. Potential, Mom said."

"Potential for what?"

Sofie sat up and, toe against heel of the other foot, pushed off one shoe, then the other, then sat back onto her bed and leaned her back against the wall.

"He wants me to be the first Menlo-Atherton High School student to run the Boston Marathon next April."

"The **Bos**ton! God, that's like the **Olympics!**"

"That's what my mom says. But she said it stunts kids' growth to run so far. She heard that. Do you think it's true?"

"I don't know. That'd be hella lame for us!"

"Well, he told *Ina*—my mom—that new scientific research shows that's not true, that it's okay now."

"But, kids don't ever run that far I don't think, do they? No one from my school has ever run a marathon."

"For the Boston, you have to be 18. Coach looked up in my school file, and saw I'll be 18 a month earlier, March

21st, and I told him it's also the spring equinox."

"My God, Sofie, you'll be famous! I'd better get your autograph now."

"I'm wondering, though, if he's just trying to save his job. He's new to our school, so he's up for tenure in a year."

"But he says you have po**ten**tial! He must be thinking of you, too."

"Yeah, he called my mom and me in. Told me I'd have to follow his training plan, and I have to raise my grades. Said I have to get to bed early."

"**No** one goes to bed early! Our time **starts** at eleven o'clock."

"About my grades and staying up late, Mom's blaming Raoul. So she thinks Lola can get me straightened out."

"What do **you** think about that, Sofie? Is she going to spy on you?"

"I can't figure her out yet. I sure haven't been going out at night now, with her sharing my bedroom. Raoul's threatening to break up. But Lola's kinda cool. She doesn't tell my mom everything. And she's fun."

"Yeah, I saw how she loved running last Sunday. You're so lucky."

"Well, I guess I'm happy she's here with us, but it's her or Raoul. I suppose that your dad also keeps a watch on you, and you're happy to have him around?"

Tiffany let a little time pass, and then said, "Well, it'd be better if he could be supportive."

"Oh, your dad seems cool. Maybe you just take him for granted."

"Hmmpf."

"And you know what else, Tiffany?"

"Yeah?"

"Coach told my mom that some Boston Brahmin's put up a four-year scholarship for the first 18-year-old finisher boy **and** the first girl!"

"Wow, how much?"

"Full four years, he said. As much as $40 thousand per year, so $160,000 each!"

"Wow, Sofie, you'd be a **pro**—making that much from running! Like the guys in football."

"But with **my** grades, I can't get in anywhere, except Foothill or another community college."

"Well, with a full scholarship… Hey, you go, girl!" And they both squealed.

"So my lola's job is to get me into bed early, no sneaking out."

"And Raoul?"

"I've been having a little trouble with Raoul, anyway, besides his threat to break up."

"Oh… Like what?"

"Well, I don't like his friends. Losers. Lola asked me abut him, and she says I'm gonna have to get all new friends. But not you, of course."

"But hey, I'm your dear friend, Sofie—I'll stay with you. Though with him gone, we'll lose our source, our supplier."

"Yeah. Lola asked me if I could stop 'smoking that *damo* [grass].' It's one reason Mom asked her to come."

"You wanna stop?"

Sofie was silent for a moment and then said, "It's not just Raoul, as you know."

"You mean about running?"

"Yeah. I think I run better when I'm high."

"Well, **you** might; **I** don't! Nothing helps me run fast."

"Well, I mean, when I'm high, I don't worry so much about how I'm doing. I just enjoy running, and I think I run faster."

"Well, then—so whatcha gonna do?"

"Yeah. Gotta figure that out… Hey, P.A. [Parent Alert]. Bye." And Sofie hung up.

1-8. Over The Hill?
Friday, May 25, 2007

Rima parked her granddaughter's weathered silver Toyota Tercel in the parking lot next to Redwood City's main library, and on the green light walked across Middlefield Road to Milagro's Mexican Restaurant. Spotting Gloria waving to her from an outdoor table on the sunny side, Rima made her way through the other patrons and noticed that Gloria held a filled cocktail glass in her other hand and had stretched out her tan, bare legs to catch color from the afternoon rays.

"Here you are!" Gloria exclaimed. She reached toward Rima for their perfunctory hand and cheek-to-cheek squeeze, and then raised her arm again to wave in a waiter to take Rima's order.

Rima settled herself into the chair next to Gloria. She waited for the waiter to leave and then laughed, "You white *Milikanos*!

"What, dear?" smiled Gloria, expectantly.

"Always exposing your **skin** under the **sun.**"

"Of course. Vanity over health; form over function," laughed Gloria.

"Where I come from, down in Zamboanga, the women go **in**side during the middle of the day, and they bleach their faces and their feet."

"Oh. How do they do that?"

"Well, they grind up seashells into a powder – they're lime, you know - and then they make it into a paste with water and smear it on their faces and feet.

"Ooh, ghostly!"

"Yes," laughed Rima. "So you pass by houses in the afternoon and many women have white faces and feet. Never mind if the neighbors see them that way!"

"And never mind if people see me sunning," laughed Gloria.

"So," and she grasped Rima's hands, "how do you feel

by now, dear, after four days of rest? Still sore?" She
smiled into Rima's eyes.

"The soreness is going away." Rima set her purse on
the tiled terrace under the table, settled her elbows onto
the chair's armrests, inhaled, and then exhaled a big sigh.
"Oh, I'm so happy to see you again. I hadn't realized it
would be such a **big** experience: it was so hard, and
painful, and … I feel so changed!"

"And you, Rima, uhh, Rima Masuhud Osoro, right?"

"Osorio."

"Sorry, Osorio. Well, you can do it! You can run, and
you can overcome the difficulties."

"Do you really think so?"

"Oh, some people quit with pain. Some say pain is the
Lord's way of telling them they shouldn't be doing this."

"Well, I sure feel better now than I did at the finish."

"You'll learn to trust your body; you'll mostly feel
better within a few minutes after the finish, every time."

"Every time?" Rima turned her eyes to the approaching
waiter, and then to the glass of lemonade he carefully set in
front of her. He then placed a huge stone *metate* filled with
guacamole onto the table and followed it shortly with a
basket of tortilla chips.

"Gloria, how did you get into this?"

"Hmm?" Gloria looked up from her glass.

"Running. How did you start running? I mean, how
does anyone start up?"

"Well, where to start. Here, let's start with our snack."
With a smile, she reached her hands out to squeeze both
of Rima's for a little secular "grace."

After they dipped their first tortilla chip into the
guacamole, Gloria said, "First, 95 percent of us need the
social connection. We need to have someone waiting for
us at the trailhead."

"Oh, I can believe that. I didn't join Bay to Breakers by
myself."

"Hey, Rima, I have an idea; how about trying out my

running group? You could consider joining."

"I don't want to be seen. I'm so slow."

"They're all different paces, even several walkers."

"Well ..."

"And, by the way, will you join us next Wednesday? We'll run up in Huddart Park."

"Is it hilly?"

"Oh, yeah. But I walk the steepest part. And that's okay."

"I mean, Gloria, how did you decide you wanted to run? And how old were you?"

"I was 43. I couldn't zip up my skirt."

"Weren't you afraid you'd wear out your body?"

"By now, I believe the sports physiologists. They say, "Use it or lose it"; our bodies are made for moving, or they'll rust.

"Well, my diabetes and arthritis ... I have to think about this."

After they each had another tortilla chip, Rima added, "But at least 'slow' didn't put me out of Bay to Breakers."

"Right, you were a finisher. You're a winner, like all the other finishers."

"Yeah, I guess you're right, and plenty of runners— well, walkers—finished after us."

They reached for another set of chips to dip into the guacamole. They dipped and then ellipsed the filled chip to their open mouths, licked their lips, and reached for their napkins to finish the cleaning.

The shadow of the restaurant's overhang had slowly been overtaking Gloria's chair. She looked up, stood to scoot her chair back into the full sun, and then repositioned her legs to take in more sun.

Rima pondered Gloria's offer to run the next Wednesday. *How exhilarating to be part of this excitement! But, my old dark thoughts these last few years, like "over the hill," or "can't do that anymore"; maybe now I could set them aside.*

"You know, I loved that our girls treated us like it was

normal for us to be part of that event, even though they did zoom ahead of us. I was so slow, and I slowed you down because you stayed back with me."

"You don't have to be side by side the whole time to do it together. And they knew, even though we came in behind them, that we had to do the same hard work to finish that they did."

"*Siempre.*"

Gloria took a slow sip of her margarita, and looking toward the western sky, said, "You know, the first time I went to Alaska, I told a clerk in a store there, 'You local people seem so friendly to one another. Why?' You know what she said?"

"Tell me."

She said, "We've all been through the cold, dark winter together."

"Oh, they feel camaraderie in suffering together."

"So, dear, on a marathon, even if you only get a glimpse of the elites up front before or after the race, at least some of the fast ones know that the really slow finishers have had to work even longer, and maybe even harder, to get to the same finish line."

"They really notice?"

"Some. See how Jerry stays at the finish to cheer us slower ones on?"

"Hmm." Rima straightened up to look into Gloria's eyes. "Hey, what'd you think of our girls on Sunday's race?"

"Well, Sofie finished strong; 52 minutes, wasn't it?"

"Yes, 52:22. She showed me our results on her computer as soon as they got posted on Monday evening."

Rima took a long drink of her water, set the glass down, and looked up at Gloria. "Did you know that she was questioned after the finish?"

"How do you mean?"

"She said a volunteer asked her to walk off to the side with him. Then he asked her where she had started running."

"What!"

"She didn't catch on at first. She said, 'At the start, of course, with my grandmother and my friends.' Then he said, 'Sure you didn't start later, maybe on Hayes Street? You came in pretty early.'"

"No! Well, we can vouch for her, of course."

"Well, on Monday night she saw that she got credit for her real time."

"So he suspected her of cheating." Gloria clenched her jaw.

"Yes. I suppose they questioned her because she was so fast and so young."

"Well, I'm also wondering about, actually, about racism. I mean, they don't question everybody, do they!"

"Now, Gloria ..." *I wouldn't want her to make a public case,* Rima thought.

"I'm thinking of calling the race director. I want to make sure that Sofie has a clean record with the organizers."

Rima shifted her legs to a crossed position. "And your Tiffany did fine as well."

"Yeah, she's a little faster than before because she tries to keep up with your Sofie."

"Well, I have something else to tell you about Sofie."

"Oh?" Gloria looked past the food and drink to Rima.

"Her cross-country coach wants her to qualify for the Boston Marathon!"

"No! You know that **I'm** trying to qualify for the Boston, don't you?"

"Yes, I do."

"Wow, she's that good, then?"

"He says so. But her grades have been going down..."

"Isn't that why your daughter called you to come here in the first place?"

"Yes, and she might get bumped off the varsity cross-country team."

"Oh, that'd be awful! Any way you, or we, could help her?"

"I've been helping her with her homework. Mainly just sitting with her."

Gloria was silent for a moment and then almost jumped in her chair to lean toward Rima. "Yes! If you'd join me for regular runs, that'd help Sofie with her running as well. Would you be willing to try it for one month?"

"Hmm … A month…How many times a week?"

"Three."

"So, 12 runs total?"

"Yeah."

"Mm … I don't know … Well, I guess I could do that many. Okay, it's a deal." Rima reached both of her hands to grab Gloria's outstretched right hand, and they squeezed. The terrace had filled by now with young 20- to 30-somethings arriving to meet for TGIF after work, and an aura of relief and flirtation filled the air. Gloria signaled the waiter for the check.

1-9. Who Drops Out?
Wednesday, May 30, 2007

"You made it!" Gloria called to Rima and approached Rima in her granddaughter's modest car that had just pulled into the still-dark parking lot at Buck's Restaurant in Woodside.

"Oh, I'm very sorry I'm slow; I don't have your cell number with me."

Rima hurriedly buckled her water pack around her waist, tucked her car key into the pack pocket, grabbed her gloves, and jumped out of her car, locking it while closing the door.

Newcomer, late! she muttered to herself. *Making nine, 10 people wait.* Two of the runners jogged in place; others rubbed their gloved hands together, elbows close to their sides.

Gloria quickly introduced, "This is Rima, a newcomer to running. She lives in Redwood City. And Rima, this is Julie; this is Vern, Keith, Marilyn, Nancy." They each shook gloved hands with Rima.

Naku. Several are older than I am!

"Let's go," called Leonard, a slim, compact man with short salt-and-pepper hair who looked to be in his early sixties, and they took off as a group into the early morning ground fog and winter dark of the trees hanging over Woodside Road. They headed toward their Wednesday morning usual ten-miler, up Huddart Park on the bayside slope of the Santa Cruz mountain range.

For the first two miles, before reaching the lower park entrance, they climbed up rural roads lined with tall trees and gardened estates, and they soon grouped themselves with pace mates. Gloria stayed toward the rear with Rima, and they were joined by Nancy and Leonard, who were curious to learn more about this new person.

"You're new to running; isn't that what Gloria said?" asked Leonard.

"Yes, very new." She quickly inhaled, and then added, "I told Gloria I'd try it for a month."

"Well, these Wednesday morning runs are very hilly, but by the fourth week, you'll notice big improvement."

They pad-pad-padded single file along the side of Woodside Road, passed occasionally by pickup trucks that were driven, Gloria said, "probably by men on their way to work in estate gardens." Turning right uphill on the quieter Albion Road, they re-formed into their smaller talking groups.

"Got up too late this morning," offered Rima.

"Oh, I was ready to call you," replied Gloria. "Just to remind you for the future, this group has a five minute guideline. That is, they'll wait for five minutes, if they know someone is coming."

Rima was relieved to notice that their pace was slow enough that they could talk normally.

"Very steamy breath this morning," observed Nancy. "Cold."

Leonard added, "Sometimes we say getting out of bed early is the hardest part and so the rest will be easier." Then he called out for those in front to hear, "Car, behind!" and all moved into single file at the side of the leaf-covered road flanked by barely visible houses up long, curving driveways behind gates. The car now ahead of them, they again grouped into twos so they could talk more easily. "And, you don't have to be physically fit to get out of bed."

"But it's hard, especially in the cold and dark," responded Rima.

"And maybe you have your dear warm human next to you, and..."

"And a warm cat at the foot of the bed," added Nancy.

"And I had two glasses of wine at dinner last night, so that makes it harder to get up."

"And hard if you didn't sleep well," said Leonard.

He turned his head to look at Rima, who was breathing

heavily as she worked to keep up with the others climbing this rural, hilly road. Gloria had made sure that Rima had black running tights and gloves, their "uniform" on these cold mornings. Rima wondered what Leonard was thinking about her. Her clean white running shoes, clearly new, would be muddy by the time she'd finish. Her brown fleece jacket, *not much to tell about me there. Somewhat rounded shoulders, slightly bent over from the waist, not much spring in my step. Well, I hope I'll be improving my posture if I stay with it.*

"You do have to have courage," he said. You know how hard it can be to get out of bed early; that's the very hardest part. So now you have a hint of how much you'll suffer while running, not as much as getting out of the sack."

Hmm, some hazing here? wondered Rima. "Are you guys all early birds?" she asked.

"Seems like most runners like to start out by dawn," answered Nancy. "Mornings are the best, and you feel better all day long."

"And some people decide running isn't for them because they'd rather join a later group, like Pilates classes."

They reached the lower entrance to Huddart Park, the not well known one used only by people on foot and park rangers, who had keys for the gate. Some runners ducked through the large metal gate while others ran around the end post. Two continued up the asphalted road to the first meadow, while the others turned onto the trail that took them over a small wooden bridge. The creek below had swelled with rushing brown water from yesterday's rain.

"Wow, look at the creek; it's awake this morning," said Nancy.

"Yeah, from the rain." Leonard turned to Rima. "The giant sleeps all summer under these tall trees, and then wakes up after the first rain in late fall. We thought it had gone back to sleep. But look ..."

The runners headed up to a water fountain where they

drank, then continued running to meet in the lower meadow, where they waited for the slower runners and walkers. Then they ran up the narrow trail to Werder Meadow, another mile on a narrower path alongside toyon bushes and under madrone and redwood trees. Now they ran single file, but they moved slowly enough to continue their conversations.

"So, who drops out of running?" panted Rima. "Late birds? ... And who else?"

Gloria was the first to respond. "You remember Michelle? I told you about her a week ago?"

"Oh, yes."

"She had a mastectomy two years ago."

"Oh."

"I don't know if that's why, but she said she decided she likes the gym better than the outdoors, and she said one marathon was enough, and too much for her."

"Oh ... who else drops out?" asked Rima. She turned to Gloria to pretend a whisper, "Maybe you can tell me what pitfalls to avoid."

"Well," said Leonard, "I know several elite runners, like elite athletes in other sports, who dropped out when they started to decline."

"Why? They can't stand the decline?"

Nancy interjected, "I've read that it's especially hard for the really fast ones to accept the decline. If they can't win, they opt out."

"Kind of like the beautiful woman who loses her *raison d'être* when she loses her youthful blush."

"Yeah, maybe it's like that."

"My answer," said Leonard, and he glared with a smile at Nancy, "you know, this guy who analyzes all the published marathon records in this country? ... For the half million finishers each year?"

"You mean the *Marathon Guide* man?" asked Nancy. "John Elliott?"

"Yeah. On his MarathonGuide.com. His analysis shows

that everyone reaches their peak performance in 10 years, whatever age they started. ... You know, fastest time, PR or personal record."

"Even 16-year olds?"

"Apparently."

"How can that be?"

"Because for distance running, it's not just brute strength. The mental is at least half of it, and it takes that long to build up pacing knowledge, best form, best nutrition, maybe lose weight, and especially build mental strength—whatever one's age."

"And, of course, for everyone, they're 10 years older," added Gloria.

"Yeah, ten years to peak, kind of surprising, especially for older runners," said Nancy, "because common knowledge has it that in the later years, speed drops off sharply, and also, numbers of athletes."

"Hmm."

"Like, remember that Marin Runners' Club front runner guy who kept a record of his speed while having a sex change to a woman?

Nancy interjected. "Jim Furman, became Jen Furman."

"Thank you, Nancy." Leonard smiled at her, Rima thought just a little indulgently.

Leonard continued. "In the one year of female hormones and all, he—she—slowed down a lot, in spite of her efforts to maintain the male speed."

"I remember that one. Oh yeah. Read about him, uh, her, in *Runner's World*."

Through the tree tunnel ahead of them, Rima saw open sky, still white-gray with morning fog that was starting to burn off, and a few faint patches of blue. Up a little grassy hill and they were at Werder Meadow and another water fountain.

They started up again, toward the group's usual high point and turnaround, another two miles upward. Gloria turned to run backwards, in order to look into Rima's eyes." Remember the *Runner's World* I loaned you, the report on elite women runners before and after menopause?"

"What was … that one?" Rima asked, panting again to stay up with the others.

"They all slowed down in their finish times within the year that menopause started."

"So is this a reason for women to drop out of running?"

Leonard was the first to respond. "I know a lot of runners, men and women, who have said, 'It's time for me to retire,' or, 'I'll stop while I'm ahead.'"

"Oh?"

"And they tend to be people who were accustomed to running in front, like the podiatrist at Kaiser, sub-three-hour marathon finisher…"

"Fast!"

"I asked him if he'd run Boston again, and he told me, 'It's like trying to date an old girlfriend again; it'd never be the same.'"

They all laughed.

Nancy added, "And you remember, Gloria, that article I told you about from the *Marin Independent Journal* a few years ago?"

"Which one?"

"Elite woman runner who decided to go into ballet instead."

"Yeah, dropping out, like that. And then the runners who get arthritis in their knees and so they take up bicycle riding, where there's no impact."

Gloria added, "And some marathoners go down to half marathons as their longest."

Their trail continued to take them upward under bay and redwood trees, and soon they reached Toyon Group Camp, some five miles and about a thousand feet above their start point, Buck's Restaurant.

"Oh, it's very warm, up here," said Rima.

"Hey, you notice," said Gloria. "The fog burns off, the sun rises, and frequently we have an inversion layer up here of warmer air."

"I like the warmth. So, can we go back to our topic? Do injuries put people out?" asked Rima.

"Oh yes. Henry had a massive stroke in March, and we're all very sad."

"Oh, *Dios mio*."

"Yes, he was running so well"

"And Nora was hit and killed."

"No!"

"Yes, a year ago, when she was on a training run in Santa Barbara... It was a van driver on an early Sunday morning. He was drunk and on substances; he confessed to the police."

They paused for Gloria to pull up her knee braces for the downhill run. In the process, she looked up to Rima. "I wear these only for steep downhills, and I'm not sure they do any good. Placebo affect, mostly."

"So is this a risky sport?"

Gloria responded first. "More injuries take place on downhill running: more impact. But downhill sure feels easier, doesn't it!"

"Running's not nearly as risky as biking," said Nancy.

Leonard had the final response. "Well, we do have 100 percent certainty of fatality, eventually. But it's not as risky as **not** running, honest," and they all laughed as they turned around from the long climb to reap their reward, the downhill run. Even Rima raced with the others under the trees, green and brown colors blurring past them on both sides, the sweet smell of damp earth and fallen leaves under their feet.

1-10: Kids Love to Run
Friday, June 8, 2007

"Eeuw!" Tess frowned. "That black toenail needs to stay covered. Please don't wear sandals at my party this weekend, *Inay*, okay?"

With glossy straight hair turned under at the neck into a chic bob, sunglasses worn as a headband, light blue pants, a printed blue blouse, Tess wore the harried expression of a professional rushing to get to her nursing shift on time at the hospital.

Rima scootched to the side of the front door threshold where she sat to put on her running shoes. She grumbled to herself, *if I use black toenail polish, they'll never notice.... And the toe doesn't even hurt. It just looks like it should.* To her daughter she said, "*Sus, anak,* of course not." Soon, she would accompany Sofie to the track.

Tess grabbed her purse and jacket, and then squeezed past her mother. Tossing her things into her fading silver Honda Accord, she climbed in and quickly backed out of the driveway. She had an early appointment at work.

Soon after, while driving her grandmother, Sofie asked, "Why does my mom dis my running so much?"

"My guess is that she thinks it isn't ladylike. What's yours?"

"Maybe. Well, I don't think it's ladylike to be pudgy, like all those girls who just sit around, who have like air bags for boobs, and for waists they've got muffin tops hanging over their pants."

Rima's eyes fixed on the red light; Sofie waited for the green. "Back in Zamboanga, my *titas*, my aunts, always told me to stop running because I would get sweaty."

"But how come you can think of doing it now, Lola?"

"Hmm. Haven't thought about that much. Maybe it's because my *Tito* Samad let me go night fishing in Zamboanga when I was a kid."

"How come?"

"Because, you know, my dad, your great-grandfather Ali Masuhud, drowned while fishing—actually dynamiting fish—and I was the oldest kid. My mom had to take care of all of us, and we needed the fish, some to eat and some to take to the market in the city to earn pesos."

"Mmm." Sofie looked carefully at the traffic ahead of her.

"Something funny, we called the dynamite *korgeyt*, Colgate to you, because it came in a tube, like toothpaste."

"People down in that remote province knew about American toothpaste?"

"Yes, but only because they saw it in the market in the city."

"Oh, your poor mom. My great-grandmother, right? Losing her husband; having to manage. Oh, I'm sorry for all of you."

Sofie drove a little more slowly than usual because she wanted to hear more of the story. Nowadays she usually rushed with her grandmother to the high school track to get their 45 minutes of workout in before the freshman PE students came out at 7:55.

"Did girls fish, then?"

"No, the other men were very critical of Uncle Samad's letting me go out with them. Fishing there is only at nighttime."

"Ooh ooh! You went out at nighttime with the men? Did the other girls talk about you?

"No, no, *Tito* Samad protected my reputation. Silly girl."

"Maybe they called you a tomboy?"

"*Binalaki* in Tagalog. The English word "tomboy" has a different meaning in the Philippines. Gay."

"Oh, confusing!" They both laughed.

"I guess I was a tomboy in US terms."

They looked ahead at the early commuter traffic, and then Rima said, "You know, at nighttime, the sea water lights up with little fires when the outriggers touch down, as we move along."

"Why?"

"They say it's the phosphorus in the water, like on matches."

"Wow, I want to see that."

"At first the men had me just hold the *kolayet* ..."

"The what? ..."

"The lantern. Fish come up to the surface, attracted to the light."

"Oh, is that why you fish at night?"

"Yes, you figured it out, *Nene*'."

"After awhile they let me go under the water to release the net if it got caught on the corals, and they taught me how to mend the nets in the afternoon after school." She paused and then added, "But the school kids didn't treat me like the other girls."

"Because of the fishing?"

"That's what I thought."

"You had a school on that tiny island?"

"Oh yes, an elementary school. How do you think I got into high school!"

"They had a high school?"

"*Anak!* Don't you remember anything? I was sent to live with the Sorbino family in the city to attend high school."

"Sorbino ... that's a Spanish name, so probably Christian, isn't it?"

"Yes, and that's how I learned about Christians. When I moved into Zamboanga City, I didn't live in the Muslim barrio. Mr. and Mrs. Sorbino adopted me..."

"Adopted?"

"It's not like adoption here. It was more like sponsoring me. And it was very common in the Philippines. Still is."

"Is that how my mom became a Christian?"

"Well, do you remember that your *lolo* was a Christian?"

"Oh, yeah."

"Yes, I met your *Lolo* Paolo in high school in the city, and only on some weekends I had the chance to go out to Sakol Island to visit my family."

"What did he think about your night fishing?"

"Well, he didn't really know much about it because when I went to high school I didn't have to help support the family anymore."

"Maybe he wouldn't have been interested in you either, like those boys you mended nets with."

"Maybe not. He and I studied together."

Sofie braked the car to another stop. "Hey, we're hitting all the red lights this morning, *Lola*, but I'm glad because I love your stories."

Rima smiled.

"Was it okay with *Lolo* Paolo that you were smart?"

"Maybe he was liberated. But, then, later he told me that he liked my legs, too."

"Your legs?"

"Yes, maybe the muscles because I liked running as a kid."

"Like all the other little girls, right? I remember, *Lola*; you reminded me that all little kids like to run."

"Ha ha, you do remember! You're right, all little boys and girls like to run everywhere in the world. But I ran a lot even when I was older, already a teenager."

"More than other girls?"

"I guess so. People always told girls to stay out of the sun or they'd get black and to not hurry or else they'd become sweaty."

"And I suppose the other girls didn't sit out by the seashore mending nets."

They both laughed.

"But you got to do more than the other girls, didn't you? You went to high school in the big city of Zamboanga and then clear up to Manila for college, right?"

"You're right. I guess something good for me came out of my *ama* having died when I was a kid. Silver lining to that cloud."

"Oh, *Lola*…"

"You know, it turns out that becoming different in your own group can free you to enter the wider world."

"And maybe that's why you dare to run with me now, *Lola*. You're the only grandma who runs; that's what the other kids say."

"Well, your mom doesn't like me running either, does she?"

"She says it's ridiculous at your age."

"She does, doesn't she. But she puts up with it because she knows I can help you run right into a good college."

"And she likes your help for me." The light turned green and Sofie started the car up again.

"And by now, you and I both know that many other 'women of age' are running. I'm not so unusual, after all."

"Oh, no, on our runs I see plenty of men and women who look as old as you, Lola. Even more gray hair, a lot of them."

"But Sofie, aren't you afraid you'll damage your reputation, hanging around with your grandmother?"

"Oh, I tell them you're my good luck charm; you help me get out on the trails on the weekends."

"I'm honored." Rima smoothed down her pants on her thighs, smiling. *Oh, maybe she's developing more trust in me. I'll continue working hard to earn it.*

"Hey, look, we still get the track to ourselves for a little while." Sofie parked in the student parking lot, and they immediately set out with a slow warm-up jog to the track.

1-11. Running Toward the Golden Gate
Sunday, June 10, 2007

"It's one of the most beautiful trails in the world, guys, and you can walk the steps and the hills," Gloria had promised them. Rima had to swallow all her pride to show up for her first organized race with Gloria's San Francisco running club. As they pulled into the Seal Rock parking lot to start the Golden Gate Vista 10K race of the DSE, Dolphin South Enders, they saw maybe 150 people gathered. Most of them wore colorful running shirts and shorts and dusty white running shoes. Some of them were stretching, a lot of them gathered in small groups, chatting and quietly laughing.

"*Lola* Rima and Sofie, are you as worried as I am about showing these, these ... seasoned runners in this club, what you can do?" asked Tiffany.

"Oh, you'll see; they're very welcoming," said Gloria. "They'll help you feel comfortable."

"Mmm," said Tiffany, but her eyes showed hesitation. Rima thought, *I've gathered all my courage as well to show up here.* She noticed that Sofie appeared calm.

At 8:55, the race director called into a megaphone for the runners to line up at the start, and at 9:00 they headed toward the soft, damp earth trail that was cut into the steep north side of Land's End's tree-covered park. Gloria had encouraged each of the four to run at her own pace, and soon Rima was panting at the too-fast pace of the other three, so she slowed down. She worried about whether she should be here at all, but with a quick look around, Rima discovered that she was accompanied by pace-peers, some of them apparent age mates, but also younger women and men. And many ran behind her at even slower paces. *Oh, maybe I won't be the last finisher,* she smiled to herself. *And Gloria's right; the faster runners don't give a hoot about my pace; I'm not in their way.*

For the first mile, the trail led the runners almost horizontally along the steep, tree-covered hill that marked the south "cheek" of the mouth of the San Francisco Bay.

It's so beautiful! Oh, I'm so happy my Sofie is here to share the experience with me, she thought. *We're running toward the sun and the Golden Gate bridge—I can see it through the trees. The two towers, so high! ... Way down there in the ocean, that's a container ship, headed under the Gate and toward port inside the bay. Maybe came from Asia? I wonder which country? And over there ... still a little fog ...Here, so many ferns ... I smell damp plants ... birds sing high in the trees above me here ... so many of us humans, but we run so quietly on this soft earth. Oh, I miss my tropical warm humid air and white sand, but San Francisco's "Land's End," what a spectacular place to visit!*

"Hi, I'm Sherry," said the woman quietly running beside her. "First time to a DSE race?"

"Yes, I'm Rima and I'm new to running."

"Oh, this is a hilly one to start out on, but you'll do fine. We're coming to the steps now, maybe a hundred, just walk them."

They walked side by side, breathing heavily.

"Hey, Rima, let's slow down a little. When ... you're ... puffing too much to ... talk, then ... you're going too fast ... for me, too."

They both slowed a little. "Phew! That's much better. This must be a major key to success, Sherry."

"Yep. Keep it slow enough to be able to talk."

Toward the top, Rima quietly exhaled, *phew*, and Sherry smiled, puffing as well.

"Why'd you decide to run ... Rima, wasn't it?"

"I'm looking over the abyss into 60." Rima panted her reply, and Sherry laughed. Rima continued. "I ... can't ... keep my balance on one leg while ... pulling on my pants. I'm ... uh ... running away from invalidism. How about you?"

"Oh, I started running 20 years ago. My mom died of cancer, so I decided to live a more healthy life. Thought it might be a way to stay away from cancer, and maybe even lose some weight."

"Oh, did it work? —I mean about losing weight."

"Well, I have lost 20, but ..."

"Oh, that's a lot!"

"Well, but I need to lose 20 more, and it's not coming off. I think there's something to 'set point.'"

"You look good."

"In July, this'll be my fifth San Francisco Marathon and …"

"Wow! More than one?"

"Yeah, I've come to like the way of life, this running."

"How?"

"Well, I feel so good for the rest of the day; I'm more perky and cheerful."

"**I'm** gonna need a nap!"

"That's just for the first few weeks. It takes awhile to work up to the start point if you've been sedentary for awhile."

"Boy, have I!"

"So, just plan that you'll suffer a lot at first, but it'll be temporary."

"I'm gonna slow down now, Sherry. Nice talking with you," and Rima was alone again. Now she could focus on her breathing, her foot padding. She walked up Lincoln Boulevard and turned around at the top—their course was marked by small orange cones, and a DSE volunteer, Vince, showed the way. She ran down toward the trail under the trees. *Sometimes, even though my lungs and my breathing are all working so hard, my feet just quietly step along, almost independently. I can trust that they'll continue moving along with a steady rhythm,* she mused.

An hour after she started, Rima returned to the Seal Rock parking lot and the finish line. Looking behind her, she was relieved to see several runners. *Yippee, not the last in! But phew, it's hard, this starting up!*

In the car, the four women exchanged reports, and then the girls fell asleep in the back. Gloria said, "I've made some great friendships here. Runners are good people."

"How?"

"They're not pretentious. Out here on the trails, there's no marker of wealth or poverty. The only necessary equipment are shoes, and the price range is very small, mostly 80 to 100 dollars."

"That's right. I hadn't thought of that. It's cheaper than, say, bicycling."

"Oh yes. And people tend not to talk about their careers. So your persona is not your career, out here."

"So there's less posturing?"

"Yes, that's it."

"Well, speech does sort out level of education, and for folks like me, if you're an immigrant."

"Of course, you're right. But in sports, especially this one because you don't need to buy equipment or pay for access, like at a gym, you'll find more mixing of genders, ages, ethnic groups, economic indicators, than in any other grouping I know of. You'll find plenty of other immigrants as well."

"Wow."

"And runners are very supportive, at least here in the back of the pack."

"Not up front?"

"I suppose they're pretty competitive, like in other sports. But they do support one another, I hear, and they do treat us like real people, as well."

"The older the slower?"

"Sort of. But we have young newcomers who often start out slow. And some fast oldies. But some of these slower oldies were never real fast, especially the ones who started late."

Southward and on the peninsula by now, they both pulled down the car's visors; the sun shone brighter down here.

Gloria said, "And you'll find that you're not so unusual, starting running at a later age."

"Why is that?"

"Up until 30 years ago, endurance runs like the marathon were only for elite runners, and almost entirely men."

"What changed?"

"Title 9 was a big change."

"Tell me."

"That public schools had to put 50 percent of their athletic support into girls' sports. So the girls born after ... uh ... 1955."

"Oh, that includes you, not me."

"Yeah, the school environment significantly changed for a lot of them, and even Hollywood."

"Huh?"

"I think they all go to the gym now."

"But how did that affect us who were born before 1955?"

"Well, accepting women into the marathons in the late 1970's somewhat diluted the elitism of the marathons."

"The male elitism?"

"Yeah. And in 1972, the same year as Title 9, the founder of the New York Marathon, Fred Lebow, actively promoted women into his race."

"And let's see, the first women's marathon in the Olympics wasn't until..."

"1984? Yes, in LA. Joan Benoit Samuelson."

"She's famous! I heard of her in the Philippines."

"So the organizers gradually realized that they might as well allow non-elites. And that's us. And the marathon cities were happy to get more tourist money. I heard it was around 1988 that the Leukemia Society of America—they've added "Lymphoma" to their title now—started supporting people to run marathons in exchange for their fund raising. I think they were the first. They really brought in the older and slower first-time runners. Their success has been copied by many organizations since then."

Rima was silent for a while, and then said, "What a new view of the world, to invite older, sedentary people to become athletes."

1-12. What Does a New Runner Look Like?
Wednesday, June 13, 2007

The two women and two girls lingered at Buck's Café after their fellow runners had finished their breakfasts and raucous chatting and had left. Still with rosy cheeks from their two-hour run into the forested hills, the four were celebrating because the girls had just finished school for the year. In their dry street clothes—damp running outfits packed into the car trunk—in this familiar café, they felt especially cozy and warm.

Rima asked, "So how much can I expect to pay for running, folks?"

Gloria responded, "Remember what I told you, that as sports go, it's cheap?"

"Poor man's sport?"

"Well, full spectrum of income, I think, but you hardly notice signs of income. Though, when you talk with them, you notice that distance runners do tend to be well educated and achievement oriented."

"Well, I'm educated but poor."

"About cost: mainly, you need good shoes. You can easily get a 10 percent discount at the local stores, but expect to pay around $100 every 350 miles, and if you're training for marathons, that means three or four pairs a year."

"*Dios mio.* What's the most prestigious brand?"

"Brands don't really stand out, whereas they do in street clothing or, say, bicycles or cars."

"Why not?"

"It's not that… It's not that runners can be credited for being especially non-materialistic…"

"Why, then?"

"Function over form: I think it's because customizing for the myriad foot configurations drives most of the decision. Do you agree, girls?" She turned her head toward the two.

"Yeah," Sofie offered, "We counted about 10 brands on our varsity track team."

Tiffany added, "Same at Menlo School, all the brands, and in a place where most of the kids drive posh cars to school."

"And some of us oldies wear a fuel belt; if you sweat a lot, you'll need one for your water bottle, especially for the training runs that don't have water stops. That's another 30 dollars."

"What do you carry in those fuel belts?"

"Water, first of all. Maybe with some energy drink powder like Cytomax or Gatorade to pour in it, but they're sticky."

"What else?"

"I.D. I carry my driver's license, a credit card, 20 dollars, and my health insurance card in a skinny wallet."

"What else?"

"Advil, salt tablets, a tissue in plastic so it doesn't get wet with my sweat…"

"No phone?"

"Sometimes. I used to carry my little camera, but now the camera in my iPhone is enough… But on a lot of our trails, we don't have cell access."

"Anything else?"

"Let's see: sometimes a bandage for a blister? Yes, in the plastic bag. And lately, because we've been getting bee stings, Benedryl gel, which I sometimes offer to others."

"Oh, dangerous sport, this running."

"And don't forget the GU. Power Gel or GU, or Shot Bloks."

"Oh, that syrup stuff. How much?"

"I take one after the first hour, and another every 45 minutes to an hour after that. So, I take six for a marathon, but that's more than most people."

"Wow, the calories!"

"Yeah, a hundred per package. But we women burn off around 80 per mile."

"So that's about two thousand for a marathon, minus…"

"Yeah, minus 600 for GU and another 400 for energy drinks, so…"

"So I'm not really gonna lose weight on a long run, right?"

"Well, no. Women say they don't lose unless they cut down on regular food."

"And men? It's not fair; with their muscles, they move and they lose."

"Dr. Wally Bortz, you know, our local M.D. celebrity who promotes healthy aging, says we have two "fat vices" which have contributed most to our national obesity, and these are gluttony and sloth. He says the first is the more important, and you won't lose unless you cut down on the calories."

"Oh, I'd hoped that just the running would help me lose weight. So, hmm, do you have room for all that stuff in your fuel belt?"

"Yeah, there's room, see? And if it's cold, I have a jacket, a beanie, gloves, and maybe even one-time-use hand warmers; then the gloves and beanie go into the jacket's zipper pockets. On races, I toss the hand warmers to kids on the sidelines."

"So what about sports clothes?"

"Well, you can tell an elite runner, a regular runner, and a newbie."

"By their clothes?"

"Oh, yes. The elites wear really skimpy clothes like bikini bottoms and sports bra tops—that is, the women. And no fuel belts. Lately, some wear arm sleeves, or compression sleeves."

"What are those?"

"Like gloves from the wrists up to the arm pits, and then maybe with gloves—separate items—on as well."

Oh, they'd cover up my crepe-paper upper arms!

"Also lately, some wear compression knee socks."

"Hats?"

"Mainly only in big heat, and frequently just visors, so the heat can escape the head."

"How about the 'regulars'?"

"The regulars? Mainly, techno fiber shirts that wick away the moisture, and short shorts. Sometimes techno-fabric finishers' shirts from a marathon. They started giving out these shirts just about five years ago, and now some people even decide on their events according to the kind of shirt they give out."

"So people wear shirts advertizing previous events?"

"Some. Some others think it's a little *déclassé.*"

"What other kinds of shirts do they wear?"

"Well, for almost every event, even the 5Ks, a shirt comes with the registration fee. They're usually 100 percent cotton and the most common color is white, and a lot of them have little black ads on the back…"

Tiffany interjected. "They look like a bag covered with flies, like you have in Australia when you take a walk. Ugh!"

Gloria continued. "Most of the regulars don't wear the same-event shirts until after the race, and then just once, same or next day."

"So what do you do with them, then?"

"A couple times a year I take a sack of shirts to Goodwill."

"Anything else about shirts?"

"Well, Nike's in the forefront on fashion. They bring out a new color about twice a year, and they make shorts, tank tops, short-sleeved tops, and usually thin warm-up jackets, all in matching colors."

Tiffany called out, "Don't forget the shorts fashion, Mom."

"Oh, yes. About three years ago, Nike started making their shorts with side vents with scalloped edges, and some piping detail, so the side vents are really noticeable. And now other brands are doing them as well. Straight sides are *passé,* looks to me."

"Don't forget Lululemon and those other sports clothes boutiques, Mom."

Rima asked, "How about pants?"

Gloria responded. "What I see with the regular and elite runners, they avoid pants, unless it's real cold. I've detected a temperature divider: 45 degrees and lower, both men and women tend to wear pants for training runs and for organized events."

"But long runs start cold and end up hot."

"Yep, so people have to decide whether to suffer at the beginning or the finish."

Rima asked, "Aren't women shy about their thighs?"

"Well, I'm interested in seeing that after a couple of years of running, women tend to cast off their running pants, at least when the air temp is above 45 degrees."

"Maybe their legs get better looking after a couple of years of running."

"Actually, that might be a factor, Sofie. But I think they also cast off their self-consciousness about their legs. And maybe other hang-ups as well."

"There's also the matter of sun damage. Thin women are more likely to wear tank tops, and those are usually shirts with the razor backs, which free up..."

"... and show off..."

"Yep, the shoulders and the pecs."

"And if it's cold?"

"Some wear a thin windbreaker that they tie around the waist after they get warmed up. Some wear long sleeved—but generally microfiber—shirts. If it's really cold, then both. If it's raining, then a rain jacket instead of a windbreaker."

"And gloves: they're the first thing to go on with cold. Then beanie hats and pants, then jackets, then long sleeved shirts." Inside their gloves, some even wear one-time hand warmers that they buy for a little over a dollar at the big sporting goods stores.

"What about pants?"

"Tights, almost always black…"

"You can't even **buy** any other color!" said Tiffany.

"… And ideally with six-inch zippers at the bottom for pulling them off over shoes."

"Why?"

"Shoes are a such chore to put on, with careful tightening, rabbit ears adjustment, and all."

"Rabbit ears?"

"Oh yeah. When I bought my first pair, years ago, the store clerk laced what he called "rabbit ears." At the top two holes, instead of crossing the laces over, he threaded each lace on same side, making a little loop. After that, when he crossed the laces over and into the loop on the other side, the loops made a much better hold for the tightness you want."

"Wow, I have so much to learn."

They all turned to watch 3 men with big cameras come in and greet George at Buck's cash register, who directed them to their setup location.

"I wonder who today's celebrity will be," said Sofie.

"And Jamis will put another notch on his wall, of television crews doing interviews in this restaurant," added Tiffany.

They turned back to their little group and took sips of their coffees.

Rima asked, "Can we please continue about what runners look like? How about hair?"

Gloria responded first. "Well, let's see. —There's not a lot of hairstyle difference between the three groups of runners: elites, regulars, and newbies. Women swimmers tend to have very short hair, and you've watched the U.S. national women's soccer team? —Those women tend to have pony tails."

"Yep, and runners?"

"A lot of pony tails, mainly on the younger women, so the sweat doesn't drip off their hair onto their backs."

"Yuk!"

"And some have short hair, just above the shoulders, and longer than on the swimmers."

"But a lot of runners also swim! Triathlons, cross-training…"

"Yeah, so you see a big overlap here."

"So what's the newbie runner look like, Gloria?"

"Girls, help me here."

"Long shorts or pants. Yeah, and of heavy fabric. Basketball shorts. Or loose warm-up pants."

"Cotton shirt!"

"Street clothes: loose shirts and pants, sweats."

"Not real running shoes. Like fashion sports shoes."

"Jewelry, like necklaces and bracelets."

"What about iPods? —White wires?"

"Well, some wear and use them when they're training solo, but all the organized runs nowadays strongly discourage them at their events; they say for safety reasons, and maybe for their insurance … liability."

"What else can you tell about a newbie? … I guess I want to avoid this, right?"

"Maybe, most of all, it's their form. Girls?"

"They start out too fast to maintain the pace."

"They don't have good running form."

"Like?"

"Uh, steps too big, so too slow turnover."

"No spring in their steps."

"Shoulders forward."

"Arms all over the place."

"Head down."

"No smile. —But most others don't have a smile, either. Only when they pass by spectators."

"Paddling with their feet; usually with feet turning outward, like the second position in ballet."

"Oh, yeah, and the further back in the pack, the bigger they are, that is, overweight."

Gloria said, "You know, maybe most of us started out in the back of the pack, overweight with white cotton shirts and heavy shorts down to the knees. —And that's okay, right? But we all want to move up. Us oldies will never be elites, though. No fifty-plussers up there in front."

"So I have to give up on "passing" for elite, I suppose,

hmm? What else? —Behavior?"

"Well, the front runners are more likely to be doing short warm-up runs before the start and then going through the standard eight stretches. The elites in big races even get special transport and their own waiting room."

"Hey, will you all show me how to look like a runner? Make sure I get it right?"

"Of course, Rima. Mainly, you already know by now."

"Elites don't talk to pace mates like we do in the back of the pack. They're completely focused on their performance."

"And the regulars?"

"The farther back in the corrals before the start, the more likely friends will have come together and are chatting. Way back, those might stay together for the entire event. Closer to the front, and after taking off together, runners drift into their individual paces, so they run solo for most of the event."

"If you're gonna eavesdrop, it'll be mainly with the back of the packers; the ones in front talk a lot less."

Rima asked, "Well, who has the most fun?"

All three laughed. Gloria said, "The ones who don't get injured. So, almost everyone has fun, front and serious competitors, or back and sharing the experience with friends, chatting along; first-timers who are especially delighted and relieved to finish."

She added, "The most emotional ones are the first timers; a lot of them cry on finishing, relieved that the pain will soon be over, that they've met the challenge after five or six months of training. For all of us, it's such a big experience. We have pain for awhile, but we know it'll go away, and the rewards are great."

1-13. Not a Premonition?
Friday, June 15, 2007

"Wow! The lake is glassy smooth this morning. So calm," admired Rima.

Rima and Gloria had driven together to Sawyer Camp Trail and parked at the stone lookout over Crystal Spring Reservoir, situated right on top of California's great San Andreas Fault.

"Yeah, it usually has white-caps."

"And look," she pointed. "The sun enhances the iridescence of those ducks out there, see?"

"Beautiful. Dreamy."

They started out slowly along the perimeter of the lake, up the first hill to Gloria's usual "stretching bench."

"No other humans—just us and the other early morning species. Weekday mornings are wonderfully quiet here." Stretching, they gazed out at the lake and above to the clear sky.

They ran, listening to the soft padding of their shoes on the asphalted trail and noticing the half mile markers along its side.

"Gloria, I'm not a premonition person, but I had a bad dream last night about leg cramps stopping my running, about not finishing a run, getting a, a DNF, didn't you call it? —a 'did not finish."

"Oh, maybe you're worried about the cramps you got on our run the other day?"

"Yeah."

"You'll overcome those with training, honest."

They glimpsed the lake as they ran under the trees that arched over the trail. One squirrel chased another on branches overhead. "No deer yet this morning," said Gloria.

Rima continued. "By 'not a premonition person,' I mean that my bad dreams don't come true. I hope I can count on that."

Gloria responded, "Well, I don't worry about my own nightmares, but I know some people get scared thinking that they're dreaming real forecasts."

"I'm trying not to let that dream bother me, but I guess I do always have to gather courage in order to go on a long road trip ... and the plane trip here from the Philippines, of course ... and some bad images do creep through my positive resolve."

"Maybe try the usual: visualize success."

"I'll try. Anyway, can I tell you my fear? Maybe you'll help me have a catharsis."

"Sure." While continuing to run, Gloria took off her windbreaker jacket, rolled it into a narrow "tube," and tied it around her waist.

"Okay, when I woke up, I immediately worried about doing a long run."

"Well, doubts do creep into everyone's thoughts. Do you think you can chase these away?"

"I'm trying. And thanks for listening."

"Dear Rima, we'll follow the best advice, which is to plan for success. Cramps? More water, more electrolytes, right?"

Yeah ... We can't prepare for everything in the future. At least we did prepare for a beautiful day out here. Sunny, so little wind, so quiet, and I am grateful that you brought me here."

"The first three miles of the trail passed local flora: a bay laurel grove, a meadow, manzanita and toyon bushes, and California buckeye trees. Overhead they saw and heard Stellar's Jays and an occasional seagull. They smelled sweet fresh-water plants. They reached the low point of the six-mile trail, where it widened out for public restrooms and a couple of benches. They drank from the water fountain, and they noticed the enormous wooden water tank on the other side of the trail, mossy from water leaking down its side.

The two women turned back to the trail, which continued under a leafy tunnel of spring green, now heading uphill toward the dam crossing the Crystal Spring Reservoir at the mile five marker.

"How's your Sofie doing?"

"She says she'd love to run in Boston. And she says she's trying to leave that boyfriend, but it's hard. He knows how to pull her back in, and he doesn't like me being around to keep her home. She's hoping that heading for Boston might turn her away from him."

"And her grades?

"Probably a big improvement. She got an A on a term paper, and she studied hard for her finals. She said thinking of Boston helps. And did you know that she and Tiffany are on the 'Net with each other every night?"

"Great. I think they're good for each other, don't you? Doing homework together, talking about college, and the running, of course. And I bet you've been helping Sofie with her homework."

"Oh, just sitting in the same room, reading a book while she's studying is enough help for her. I think she's a little lonely, trying to leave that boyfriend and his friends behind. Your Tiffany is a good friend for her."

They puffed up a steep tree-covered hill, and here the trail opened out to the wide blue sky above the dam and the lake. As the trail became horizontal again on the dam, they picked up their pace.

Gloria's breathing calmed down on the flat trail, "You know, Rima, Sofie will need to qualify at a previous marathon. And I need to qualify somewhere as well."

"Yes, I know."

"I wonder ..." and she turned to look at Rima. "Do you think you might want to join us? We could all try together, maybe even Tiffany."

"Oh!" Rima turned to look ahead, and they continued across the dam in silence. As they entered another tunnel of trees, the trail now rising steeply, she responded. "I'm just managing to get through this 30-day trial you sprang on me."

"And you've been doing fine, right? And, you're telling me that having this big goal is getting Sofie away from her bad influences, and she seems to be thriving on your support. And you'd get healthier as well, right?"

"Oh, *Dios mio!* What would it involve?"

They slowed their pace to a walk up the steep climb, and when they reached the crest, they stopped at an opening in the trees and another water fountain. A short run down to touch the six-mile marker, a short effort back up to the crest, and they stood to rest.

"First, chase that bad dream of yours away."

"I'll try. It's about my body, though."

"Training does wonders, you'll see. It makes all the difference."

"Well, I already do notice big improvement with these four weeks of running."

"I knew you would. So let's find the best qualifying marathon for the four of us."

Rima took another drink from the water fountain.

Gloria continued. "Let's see, we need a few months to train. I've been thinking that the Portland Marathon comes at about the right time, and it has a good course for trying to qualify."

They started their run downward under the trees and back to the open expanse of the dam.

"When does it roll?"

"October seventh, Sunday. Most marathons are on Sunday mornings."

"Hmm, I'm hesitant. With the diabetes threat, those cramps, and this arthritis thing … my knee … it's all pretty scary."

"But look at you now; you're doing fine. With a gradual onset of running, those problems won't get the best of you."

How long would it take to train? I mean, would I have enough time?"

"We have almost four months until the Portland, just enough time. The Leukemia and Lymphoma Society—they call themselves the TNT—the "Team In Training"—has a four-and-a-half-month training season, from couch to marathon finish. We've already started, and your body will do fine. Lots of people with diabetes and arthritis continue to run."

"How, I wonder?"

"You'll see, and I'll help you. Oh this is a **good** idea, don't you think? I'd so love to have you join me."

1-14. Where Does It Hurt?
Friday, June 15, 2007

Rima came home from the grocery store to find a note from her granddaughter.

"Out with Tiffany. Back at 5:30." *Lonely. It's only ... here in America, in this... empty house...... So much more aloneness here.*

Rima looked for Sofie's dear old cat, Kanela and, sure enough, she was sleeping in her usual spot on the window seat, basking in the late afternoon sun. Her gray and reddish-brown fur glistened faintly in the light, her slight Siamese heritage showed in her dark points; her ears, muzzle, and paws. When Rima lay down beside her, Kanela opened her blue eyes. They lay face to face, gazing into each other's eyes. The cat's black pupils had narrowed in the sunlight to vertical lines.

We're kindred souls, Rima thought.

She talked very quietly to the cat. "So much English, everywhere, when I arrived here. It was too much for me. But when you first meowed to me, I thought, 'Oh, a familiar tongue, like back home.'"

But so far this afternoon, the cat didn't show that she was pleased. Rima lightly stroked her from her head to her shoulders, and Kanela squeezed her eyelids slightly together and sighed.

"Kanela, why have you gotten stingy with your purring lately, and why is your coat looking raggedy? And *mahal* Kanela, why do you sometimes lose your dinner?"

Watching for a sign of discomfort, she gently reached both hands over both her own head and the cat's and softly pressed around the cat's whole body, while continuing to look into those blue eyes. "You don't complain about any place I touch you. Where does it hurt, *kuting*? When I arrived here two months ago, you were such a purry kitty. It can't be age, can it? Is 12 so old? Is it anything I've done? Are you sick? Or maybe just arrogant?"

Kanela turned her head and gaze away from Rima, but continued to sit demurely with her forelegs neatly folded under and her tail quiet. They both lay still, with heads touching.

After a few minutes, Rima quietly asked, "How about if you exercised more? If exercise works for humans to ward off invalidism, how about for cats? Will you want to play again with a crumpled paper? That's exercise, isn't it? Hmm, why wouldn't exercise work to keep cats healthy if it does for humans?"

Kanela shifted her weight slightly and adjusted her hind legs under her.

Is she comfortable?

Rima's thoughts turned back to her big concern, for her 30 days' promise to Gloria about running would finish in 10 days—five, if she counted the Bay to Breakers.

"Kanela, what do you think? Should I push on with the training to try for the Boston marathon?"

Kanela didn't move.

Rima reached out her hand to lightly pet Kanela's head; the cat raised her head to meet the hand, and then raised her chin to be scratched. "Aah. I feel your purr at last."

"Funny, how we often communicate with each other. You know when I need comforting and you come to sit next to me, and you—usually—purr."

Rima raised up onto her elbows while continuing to look into Kanela's eyes. "You know, Kanela, I talk to you like some people talk to 'that man in the sky.' I never did go for a person-god-father who would care more for me than others if He got more praying from me."

She petted the cat's head and back, Kanela continued her quiet purring and Rima felt the cat's quiet calm settle into her much bigger body.

"But you, Kanela, it works to talk with you. Hey, this is kind of like what I like about prayer; I mean, the positive power of prayer—it works even if it's secular."

A few strokes of the cat's back, and Rima continued to talk very quietly, so as not to disturb Kanela. "Let's see: I remember prayer in my *difunto esposo's* Catholic church in Manila. It was so similar to prayer in our *masjid* down in Pasil Manta. Both religions have ritual prayer, even though the details are different. But then, in both we had our own individual prayers. They had the same steps. Let's see," and she named the steps:

Be grateful for what's going well today;
Express concern for others in need;
Sort out and define today's concerns; and
Sort out and reflect on decisions that need to be made.

Kanela slowly stretched out one front paw to Rima.

"Oh, I should continue petting, I see." said Rima, smiling, and she complied.

Rima looked out the window for a while. "Kanela, I think I want to go to Boston. To get there, I need to find more optimism, and do more training, and focus on fun, but most especially, I'll do it to help Sofie. And I need to get healthy. Gotta figure all that out. I think I want to do it."

Rima's eyes focused not on the world outside her window, but on her thoughts.

"Hey, we both need to get healthy. We need to learn what's wrong with you."

She squeezed the ruff on Kanela's neck, and the cat responded by closing her eyes and purring a little louder.

"Kanela, you listen, but you don't tell me what's ailing you, so we need to take you to the vet. You're a great listener, though, and I'm always grateful to you."

1-15. How Do You Get To Boston?
Saturday, June 16, 2007

"Hard to pull dry pants onto salty, sweaty legs, hmm," Gloria said, as she tugged her designer jeans up.

In the parking lot of Wunderlich Park in Woodside, under live oak trees and below the horse stable, they stretched outside of Gloria's car and then sat inside it. Rima sat in the back seat so they each had their "dressing compartment," mildly vigilant for any other humans who might see them changing into their dry clothes.

"And another hazard about putting on pants in the car, for me, probably not you," laughed Rima, "is that my legs threaten cramps when I lift my bum off the seat."

"Me, too!"

"Well, you know that 10 miles is very far for me. After running five miles up that steep climb to Skyline Boulevard and then down again, phew! But fun!"

"New trail, new adventure, right?"

"Oh, yes, and I do like this trail. Most of it's under trees on this warm day, and halfway up—and down—such a beautiful meadow with that panoramic vista."

"Yes, you saw; the view goes clear down to San Jose, and today we could see the Hamilton Mountain Range beyond, and even UC's Lick Observatory."

They continued dressing; they brushed their wet hair back, stuffed their sweaty, damp clothes into their bags, and set their dusty running shoes down on the floor.

Rima said, "I've been wondering, how can some people run so fast? And go for so long? Is it just practice? Or can learning help? I mean, like reading about sports research." She took another swallow of her bottled water.

Gloria sipped her Cytomax before answering. "To do well, you'll want to learn a lot."

"What all? Please tell me."

"Well, let's see. I don't know everything, but I do have a long list of topics for endurance running. Ready?"

"Yep."
"Okay."

Pacing: for each run, and across training sessions. Lots of advice here, lots of concepts, some conflicting, whether length of stride vs. speed of turnover
Posture: *chi* running, forward diagonal (Watch kids on the playground.)
Breathing: rhythm; inhale into abdomen
Shoes, socks, lotions, other clothing; barefoot
Nutrition and hydration, before and during runs
Cross training: core training, yoga, swimming, biking
Positive thinking: maybe half of your success!
Scheduling for our events. And let's not forget:
Pain endurance: "Oh yeah, I know that one!" Rima said.
Record keeping: helps you analyze, for future planning
Research: Plenty to learn! Let's focus on older bodies!
Companions

"Lord, will I have time to learn all this?"
"Oh, Rima, you'll do fine. A little at a time."
"Where do I start?"
"Well, remember what I told you before, that the first two tips for endurance running are, first, to run slowly enough that you can talk. That means you'll be well within your aerobic range, and you won't burn out fast. The second is to increase only gradually: don't add more than one mile a week.

"You just said not to add more than a mile a week. So if it's 26.2 miles for a marathon, that'd take 26 weeks. That's six months, right? —And then there's the point two mile."

"So that would put me... About a half year out from any marathon, is that right?"

"Yes, with two modifications to your calculations: you'll have a three-week taper before the marathon."

"Why?"

"It takes everyone's body three weeks to completely heal from the micro-tears we get when we're building muscle. That's how muscles build. So, with the taper, you'll be in the best shape for the marathon."

"And what's the second modification?"

"You're not starting at just one mile. You're already under way."

"You're right, huh. I'm sort of up to 10: the 10-miler at Buck's on Wednesdays, and this very hilly 10-miler this morning."

"And you started out four weeks ago with 7.4 miles when you ran the 12K of the Bay to Breakers. That was a little far for a first run, and you told me you were pretty sore afterward."

"Oh yeah. So, I've got 16 more miles to add on, in 16 more weeks; is that right?"

"Yes, but TNT coaches their runners up to 20 miles, not all the way to 26.2, and in just 4-1/2 months. So, let's train up to 20."

"Why not all the way?"

"They say they had so many people on their 26-mile training run who got injured and then expressed big disappointment. The injured ones said, 'If this had been the real thing, we'd have finished the marathon. But now we can't run the real thing."

"Uh, okay, then, 20… Part of my question, Gloria, was how come the front-runners are so much faster? Is it just that they've trained a long time and they're young?"

"Well…"

"And is there any hope for me?"

"Well, Boston and all of the big organized races now have five-year age groupings for each gender. So you'll be competing against your age and gender peers."

"*Allah Akbar* I don't want to compete! But I might want to be included!"

"I mean, you get to run with your age mates, and even plenty of the younger ones."

"So there'll be other 60-year-old runners?"

"Oh, yes—Hey, I printed out this for you." Gloria fished into her glove compartment and brought out a little chart. "This shows the finishers of this year's Boston Marathon two months ago and percentages for each group of the 30,000 finishers.

Rima examined it closely.

Participation by Older Women and Men in the 2007 Boston

	Women		Men	
Age Group	% all runners	% of all women	% all runners	% of men
60-64	.57%	1.45%	2.6%	3.4%
65-69	.18%	.46%	.82%	1.35%
70+	.07%	.19%	.42%	.69%

Source: MarathonGuide.com

"So, umm, .57 percent of 30,000 finishers; that's... umm … 171 women in my age group. Wow, I had no idea! But men, more than double the women."

"Quick calculating, Rima!"

"Thanks. Science teacher, last 30 years."

Gloria continued. "And, you'll be astounded; the whole field has been growing fast in the last few years, but within the field, the percentages of women, slower runners, and especially older runners, both men and women, are rising faster."

"A whole new world. I'm amazed. I thought Americans only drove cars."

"It's not just this country; endurance running is catching on in many other countries as well."

"I wonder about in my Philippine Islands…"

"We can look it up when we get home. Here in the US, last year, we had almost a half million marathon finishers, and about 40 percent of them were women."

"Oh, Gloria, you're enticing me. But I would—I

would—I haven't decided yet—I'd be competing against... uh, injury and pain."

"Of course. You're starting too late in life to be a front runner. You can improve a lot and enough, but you'll never be in the front of the pack. Can you handle that?" They both laughed.

"But, can this old body get **any** improvement? Or would it just get worn out?"

"I **know** that you can improve. You can train well enough in four more months to finish your first marathon."

"I mean, I already feel more muscles in my legs. I hadn't known that 60-year-olds could still grow muscles."

"Yes, even 90-year-olds can grow muscles—shown in good peer-reviewed research—and aging bodies can still build endurance."

"What slows us down, then?"

"Well, VO2 max is kind of the bottom line."

"What's that?"

"The maximum amount of oxygen that your body can process in a certain time, and the speed of processing it. And then, the ability to sustain that VO2 max over the endurance event."

"So can't you build up VO2 max along with your muscles?"

"A little, but not much. The easiest way, that is, the least difficult, the experts say, is to lose weight. For all your oxygen intake and exhalation, processing through less body mass is more efficient."

"Yeah. Of course losing weight isn't easy. Especially after menopause."

"What I mean is, the VO2 max decline with age is pretty steady for everyone."

"How much?"

"They say a drop-off of about 1 percent of VO2 max per year after age 35, I think it is."

"That puts me at least 25 percent down, right?"

"Yeah, probably. That is, from where you would have

started out at age 35."

"So, is there any hope for me, then?"

"Sure, to qualify for Boston. They have qualifying times for the different age groups and genders. Look at the BAA site online. Your competition is the time they post for your age group. And, you get an 18-month leeway. That is, you can qualify for your 18-months-later age."

"So what finish time would I need to have?"

"For age 60—and it's the age you'll be on the Boston race day next year, not the day you qualify, that's... four hours 30 minutes."

"You have these in your head??"

"Some of them. It's because I've been trying to qualify for awhile."

"Wow, fortitude. And what pace is four and a half hours?"

"Uhh, four point five hours times 60 minutes is..."

"That's 270 minutes," said Rima.

"Yep. Again, fast multiplying!"

"Back when I was a kid on Sakol Island, We had plenty of 'math in your head' exercises in our little elementary school."

"Hmm, so Filipino schools maybe were better than my..."

"So, 270 divided by 26.2 miles is ... 10-plus minutes. Do I have it right?"

"Yep."

"Plus eight minutes left over, divided by 26, is about point three, right? So, 10.3-minute miles."

Rima repeated, "10.3, 10.3," and quickly added, "You know, of course, that I haven't decided whether I can do this, don't you?"

"Of course, of course, I'm just sayin'," said Gloria, and they both quickly laughed.

"Here, I brought bananas for us." Rima pulled them out of her bag and gave one to Gloria.

Gloria continued, "Do you like learning this stuff?"

"I love learning these demographics, and what I'd have to learn to improve."

"Great. You can also look online at an age rank calculator to see how well you'd do in an organized event in comparison with all the other 60-year-old women in the country for the year in that same length event."

"How well do **you** do on that calculator?"

"Let's see if I can remember. I'm in about the 63rd percentile. I'm trying to improve to about the 65th percentile. That's what it'd take for me to qualify."

She smiled slyly and reached into her glove compartment. "I've got another chart for you." She handed Rima another printout, this one of Boston Qualifier times.

Selected Women's' Qualifying Times for the 2007 Boston

Age Group	Q Time	Age Rate %	As if age 35
18-34	3:40	66.44	3:35:28
50-54	4:00	64.67	3:35:48
55-59	4:15	63.72	3:37:43
60-64	4:30	63.41	3:38:58
65-69	4:45	63.60	3:39:19
70-74	5:00	64.45	3:35:26

Source: BostonAthleticAssociation.org

"Oh, and what's **your** finish deadline here?"

"For 55- to 59-year-old women, it's four hours, 15 minutes." Gloria pointed to the chart.

"Wow!"

"Yep, nine-and-a-half-minute miles. That's a real stretch for me, but I'm trying."

"And let's see; what about the girls?"

"See here?" Gloria pointed to the chart. "For every woman aged 18 to 34, it's three hours and 40 minutes."

"And that percentile?"

"See, it's about the 66th."

"And what's their pace?"

"I already calculated it. It's 8.4-minute miles."

"Eight minutes 40 seconds?"

"No, eight minutes and four tenths of 60 seconds, so 24 seconds!"

"Wow, eight minute, 24 second miles."

"I don't get it."

"You don't get what?"

"Well, you remember at Buck's last week, at breakfast, the guys said they read in *Runner's World* that of the 400,000 marathon finishers in the US last year, only 5 percent of them ran fast enough to qualify for the Boston?"

"Yeah, I remember."

"So, wouldn't that mean that you'd have to be in the

95th percentile, not the 65th?"

"Hmm," said Gloria, "Good point. Let's try to figure out why not the 95th."

"Uh, Maybe by age 60 most drop out?"

"That certainly happens. Injuries, but maybe mainly loss of motivation. You can see the numbers on *MarathonGuide.com.*"

"And, uh, not everyone tries to qualify for Boston?"

"We know that's true. But that's not enough, is it?"

"No, probably not."

"How about this: in the last 20 years, a lot of walkers entered the marathons, and they tend to be older women, aged 50 and above."

"Oh, that could bring the finishing times way down, right? But that'd bring your percentile way **up**, right?"

They pondered. Gloria started the car and headed toward home.

Rima gazed at the road ahead of them. "Eight minute, 24 second miles… Do you think our girls can do it?"

"I think Sofie can do it. For both of them, it's a matter of getting in the training, and…"

"And?"

"And getting the motivation and keeping it."

"So! How are you going to improve, Gloria?"

"Well, you know those coaches who wrote the book *Sports Speed?*

"No. Oh, did I see it on your bookshelf? It's an old one, right?"

"Yeah, at least 10 years old."

"And by, uh, three coaches…"

"What about them?"

"So these coaches say speed consists of two attributes, about 50-50."

"Youth?"

"No, and we can't do anything about that one. But, of course, young athletes in general have more of each of these."

"Two attributes? The suspense is very expensive."

Gloria laughed. "The first is not a surprise: length of

pace and speed of turnover of the feet."

"Which is more important?"

"They show the careful calibration to customize for each individual. But after the 1984 Olympics in LA, a UCLA study."

"Hey, I know that one! We watched a lot of the Olympics at the high school where I was teaching in Quezon City, in Metro Manila. Tell me if I have it right: the first 10 finishers in the men's marathon had a faster turnover than the subsequent ones."

"Right."

"And they were Kenyans and Ethiopians, of course, and their pace was around 90 steps per minute."

"Wow, You do know, Rima."

"So their pace was more important than their length of step, right?"

"Well, in careful balance."

"And what is the 50 percent surprise, Gloria? It's hard to wait."

"Well, to me it was a surprise: springiness of step."

"Springiness? Why?"

"Because, they say, with each step, the energy you expend to make that step goes into the ground, **unless** you use it to spring off into the next step."

"*Dios mio*, I thought maybe that all that springing up and down of the front runners was wasting energy. Why not keep a steady horizontal movement? Oh, so that's why the front runners look springy: the mechanics of tension and release, that's half the reason they're faster. Why didn't I think of it before? I've been teaching the fundamentals of compression - that is, tension and release - in my high school science classes."

"You know, Rima, that reminds me of the physical therapist who treated me after I broke my ankle a few years ago. She encouraged me to do heel to toe raises with the balls of my feet on the edge of a stair step."

"Oh, why's that?"

"Well, she was recruited by Notre Dame University as a cross-country runner, and she said the coach had the team do 100 heel raises on each foot, separately. And when I tried, I couldn't do more than 20 with both feet, together."

"So, that'd be an exercise in which I would not be handicapped by age. My new mantra could be: springiness is half of the effort to get faster. It's non-aerobic and I can do it at home; so it's easier, and takes just a couple of minutes."

"Yeah, let's each do them at home every day."

"You don't need every day. They say three times a week will get you there faster. You need recovery time, especially if you're older than 40."

"Better call me up to check up on me. Maybe there **is** hope for me."

"For your next practice run, is Saturday all right, then?"

"Yep, I'm in. Still in my 30-day trial. Can't promise yet about a marathon."

"Oh, the suspense! Here we are at your house, your ... what did you call it the other day?"

"My *bahay kubo*, little nipa thatched hut." And Gloria tried to sing the simple, catchy tune along with her, as Rima stepped out of the car and turned around to pick up her bag of sweaty running clothes.

Bahay kubo, kahit munti
Ang halaman doon, ay sari sari:
Singkamas at talong, sigarilyas at mani
Sitaw, bataw, patani.

Nipa hut, even though it is small
The plants that grow around it are varied:
Turnip and eggplant, winged bean and peanut
String   bean,   hyacinth   bean,   lima   bean.

1-16. We're Up and Running!
Wednesday, June 20, 2007

"Happy summer solstice." Gloria and Rima called to their fellow runners who had finished their breakfast at Buck's and headed out to their cars. The two stayed seated to talk.

Patsy, the waitress, poured decaf refills.

When they were finally alone, Gloria said, "Four days to the conclusion of your 30-day trial; the suspense is killing me."

Rima smiled. "If you count the Bay to Breakers, my first run, then today is 31 days—and a big celebration."

Gloria's eyes opened wide. "You mean?"

Rima said, "It's a big day for our planet; I mean, summer solstice. And, running is good. Thanks for getting me here, Gloria.

"And?"

"Okay, let's do it!"

"Yay, Boston, here we come!"

She raised her water glass, Rima did the same, and they clanked them together, laughing.

"I'm so delighted you're my running companion," Gloria said. "So let's talk about the path ahead."

"Well, if, if ... " said Rima. "To me it's a big question, whether I can qualify."

"You've been running nine-minute miles the last two weeks, so you can surely finish a marathon in four and a half hours—that's a 10.3-minute per mile pace—to qualify for the Boston."

"I've never run over 10 miles."

"Gradual buildup, heel lifts, maybe yoga, good nutrition, enough sleep. Let's do it."

They shook hands in mock formality, laughing.

"How about your Tiffany?"

"She said it'd be cool. Though maybe boasting at school is her biggest motivation."

"Well, Sofie would surely like Tiffany to be her running buddy."

"She says the kids at school ask how many miles, and

they're surprised when she says that all marathons are the same length, 26.2."

"**Miles!**" they shout. They can't believe it."

"So where would we try to qualify? You talked about the Portland the other day?"

"Yes I did. Let's look. I've been carrying around this list of marathons that I printed out." Gloria pulled a photocopy out of her purse.

"Wow, you always have data."

"Fun, for both of us, right? Let's see, about the timing: The Boston is mid-April. That gives us 10 months."

"I can't believe I'm agreeing to this; I'm so excited!"

Gloria smiled and returned to her paper. "We'd have to register by, say, January, to make sure registration would still be open. Seven months to qualify somewhere else."

"I did think of that; I'm committing to not one, but two marathons."

"And, I think we should have a backup, a second marathon, in case we don't succeed on our first try."

"Oh, two marathons, **three** with Boston? *Naku.* What am I signing up for?"

"With marathon registration in your pocket, it'd be easier to keep up the training, right?"

"Logical, but practical? My poor body."

"I have faith in you, Rima. Now," and Gloria spread out her paper. "The CIM in Sacramento is the fastest in the west."

"Fastest?"

"Yes, its net downhill drop is 350 feet, with very little uphill. And it's also the latest marathon we can try for, December 2nd, and stay within time to register for Boston. So we need our first one before that."

"Oh, the Portland one, then?" Rima pulled on her reading glasses and leaned forward to look at Gloria's list.

"Yes. It's on October 7th. See here?" Gloria pointed.

"Can we do all that in just three and a half months? And then just two months later the CIM?"

"Sure. Of course, we'll have to try to register today to make sure they're both still open."

"Oh, I hope we can get in—and the girls too?"

"Yes, I'll register for four as soon I get home in front of my computer."

"And you'll tell me the registration fees for me and Sofie."

"Sure. Let's talk about this with our girls tonight."

"Yes, of course. I hope they'll be as excited as I am. But I'm scared, too!"

Rima drank her coffee, and then set the cup slowly down.

"But, Gloria, about distance, you've gotten me up to just 10…"

"Yep, we're already under way with our 10 miles on Wednesdays. Our weekend runs we'll gradually lengthen. And then we'll add speed work on Fridays. We can do this!"

The waitress brought another refill. Rima looked around and was reassured to see a couple of empty tables; therefore they were probably not overstaying their welcome in their favorite café.

"And your Tiffany?"

"She'll manage. Your Sofie will motivate her. And she can sign up for cross-country at school in the fall."

"About the weekends, usually Sundays…"

"Oh, I didn't think. Is it about church?"

"It's not that; I was raised a Muslim, *Allah Akbar*. It's about how I love these trails in the woods, and Sundays are fine. Gloria, do you find that the older you get, the more you appreciate nature?"

"Oh, yes! You too? Such a spiritual experience, maybe as spiritual as a church."

"There's something spiritual about running itself, don't you think? And sometimes you even notice more, not less, when you run."

"Yes, maybe because you focus on this moment, this place."

"And I'm aware that humans are not everything."

"How do you mean?"

"I mean, I pad-pad along the trail, and I see animals

watching me unafraid, maybe because you have no deer hunters around here?

"Right, it's a nature reserve."

"And plants sway in the breeze and bend with the sudden gusts, and I do, too.

"Oh yes," Gloria closed her eyes and smiled. "Like the plants, we're affected by the wind."

Gloria very quietly started singing, "How many roads must a man walk down, before you call him a man?"

Rima smiled, "Hey, I know Bob Dylan." And they whisper-sang together,

How many seas must a white dove fly,
Before she sleeps in the sand?
And how many times must a cannon ball fly,
Before they're forever banned?

They raised their voices – but just slightly, so as not to disturb the tranquility around them - in jubilation.

The answer, my friend,
Is blowing in the wind,
The answer is blowing in the wind.

Delighted that they both knew all the lyrics, they squeezed their hands together, laughing, and still reflecting.

"You know, up there in the early morning, I feel some safety because you and the other runners are nearby, but I'm happy to see more other species than humans."

Gloria smiled with a recollection. "Oh yes, I imagine Ohlones, our local Native Americans, you know, before the Europeans came to mess up their lives, up here in these coastal mountains during the summer. I suppose they still come up here. You know, don't you, that Ohlones still live here, especially in San Jose? I imagine in the past that they also looked up and noticed the cloud cover lifting after sun-up. We run in Ohlone footsteps, and we can notice better if other people aren't around."

They each reflected on their feet padding the earth.

"Oh, Gloria, you know that bay laurel grove we pass under just before we return to the lower meadow?"

"Yes…"

"Remember looking up the steep bank beside us, under the bays, where it's cool and dark?"

"Yes; we sometimes see two or three deer quietly watching us. These summer mornings, you can smell the bay laurel oil."

"Yes, it's such a mellow fragrance. It fills the air, refreshes my lungs."

They smiled together, and then both women closed their eyes to continue this reverie.

Rima spoke next. "You know, when we start out on our run, usually my body is very sluggish…"

"Yeah, heavy, we struggle to get enough breath."

"But after a kilometer—a half mile—I've "gotten *mga —manga* - grungies out of my system as well." That's an American word, right? Also nowadays in Pilipino. It seems that sloth had been filling my body, clogging my cells. But, soon after I start sweating, I feel I can run free."

"I agree."

"Then my steps become more springy."

"Yes, you've warmed up."

"I think I love this running you got me into. And Gloria, I much prefer running on dirt paths: my feet on the earth, between the roots and rocks, and when I see them, I know what's under the trail as well."

"Of course we do have to pay more attention to where we step."

"Yes, and under the trees in the early morning, I even love spotting your banana slugs, how they stretch across the trail."

"Ha! As if they have a pact with us that we'll step over and not on them."

"When the sun's up, not yet shining through the trees, already some birds start their noises."

"Yes, our jays squawk at one another."

"And they squawk at the squirrels as well. I see them on the tree branches."

"Yes, the squirrels' nests are also up in the trees. They chatter too, and they run down to the ground and back up, and the birds shout after them."

"Oh, heavenly, even the squabbles in your nature here. What else? Oh! We see silver trails across the path showing that snails have passed by. And you know? When we come out into the sunshine, we see so many insects hovering just above the plants, especially the plants with flowers."

"I'm delighted you notice all this."

"And occasionally someone not in our group walks or runs toward us. Like, remember awhile ago back there this morning, we saw that man come up the hill, "

"Yeah, salt and pepper hair, looking pretty spry out there by himself..."

"Yes, we've seen him now and then, and each time we've murmured 'morning' as we pass one another."

Gloria added, "We do our part to keep this trail a friendly place, not like at a shopping mall. Not many people out there, early morning. We maintain our distance; we honor his solo outing ... but we're not complete strangers because we're sharing this spiritual experience."

"You know, I think I enter a different state. My thinking becomes less analytical, more aware of the long shadow cast by the small stone sticking out of the trail ahead of me."

"Aware, but below consciousness?" asked Gloria.

"Maybe. I'm aware of the stone, and when I get there, I'll lift my foot higher and step over it."

"Yep, gotta stay mindful about where our feet go."

"Oh, when the sun comes up higher, the dew rises up off the grasses, do you notice?"

"Yes, and?..."

"And how the air becomes misty, bees buzz, they hover above the little belly plant flowers—you know, the very low ground cover plants. I'm mesmerized as well, dreamy, but I hope I'm alert. My pace sounds steady, and I notice that my breathing stays in rhythm with my steps."

"You've heard me say it before, 'Oh, let's stay out here all **day** and forget about our responsibilities.'"

They smiled at one another and nodded.

Gloria reached again for Rima's hands and squeezed them. "Well, these trails will get us to Boston."

PART 2: FROM BUCK'S TO BOSTON?

2-1. Food for Running:
Saturday, June 23, 2007

"It's so quiet in this cathedral." Rima looked up into the redwood trees standing tall, their tips above the fog this morning. She and Gloria leaned into the steep hill of Wunderlich Park again and quick-stepped upward.

"Yes, no other humans. But look at that deer up there. Such springy leaps!" She pointed to a doe that jump-ran parallel to them through the underbrush. She added, "No sense for us to run yet; we can get up to our full aerobic effort here without trying to lift our bodies off the ground."

"*Totoo*, I agree. I breathe heavily enough just walking up this hill."

The two started out early on this 60-degree Sunday morning, noting the fog overhead and lack of wind. They wore shorts and short-sleeved shirts, and each carried just a water bottle in their fuel belts.

"I'm becoming accustomed to being out here with very little clothing and nothing in my hands. It's liberating."

"It took me awhile before I stopped missing my purse. I used to tie my car key onto my shoe laces, but now it's in my fuel belt pocket, or on shorter runs, in the little pocket inside my running shorts."

"We're free. No cars up here with their noise and fumes. No papers, no telephone."

"No obligations. Well, the girls have their school coaches. But for us, we do have to watch our step, that is to step mindfully, especially when the trail is rocky. We'll step well, we'll stay strong, we'll be vigilant against danger."

"And this trail will lead us to Boston, didn't you say?" Rima laughed; Gloria joined her.

The trail leveled for a short distance, and here Gloria started running, with Rima following a few paces behind.

After a hundred feet, the trail again went uphill through madrone trees, and the two women slowed again to their quick walk.

"Gloria, am I going to have to eat differently? I've lost just two pounds since I started running a month ago. Do you think I'll lose more weight? I'd like to."

"Well, I get the idea that your traditional diet is good."

"Oh, rice, fish, bok choy—you call it; we call it *pechay*—and fruit?"

"Yes, sounds healthy."

"Well, I've been reading, trying to learn if I need different food while training. I try to search for the facts on Sofie's computer. It's hard to find research results, and to sort out expert information from all the other stuff out there."

"Yep. More vegetables and fruits—foods with lots of colors—and as many raw as you can manage; whole grains only, enough protein, organic, and cook your own."

"Well, that describes our food out in the *boondocks*, except that down in Zamboanga, if we could afford it, we bought white rice."

"I thought you told me that you cook brown rice."

"Yes, I now learned it's much healthier, and here in California, I've even talked Tess and Sofie into brown."

By two and a half miles they had climbed around 400 feet, emerged from the trees, and arrived at the meadow. It offered a panoramic view of the southern end of the San Francisco Bay and the city of San Jose.

"There's too much fog this morning to see San Jose clearly," said Gloria. She turned back to the trail. "Shall we? Another 800 feet uphill, another three and a half miles, to the ridge up there," she pointed. The thick marine layer of fog hung below the ridge; at the top, they couldn't see any profile of trees.

"Let's get back to food and deciding what to eat; is that all right with you?" asked Rima.

"Sure."

"Coming into this field as a novice, that is, with no formal training, it's hard to learn without a guide."

"How do you mean?"

"Of course you're my guide, and I'm grateful to you. I try to learn on my own as well. Now I wonder, what do you have to know, to know what you're doing?"

"Ha!" Gloria smiled.

Rima continued. "So, expertise, controversies, where are the frontiers? How does one access all that? The nutritionists, the sports medicine experts... And can you understand their jargon?"

"Uh, I guess you're right, Rima. I mean, I don't know a lot of medical terms and concepts, so I guess I rely on experts communicating to lay people, aggregating and curating the research for us, and I hope I can listen to the right ones."

"Oh, you do have a sophisticated approach, Gloria. Help me, because I want to sort out the criticisms within the field to get the best professional advice—blame it on my science training, and teaching the scientific method to children for so many years. And in a field like food... it takes years to notice consequences of eating habits, right? I mean, researchers can't easily do many-year food experiments on people. So, instead, they go around to many cultures and learn about different traditional diets; that's the best that they can do. We've had nutritional studies in the Philippines."

At a steep hill in the trail, they walked again, side by side.

"Rima, have you heard of *The China Study*?

"I've seen it listed. Tell me more."

"Well, it's the biggest nutritional study ever, if it's all true. The Chinese government, in the 70's and 80's, I think, gathered info on the daily diets of people of many regions in China for, I think, 10 years. And along with diet, they got data on several measures of health. They compared the two sets, eating habits and health, and showed some startling results—mainly that vegetarians didn't get cancer or a lot of other diseases, whereas animal eaters did."

"Oh, I want to read it."

"And then there's the Crete study. That data was gathered at the end of the Second World War, and those researchers reported that the traditional diet of Cretans was especially healthy." People here in the U.S. call it 'The Mediterranean Diet.'"

"Oh, also very interesting. What I really want to avoid is just believing. That is, I expect to maintain healthy skepticism. I'm willing to take some risks, but I'd like these to be calculated. I want to gather research data to learn of dangers I might not have thought of."

"Admirable, Rima. You'll want to learn what to eat before starting out running, even in the early morning; what to carry with you to eat on a long run; and food for recovery. You can decide in advance, but your body might force you to adjust your plans."

"Will my stomach also get stronger as my legs and feet get stronger? I've felt queasy toward the end of some of these 10 milers."

"Oh, yes, everybody says that starting out; they could hardly eat after running. Apparently the body sends all the energy to the feet and legs, and then the alimentary system doesn't manage well on its own."

"So I **and** my **body** have so much to learn."

They slowly climbed toward the ridge into the low-hanging fog, the tallest trees pushing up into it. Under these trees, Rima noticed, "Oh, look, heavy drops. The path is completely wet here. Surprising, huh? Wet just **under** the trees."

They continued their climb, with Gloria going a little ahead. A little higher, again under the highest trees, they saw the ground was even wetter. "I'm feeling drops on my shoulders." called Gloria.

"Yeah, listen to the rain all round us, but it's only falling under the tall trees," responded Rima. "This is like our tropical forest—maybe no clouds above, but so many drops down here that we could call it rain."

"And in these clear stretches where there are no trees overhead, the path is dry. It's just the opposite of what one usually sees with a light rain."

For the next mile this pattern became ever more pronounced; they took maybe 20 steps under trees, on a wet path with rain falling around them, and then 20 steps that were dry in the spaces open to the sky.

"When I was a child," Gloria said, "one afternoon we had a sudden downpour, which is very rare in Southern California. We ran out into it, and I learned from my older siblings the chant, 'It's raining, it's pouring, the old man is snoring!' We chanted it over and over, we danced and splashed, and then the rain was finished."

"What a beautiful memory."

"Yes. But then we were back to our summer drought as usual. That night my grandfather told me that the newspaper the day before had an article about seeding the clouds with salt crystals."

"It's so different than in the Philippines, your Mediterranean climate here, with no rain in the summer."

Gloria looked up again. "Yes. So now I'm wondering; these tallest trees, the older redwoods, must have been **leafing** the clouds. The leaves must be collecting tiny water drops in the clouds to come together, and then the bigger drops fall like rain. And maybe this is why the rain falls only under the trees and not in the clear spaces."

"Our mysterious cathedral," said Rima.

2-2. Why Don't You Run Fast?
Saturday, June 30, 2007

"So, Rima: are you getting any faster?" her former college classmate asked. Rima sat with Marilu and her daughter, Cindy, in the front nook of Buck's. They had taken a morning stroll through Edgewood Park to view what was the very last of the spring wildflowers. Marilu settled into her seat, her jacket carefully folded over her chair back, fresh lipstick applied, closed purse on the empty seat beside her, and order given to the waitress. She looked expectantly into Rima's eyes.

The stroll had been a disappointment. Marilu, her classmate back at Ateneo de Manila University, had come from Cebu in the Central Philippines to visit Cindy, who lived with her husband and young children in Redwood City. Rima promised them her own "morning spiritual high point" with a panoramic view of the San Francisco Bay. Strolling through the meadows and under the valley oaks and bay laurel trees of the park, they saw a few flowers left over from the spring profusion. But sadly, the morning's light gray-rust colored haze was so thick that they could barely make out the Hamilton range of mountains beyond the bay to the east. Rima thought maybe that's why the two women didn't appear to fully appreciate why she loved this park so much.

Maybe they'll like the restaurant better. They're both "indoor" people, and sometimes we see a celebrity or two there. They'd love that.

"*Inay*, sports car hanging from the ceiling," Cindy had pointed, as they entered. "And dozens of baby shoes, copperized." They had grabbed each other's forearms to point out one after another amusing display.

Sitting in the runners' nook, Rima pointed at the wall to the one nod to the runners who met here each Wednesday morning: a photo of 16 finishers of the Medoc Marathon in the southern part of France, two Septembers previously.

"Oh, they're very healthy looking. Trim." said Marilu politely, after standing up to peer at the framed photo that hung on the wall near their table. Then she sat back into her chair to study the menu. Cindy added, "They're not **all** old, Mom; see these young ones?"

Marilu waited for Rima's explanation—justification? — of her slowness.

Rima thanked the waitress for her decaf and then turned her eyes toward Marilu. "I'm one of the slower runners of the Wednesday morning group. Several of our men are in their early 70s, and they and most of the women and all of the younger people run faster than I do."

"But why don't you run faster? You've always wanted to excel at everything, so why not this?"

"Sus! Disapproval takes a lot of forms, Rima thought, but she asked calmly,   "What do you mean, Marilu?"

"I mean, how come even those older men are faster than you?"

The waitress brought Marilu's and Cindy's platters of French toast topped with fresh fruit slices and whipped cream, and Rima's usual order of two poached eggs with a piece of whole wheat toast, no butter.

Marilu enthusiastically dug in, her knife and fork firmly held in her slim, manicured fingers. "This is exquisite French toast—completely soaked with egg mixture. How do you like it, *Nene*?" she inquired of her daughter before she popped another bite into her neatly lipsticked mouth.

"Well, for one thing, some of those men ran cross-country in high school, and they've been running ever since." Rima dipped a little triangle of toast into an egg yolk, her favorite "American" way to eat eggs.

"But can't **you** get faster? Or are some people just innately faster?"

Rima grumbled to herself, *this is a variation of "what do you get out of this? Why are you doing this at your age?* After just one month of running, she'd already heard so many criticisms from family and non-running friends, especially old friends from the Philippines.

Marilu added, "Aren't you worried that you're looking foolish? It wouldn't be quite so silly if you ran fast enough to justify your running with **speed**."

Rima knew how to respond calmly.

"First of all, I'll never run as fast as some of those men and women because they started early and I started at age 59."

"Why not? Maybe you just don't try hard enough?" Marilu's mouth smiled, but not her eyes.

Rima ignored the taunt, and calmly added, "Second, it's too late to develop a bigger heart and a system that can use oxygen as efficiently as runners who started when they were young."

"You told me that old people can build muscles and cartilage; why can't they develop a better oxygen system?" Marilu pressed.

"Too late. There's good research on the aging athlete. Even very elite runners gradually lose the ability to process oxygen after age 30, and the decline is fairly steady, at least up to my age. After that, it may be even a steeper decline."

"*Sus*, how can you stand it, Rima? I'd think you'd feel embarrassed."

"Mom, *magkalma ka*, calm down," Cindy leaned forward to reprimand her mother.

"Thank you, Cindy, but never mind," Rima said, and she looked first at Cindy, and then to her mother. "Well, to answer you, actually, I **am** a little ashamed. Usually we like to do things we're good at, especially when it's something competitive like a sport."

The waitress brought refills of coffee, and she refilled Rima's water glass as well.

"So how **did** you get this crazy idea, and at your age?" Marilu demanded.

"Mo–m!" hissed Cindy.

This time Rima let Marilu's criticism hang in the air.

"Well, you know, Marilu, it took a lot of courage. But I decided that for my 60th birthday if I would do anything— that is, anything at all new—I'd have to start without the advantage of youth."

"Of course, silly."

Rima smiled and said, "It's like Regina Spektor sings, 'Today we're younger than we ever gonna be.'"

She drank her coffee and added, "I mean, thinking you have to be good at everything you do could really be a handicap, couldn't it?

"How do you mean?"

"I mean, if you insist on being competitively good, then you'd just do less and less, especially new activities; right?"

"So?" Marilu reached for her purse, snapped it open, and dug around for her credit card.

Rima waited for Marilu to look up. "So, how could you look forward to anything?"

"Maybe just be dignified and accept that by 60, people don't do these things, Rima!" and she looked around to catch the waitress's attention.

"Well, I decided not to accept, and you know what, Marilu?"

"What?"

"The benefits are really strong."

"Like?" Marilu exhaled, perhaps relieved that the confrontation she had started was taking a friendly turn.

"Like, I feel a lot better. I sleep better, my digestion is better, I weigh less, I feel more limber, I'm happier, and besides, I've met all these older people who also 'are not acting their age.'"

"Hmmpf," Marilu interrupted, with a broad smile. "Arrested development."

"But they're not being juvenile, they're being optimistic."

"You always were a little rebellious, Rima, dear." Marilu tapped the edge of her credit card onto the palm of her other hand.

"Maybe you're right. You already know about my childhood."

"Yes, down among the Muslims in Zamboanga… where the monkeys have no tails…"

"Mo-uhm!" interrupted Cindy.

Rima ignored the common pejorative toward the Muslim minority in the southern islands.

The waitress came with the bill. Rima gave her 10 dollars and Marilu gave her a credit card for the remainder.

"Your *tito* let you take a wrong path, my dear, by letting you go out night fishing."

She's back on the confrontation, thought Rima, but she stayed with her friendly responses. "Why? Think where it got me."

"Yes, where? Sometimes you do inappropriate things, my dear."

Rima thought, *oh brother, back to the old late-night college arguments, even about whom I should marry!* She quietly said, "Well, maybe I learned while traveling along that path to be brave. Not fast, but brave enough to go out even though I'm **not** fast, and I never will be, by now."

Marilu leaned down to the tiny mirror she had retrieved from her purse to freshen her lipstick. "Well! Are there others like you here in California?"

"Some older runners. When I signed up for the Double Dipsea race two weeks ago, Ken, the organizer; you know what he told me?"

"What, dear?"

Rima noticed the condescension, but calmly said, "He said that I'm the only 60- to 64-year-old woman who is registered, so I'll probably get first place, and...."

"So what's **that** first place worth? Not much! Last place as well."

"That's what I started to say! But he stopped me."

"Why?"

Rima continued as if she hadn't been interrupted. "And he said, 'Don't say that. Thousands of women your age live in the Bay Area, and you're first of all them, too!'"

"That's a stretch."

Food and finances were finished, but the three stayed in their seats in order to find a way out of this tense topic. Rima hoped, *Maybe other customers can't hear. I bet Cindy is hoping the same.*

Rima exhaled emphatically. "Well, I guess we look for

the positive. For me, it's not that I'm **ahead** of thousands of women. I'm not really competing, and, actually, that's one reason I love running."

"How's that, again?" Marilu had started to stand up, but with this she sat down again.

"Well, not being one of the competitive front runners, I do it in order to finish, even though—maybe **because**—I can never be fast. I run because I can."

"Don't you wish you had started in high school?"

"Yeah, I do, now and then, because I'd be faster now, but, of course, a lot slower than as a teenager. And besides, as you know, we didn't have organized running in school."

"No, you're right." Marilu fidgeted with her car keys.

"Back when I was a kid, I loved running, but it never occurred to me that adult women could run, because women weren't supposed to run, right?"

"Right. Not ladylike."

"Remember when we were kids, Marilu? They'd say, 'Don't run, *Nene*,'" and then the two chanted together, "'or you'll get swea–ty!'"

They laughed, stood up, and briefly squeezed their hands together in a gesture of solidarity, and then the three left the restaurant.

2-3. Nothing Like the First Time:
Sunday, July 29, 2007

"Did you sleep, *Nene*?"

"Uh-uh. You?"

"Nope. Let's hang onto your coach's words, that it doesn't matter."

Anticipating this special day, Rima woke Sofie up at 2:30 a.m. for their first half marathon, the first half of the San Francisco full marathon. Gloria and Tiffany would be picking them up at four a.m.

The four would arrive in the city around 4:45, and they knew the routine by now, from shorter organized runs. They'd park in the dark. The streets would be misty and still except for small groups of people dressed in running clothes, all quietly converging on the start line. Today, this line would form in front of the Ferry Building on the Embarcadero. A half hour before the start, they'd take off their caps, jackets, and pants, and put them into the plastic bags that they'd gotten their "goodies" in at the expo two days earlier. They would make sure their individual bib numbers showed on the outside, and then find the "gear check" truck where they'd leave their bags of clothes.

Gloria showed them the way to the restroom on the second floor of the Embarcadero parking garage, and then they hurried to the start line. Gloria had registered them all as "two-hour" finishers, so that they'd start together in the third corral, behind the elite invited runners in the first corral, and those expecting to finish the first half in under two hours, in the second corral. The corrals would be opened to start running in waves, a few minutes apart.

They knew they'd been lucky to get their registration for the first half, for it filled quickly, probably because it included the run across the Golden Gate Bridge and back. They read that 4,200 full marathoners had registered; another 5,000 had registered for the first half, and some 3,000 for the second half. They were lucky with today's weather as well: low 50's to start, very little fog, and, as Tiffany said, "It's already burning off."

The speech, the cheer and countdown, the start gun, at 5:30, and they were off. Soft pad-pad, as hundreds of runners quietly jockeyed into their own pace spaces, faster runners to the left, slower to the right. All were mindful of cobblestones, curbs, and tram tracks, as well as others' feet. Above the bobbing movement ahead they saw Coit Tower to their left, still lighted. To their right, the Oakland-SF Bay Bridge was lighted all the way to Yerba Buena Island and beyond to Berkeley. Closer to the runners, the San Francisco Bay was surprisingly quiet in the pre-dawn dark.

"I've never seen it so calm," said Gloria. "Glassy."

They ran past the piers and Fisherman's Wharf and headed out toward the Marina, where to their far right they saw the sun start its rise above the Hamilton range to the east of Berkeley. A few moments later, the full globe was reflected in the bay, giving double the new light for the runners.

"Just runners and volunteers," said Tiffany.

"And those street cleaners," observed Sofie. "See them?"

Along the Marina, Rima noticed a couple of walkers throwing tennis balls to their black labs at the water's edge.

"*Sus*, we're lucky to have this experience. Thank you, again, Gloria, for getting us here."

Gloria smiled.

Just before Fort Point, directly under the Golden Gate Bridge, the course took them uphill to the Golden Gate Bridge, which they ran across to the northern viewpoint and then back again, returning to the San Francisco side at around Mile Nine.

The first half marathon finished in Golden Gate Park. Now with their medals on ribbons around their necks, and packaged snacks and bottled water to pick up, they walked out to Fulton Street to catch a shuttle bus back to their car at the marathon's start in downtown San Francisco.

Sofie said, "I thought I was well trained, but that was hard!"

"Hilly," added Tiffany.

"Around Mile 12 I got cramps," said Rima.

"Oh, no!" said Gloria. "Where?"

"Right calf, then both quads, then right IT band. Had to walk to the finish."

"Mom says the last mile is always the hardest," offered Tiffany.

"These were—what do you say? —Charley…"

"Horse?"

"Charley horse cramps in the quads. I want to avoid **those** next time."

"Rehydration," said Gloria. "But it's tricky."

"How?" asked Rima. "I've got plenty of sweat. And the weather was perfect today. And humidity, water intake, hills… So what do I do when I get a cramp—or many of them—like today? I tried stretching, but I got even more cramps when I stood still to stretch."

"Carry salt with you, and electrolytes and water. Take water and electrolyte drink at each water station. We'll fix you up better for next time."

Out of the bus, they took the elevator of "Embarcadero Four" down to Gloria's car.

Gloria drove home with Rima sitting beside her, and the girls nodded off in the back. Rima thought, *this is part of our routine as well. I'd better talk to make sure that Gloria stays awake.*

"The weather was perfect, wasn't it? No excuses there. And did you see and hear all those runners who came from far away?"

"Like what?"

"I heard some say that they couldn't believe the beauty; they kept stopping for photos."

Gloria quietly drove, and she nodded her head. "I heard people say they were surprised to start in the dark, and how delighted they were to see the towers of the Golden Gate Bridge miles before we reached them."

"And there wasn't any fog. You thought we'd probably have the usual summer fog, but we were lucky, hmm."

"Yeah. Usually these people coming from far away wonder where the bridge could be because they can see only fog."

"There were lots of purple shirts."

Gloria drove up the Fourth Street ramp, and then pulled into the lane for Freeway 101 South, heading down the peninsula and home. "Yeah, they're members of the TNT, and their home cities are printed on the back of the shirts."

"Yes, and from so many states! I heard a runner with Kansas on her shirt say, 'Oh no, another hill!'"

"Well, with our hills, no one does a PR in San Francisco."

Gloria adjusted her sunglasses and the car's visor to protect her eyes under the midday sun.

Rima said, "Phew! Another affirmation of life, Gloria, and thank you for driving, once again. Our girls did great as well, didn't they?"

"Oh, yes. Your Sofie ran fast, as usual, and even though Tiffany was scared she wouldn't make it, she did fine."

"I hope she'll feel encouraged for the future."

"Yep. She said she'll wear her new T-shirt tomorrow, maybe to the mall. She said its prestige lasts for just one day."

"Sofie as well. They probably agreed to do it, even now on summer vacation. No one else in their schools ran, did they?"

"I don't think so."

They were silent for a while. Soon they passed the Highway 92 turnoff for Half Moon Bay.

"You know what Tess said to me yesterday?"

"Hmm?"

'She said, 'I don't know **how** you do it'"

"Oh, how'd you respond?"

"One foot, then the other."

Gloria chuckled.

"Of course it's not that simple, is it?"

"Hmm."

"Maybe she's starting to accept my running. But I wonder why I told her that. I still can't figure out how to avoid cramps, even with expert advice."

"You'll overcome them, somehow."

"I mean, every non-runner out there thinks either, 'Of course I know how to run. It's human, so what's so special about it?'"

"Hmm."

"Or, 'I could never do that—only people with special bodies can do it.' And neither is right, or, rather, completely right, is it?"

"No. But **you** have what it takes to succeed, most of all, which is determination."

Gloria appeared a little dreamy. "Rima, keep talking. Keep me alert."

"Yes, Ma'am! This afternoon I'm going to let Tess know I misled her about who can run. And you're teaching me, Gloria, that you don't need a special body, you just need to have basic health, without ailments like arthritis, and a strong determination to overcome adversity."

"Yep."

"So I'll repeat your advice, that you need to start slowly and gradually, and you probably need companions, like I do. That's what I'll tell her."

"You don't expect to recruit her, do you?"

"Oh no. Just explain."

"Well, I know you'll do fine on our next big event, which will finally be a full marathon, and it'll be your first. There's nothing like the first time!"

"Yep. Gulp."

"First time: I kind of envy you. And how are you going to prepare, my dear?"

"Four ways, O learned one."

"Tell me".

"One: heel rises."

"Good."

"Two: more cross training, like swimming, biking, and yoga. Maybe I'll start going to the yoga class at Burgess gym."

"And?"

"Three: Lose more weight. Ugh! Mainly, eat less."

"Yep, and?"

"Four: Figure out the rehydration."

"Yep, you've got it," Gloria slapped her steering wheel.

"How much time do we have, again?" asked Rima.

"Until the Portland?"

"Yeah."

"October 7th."

"Let's see. Two and a half months left, then," said Rima.

"But, remember the three weeks of taper at the end. That gives us, umm, seven weeks."

"Lord, Gloria, how can I do all that in just seven weeks? *Susmaryahosep.*"

2-4. Run For Their BQ:
Friday, October 5, 2007 – Sunday, October 7, 2007

"Over here!" Tiffany waved to Sofie.

The girls met at Tiffany's favorite Friday night hangout, that is, when she had no date. Cafe Borrone in Menlo Park was a favorite hangout of high school kids, both from public and private schools, and even some Stanford University students. They called it Borronie's. Fall had officially started, but the evening was still warm enough to sit outside in the twilight, and Tiffany had been holding down a table, doing her homework, for over an hour. Sofie gave her a quick hug and sat next to her.

Tiffany set her laptop aside and looked up. "Sure wish I could run like you."

"Well, I'm nervous as a cat."

"Me, too."

"Let's drink to **that**!" They clinked together the cassis Italian sodas that Tiffany had ordered.

"Wow, tomorrow will be my first plane ride, Tiff."

"No!"

"And in just **two** days, we'll be running our **first** marathon! In Portland! **Eeek!**" They each took another ceremonial swig of their drinks, then raised their glasses high before setting them down on the table.

Tiffany looked up at the darkening sky for a moment, then said, "I wouldn't even be going, but mom…"

"Oh, Tiff, I **need** you."

"I know, you keep saying that."

"I **mean** it."

"But you have your *lola* and my mom."

"Well, your mom needs you, too. We're all in this together, remember?"

"My mom needs me for herself, not for me."

"Oh, come on; she wants to share the experience with her darling daughter."

"And besides, I'm not fast enough for her to boast about."

"All finishers are winners, Tiff, remember?" Sofie

reached for Tiffany's hand to squeeze it.

"Well…"

Up early the next morning, airport, plane, taxi into their hotel, then immediately over to the expo for their bibs and goodie bags. Back to the hotel, then out for pasta dinner with Gloria's three friends from her San Francisco DSE Runners' group. Nervous anticipation, but they shared lots of laughter and photos. By 7:30 in the evening, they were back in their hotel room to prepare and try for optimal bedtime.

"Here's how I lay out my stuff, guys," said Gloria, and they all followed her example. Each used a chair to lay out an invisible runner.

"We'll be filling these tomorrow. Woo hoo!" said Tiffany, and they laughed.

"Who will shower tonight and who prefers tomorrow morning?" And so they choreographed their early morning routines for optimal efficiency.

Four o'clock Sunday morning, October 7th, Gloria picked up the phone that was ringing for the wake-up call. Immediately after, the room's alarm clock rang and Rima turned it off.

Five o'clock and the promised hotel breakfast for marathoners wasn't ready. The four had joined a couple hundred runners sleepily milling around in the lobby, trying to be patient. At 5:20, the four gave up and returned to their room to eat their energy bars and bananas, and they made green tea from bags they had brought, heating water in the room's coffeemaker.

Six o'clock found them crowded into a full elevator going down to the lobby.

At 6:15 they reached the start area. Gloria used her cell phone to locate Keith and Julie from the DSE Runners' Club, who then squeezed through the crowd to find the four women. Gloria asked a fellow runner to take a photo of the six of them before the start. The long Porta-Potty line took them 20 minutes. At 10 minutes before start time, they took off their pants and jackets, stuffed them into their plastic gear check bags, donned their black trash sack "suits," and found the covered U-Haul truck. They tossed their gear check bags to the young man standing in the truck, who appeared overwhelmed by the white bags that were coming too fast for him to catch them all.

At the start line now, the four lined up far back in the crowd, "But we have our chips to show our real start time, right?" asked Sofie. Rima's number was 7231; she wondered if the crowd of runners was really that large and more; 7,000 had been estimated on the marathon's website.

The four hugged, wished each other well, "BQ, BQ!" and agreed that they would be separating shortly after the start. They had their key cards in their fuel belts, so their next meeting would be back in the hotel room after all finished.

Someone was on a loudspeaker, but they could barely hear the few cheer words. And then the sun broke through the clouds and lightened up the crowd. The wheelchair contenders were sent off, and ... at 6:58 the start for runners was proclaimed, two minutes early.

Three minutes passed with slow shuffling before they finally reached the start mat, and here the crowd immediately thinned out by finally running. The six ran together for five minutes and then separated into their individual paces.

Rima was on her own now. *The temperature's maybe 49 degrees, no wind, no rain.* She felt fine: relaxed, breathing easily, four steps for inhalation, four for exhalation. Coordinating steps with her breaths was her way to ensure she was starting out slowly enough to last for the four and a half hours (and hopefully not more) of running coming up.

Rima's shoes felt good, as did her feet. For rehydration and refueling, she had carefully planned the salt tablets and Power Gels she carried in her fuel belt. She also counted on drinking at each of the 12 water stops, both water and Cytomax. Running up the hills felt fine, so far. She checked her watch and the monitors at each mile marker, and she was pleased that the 10-minute pace felt so relaxed. She knew she was on track.

At 13.1 miles, the halfway mark, and still feeling very relaxed, Rima noted her time was right on schedule, two and a quarter hours. She'd have to do a "negative split half," that is, faster second half, to allow for a possible Porta-Potty stop, in order to get her BQ. *But I planned for this, didn't I? Now, I kind of wonder why; I'll have to work harder.*

Could she really keep a faster pace? That'd be astoundingly faster than her times in all the long training runs. They hadn't pressed at all during those runs. *Maybe all these salt tablets, gels, and the Cytomax drink will give me the necessary electrolytes and water.* Yes, lack of those had been the reason for her leg cramps in the higher miles these last few weeks. *Missed sufficient electrolytes and water.*

Her legs started to feel heavy. *Lactic acid buildup*, she muttered. The hills were mostly behind her, so maybe she'd do fine in spite of the heaviness. She took another gel and a salt tablet. The attendants at the water tables were quick to refill her pint-sized water bottle with their diluted Cytomax.

At 16 miles, Rima got a sharp cramp in a quad muscle of her left leg. She pulled to the right to a telephone pole, lifted her left leg up behind her and bent it at the knee to stretch out the cramp. *Oh-oh, right leg now, cramped at the hamstring, and at the foot, the plantar fascia.* She knew she'd have to resume moving to avoid the lactic acid buildup and even more cramps. After a couple of minutes the cramp subsided.

Starting out again, but very wary about cramping up again, Rima was easily able to move back up to the 10-minute pace, she estimated, judging by the swing of her arms.

Several more times in the following miles, first one, and then the other leg cramped in one after another muscle. She tried reaching down to the adductor of her right leg to deeply press out the threat; and each time, in order to press, she slowed to a shuffle. But completely stopping brought on more cramps.

Deep breathing. She reminded herself that in the last few

weeks she had had good success with deliberate deep breathing and inhaling into the abdomen. Now she moved to a breathing rhythm that was new to her: inhalation two steps, forced exhalation, one step. It felt right.

Up until the 13.1 half marker, she had traveled with the 4:15-hour-finish pace group. Several times she had gotten ahead, knowing that at the water stops she'd fall behind because she'd need more water than the others, but then she'd accelerate to catch them again.

But with that cramp and stretching at the 16 mile marker, the group had gotten too far ahead for her to catch up. She hoped that her PR to the 13.1 hadn't signaled too fast a start. Gloria had told her several times, "start out fast, die like a pig."

She wanted to reach 20 miles at 10:30, and almost succeeded: 10:31. She felt heartened; she still had a good chance to succeed. At this rate, she was on her way to Boston! *And only a 10K to go.*

The cramps, though still threatening, had subsided and her pace was still good. *This might work. It's so beautiful out here. I'm part of a big adventure.*

Twenty miles at 10:31, and the 4:30 pace group was still somewhere behind her. Though she didn't look back, she also didn't hear them. *Good. Let's see, three hours 31 minutes is... 211 minutes, divided by 20... Uh... That's a 10:34 pace. Ten-minute 33-second pace is four hours 30 minutes. I don't hear the 4:30 pace group behind me. That puts me at the finish at about 4:29, and I crossed the start mat three minutes after the clock start, so, 4:26 on their clock, with four minutes, 59 seconds as a buffer, plus about three minutes..... Am I thinking right?*

Spectators cheered her on; she smiled to them and picked up her pace each time she came upon a group.

So maybe I'm on my way to Boston. Now if I can just continue to keep the cramps away. Another salt pill, another gel, ... water to process both.

Mile 21, going a little slower but still within her buffer window, Rima concentrated on good thoughts:

If this race is mainly psychological at this point, then I'm going to succeed.

I'm super relaxed.

Muscles... you'll rest in an hour.

I could go down to 10.5-minute miles and still make it.

I'll try to feel like I did at five miles last Wednesday: very springy feet, plenty of air.

Leonard recommended that I think of just a short run ahead of me. So, I have just ... five miles to go.

Relax the hands... they feel a little puffy. Shake them out a few times... Better. Now, Sofie's Coach Ramirez told runners to pretend we've a potato chip—like this—in the three fingers of each hand.

Several times she had to stop to press her fingers into cramped areas and to stretch. Her time had slowed to about 12-minute miles. Now she could just make out the Mile 22 water-stop marker ahead of her. She took her last salt pill and her last gel. Reaching the water stop, she took several swallows of the energy drink.

Suddenly, and very strongly, at the 23-mile marker and at 10:58, the left adductor cramped. Rima pressed her thumb deeply into it above her knee as she hobbled over to a pole beside the road to stretch her leg. But as soon as she stopped moving, several other muscle groups in both legs cramped up. She had to immediately resume moving. She tried five or six times to run after more attempts at stretching, but with each first impact step, several muscles cramped.

She walked. The cramps loosened slightly, and then a little more. She could walk.

Out of salt pills and gels, but has the last pill had time to metabolize? She hoped, *might it still kick in soon?*

She tried power walking, but noticed that she couldn't speed up beyond a 15-minute-mile pace without her legs cramping.

Uhh, that puts me in at 48 minutes from now; 11:38 a.m. I'm not going to Boston. Maybe the salt will still kick in, but it should have by now.

Do I see salt? "Salt! Salt!" She called to a woman on the side of the course offering a tray full of pretzels. Rima grabbed a fistful and munched through them quickly. *Maybe this will get into my system fast.* She gulped several swallows of water.

A couple of minutes later, Rima tested running again, but the first fast step brought back two cramps in her legs. This time, while walking, she bent over to press on the adductor of her left leg, then the IT band above the knee on the outside. She reached over to the other leg for the same treatment.

Just walk fast now ... maybe run at the last.

Mile 25, Mile 26, her several attempts to run failed. She tried running with her knees a little bent, a shuffling run. *Can't do better than a 15-minute mile.* Rounding the last corner, she saw the clock at the finish, 4:39:45 ... She tried to accelerate her new gait, this funny shuffle, but couldn't beat the clock's move to 4:40.

"And Rima Masuhud Osorio, from Redwood City!" She heard the announcer's voice boom over his loudspeaker.

Now it all happened very quickly. She crossed the finish mat, under the balloon arch. She burst out in tears. *I finished! Oh, I finished! I knew I could! I'm so grateful!*

She stumbled ahead. A volunteer woman cut off the plastic ties that fastened her time chip to her shoe; a finish medal was put over her head and around her neck. She walked through the crowd, picking up little cubes of Cliff Bars that had been cut and set out on trays for the finishers.

Gradually, slowly walking, her legs loosened up. *Such relief.* In her somewhat muddled mind, she could hardly comprehend that defeat was embedded into her finish line success. *I'll try to accept that later, when I can think better. Now, mainly, blessed relief.*

She walked past other finishers. *Strolling. How did they all decide to slow down so much after finishing? It's kind of like everyone stands still on an escalator, but why? I still want to walk fast, and fast is more likely to keep the cramps away.*

She walked more purposefully toward the gear check. *Ready for my jacket and pants; I'm getting chilly.*

That evening, back in their hotel room, the four

runners found that the individual results had already been published online, and looking on Tiffany's laptop, there it was: "Rima Masuhud Osorio, 4:40:15 clock finish, 4:37:08 chip finish." Seven minutes too slow to qualify for Boston. She had been on her way for the first 23 miles. But then...

The others? Sofie had qualified with 3:12:12 hours, three minutes ahead of her deadline for Boston. "Oh, Lola, I'm so grateful. And thank you so much, all of you, for getting me here and to the finish."

Gloria had dropped out at Mile 20. "I'll tell you later; can't think straight now." And Tiffany had dropped out at Mile 18, when the course led her near the hotel. She had arrived at the room just as Sofie stepped out of a cold shower, cold enough to calm down her muscles. Tiffany flopped down onto their king bed, and then rose up minimally to untie and kick off her shoes. "Now what?" she sighed.

2-5. Polishing, Interrupted
Sunday, October 7, 2007

Stanley loved to polish his old Porsche 911S, to admire its round curves and to optimize the hunter-green color. Out in his four-car garage on this warm Sunday afternoon, the rumble of his cell phone vibrating on the wooden workbench interrupted his reverie. He reluctantly put down his soft cotton polishing cloth, and said, "Hello, Keith, wassup?"

"Rima asked me to call you for Gloria."

Stanley abruptly turned away from his car to walk toward the house. "Why didn't she…?"

Keith cut in. "They were running out of cell phone battery."

"Yeah. And?"

Keith paused, and then said, "Rima said Gloria will call you in a couple of hours…"

"Because? Come on, Keith, out with it!"

Keith stumbled again, "She's going to be okay…"

"Who? My wife?"

"Jeez, let me say it!"

"Okay." Stanley, in the house now, poured himself a glass of filtered tap water and took several swallows.

Keith slowly said, "Gloria fell and scraped her knee. Probably no bone break."

Stanley's glass clanked down onto the esmeralda green granite counter. "Again? The right knee again?"

"I think the right. They took her to the hospital."

"For what? An X-ray?"

"I don't know. I was ahead of them so I didn't see her slip. They're still there. Julie, Rima and the girls are with her. They were talking about an X-ray, but …"

Stanley was in the walk-in closet of their bedroom by now. Positioning the cell phone between his ear and his shoulder, he struggled to change his clothes. "Dammit! This is the third time she's fallen on that knee. She didn't finish the race?"

"I think not," Keith sounded apologetic. "She dropped out at the uh, uh, I think Rima said around 20 miles."

"And she wanted to qualify for Boston today. Going too fast, maybe."

"Maybe. It had been raining before the start, you know."

Stanley pressed his right foot into his Puma sport shoe. "Boy, Keith, don't you get tired worrying about your wife at these races? Oh, yeah, but you go too..."

"Well..."

"Gloria's over fifty-five now, for Chrissakes! Uh, thanks, Keith." He hung up, and then mumbled to himself, "What am I doing with these clothes?" He had agreed to pick the runners up, but realized now that he'd have to wait for hours before going to the airport.

2-6. I Run This City!
Sunday, October 21, 2007

The four women held hands in the dark in order to push toward the start line of the Nike Women's Marathon. They would run just the first half with the milling throngs that were together at the start, including the full marathoners. They could feel the shared warmth of so many bodies, hear the hush of nervous anticipation. A few people jumped up and down in place since there was space for only a tiny warm-up in this tightly packed crowd filling San Francisco's Union Square.

Whispers about "I can't see the start line; how far away is it?" "It's around the corner; too hard to see over the crowd." 63 degrees and no wind, so no need for warm-up clothes; shorts and short sleeves or tank top, and they didn't suffer from the cold. Perfect running weather was 8-10 degrees colder, cold enough to cause shivers before the start.

I hope the warmth doesn't bog me down, doesn't bring on cramps," thought Rima. She had taken a teaspoon of salt before leaving the hotel and washed it down with water. The water tasted refreshingly sweet after the sharp, unpleasant taste of the salt. She had tried to minimize the shock by dumping the salt onto the back of her tongue.

Gloria heard it first above the muffled talking of the throng: "Ten!" and she added "Nine!" Then those around her took up the count. They all shouted in slow, deliberate rhythm, "Eight! Seven! Six! Five! Four! Three! Two! One! Yay!" Rima looked at her watch: exactly seven o'clock.

The crowd around them continued to stand; they noticed no movement. Someone asked, "Was that the start?" and Gloria responded, "Yes, look," and pointed to the big television screen above the Tiffany store, on which they could see front runners take off from the start mats under the high, inflated arch. Nine minutes after the clock start, the four crossed the mat and the start of their chip times. Gloria reminded them that for each event clock they'd see along the way, they'd subtract nine minutes in order to have their chip times.

They ran downhill toward the bay, jockeying between other runners to find a way to build to their paces. It was so crowded! Some jumped up onto the sidewalk in order to quicken their paces by passing by others. The crowd wasn't paying attention to the usual rule of the race, "slower to the right, faster to the left." *So many, no way to get ahead, to get around, this moving mass in the street,* thought Rima.

They turned one corner, then another, running into daylight. Within 10 minutes they had reached the Embarcadero, where they could now see the bay, and then they all turned away from the sun to run westward along the bay. Fog overhead, so only filtered sunshine. Heard seagulls calling, no vehicles. They heard the soft pad-pad of running shoes on hundreds of feet all around them.

At the Mile 1 sign, Rima said, "Already? It's gone so fast, talking." First water stop, tables on the right side, dozens of high school volunteers handing out Gatorade at the first tables, water at the last tables. "Which high school are you from?" asked Gloria. "Galileo," two responded. "Well, thank you, Gali**leo!**" she called as she resumed running.

Shortly after Mile 2, Gloria said, "You'd better go now; I don't want to hold you back any longer."

"Okay, then, we'll meet at the gear check after the finish." Rima picked up her springiness and her stride and left Gloria behind.

Rima loved numbers. She played with them; they entertained her throughout the run.

Must be around 2.6 miles. One-fifth of the way already for us half marathoners. She looked at her watch: *28 minutes since I started, so almost 11-minute miles. Oh, I'll have to pick up the pace a lot! But the start was so crowded, that's why my pace has been so slow. Here, cobblestones and trolley tracks along Fisherman's Wharf. Even so, now that the runners have spread out, I can run faster here.*

She smelled the salty, cold water bay, the kelp. Boudin Bakery, probably deliberately, emitted the fragrance of their freshly baked sourdough bread.

She reached the Mile 3 marker, and then the Kilometer 5 marker and water stop, and she heard nearby "Where's the hill?"

The woman's companion responded, "Just around this turn, see?"

A hundred steps further, then "Oh my God!"

Rima noticed that their TNT shirts had "Kansas City" on the backs. She saw many more shirts proclaiming Baltimore, Indianapolis, Ocala, and Toronto. *Wow, Canada!* She had heard that most of the out-of-towners found the hills daunting. This hill past Mile 3 was very short and covered by eucalyptus trees. Feet tromped on fallen leaves, lifting Euk oil fragrance up to runners' noses.

Let's see, Kilometer 5 of 21 kilometers total for the half, so I'm almost a quarter of the way to the finish!

Crest of the little hill, grassy slope downward, down to the Safeway owned by Gloria's friend and fellow DSE runner. *Slow runners here.* Rima ran along the edge of the grass in order to bypass the slow ones. Back down to the street, asphalt again, and a wide pedestrian lane clear out to the Golden Gate Bridge, *which would be after Mile 6,* she thought she remembered from the course map given her at the expo on Thursday night, in a big tent at Union Square.

Mile 4, next water and Gatorade stop. *In a half mile, I'll be more than a third of the way, and I'm feeling fine. I'm warmed up now; it takes me about four miles nowadays to warm up. My hands have to be constant windshield wipers. Sweat's dripping into my eyes; it's so humid out here. —Rained recently, warm out by now. 63 degrees to start, and it's scheduled to not get above 68 degrees by the finish. Still a little warm; 55 degrees is better. Gotta drink a lot. Almost one hour into the race; I'd better take another salt capsule. And time for my first Power Gel, every 45 minutes. Next one is at 9:00 on my watch, and subtract nine minutes for my true running time.*

Just after the Mile 6 marker, Rima saw the Kilometer 10 marker, and beyond it loomed the steep hill up to the Golden Gate Bridge. She knew that the road on the bridge stood 270 feet above the water. Far ahead of her and up high, she could just make out the line of bobbing bodies. She was connected to them; it looked like a continuous undulating light-colored, multicolored rope, and she was a part of it in her blue shorts and top. *High fog, high enough that the towers of the bridge are visible, burnt orange. Lighted from the east, even though the sunlight is still filtered by fog.*

The course didn't cross the bridge. Rather, the runners moved along Lincoln Boulevard on the south, the San Francisco side, of the bridge. At the underpass tunnel, runners shouted "Whoo **whoo**!" to hear their echoes. Slow uphill beyond the tunnel, feet padding around her, their sounds reminded Rima of Sulu Sea's soft waves against a shore of pebbles, knocking against one another as the water passed over them and then receding again. They climbed up a steep hill past former officers' housing in the Presidio, Fort Winfield Scott, Mile 7 and a water stop.

Smart, to place the stop almost at the top: most of us back-of-the-packers want to walk while drinking so we won't spill, and then we'll be happy to run downhill.

She heard a fellow runner express her relief at the downhill, even though it was steep in its curve downward for 150 feet. That woman's companion warned her that another uphill was coming. Up another 150 feet, and then another very steep downhill with no trees, and to her right, the view opened to a grand vista.

Rima gasped, *The wide Pacific Ocean!*

Past Mile 10, downhill past the Cliff House, heading to the Golden Gate Park and the finish of the half. Rima passed many runners on her downhill run. They didn't seem to want to, or were incapable of, shifting into a higher speed for the downhills.

I can power-walk up hills as fast as I can run them, and I'll save energy for what's coming later. And downhill I can run much faster.

I'll bend my knees just a little to absorb the impact of the downhill.

The expanse of Ocean Beach spread out before them for miles; she had heard it was about four miles long. *Still high fog, not burning off, but almost no wind. Temperature feels the same, maybe still 63 degrees.*

Ten miles: we half marathoners have 3.1 to go. The event clock here on the side of the road shows the clock time of 9:50 a.m. Subtract nine minutes, that means one hour, 41 minutes for me. So 100 minutes. My average is now a 10-minute mile; I've made up for my early slowness. Good. I'm still feeling fine.

So many purple shirts! Women, a few men, maybe 5 percent of all the runners, and they're from all over the country, even Canada. This really is a TNT run. So many really, really heavy women I'm passing; they're mostly walking.

"Hello, Indiana," she had read on the back of three purple shirts. She pulled up alongside of them.

"Did you start before seven?"

"Yes, we were allowed to start at 5:30, earlier than the rest" said one.

"Oh, with a deadline at 1:30 this afternoon for the full, that means you have eight hours to finish the marathon," Rima observed.

"Yep, and we're going to need it all," responded another of the women.

"Well, you're doing great!" and Rima left them behind.

Slight uphill into the park, past the Queen Wilhelmina Windmill, and a little beyond Mile 11, the half marathoners separated from the full marathoners for their final two miles and their finish at 13.1.

Two-thirds of us are turning to the half finish. So, most of my fellow runners are also half marathoners. Two different color bibs, but it's hard to see the color of their bibs unless I turn around to look at their fronts as I pass by.

Rima looked at her watch. *It's 8:57, and I'm still on schedule with a 10-minute pace. My body is still doing fine, no cramps. Hold up, body!*

Downhill to the Great Highway and the Pacific Ocean

again, right turn for the straightaway to the finish. Rima saw that some of her fellow runners limped and some pulled to the side to stretch out apparent cramps.

Ahead she saw the Mile 13 marker. Spectators had gathered on both sides of the road, cheering, shouting, and clanging cowbells. She heard, "You go, girl! You show those young'uns!" Rima looked around to see a trim woman in running tights with short, spiky, gray hair, her mouth open wide from shouting and smiling. *That must be for me.* Rima's steady, two-plus-hour smile broadened.

Coming toward the grand finish arch, she found energy to quicken to a slow sprint. The spectators roared for her. The announcer on a loudspeaker called, "And here's **Rima**!" *No more family names for this race, just Rima. And that's okay.* She crossed over the finish mats and walked across a red carpet. A tall, young, tuxedoed fireman with a big, knowing smile handed her a small turquoise Tiffany box, and

whisper-quietly, up close, said "congratulations."

2-7. Oldie But Goody
Saturday, December 1, 2007

"Because it's the last chance for our BQ, Gloria, aren't you even more nervous than usual?" Rima asked as Gloria drove them through the gray December rain toward Sacramento and their hotel. The next day they'd run The California International Marathon, the CIM. The girls were both asleep in the back seat of Gloria's BMW with pillows and a shared blanket.

"I'm inherently anxious; you know that."

"You seem even more jumpy today."

"Yeah, but don't worry; I can drive fine," Gloria laughed, and then braked a little and turned her windshield wipers up to handle the spray splashing from the diesel truck in the lane to their right.

"Maybe the nervousness helps you perform? "

"Maybe."

One of the girls bumped her foot into Gloria's seat back. Startled, she glanced into her rearview mirror, but then realized that Tiffany was simply adjusting her sleep position.

Gloria added, "well, you know actors say that just the right amount of stage fright helps them remember their lines."

"How about for running, Mom?" Tiffany mumbled as she again pushed the back of Gloria's seat with her legs, this time to get into an upright position.

"Just enough helps you stay in the right zone."

"You mean 70 percent max heart beat rate zone, Mom?" Tiffany rolled her eyes, knowing that from the front seat, her mother couldn't see her.

Rima heard Tiffany's sarcasm.

Gloria kindly answered, "Well, maybe that part of the zone, too."

"What else then?"

"I mean, just the right focus."

"On ... ?"

"On ... on visualizing success."

"Oh yeah, that's what Sofie's coach said, 'Visualize success.'"

"And have the sense to start out slowly. **Slowly**."

"But the excitement in the air will be too strong to fight." Tiffany snuggled back into her pillow.

"How can **you** stay so calm, *Lola* Rima? came a muffled call from the back seat.

"Calm? —At the start?"

"Well, yeah, then, too."

"I count my breathing."

"Huh?" Tiffany caught her own impoliteness. "I mean, how?"

"Long, slow breathing at first: four steps on inhale, four steps on exhale, and that means that I'm going slowly enough to not use up all my glycogen stores at the beginning."

"The what, again?"

"You know all this, Tiff; your mom taught it to me. It's the energy we have stored in our muscles. If you sprint, you use it up too fast."

"Oh. Four in, four out—uh, what else, Rima? How come you're not even as nervous as my mom?"

"Oh, I'm nervous, alright."

"Tell me more, tell me mo-o-ore." Tiffany sang the choral refrain from the musical *Grease*.

"Right!" They responded in chorus, not only Gloria and Tiffany, but now Sofie as well, who was waking up.

"Do you want to name one of your doubts?" Rima was aware that she had shifted into her old teacher gear.

"Uh, that I'll have to pee early on in the race. And early on, the Porta-Potties all have long lines."

"Oh, yeah. And that's why we all stand in line to go once before the start, right?" said Gloria.

"Here's another one," Sofie called out with her sleepy voice. "How about number two and I can't wait, even for the next Porta-Potty?"

All four laughed with recognition, and Gloria gave her reassurance. "We're in rural countryside at the start of this course, so look for bushes and trees, especially down side streets."

"And find a stick or rock to dig a deep hole for your Kleenex that you pull out of your fuel belt, you've always told me," giggled Tiffany.

"What was that voodoo you told me about, *Lola?*" asked Sofie.

"Not voodoo, but back in Zamboanga, we would call the Kleenex and all that you leave behind *bakasnen*, the leavings, which you'd want to bury—fingernails, strands of hair, anything—because bad people could use your *bakasnen* to whisper incantations and put a bad spell on you."

"Fits in well with concerns about sanitation," said Gloria.

"Oh, Mom!" Tiffany muttered.

Gloria focused on the road; rain was coming in gusts now onto the windshield. "Sure hope this rain stops by tomorrow."

"Well, the forecast is good," said Rima.

Gloria turned back to the topic. "So, what else are you afraid of, girls?"

"Uh, if I don't finish? **Duh!**" And they all laughed.

Rima added, "But we'll all finish, right? Your coaches have given you both plenty of pep talks, no?"

Tiffany said, "Well, uh, what if my body deceives me?"

"Like how?"

"Like this IT band problem I've been having; what if it flares up?"

Gloria interjected, "And what can you do about that?"

"I know, I know," sighed Tiffany. "First, press into it with my fingers, and, and...."

Gloria interrupted, "And remember to stop to stretch it."

Tiffany sighed and slumped down onto her pillow.

Rima thought, *oh, Dios ko, I didn't mean to bring on a reprimand from her mom.*

Gloria continued on with the now-gloomy rehearsal. "What else, girls?"

Sofie obliged a response. "Uh, drink more water and take a salt tablet.

"Yes, and anything else?"

"Oh, yeah," Tiffany said, "You always remind me to visualize finishing and to get my mind off of being sore and tired."

"So that's another way to think about getting your head in the zone."

"How, again?" asked Sofie.

"Get your mind off the soreness and the tiredness. Calculate your pace. Like Rima does, for instance, count how many steps to the next mile marker."

Rima added, "It really does help to find positives, doesn't it. I notice the sun coming up, making the dew sparkle on the grasses. I recall how I felt running under the finish arch of the half marathon at Golden Gate Park."

Tiffany grumbled, "Boy, what would I tell the kids at school if I **didn't** finish?

All three again jumped on her remark. "Tell yourself 'I **can** finish and I **will** finish!'" they shouted in unison, laughing.

They rode in silence for a while, each reflecting. Gloria appeared focused on the route to the hotel 10 miles ahead. The girls pushed their blanket into the back of the car. First Sofie, and then Tiffany, took a couple of swigs from the water bottles that they had stored in their door compartments.

Tiffany's reflections bubbled up into a question. "Hey, guys, the three of you have already finished marathons; I'm the only newbie here. Can you tell me what to expect? Like, how you do you feel toward the end and after the finish?"

Gloria exhaled, "Well…"

Rima gave a short laugh and hesitated.

Sofie said "Ummm."

Then all three burst out laughing.

"What?" Tiffany asked

Then Rima said "Maybe I speak for all of us: that's a big question," and all four laughed.

Gloria said, "And let me add that we'll be turning off the freeway in about... uh, seven minutes," and she positioned the car for moving into the rightmost lane.

Rima quickly added, "But we do want to answer you, of course!" And they laughed again.

"Well?"

"Well, where shall we start, ladies?" said Gloria.

"Uh. Let's review the beginning, and get to the finish later. Let's try to recall some things that we noticed during our first marathon," said Rima. "How about ...uh ... surprises, during the whole experience, okay?"

"Sure! —I can think of one right now," Sofie said. Before the start, I always notice how everyone just stands around, randomly. But then just a few minutes before the start, even if no one says anything, they suddenly get orderly. They go and line up."

"Yeah, and how do they do that?" Tiffany played along, as if the whole experience were new to her.

"I guess they're all paying attention to the time. Timing is such a big part of the whole experience."

Gloria turned off the I-80 onto I-5 North. She interjected. "... From start to finish, actually."

"Yes," Sofie continued, "And before the start, they all try to drive or get bussed to the starting place on time, and then they try to get to the Porta-Potty, and then take off their extra clothes and get them into the gear check bag, and that one into the gear check truck, and then they position themselves in line, and they want at least 15 minutes to spare."

"Remind me of any other surprises, guys," Tiffany said, a little pout on her lips.

"I have one, said Rima. "Most of us have our private motives, but we try to meet them in a public way."

"Well, like other sports, right?" Tiffany scoffed.

"Well, we'll be with thousands running toward the same goal, and … "

"And?" This time Tiffany asked more respectfully.

"And, thousands and thousands will be standing along side of the road the whole way, cheering us on."

Tiffany said, "Oh, yeah, you've told me. That **will** be a big surprise, because we're gonna start out in the dark, like in the Nike Women's Marathon, and this one is out in the country. And it'll be freezing; there'll be frost on the weeds!"

"Yep," said Gloria. "You'll be surprised at how many parents have their toddlers out there to cheer us on, tiny kids in their jammies sitting in their little red wagons with blankets around their legs."

"Wow," Sofie and Tiffany both said.

"Let me add to that," Gloria called out, "The runners are probably all strangers to us, but we all know a lot about each other because we're all headed for the same goal."

"And we've all worked very hard over months, some maybe years, to get this far," interjected Rima.

"Oh, here's our exit." Gloria smoothly steered onto J street.

"Yes, and we all know that we're about to take on one of the hardest tasks of our lives," said Rima.

"Phew!" Tiffany said. "And **everyone** is scared? —As scared as I am? —As you are, Mom?"

Gloria answered, "Yes. We're kind of like the military, waiting for our orders to go into battle, and it's dangerous out there."

"But," Sofie added, "we're here because we want to be here, not because we were drafted." She added, "Like guys used to be, for the military."

Rima said, "And also, there's happy excitement in the air, right, guys? Because we finally get to start! And this is fun!" They gave a hesitant chuckle.

She added, "And all those strangers around us? Because we know so much about each other, we feel like companions. Even I feel like one of them, although I'm two or three times as old as most of the people around me. And they treat **me** like a companion, too!"

Tiffany asked softly, "And everyone is gonna finish?"

After a short silence, Rima answered, "That's the big unknown for everyone."

"Everyone worries about finishing?"

"I think so; every body is pushed to the limit. My friend Denise says, 'Body, don't fail me now!'"

"Oh, yeah!" Tiffany said.

Gloria said, "About 95% finish most road marathons, I've read."

"Statistically, then, we're good," mumbled Tiffany.

Gloria continued. "And then, we're all concerned about the weather. Did I prepare right with training, water, food, clothes, sleep, and will that threat of an injury stay away? But hang on to this, Tiff: I know I can push through difficulty, every difficulty, unless it would be a serious injury."

Tiffany slowly answered, "I'm not sure I can work that hard... I sure am nervous."

Gloria drove along J Street until, passing 12th, she saw the valets out in front of the Sheraton Grand Sacramento Hotel, and pulled to the curb.

"Sure you can, Tiff."

2-8: The Pain is Temporary; Pride is Forever
Saturday, December 1, 2007

The girls happily explored the big west-facing hotel room that contained two king beds. All four unpacked, but Rima still focused on Tiffany's question in the car, "What does toward the end and after the finish feel like? And Rima added to that thought, "... especially later?" Too many thoughts in her head to discuss it today. *But, hey! Recalling my feelings in the Portland might help me to do better here.*

"Sofie, may I borrow your computer?"

"*Siempre, Lola.*"

Rima sat at the room's desk near the window, She pulled up notes that she had typed on Sofie's computer not long after the Portland experience eight weeks earlier, and set out to slightly modify them:

Some of My Feelings
After Running the Portland Marathon

Waiting at The Start:

How intriguing the experience! —Such energy in the air, zingy like the moments before a summer storm starts dropping the first huge droplets of rain.

I've never before seen these other runners, waiting with me. Most of them appear to be here solo, but it's easy to start a conversation because we already know a lot about each other. We're all here to do the same thing. Some of what we know about each other:

We've all been training for months.

Surely we've all had injuries, doubts, hopes, complexes of interaction with others in preparation.

We don't want to tell others what our real goals are for this race. If we're asked about our expected finish time, we'll be more modest than we privately hope to finish. We don't want to jinx our time; we don't want to let the energy out of our hope.

We're sharing the experience with a demographically mixed group. Some have traveled far, have another first language; some of us are local.

Some are experiencing their first marathon; others are veterans.

We all ponder whether we should take some food right before the start: banana? GU? I'll take a salt tablet.

Just before the start, everyone goes quiet. I suppose we're all visualizing what's coming. I did my best to visualize success: be light on my feet, hold good posture, do deep, conscious breathing; enjoy each moment; expect success.

The Start:

At last! What a release of pent-up energy!

The aura! We're floating on everyone's energy—but gotta keep it slow. Let my breathing set my pace.

We're all pretty crowded, shuffling, but as soon as we cross the start mat, we'll spread out enough to run.

Some are passing me; I'm passing some.

When will my sweat start? When will I have to start stripping? In just a few minutes, I know. I'll take off my jacket, and then my gloves.

Ooh—The body is a little heavy; I hope that it'll lighten up as I warm up!

Sky is starting to lighten; I'm happy we're running westward (tomorrow, on the CIM), away from the sun the whole way.

The weak places of the body: I hope they'll stay quiet!

Take a package of GU in 4–5 miles.

I can count on feeling very determined to do well.

Oh, I see a man with gray hair; I wonder if he's as old as I am? And oh! There, a woman with gray hair; is she in my age group? —Is she in competition with me?

First Mile:

Wondering about this adventure: will it go well? Will the negatives fade away? —Or will the negatives stare at me? Can I push them away? Will the body hold up?

I said to my dear Sofie, Gloria, and Tiffany: "I wish we could feel this way at Mile 25!" "Ha!" was their response. Tomorrow, I'll say it again.

We run together for a short while, and then we say "Goodbye. Have a good race; see you at the gear check pick up."

Easy, these first few miles, at least as soon as we warm up. Deceptively easy. The body goes through several stages: warm-up, easy miles, but by Mile 16 our bodies become significantly different, and we won't know just how different until we get there. Can I avoid leg cramps? It's a big unknown out there. And will we have a strong headwind, like they had here last year?

Even though still dark, already we can see the first spectators, some of them children. They're waiting not just for the elites out front, but even for us slower ones. "Thank you!" I call. "Good luck!" they respond. So many people come out to see us pass by, and not just the elites out front.

Jackets, trash sacks are tossed to the side of the road; I hope all the good stuff goes back to Goodwill. The marathon organizers must pay for this service. I bought this great French ski jacket for $15; pink, large child's size and the sleeves are a little too short for me. If it weren't for that problem, it'd be hard to throw it to the side.

That so many people finish a marathon nowadays doesn't mean that it has become easier. It's not like climbing Everest, with a Sherpa dragging up a wealthy socialite wearing an oxygen tank. In fact, the slower ones may be working harder than the elites, because they're working for a longer period of time. Marathons have perhaps become safer because we know more about hydration and electrolytes and nutrition, but they're not easier.

Hey, I can still do this, like the young ones—I can push myself harder than almost anyone, so my pace is not bad for my age. Mostly, people in my age group drop out, I see from the statistics that *Athlinks.com* posts. The ones who stay in are relatively fast.

Reading on, Rima saw that she hadn't written up Miles 2-26, but had jumped to the finish.

Finish:

Short sprint to the finish, and oh, the relief! Success, deep fatigue, but I'll feel better soon! I did it! These feelings last for a long, long time.

Everyone in every marathon nowadays gets a finisher's medal. The organizers want to let us know that we're all winners, having finished.

Rima saved the file, put Sofie's computer in sleep mode, and closed it. She brought it up to her chest and wrapped her arms around it, feeling its warmth.

This time I'll qualify for Boston, she thought. *Last time I learned that I can push my body to the limit, and I came close to succeeding. I've had some doubts, and I might have forgotten how capable I can be. I'll continue to tell myself that soon after finishing, I'll be relieved of the pain. I'll be relieved of any doubt I might have had. I'll visualize success, visualize the finish. And I'll cry with relief, with pain, and with happiness at my success. Once experienced, never forgotten.*

I finished (Portland); now I can take on other challenges as well. I hope I can coast on this success for many, many days. And tomorrow, may I finish as well, and qualify—Gloria and Tiffany as well. Sofie already has her BQ and her Boston registration; she's just along for the run with us. I know she wants to have a good finish time.

2-9. Last Chance to BQ:
The California International Marathon
Sunday, December 2, 2007

"Attention, runners, can you hear me?" the bus driver spoke into his sound system and everyone stopped to listen. "Good news; this is my only trip to the start, so you can wait in the bus with the heaters on, if you want to."

Cheers, clapping, foot pounding: what a windfall! All had expected that they'd have to wait in the low 30's fog and dark for more than hour before the 7:00 start.

At 5:00 they had boarded one of the chartered buses to Folsom and the start line. Heaters and the filled seats warmed everyone inside. Sofie exclaimed, "Look, less Tule fog than last night. You can at least see some lights down those country roads."

Out on the start line, a few words of cheer over a loudspeaker, and the four women did their ritual group hug. "Another adventure: BQ!" Dawn slowly lightened up the rural area, but the sun wasn't yet up; frost still covered the ground. At 6:55 the announcer signaled the wheelchair contenders to start.

Some 6,000 runners became very quiet. The sky was still quite dark, no wind, no thick fog, and at 7:00 the start was announced on time. The four women had gotten up very close to the front, so they crossed the start mat just a half minute after the gun, and they immediately parted ways. The road led slightly downhill, and Rima felt fine: relaxed, breathing easily with her four-four rhythm, (four steps inhale, four exhale), her way of ensuring that she would do better than in Portland, starting out slowly enough for her anticipated four and a half hours of running ahead.

Feeling fine. Shoes feel good, feet as well. Everything parceled out in the fuel belt: salt tablets, Cytomax powder, Power Gels. Up this little hill: no trouble. Checking her watch and the monitors at each mile marker, she was pleased that the 10-minute pace felt so relaxed, and she knew that she was doing much better than she had in Portland, eight weeks earlier.

Spectators lined the rural road from the start; they had been waiting in the dark. *Brave people, and solid support. Loyal to their big annual event.*

At each mile marker, a volunteer continually called out the time. Passing Mile 1, the volunteer called out "9 minutes, 40 seconds," and then "9:41." *I'm being influenced by the faster runners, by starting up front, and surely the excitement of the event as well. I hope I'm not starting out too fast.*

At Mile 2, Rima heard "18:50." *And I'm still floating with the excitement of it all. Another six-tenths and I'll be a tenth of the way finished. If only I could feel this way to the finish! I'll try to visualize it.*

Balloon arch over the road to mark the half ahead, 13.1 miles, and I'm still feeling very relaxed. She noted her best time yet, 2:09 hours. *Can I really keep up this pace? This is astoundingly faster than Portland. Will all these salt tablets and the Cytomax keep me in the necessary electrolytes? Oo, yes, that was my problem in Portland, not enough electrolytes, so I got cramps.*

My quads are getting cold; I sure hope that won't bring on cramps.

At the Mile 16 marker, Rima reflected, *cramps had started by now in Portland...*

With wet clothes and a side wind, Rima struggled, but she kept up the same pace.

By Mile 25, *Still no cramps! Just threats a few times.* Rima had downed six, six! salt tablets and a lot of water. Throughout most of those miles she had used her new breathing rhythm: one step with forced exhale, two steps, strong inhalation. It felt just right.

And, maybe 40 or 50 times throughout the race, she had reminded herself to step up her tempo. *I was afraid I had started out too fast—and would suffer later—but I'm still okay!*

Approaching Mile 26, Rima ran alongside California's state capitol building. The course made two left turns ahead, and the event finished in front of the capitol. She saw ahead of her another balloon arch, and she could make out "4:28:31" on the event clock. *I'm going to Boston!* Over the microphone she heard, "And Rima Masuhud Osorio from Redwood City!"

High school monitors kept an eye on the gear check bags that were laid out on the capitol lawn. Cold by now from the brisk breeze on her sweaty clothes, Rima immediately bundled up in her own warm, dry jacket. After another half mile to the hotel, up the elevator, pulling the key card out of her fuel belt, and she entered the room to find Sofie sprawled on the window seat, legs in the air, twirling her ankles.

Sofie sprang up, approached her, and smiled expectantly.

"Oh, Sofie, I qualified! I'm feeling pretty emotional." And indeed, Rima's eyelids showed red rims.

They hugged. "And you, *Nene*?"

"I beat three hours, 2:53:03!" They hugged and patted each other's backs.

They waited more than an hour for Gloria and Tiffany. "It won't be good news by now, right?" asked Sofie.

But they came in smiling. Gloria said, "We're still going. We're gonna pay for a charity registration."

2-10. Gloria, Grousing
Saturday, December 8, 2007

"Hey, Gloria! How about if I go to the track with you on Saturday mornings?" Stanley had offered. "I'll be your track buddy." As undergraduates, they had met at Stanford, and nowadays they liked attending concerts and conferences there. "Dear alma mater, here we come again."

"I'd really like that." *Wow, he's inviting me on a date! And besides, Tiffany always sleeps in on Saturdays; there's no companionship there. My running friends, even my dear Rima, usually have family, errands on Saturdays.*

The first Saturday they shared a good experience: they jogged one warm-up lap together and agreed to separately do 20 minutes of laps and runs up and down the bleacher steps. Then they met for a cool-down lap. The following Saturday they again shared success. Driving home, Stanley even said, "I feel so much better!" Gloria smiled.

Missed last weekend—the CIM. Today would have been their third Saturday morning together, but he had flaked out. She could count on her car, at least, to start up smoothly, and she was off. *So now I'm in a huff. Damn!*

Who can I commiserate with? She fingered her cell phone.

No one; have to keep up appearances, she grumbled.

Gloria stifled her urge to explode.

And, gotta stay on the road. *She slowed down.*

Turning on the windshield wipers to clear off the condensation, she pushed the "defrost" buttons, front and back.

On the one hand, life is easy; he provides so well. But he's so lazy with his body, and he's ballooning. And he's so tight with his – his, he says - money, unless he decides to spend it. He's so reluctant to spend anything on my running. 'Boston—too expensive for you to go to that marathon.' Hmmpf! Not having my own income, I have no power. It's really tough.

She fumed. *This isn't the way to start a morning track session!*

She tapped her fingers on the steering wheel.

I've been looking forward all week to this morning half hour on the track with him. Stood up! There goes our weekly date.

Gloria had Middlefield Road to herself this early morning. Her car was surrounded by foliage that glistened as it gently moved in the breeze. She reached into the overhead compartment for her Ray-Ban shades. *It's a beautiful, quiet morning, but I'm disturbing it by grousing!*

God! His new diagnosis—pre-diabetes—no exercise... he could become an invalid. Doesn't he care about his quality of life? Oh, Lord! Who would become his full time caregiver? Is this my future? And all because he doesn't take care of himself. He's selfish, letting himself go like this.

Leaves swirled in gusts ahead of her car as she made her way through the residential streets to the track. High definition: everything so sharply outlined, rainbows around every leaf.

Can't give him any advice, no matter how gently; it always backfires. He digs in. When he offered to join me on the track, I thought he wanted to start taking care of himself. He couldn't keep it up. God.

Like, this morning: I asked very gently and innocently, didn't I? "How many minutes before takeoff?"

"Pfff. I don't feel like going; a headache just started."

"Take two Advil."

"You sound so annoyed, Gloria."

Recalling the response she had given, she smiled ruefully. *"If you could do something for your health but don't, then I wonder if you'd rather suffer."* Now she thought, *I bit my tongue and didn't add, "and feel sorry for yourself."*

"It's masochistic, going out there to get a lot of pain."

"You said you felt great afterward, last Saturday."

"I don't feel like going today."

Gloria felt her anger travel to her foot on the accelerator. *Drive calmly, girl,* she reminded herself.

Her thoughts returned to the confrontation of a just a few minutes earlier.

"By the way, you were the one who offered to go on

Saturday mornings, remember?" Now she thought, *I did slam the door, didn't I.* She smiled again, and felt a little ashamed. *Didn't take the high road that time when I left. But what can I do? I have no power. Damn!*

With a green light and almost no traffic, she turned right onto Embarcadero Road, which would take her directly onto the Stanford campus and very close to her destination, the Angell Field track.

She just couldn't leave the argument behind her. *I wanted to add, "I don't want to live—and die—like my mother!"*

Dear Mom, got worn out taking care of Dad … his last years… Even though Mom hiked every morning back in the sagebrush hills with her Mocha, dear dog. But invalid care stressed her out. High blood pressure, TIA's, the dementia.

Her big argument with Stanley last summer sprang into the road in front of her.

She recalled saying—hissing! —back then, "You asked me to contemplate, if you got sick and I were still healthy, if I'd take care of you."

"Yep, our vow included 'in sickness and in health,' right?"

She recalled continuing without responding. "'And do you remember, Stanley? I had replied, 'Yes, gladly, **if** you would take care of yourself. If **not**, I'd still do it, but I'd resent it.'"

Stanley had remained seated, and then he pulled his feet together on the floor, waiting for the next snap.

Gloria pressed through. "I sure remember your response! You shouted, 'Is this a conditional marriage? If so, we might as well just end it now!'"

And I had responded to that with "Anyone who thinks they would not resent it isn't being honest with herself—or himself."

In the quiet of her car, Gloria imagined adding, *"And by the way, Stanley, please contemplate another real worry…"*

She imagined his response: he would position himself for defense. He wouldn't turn his head to look at her. She imagined continuing, *"If I got stressed out by your lack of exercise and all that ice cream you eat, I could get dementia like my mother did. And then you might have to face taking care of me! And I would try hard not to blame you for the dementia."* She reflected, *I'm glad I didn't say all that. It would have backfired.*

She crossed El Camino, entered the university campus, and turned left into the Angell Field parking lot. Her car was filled with her anger, but outside, the university's football stadium and the eucalyptus grove behind her appeared quiet.

I don't want to bring my anger out into all this beauty. She looked around. I'm the third car here. I'll be content to have the track mostly to myself. Think "resolute," Gloria.

She parked. *It's so easy to get to the track. I'll take just the car key and water bottle.* She continued her reflection. *I'd like to avoid that scenario by running. I'm running away from dementia.* And having gotten that thought out in the open, she started to calm down. She entered the track with a walk of the first lap, breathing more deeply and slowly.

Running is my only way of surviving… his half-assed support! I'll run, maybe run this anger out of my system. This is my way to get power, in my legs!

On the straightaway of the second lap, she picked up her tempo, and her breathing grew heavier and faster.

Running is sometimes hard, especially the start, but around Stanley, keeping my mouth closed is even harder.

2-11. Running Out of Time
December 12, 2007

Wednesday morning at Huddart Park, in the predawn dark and cold wind, the runners were all bundled up with fleece caps, gloves, jackets, and long tight running pants. Starting the climb toward the park, four women - Rima, Julie, Marilyn, and Nancy - stayed back with Gloria while she checked out her knee, which had given her some trouble after the CIM 10 days earlier.

"It's starting to loosen up," she reported. "Patellar tendonitis, I guess."

"Great that it's getting better!"

"So maybe the knee isn't going to put me out."

They slowly ran upward through the quiet residential roads, gradually warming up in the two miles before reaching the lower park entrance.

"Hey, Rima, I'm so happy you qualified for Boston!" said Julie. "I knew you could do it! ... What'll you do now, Gloria? When will you try again?"

"I do want to go... I mean this April," said Gloria.

"You talked about that charity getting you in ... but ... you know, I personally, you know ... I wouldn't want to run it if I didn't qualify," puffed Marilyn, as they climbed the slope toward the first water fountain.

"Well, I do have mixed feelings about that," said Gloria.

"Hey, Marilyn, don't be hard on her; she missed qualifying by only four minutes," said Julie.

Marilyn leaned over to drink from the fountain; the others waited for her, then all walked toward the restroom to wait for Nancy.

"What are your reasons for doing a charity?" asked Julie.

"Well, Leonard asked me when will I run it? —Like, will I ever qualify? Like, this could be my last chance."

"And that's the biggest reason: I want to go with you

guys, this year," said Gloria. "I want to play with the big kids."

Several laughed in support.

"The biggest problem," and Gloria looked around, wondering if she should continue, "is…"

"Is?" asked Julie.

Nancy came out of the restroom, so Gloria led them in resuming the run.

She continued. "The biggest problem is, Stanley doesn't want me to spend the money."

"How much is it?" asked Marilyn.

"The total is thirty-three hundred for both Tiffany and me, but that includes the hundred and fifty registration, per person, and the tax credit would be over a thousand. So, it'd cost us two thousand net."

"So why do you let him always have the financial power? Why don't you just use a credit card?" asked Nancy.

"And besides, didn't he just get another new Lexus?" added Marilyn.

"Well, because we need to be able to trust each other," said Gloria.

"Yeah, I agree, " said Julie. "So what're you gonna do?"

The five women ran along Richard's Road, a dirt road under the redwoods and bays along the creek. The road was wide enough that the women could run closely together, some side-by-side. They wanted to continue their discussion.

"I've got to decide this week; I've heard a rumor that the Boston's gonna fill up."

"Oh, send your application in right away, then!" said Nancy.

"Well, I got a letter from a charity that supports school kids taking up running, and they'll hold their last two spots for us until next Monday."

"Doesn't Stanley like you exercising?" asked Marilyn.

Nancy added, "Yeah, doesn't he see how healthy

you've become? And you seem so much happier now, these last few years."

The road led up a hill, the last before they would turn off onto a trail that led steeply upward. Gloria slowed to a long stride walk, reached down to rub the side of her knee, and then resumed her brisk walk in order to catch up with the others.

"He still thinks that all runners eventually ruin their bodies; and he thinks over fifty is over the hill. And he doesn't want me to hurt myself, he says."

"Hey, Gloria, you're not gonna let that knee injury from the CIM put you out, are you? Like a cop-out to try to save your marriage?" asked Nancy.

"What does your daughter say?" asked Julie.

"She doesn't want to leave Sofie and Rima in the lurch."

Rima was silent. She knew that Stanley had agreed to Gloria's donation for Rima and Sofie to go. Gloria had even arranged for a formal donation to the school for Sofie's entrance as the first marathon contender from Menlo-Atherton High School. And Stanley had agreed to the reasoning that Sofie should have her grandmother along as support and chaperone, especially since she had qualified to run. He did jokingly remark *Little Brown Brother*, in reference to the 1960 classic history book about the Americans' patronizing attitude toward Filipinos during the Spanish-American War of 1898-1902.

The runners reached a little plateau where they all paused before going up the next hill. Gloria announced, "Well, I want to go to Boston. I'll think of something. I'll try to find the right time. This is a great place to sort things out; I'll face him, but it's gotta be within the next four days."

2-12. Mem Chu
Friday, December 14, 2007

"I'll be in front of the church by six o'clock, so that I'll be first in line and get the best seats for us when they open," Rima told her daughter. "I can't wait!"

"Oh, thank you, Mom. I'll come directly from work, and I'll be there by seven thirty," Tess responded, as she grabbed her coat, purse, and car keys. "I'm so happy we'll finally have these moments. We'll sing together... and in Mem Chu, the Stanford University Memorial Church!" Then she rushed out the door.

Rima felt grateful that her daughter had had several years of experience singing in the *Messiah*, in alto voice, just as Rima had sung back in Manila. *At least some good traits pass on to the next generation*, she mused.

She had stood for an hour in the cold in front of the church, one of the first to arrive in what would become a long line out into the courtyard. *I promised Tess I'd get here early in order to get one of the best seats: front, center, just behind the volunteer orchestra and looking up at the conductor. I love the beautiful gold and colored mosaics out here, the rich colors of stained glass windows, lighted from inside.*

Finally, doors were opened and the crowd, albeit dignified, rushed through the narthex into the sanctuary. Rima had had a lifetime of training on targeting her goal and working her way through crowds; she got the seats she wanted.

The contrast! Warm air, warm light from huge chandeliers, an enormous cathedral, happy anticipation inside this huge sanctuary. Our excited voices echo off the walls—probably reverberate more than once—with a low roar.

Maybe I'm as excited as anyone. In this famous university, and I get to participate! My too-busy daughter—we'll have a couple of hours together. This music fills me every December, and what a place to celebrate this year, in California! Tess told me the conductor is so fantastic that we'd want to follow him anywhere. Tess says that almost all of this crowd has had years of musical training, can read music, and can sing well. She says the general population in this country nowadays can't read music and doesn't even sing much. We'll be a special community for two hours, honoring this 250-year-old music and sharing. We'll all sing, we'll sing even the solos that Handel wrote, so we won't have a hint of competition, only sharing.

And Rima still floated in the warm breeze of her "BQ"euphoria. *I'm celebrating a secret from all the others here. Oh, life is good!* Twelve days had passed since she had qualified in Sacramento for the Boston, and now both she and Sofie were safely registered for the big event in April.

Singing together, sharing, that's such an important reason we love music. Hey, we shared the experience of running and didn't compete against each other, that is, the 90 percent of us back behind the elites. . And maybe that's why I don't mind that I'll never be a contender. In Sacramento, I ran the distance, sharing, not competing, with my fellow runners. But I did race against the clock.

Tess rushed into the church at the last minute to look for her mother, somewhere among the already packed pews. She looked down to where she had advised her mother to sit, in the second pew behind the volunteer orchestra, on the left side next to the center aisle. And there she was, sitting by herself, holding a wide space next to her. Tess recognized her mother's short salt-and-pepper hair and the red cashmere scarf around her neck that was Tess's early Christmas gift for her to wear tonight.

"I'm here, Mom," Tess whispered, and helped her mother pick up her place-saving coat on the bench. Rima smiled apologetically to the man on her left as she scooted toward him.

Rima looked up high in wonder at this grand cavern, where the church's stained-glass windows and wall figures sparkled from the glow of the chandelier lights. A little lower, the balconies on each side were already filled, and in back, the pipe organ rose majestically above the large filled balcony. Down at her level, among the warm oak pews, she saw a couple thousand people, all buzzing with happy anticipation, by now quickened to the edge of impatience and ready to make music together. Many were returnees, and they knew this chamber would soon resonate, carrying them all into their collective peak experience.

Everyone seemed to notice when the university choir members on stage turned to their left with smiles and applause. The congregation followed their cue and burst into applause, cheers, and even whistles, when their beloved conductor, Stephen Sano, arrived. For the last few years, this sing-a-long invited no soloists, so anyone— everyone! —could sing any part they wanted. This meant that hundreds of people stood up to sing the solo parts, and of course the entire congregation stood to sing every chorus piece. For the orchestra, only *The Trumpet Shall Sound* solo would be played by one instrumentalist.

After the first tenor solo, *Comfort Ye My People*, Rima whispered to her daughter "I'm sitting next to a beautiful voice." Tess peeked around her mother to see a tall man with an angular face, thin, graying hair, and bright enthusiastic eyes. A little earlier, she had seen him help the woman next to him (his mother?) take off her tan cashmere coat and cream-colored silk scarf.

With the other altos in the audience, Rima and Tess stood to sing the solo *O Thou That Tellest Good Tidings*. Just as they sat back down, the man's companion dropped her program, and it sailed to Rima's feet. Rima rescued it, and as she returned it, the man smiled into her eyes as he took it for the woman, who allowed a brief, shallow smile to thank Rima.

Why such a pallid, kind of impolite, gesture? Rima wondered. *Maybe she's embarrassed to have dropped her paper.*

The thousands sang, they applauded; they reveled in Conductor Sano's tradition of singing the *Hallelujah* chorus. "Shall we sing the chorus again?" he asked, to a swelling of applause and cheers. They did sing again, and followed with more applause and calls. Professor Sano held high the *Messiah* scorebook and the applause swelled even more. Rima thought, *this music brings me to a peak experience every time: the long buildup of tension, with "hallelujahs" and "forever and ever," and then the release! It sends a thrill down my spine, the second time too, and I'm singing through tears and*

trembling lips. Maybe for all of us its collective peak experience is
like a very tense baseball game, and finally, finally, our team scores,
and the spectators explode out of their seats to shout their release.

The participants reluctantly picked up their overcoats
to leave. As they slowly filed up the full aisles, they
recognized old friends, they greeted others, and they
slowed down the pack, but no one was in a hurry to leave.

Out of the inner quad and into near darkness, the
crowd passed by the group of dark bronze Rodin figures
quietly contemplating—what? —academia? Mother and
daughter huddled together with arms interlocked, and they
briskly walked in the cold to Sofie's car, which Rima had
driven and parked close to the front of the Oval. Tess
climbed into the passenger seat, to be driven to her own
car, farther away in the eucalyptus grove.

As Rima moved to open the driver's door, she stopped
to wait for the couple going to the car next to her.

"Oh, hello again," he said. "Our pew companions!"

"Oh, hello," replied Rima, quietly. She waited while he
helped his—mother? —into the car, helped her with the
safety belt, and closed the door. He started to walk around
the car to get in, but then stopped. He returned to the
passenger side and turned back toward Rima. He opened
the cupped palm of his hand toward her, indicating she
could safely proceed, and then held her door open for her
to climb in. Rima tucked her skirt onto the seat next to her
legs.

"Grand experience, wasn't it?" he said.

"Oh, yes, I'm very fortunate to be part of it," she
responded.

"You have a beautiful voice."

"Oh, thank you. You as well."

"Thank you… Well, good evening."

"Good evening," Rima responded. Tess sat quietly in
the passenger seat, looking straight ahead at the dark
oval—the lawn.

The door was still open, this man still holding it. And
what was he saying? "Uh, hey, may I take this opportunity

to invite you for coffee tomorrow morning at the Arrillaga
Alumni House—over there?" He pointed. "How about ten
o'clock?"

He waited. Then he rushed to add, "Oh, my name is
Glenn Hamilton. And you're ... ?"

Rima gulped, "Well, uh ... Karima Masuhud Osorio."
She offered her hand and they shook. "Oh, where is that
again? Uh, okay. Ten o'clock." He smiled, held up one
thumb, and closed the door for her.

She glanced at her wide-eyed daughter, put the key into
the ignition, backed the car out of the space, and joined
the slow crawl of cars driving around the Oval to exit the
campus on Palm Drive.

They drove in silence for a few moments, and then
Rima said, "*Sus*, Tess, what do you think?"

"Well, Mom, you don't have to go just because you said
you would."

Rima paused, and then said, "His voice is so
beautiful—a baritone, really. And the coffee shop,
especially here on the campus, would be very safe, *hindi
ba?*"

Tess rummaged around in her purse for her Chapstick.
"What do you think he wants, Mom?"

"Well, maybe just some conversation, maybe to talk
about our *Messiah* experience."

"Hmmpf."

Rima added, "And besides, he wouldn't take advantage
with his own mother right there, would he?"

"Hmmpf."

"Anyway, this is just a trial run. Safe."

"So go for it, Mom," said Tess, brushing her thighs to
smooth out the folds in her coat.

2-13. Path to the Ancient Oaks
Saturday, January 26, 2008

They walked. Glenn showed Rima the Baylands, Edgewood Park, the Rancho San Antonio trails.

They met on Saturdays. Soon they added the Dish to their morning schedules, early, and after their walks, he drove down 280 to work. She knew that this walking was good cross training, but she reserved her Wednesday, Friday, and Sunday mornings for running.

Glenn marveled at her courage. "You're so brave to make the trip to the U.S. by yourself and to help out your family in need and especially to take up running," he said. "Are you really going to run that marathon in Boston?"

"Boston has become a big American prize to me," she laughed. "And you're helping me get there with all these walks. But you take care of your family as well; you're so good to your mother and also your daughter," she said. "They're very lucky."

"I regret that I can't run with you. My knees. I used to play a lot of tennis."

"Oh, I'm very sorry... about the knees."

They looked into each other's eyes. They each found the other's appearance attractive and exotic. *I suppose I look as exotic to him as he does to me,* she thought. *His eyes ... what shape? ... Three cornered! A third angle, up there by the top of his nose. And his irises are so, so ... multi-colored. Gray, blue, green, brown. What's their pattern? It's so complex; like a precious cowry seashell. Mesmerizing.*

He marveled at her cool-appearing skin, even on this warm-for-January afternoon.

"I guess I can control it somewhat: as girls, we learned not to get sweaty."

"How?"

"Well, kind of like you learn to pick up the hot handle of a pan without getting burned."

"You do? I don't."

She paused, and then added, "No? Well, anyway, I can't control the sweat when I'm running long distance."

"Of course not; you have a high metabolism, and besides, sweating is healthy."

They hiked side by side down one of the Dish's four steep hills above the Stanford University campus, the beloved, contended, "natural" terrain with beautiful view that was surrounded by residences and highway.

"Oh, I'm so happy we're both—how do you say it nowadays? I hear that 'liberal' is a bad word now—we're 'Bleeding Heart Progressives,'" she said, laughing.

"Yes, always rooting for the underdog," he replied. "And always willing to make a change. But don't tell my mother; I can't talk politics with her," he laughed.

"Or with my daughter's boyfriend, I've learned," said Rima, with a chuckle, and she turned back to the trail.

They moved to quieter, wooded trails in the Portola Valley hills and stopped at the crest of a hill to admire one another.

"I cannot get enough of your eyes; they're so new for me," he said, placing his hands on her shoulders.

"The same for me; I have never seen eyes like yours up close," she said. "I cannot … comprehend them all at once."

"Oh, the same with me!" he said. "Here, let me look up close," and he pulled her toward him. "So—can't pass up the word—'almond shaped,' even though almond is a temperate climate nut and you've come from the tropics."

"I'm a nut?" she asked, smiling.

"Silly… Now, back to your eyes! Your irises are so dark that any light out here dances in them and reflects off them. So sparkly!"

They laughed and she gently pushed him away. They turned back to the path.

They agreed on afternoon picnics at a favorite rocky outcrop on the west side of Russian Ridge near Skyline Boulevard in the Santa Cruz Mountains, just a half hour's drive away. From this viewpoint they could look out toward the Pacific Ocean across a half dozen ridges. They felt especially fortunate on those afternoons when no ocean fog had rolled in, and they could see the water shining far beyond the hills.

"Dark green and gold hills, these colors in nature are so exotic for me!" said Rima, admiring their view. She saw the dark green needles of conifers: Douglas Fir and occasional redwood groves. Broadleaf evergreens were dark green as well: bay laurel groves and native black and blue oaks. Between these tree stands lay wide open spaces covered by last year's grasses, now spent but still standing and shining gold in the afternoon sun.

"See how the hills are turning green again?" asked Glenn. "We've had enough rain over the winter and some warmer weather that our new grass is sprouting up, and soon it will cover the old."

"Yes, light, bright green," she said.

Usually they first hiked down to the Ancient Oaks on the coast side of the ridge. The path led between some 20 huge trees, spread out wider than they were tall, with thick, gnarled, moss-covered limbs reaching up and over to one another, forming a canopy over the path. The path continued past the oaks down into a little glen—at this time of year with a stream trickling down toward the ocean. During most of the year the earth was dry.

The path led Glenn and Rima back uphill to their picnic spot. They returned to a broad, flat rock among the grasses, facing the wide sky and a panoramic view of the green and gold trees and grasses, the mountain ridges, and beyond, to the sparkling blue-gray ocean. They had carried their food and a space blanket in backpacks. First they laid out the space blanket, blue side up, silver under, and then their picnic of cut-up vegetables and fruits, followed by wine and cheese. They sat to eat and frequently paused to experience the view.

He reached for her hand. He was again surprised how smooth her skin was.

"I'm not a hairy ape," she laughed, as she gently tugged at the hair on his forearm. "You're so bushy, but I guess it looks good, for a man." They smiled at one another with laughing, teasing eyes.

They looked out toward the hills before them and beyond to the ocean. A red-tailed hawk rode a thermal not far above them, hovering effortlessly. In the late afternoon sun, the hills cast shadows that slowly advanced toward their picnic spot, through the little valley below and then up the hill toward the two people.

Rima chuckled and then said, "I can't get this song out of my head." She quietly sang the first phrase of *Oh Thou That Bringest Good Tidings to Zion*, her clear voice very small in the late afternoon breeze on the hilltop.

Glenn smiled and sang the next phrase, "Get thee up into the high mountain."

They hummed, both forgetting the next line, and then they joined together: "Arise, shine, for thy light is come, and the glo-o-o-o-o-o-o-o-o-o-o-o-o-o-o-o-o-ry of the Lord is risen upon thee!"

They punctuated the long O syllable over the 33 notes. Handel's melody rose up, rolled down, and rose up again, like the hills before them. They inhaled deeply and then laughed and hugged, delighting in sharing this experience and in recalling their first meeting.

Now sitting arm in arm, they waited for the sunset. The late afternoon breeze picked up the edges of their space blanket, and the air surrounding them started to mist up.

"Oh, it's chilly!" Rima said, and Glenn pulled her closer. The sky's milky blue hue started its progression of evening colors. The blue darkened, then turned toward purple as the sun sank into the coastal fog hovering just above the farthest ridge of peaks. Rays of orange and then pink shot up where the sun had sunk, and then they slowly faded into the background of purple, then blue gray, and gradually dark gray.

"Sunset lasts so long here," said Rima. "Maybe a half hour. In the Philippines, daylight just clamps shut in maybe five minutes."

"Tell me more," he whispered, close to her as he smiled dreamily into her eyes.

"On the Sulu Sea, it's the same sun but different colors,

different breezes. It's warm enough to caress your bare arms. More humid, not so cool," said Rima.

"The colors?"

"Fiercer, more intense, more brilliant. More vivid orange, pink, dark red. And gone very soon."

"I want to learn all about you," he said.

"*Ako rin,* same here," she said. "And me, you."

They laid back on the ground cover and in the growing dusk could still see into each other's eyes.

2-14. Lean Forward
Sunday, February 3, 2008

At Mile Nine of the San Francisco Half Marathon, out on San Francisco's Great Highway, the angry ocean finally blasted the heavy rain horizontally into the runners' faces. They could move forward only by deliberately leaning into the wind, which gusted so sharply and unpredictably that they continually staggered to stay upright.

By now Rima and her running companions had separated, most others having gone ahead of her. Besides the four women, several Buck's Runners started with them: Leonard, Nancy, and Marilyn. Before the rain, the crowd of runners had been strangers racing in competition; now, leaning into the gusts, they were companions, sharing not just the race, but also the elements. The weather had made this an even bigger adventure.

"Big enough challenge to write home about!" A drenched man on Rima's windward side called to her as she passed by. Protecting her eyes from the rain and wind, she kept them mostly closed. She could barely see the man or beyond him to the ocean which was churning white, its spray swirling high above.

"Yeah, when you can get your fingers thawed enough to work again," she shouted back to him through the headwind.

She mused to herself as she blustered along. *With this thin rain jacket, I think I can stay warm enough to finish. Here comes the 10-mile marker. My legs are threatening cramps; maybe these new salt tablets will keep them from really grabbing me. But those runners who are really soaked, some of them still out here won't finish.*

Too bad that our Julie didn't come: she's missing a big adventure. She could even have won again. So many elites decide to drop out with the Big Decline with age. And she's had far to fall—she's been a champ so many years, whereas I'm happy just to finish. Well, maybe I'll win my age group by default again, even with so many entrants. Some of the fastest my age must have stopped running; what a shame, but ... improves my chances for placing.

Isn't it ironic ... I win over these hotshots? But I don't want to win against my friends; I hope Julie comes back.

She checked her condition: *Core and head still dry. My raincoat and hood are keeping up their work. My hands are okay with these hand warmers—still inside my gloves. Face, pants, legs, shoes: wet, but I feel okay. I'm so fortunate; so many around me are purple-lipped.*

Through the driving rain, Rima could just make out stoplights ahead of her. *Third light ahead, that's where we turn up into the park and the finish. I can make it. Now Rima, lean forward even more and let gravity help move you forward.*

Meanwhile, Julie was home, fighting back her tears, while watching gusts of rain crash against her bedroom window. She muttered to Keith. "Can you believe that Rima might even win our age group again? I'm much faster. Damn! I've got to get off this injury, and I've got to do more track work and get back to the high mileage."

Keith's thumbs continued their busy work on his iPhone.

2-15. Living is Moving
Sunday, February 3, 2008

Early that same afternoon, Rima and Glenn walked the path up and around Edgewood Park, even though the wind was still blowing in blusts, like during the half marathon.

I'm getting accustomed to walking with this man on the weekends. It's exciting, comforting, but a little risky, getting involved.

"Brave of you, racing in the rain. Tell me."

"Oh, Glenn, it's a big adventure! At Mile Nine out on San Francisco's Great Highway, we could see rain in the ocean as we ran along toward the zoo. And on the way back to the finish in the park, we had to—oh, really! — lean into the wind, and then the rain finally got us, right in our faces!"

"So, were you worried about getting too cold?"

"Not I, but many were really suffering. I wonder if we'll read about it in the paper. But on the other hand, the papers hardly cover distance races."

She stopped to look at him. "I'm glad that you care."

"I'd like to come to see you finish, but it seems a little early to be so public."

"Oh, I'm complimented." She laughed and squeezed his hand.

"Around Mile 11, two of us picked up a young woman who slipped right in front of us; she was shivering."

"Oh, hypothermia," he said.

"Yeah, if an organizer's car or an ambulance had come by, we'd have signaled for it. I gave her my hand warmers and gloves, and we walked along with her for awhile until she said she could manage; she looked better, so we ran on."

"How about your hands, then?"

"Completely wet, but I pulled my jacket sleeves over them, so they stayed warm for the last two miles."

"Smart of you."

"Thanks.

"So, this running isn't too much for you, then?"

"Oh, no, exciting! —Of course, we were all very happy to change into dry clothes in the car and turn on the heater."

"I do worry about you sometimes."

"Your concern for me is very touching, Glenn. But as you know, I've decided to take the active path at this crossroad of my life."

"But do you have to run so far?"

"Gradual buildup makes it safe. We all work to find our balance. Everyone makes dozens—hundreds—of decisions every day, don't we?"

"I suppose so. I don't mean to discourage you; I'm just concerned. It's all so new to me."

"You dear man." She gave him a quick hug. "I hope you'll feel reassured as time goes by. I do try to always be mindful, each step, each decision. Here in California I have less difficulty making my own decisions. In the Philippines, the social control of my relatives is stifling."

"Tell me about it. Like my mother has never learned to turn loose. She loves stability and hates the changes taking place in the world today. She wants us all to show more mutual respect to family, friends, and stasis. She's having a struggle accepting my changes."

"Well, there's the good along with the bad. In my home, my little island, we all know everyone. Adults watch all the kids playing and handle problems or report to the parents."

"You care for your neighbors, then."

"Oh yes. Here, you can have more innovation, more change, faster evolution—but where's the family? You seemed unusual for an American. The first time I saw you, I appreciated that you had brought your mother to the *Messiah* sing-along."

"Family life is evolving fast in this country; some good, some unhealthy."

"Yes, it's hard for us Filipinos to understand American individual independence."

"They say it's because we have a pioneer heritage:

people who moved out west, until at least after World War
I, expected to never see their families again. And so the
people in the Wild West had less social control on each
other because they didn't have to answer to the families or
neighbors they left back east."

"But, Glenn, can anyone ever return home? Would
they accept you back, with all the changes you would have
made in your time away?"

"I guess our heritage from the 18th and 19th centuries is
that we didn't have to face the folks back home, and so we
could make more rapid changes, some of them positive,
not all of them."

"If you go home, you have to face the social control of
those who stayed behind."

Glenn looked up high. "Take these redwood trees:
probably some are hundreds of years old. They've survived
because they could adapt to different conditions over the
years. Before, deer and other animals made their own
trails. But now, so much is new, these paths and other
human interventions, for example, but the trees still live
on."

Rima responded, "they're so tall, so grand."

They walked side by side on the now-wide path under
the trees. Glenn continued. "We all have to change,
nowadays. I love to think how Ohlones likely came up into
these hills during the summer. Back then, I imagine that
they walked here on this very trail under these bay trees.
Maybe until 1850, when our ancestors interrupted their
lives. It's been a big change since then. We all wear
modern shoes nowadays on these paths."

"On Sakol Island, we all walk barefoot on the soft,
somewhat coarse sand."

"White coral sand?"

"Oh, yes, but thirty meters from the beach, the soil is
humus enough to support good crops of vegetables, fruit
trees, and coconut trees for copra."

"You had copra?"

"Yeah, it's been our main cash crop since the early
1900's, when the American military came down with
coconut seedlings and encouraged our grandparents to

plant them. Our other way of getting cash is by fishing. Fishermen and farmers exchange and some fish are taken into the city to sell."

"So did you run in the sand? Or on firmer soil?"

"Both. But at low tide, very wide shore, wet sand, firm, we could also splash in the water. We liked the beach even more than our trails under the coconut palms, but those trails are soft too, no rocks."

He touched her shoulder, smiled at her, and she turned her head toward his. "Rima, I could walk all day every day this way with you, learning from you. Please continue about the coconuts: so your people made a big change with coconuts in order to have a cash crop, right? So they were capable of change, then?"

"Oh, they had to. That was toward the end of the Spanish-American war."

"Started over sugar in Cuba, isn't that right?"

"I think so, and then the Americans moved over to the Philippines around 1898 to chase the Spaniards out and to take over."

"Oh, Lord, our warring heritage..."

"But you know, Glenn, at least at first, Filipinos were grateful. Americans told us that we could become independent and the battles didn't take place near our little island."

"Cash crop, that was a big change!"

"Oh yes, and bigger ones to come. Then came outboard motors, after WWII. By the 50's, fishermen, everyone, switched from sails to outboards, still on double outrigger canoes. So now everyone needed cash to buy gas and oil.

"Was that good?"

"Well, with motors, it became more possible to go into the city. They could get there and home again in one day, so people started going."

"City?"

Zamboanga has about six hundred thousand people, maybe less than a sixth of that in 1945. We could see movies, mainly American ones. That's what we knew about America: big houses, cars, people singing in the rain..."

"People spent their new cash to learn about America from movies?"

"Yeah, especially the young men. We sold our copra and bought stuff, like gas for the transport."

"Big changes."

"Yes, but then the smuggling and piracy started because of the faster boats, the *kumpits* from the Bisayas."

"Oh!"

"And some of our children moved to the city to go to high school. Our parents saw that education had become important. They'd be able to earn more cash than by selling fish or coconut meat."

"It must have been hard to send their children off."

"Everyone had relatives in the city, in Campo Muslim, the Muslim neighborhood. Students stayed with relatives. It wasn't so hard to say goodbye because they could come back to our small island on the weekends. But after high school, they didn't always come back to live. I was one of them, and I even went on up north to Manila, to college."

"How'd your mother manage that?"

"Oh, we all always kept in contact. And we all always sent money home. Everyone, always—I always worked, even when I was in college."

"I read in the *Wall Street Journal* that Filipinos send home a larger percentage of their income than any other immigrants. And you, too? You sent money even though you were so independent, going away to high school and then even much farther away, to college?"

"Oh, yes, like everyone else. You might say that I had several stages of independence from Sakol Island Muslim convention: I fished, then I left for high school; I went even farther away for college—600 miles to Manila—and then I married a Christian and stayed up there. I taught high school science."

"So, you had a lot of experience with independence!"

"More than most. Maybe because I was different from

an early age, going out fishing with the men."

Their path led them onto a wide meadow on a hillside, with a switchback path climbing into more trees. The rain had subsided. Downhill, a wide vista opened to low hills with houses, and beyond it, shimmering in a light mist, they saw the bay. On its far side, they could make out the Hamilton range of mountains that enveloped the east side of the San Francisco Bay Area.

"Our winter green is in full display now, see?" Glenn spread his arms out to the new grasses popping up through last season's by-now brown and horizontal, decaying grasses. "Our winter rains bring green during the dark months."

They trudged up the switchback in single file, after Rima had stepped back in order to let Glenn set his pace.

"Glenn, tell me about your knees. You used to be more active?"

"I guess that as individuals, we all have to change, at least with age. The question is, do we change gracefully or not? I have tennis knees, and I haven't really found an alternative to tennis. But I discover that I love these walks with you. It's a graceful change, don't you think?"

"Of course! And I'm happy to accommodate you."

"And you, Rima, taking up running. How did you manage that?"

"I have to grow and change, not just for myself, but also for my daughter and her daughter."

"But running! Dangerous, especially for 60-year-old knees, isn't it? Walking is safe."

"You drive out on 101; that's not safe, right?"

"Maybe, Rima, you're like our longshoreman philosopher Satchel Paige: "Never look back; your past might be gaining on you. Always look forward.""

"Well, maybe it was because I succeeded in fishing that I was able to make the next great change, to go off to the city at age 12, to high school. So my past helped me."

"And, it sounds like you don't have anything in your past to hide." He waited for her response.

"Can't think of anything. Just some sadness that my father died. But I really valued bringing fish home to the family, and sometimes even a little money when fish were sold to our neighbors or in the city. I try to look several steps ahead, like in chess."

"You play chess?"

"Yes, and I got pretty good. Mostly the boys play, but I did, too. But now I get impatient with people who don't plan several paces ahead, like drivers who don't plan for what's ahead of them on the road."

Glenn stopped to catch his breath, and Rima passed him to look ahead. Now under bay, valley oak, and madrone trees again, they saw another clearing ahead, green with blue sky above, which appeared to indicate the top of the hill.

Glenn continued. "You must have plans for your future?"

"Oh yes, but I'm not telling, so don't ask. I'd lose my energy." She laughed, squeezed his hand, skipped ahead two skips, and then returned back to him.

"You know, Glenn, I try to use the maybe 70 or 80 years of my lifetime as best as I can. I want to look back on success, but I also want to look forward to new successes."

"I do notice that you like to move, even when we're talking!"

She smiled. "Living is moving. To live, you need to move."

They walked single file through a narrow passage between sagebrush.

Rima asked, "Have you heard of the runner George Sheehan? In the 1980's he wrote a book called *Personal Best.* Gloria loaned it to me. He said, 'Once I accept death, I center on the present.' And then, 'To have a death worth dying, you must have a life worth living.'" [p. 233]

"Oh, that's thought-provoking."

"You know, watching my papa die, and later, my husband, I know mortality. I want to live a life worth living; and that means living in the present. For instance, by myself, I run with music in my head, my own music, not in ear buds with white wires. With music, I live in the present, and I reflect. How about you?"

"Oh, what a beautiful idea. We have so much to learn about each other. I listen to tunes in my head as well."

They entered the grove and Glenn slowly puffed up the path to the crest. Rima slowed down to let Glenn experience the surroundings by himself, and she wanted to stay back to listen by herself as well.

She thought, *what an orchestra of sounds. If I would write all these sounds in musical notation, the percussion section would be prominent, but in tenor or alto tones, not bass. The tones are not single, but rather, close chords.*

Uphill, my breathing holds a steady 90 beats per minute, and its high tone is maybe in the tenor range. And now, on this steeper hill, the tempo increases to about 120 beats per minute, and the high tone rises.

While running, my feet were holding a steady 180 beats per minute. Now, slowing to a walk, their beat keeps time with my breathing. When my foot moves a rock, the tone of my step rises to soprano notes. I hear a lower sound when I step on a tree root on the path, maybe the sound of a small hand-held drum.

From overhead trees, I hear a drop from the morning rain – there, another one! They fall to earth with a soft tenor thud, a brush on a snare drum.

Back there, passing through grasses, I heard soprano insects, singing in short staccato. On both sides of the path, they sit in different sections of the orchestra.

Under the trees again, birds sing the melodies on each side of me. They're the woodwinds, the flutes and piccolos, and sometimes they sound like humans whistling.

The Stellar Jays have the dominant voices, maybe in high alto range: "chee chee chee chee chee." Their dynamics – their volume – increases as I approach and diminishes as I retreat.

Smaller birds – I don't know their names – sing different songs. They wait until the Stellar Jays have stopped or passed by, and they're less influenced by my presence. They hold still up in those trees.

*Their volume seems to increase only because I approach below them.
It dims as I move beyond their perches.*

*The leaves: they're the strings, the violins and all. The breeze
softly plays them. What a huge orchestra section: thousands of leaves,
high and low, both in my sight and in tone. Gentle gusts of breeze
carry the alto and soprano sounds along for several measures,
measured by the beat of my feet and of my breathing, and then the
leaves rest for several measures.*

*Soft sounds! If I hadn't stayed behind, nature might be hard to
hear. What a grand orchestra, with so many players and under the
big sky!*

Glenn had stopped at the lookout and was looking out
over the wide vista, the trees nearby, down to the
expansive bay, and across to the Hamilton mountain
range. He turned and held out his arms to her, smiling. "I
love being here. I'm still puffing, though, coming up that
last hill. You?"

"I've been listening, another reason I love running. My
feet and my breathing are in chorus with each other.
Because it's my own music, I can change its tempo to fit
any change of my feet or breathing. This tempo is almost
always set to other composers' music, both vocal and
instrumental."

"Does the rhythm help you?"

"Oh, I think so. When I noticed that I was
coordinating the rhythms and tempos of my breathing and
feet, then I could enhance them and my pace."

"Do other runners do it?"

"I don't know; I discovered it for myself. Out here on
the training runs, after we start together we run at our own
paces, so I'm frequently by myself. I see the breeze gently
swaying the trees above me, and I think about my friends
and family in the Philippines. I wonder if they're watching
the *habagat* wind blowing the waves from the southwest
this time of year—the fishermen are always watching the
winds. Especially, I wonder about my father and mother,
and my late husband, if their life energy has gone into

those breezes, or maybe even these breezes, here in Edgewood Park."

With admiration, Glenn quietly recited, "I lift up mine eyes unto the hills, whence cometh my strength."

"Beautiful! And vaguely familiar."

"I can't take the credit; it's from Psalm 121. But I think the narrator was talking about the Lord, not the energy of our ancestors."

2-16. Head for the Hills!
Sunday, February 17, 2008

They ate together.

Since Rima's arrival eight months earlier, she had brought her daughter and granddaughter together with her evening meals, and then Tess's boyfriend, Steve, and by mid-February, now Glenn as well. They all quickly settled into a cozy family routine in Tess and Sofie's little house in Redwood City.

Both men were a little startled by Rima's Filipino dishes, but each decided that bravery would get them some delicious meals and family camaraderie. Sofie discovered dishes as well, and she was surprised to enjoy learning more about this part of her Filipino heritage. Her mother had hardly cooked all these years; Tess tended to buy take-out food on the way home, and frequently she and her daughter didn't eat together. Steve sometimes took Tess out to dinner, and then Sofie fended for herself. And Glenn, in these last few years, had handled his single status by eating a large lunch in his company cafeteria and then snacks at home in the evening.

Rima adapted her traditional dishes to what she could find in the peninsula's ethnic groceries and the farmers' markets. For instance, she couldn't find *macapuno*, fresh young coconut meat, because the coconuts always matured in transport to California. So she settled for canned coconut milk, which she put into soups, even though it tasted rather too mature to her. While still in the Philippines, Rima had switched her own starchy staple over to brown rice, which her fellow Filipinos considered unusual, and she had long ago decided she didn't want any part of killing land animals or using cow's milk. She still cooked fish, but because it was so hard to get very fresh fish on the Bay Area Peninsula, she used mainly dried fish and *bagoong*, fermented fish paste, for protein. And occasionally she topped a vegetable dish with a chicken, duck, or turtle egg.

Glenn, Steve, and even Sofie were at first a little apprehensive about the exotic ingredients, but they were intrigued, especially by the new vegetables and fruits. "How did she find these in California?" Glenn asked Tess. Baby bok choy (*pechay*, she called it) was familiar to him, but the bitter cucumber she called *ampalaya*? How could bitter be good? And swamp spinach?—*kang kong*, she called it. He and Steve and Sofie agreed that they felt safer when these vegetables were combined with the more familiar onions, garlic, tomatoes, and even the Chinese long green beans. And they readily accepted Rima's fried bananas and grilled eggplant slices.

"But where's the beef?" asked Steve, laughingly recalling the phrase from a Wendy's marketing ad, a phrase which was later used in Walter Mondale's campaign. "This dish has beef in it just for you," Rima pointed out. "We don't put massive chunks of animal flesh in the center of our plates like Americans do," she laughed. "In the center we serve a little mountain of rice, and then side dishes of vegetables with spicy sauce and sometimes fish and nuts, and yes, even beef." She paused, and then added, "We have a different concept for a meal, more like in China and Japan, where the starchy staple also is the main dish."

Rima even found tropical fruits nearby, more than just bananas. In February, *chirimoyas*, also called *guayobanos*, had come into season, some even grown in California. She knew Americans were accustomed to dessert, so she offered fruit: a papaya half with *calamansi* juice, or fresh mango, cut into cubes. Glenn found it fascinating to watch her score half a mango inside its peel and then press it inside out to slice out neat cubes. She also served pineapple circles with serrated edges after she had carved diagonal grooves to take out the little florets from the scales of this composite fruit.

Glenn didn't get around to telling his mother about these dinners, or, in general, the seriousness of his new romantic interest. But Rima knew that Glenn's mother didn't approve of his association with her. During one afternoon walk down at the Baylands, he had divulged to Rima that his mother had asked why Rima ran on Sunday mornings instead of going to church. "They're all devout

Catholics over there, aren't they? I heard that."

"Oh!" Rima was startled enough to stop walking and look into, it seemed to her still, his very exotic, "triangular" eyes.

He continued, "I told her that you were raised in the Muslim south."

"What'd she say?"

"Well, I saw her bite her lower lip, but she didn't say anything."

"Oh. She didn't say, 'She'll do anything to stay in this country'?"

"Not yet." He laughed.

They had squeezed hands and resumed walking, then with clasped hands, they pointed together at three white snowy egrets quietly standing together in the marsh.

A couple of weeks earlier, Glenn had agreed with Rima to try to help Sofie with her homework, and Sofie had reluctantly consented. After these dinners, the two moved to Sofie's desk in the living room while the other three lingered at the dining table.

On a Sunday afternoon not long after the start of the homework arrangement, Glenn picked Rima up after her training run with Gloria, Tiffany, and Sofie. The others drove home, Gloria with Tiffany, and Sofie by herself. Glenn and Rima walked again in nearby Edgewood Park; they chose this somewhat less hilly, less tree-covered park because Glenn thought the walk would be easier for him there. "I like nature dry; I don't want to get my shoes muddy," he explained. He wore his North Face navy-blue raincoat, just in case. His sand washed light-blue jeans and white turtleneck t-shirt he must have expected to stay dry.

Rima had taken up her fellow runners' habit of changing into dry clothes in the car. Though she found it awkward to pull wet clothes off and dry clothes on over clammy, salty skin, and sometimes she compromised her modesty somewhat, Rima had quickly learned that the inconvenience was worth the comfort of getting out of wet running clothes which would very soon turn cold. "Do you mind waiting outside and looking the other way, Glenn?" she called to him, laughing a little shyly. Today she changed into yet another hand-me-down set of Gloria's last year's *apres-courir* outfits, this one silver-gray. "Oh, dry and warm! Thank you for waiting," she said as she climbed out of the car and quickly brushed her wet hair back.

Moving through the open meadow toward the trees of the park, Glenn said, "Your Sofie, she's not sure she wants to accept my help."

"I know. Or mine."

"I try not to give advice, just ask for clarification."

"Oh, you know how to handle her, then."

"I'm observing that she understands the material pretty well, and she's doing the readings."

"I'm happy to hear that. I thought so; I've seen her sitting with her books in the evenings even after you leave."

Most of the trails in this park were wide enough to walk side by side. Perhaps it was the brisk breeze and threatening clouds that kept other walkers away from the park this early afternoon, and Rima and Glenn were delighted to be alone.

"You know, I'm not so worried about the marijuana as you are."

"Well, maybe I agree; maybe it's more about that boyfriend than the substance."

"Well, I'll continue sitting with her as she studies, that is, if she wants me to. I do agree with you that her running and her coach's support are keys to her pulling her grades back up."

"Thank you again for your patient help."

"It's easier to help someone else's daughter."

"Yes, and have you noticed? My Tess is even starting to approve of you."

"Well, she knows the help needs to be from someone

else. That's why she brought you here to the U.S., right?"

"Yes, and...."

"And," he interrupted, "Who would have imagined that you'd be so active in helping Sofie to run?"

"I'm as surprised as anyone."

Walking hand in hand, they passed through the high meadow on the north side of the park and then into the shade of enormous bay trees on the east side of the main hill.

"You know, Glenn, when I first arrived here last April, Tess and Sofie and I went around to each of Sofie's teachers to learn what she needed to do to bring her grades up. And you know what her PE coach, Coach Ramirez, said?"

"No, what?"

"He said that educational research shows that for high school students who are at risk of dropping out..."

"...Was it going that far?"

"My daughter got me here by telling me Sofie's grades were plummeting toward F's, and she had a boyfriend who was dropping out, and she had started smoking dope, and she was even not coming home some nights...."

"Oh, Lord."

"Back to Coach Ramirez;"

"Oh, yes, about students at risk."

"Yes, he said that the single most important thing to keep them in school is a school sport."

"Really?"

"Yes. And he said, 'Our Sofie here is an exceptional runner.'"

"Oh, really, exceptional? I have seen that she's fast."

"Not only is she fast, but the coach said she has unusually strong and enduring determination. He said with that combination she'll go far."

"Oh, is he the one who got the idea of the marathon?"

"Yes. He said she could be their school's very first student to run the Boston Marathon."

"Oh, so it wasn't Tess's idea, then?"

"Oh, no, the coach's."

"And what does Sofie think about it?"

"Mixed feelings, I think. Oh, she knows she can run it; she finished Portland and Cal International marathons with no trouble.

"Wow."

"But she's having a hard time giving up that boyfriend, and the weed is part of it. And she needs to bring her grades up to B's to do track in the spring and to graduate in June, and that's a real question." Rima pulled Glenn's hand toward her and turned to stop and look at him. "Glenn, your help has great value."

"If, if…." He lifted his eyebrows briefly and looked up into the trees overhead.

They resumed walking.

Rima opened the next topic. "You know, I think we're having more success with this *mestizo*—mixed—relationship in my family than in yours."

"Hmm."

"Your mom and your daughter, they disapprove, right?"

"Hmm. Well, my daughter… you know about most children of divorce, right? There's a built in, structural flaw for any new relationship."

"How do you mean?"

"They never want to see their parent with someone else."

"Oh, I suppose not. Oh, Glenn, I don't want to damage your relationship with your family. Do you see any hope for your daughter loosening up? Or your mother?"

"Hmm. I'm hoping as much as you are."

They walked and he reached for her hand. "Let's hold on." He turned to face her and then reached for her other hand.

"It's fine, we're here by ourselves, hmm, Rima? The touching?"

"Fine here, by ourselves. But not in public, like some

Americans and especially the Europeans. Let me show you a Filipino kiss."

They hugged, arms around each other. She leaned into the nook of his neck and gently but audibly inhaled below his ear and took in his gentle, masculine scent. And then again. He held onto her shoulder with his hands, pushed her back to look into her eyes, and asked, "Is this right?" and did his best to repeat her "kiss."

"Mm-hmm."

He laughed. "No other people here. The deer rest during the day up under those trees; surely **they**'re watching us."

"Deer, birds, okay; humans, not okay." She "kissed" him again and then pulled herself back to look at him. "Breeze, insects, okay." She "kissed" him again.

They pulled back again, looked into each other's eyes, and smiled. He reached for her hand, and they resumed their walk. The trail led them out of the bay grove onto the east meadow, where they started the switchback climb toward the peak of the park.

2-17. What's In Running For You?
Sunday, February 17, 2008

They walked single file as the switchbacks narrowed, carefully placing their feet between the rocks and roots sticking up in the trail. For a while they listened to the whisper steps of their feet, the breeze in the low grass, and the calls of birds overhead.

Continuing upward, they entered a wider trail under trees, wide enough for two, and they rejoined hands. Overhead, rays of the afternoon sun passed through branches of blue oak, madrone, and toyon trees.

They climbed up the last, steep red earth stretch to the hill's peak. The trail was steep enough that both breathed too heavily for talking. Reaching the "saddleback" in the ridge, they stopped to catch their breath and to take in the new sight: San Francisco Bay had finally come into full, panoramic view.

The afternoon breeze had cleared the view to The City, San Francisco, 35 miles to the north. To the east, nearby and below them, the peninsula cities were clearly visible, and on the far side of the Bay, the East Bay communities sat quietly along its shore. To the south, they looked down the grassy meadow to the huge hangars of Moffett Field in Sunnyvale, and beyond, past sprawling San Jose, to the low mountain range beyond. Glenn took the opportunity to lean his head close to Rima's, and he pointed. "Look, you can even see the observatory on Mount Hamilton."

"Is that the highest one?"

"I think so. It's 4,200 feet, something like that; uh, about 1,300 meters to you."

"Beautiful, such a panorama. And so quiet. Even the cars down there on the freeway are quiet from up here, like ants."

He listened, he smiled, and he delighted in her appreciation of the California beauty he was happy to share with her.

Glenn put his elbows down on the top rung of the fence and continued to survey their panorama. Then he turned to her. "So what's in running for you, Rima?

"Ha!" she laughed.

Elbows off the fence now, he turned to face her. "Is it mainly to help your granddaughter? Why else would you start now? It's kind of unusual. Here at least."

"You'd be surprised how many seniors run here. But it's even more unusual in the Philippines, actually."

"Oh, why?"

"I suppose because it's very hot in the Philippines. You get too sweaty too easily. Here, I just want to kick up my heels!" and she released his hand, raised both of hers in the air, and jumped to click her heels together.

Laughing, he said, "Rima, you delight me!"

"You know, when Gloria and Sofie convinced me to run the Bay to Breakers when I first arrived here, I couldn't even jump to click my heels. You know what I thought?"

"No, what?" He smiled.

"I thought that old bodies couldn't build muscles or in general get in shape again.

"In shape, sure we can. But running? You can't be a child again!"

Dios ko, do I hear disapproval again? Or maybe he's hoping I'll convince him that I'm treating myself well, she worried. She slowly raised her eyes to his. "You don't need to pretend to be a child again, but you can feel like a child."

"Maybe it's dangerous."

"You know what I learned, Glenn?"

"What?"

"Within **two** weeks, I learned that I could regain some muscles. Even for such an old lady."

"I think it still might be risky, even though you do look so young."

"Well, I'm already stronger. My balance is better. I think I'm in **less** danger than I was before. I'm willing to take the chance. And last May, I agreed with Gloria I'd try running with her for 30 days."

"And?"

"That was until June 20th. By then, I felt, 'Hey, I'm in training; I'm training for a big experience!'"

"And that was for ... ?"

"First, for the first half of the San Francisco Marathon in July. And then the Portland marathon in October."

"That's a lot!"

"But you know, it started to become a way of life, and I liked it. I started eating better, sleeping better. Even while in the house, now I walk around on my toes to strengthen my feet."

"Wow, you've become an athlete."

"That's a big word, isn't it? But maybe you're right."

"Sounds like you deserve it."

"And besides, Glenn," she smiled, a little embarrassed, "it's a great moving meditation. Forget hassle, mourning, worry about Sofie. I listen to my breathing. I listen to my thoughts, to my footsteps, to the birds. To the breeze in the trees, and later, to the insects, after the sun is up and on us, like now. The rhythms, nature's music!"

"All that, now? But did you also notice them as a child?"

"I noticed nature. I don't know if I noticed my breathing... But I was always a bundle of energy. I couldn't sit still in school. Didn't walk to school; always ran. *Malikot.*"

"Did the teachers love you?" and he laughed.

"Well, I learned to control myself, but I couldn't wait to get out of the classroom. Same with you?"

"Sure. Maybe most kids, right?"

"Probably; so when teaching these many years, I took my students outside a lot. Even as an adult, sometimes running across the parking lot suits me better than walking."

"But you walk so graceful, like a cat."

"Oh, thank you. It does take strength to be graceful, doesn't it?"

"Uh, sounds right."

"Maybe I do move more smoothly now, after 10

months of running. More like when I was a child." She paused. "It's a weekly reminder that I'm still alive, still capable, even though I've seen deterioration of this body, my skin sinking toward the ground."

"Well, your skin is still very smooth."

"Uh, thanks." She blushed.

"Mainly, I feel better all the rest of the day. If I notice soreness in my quads or my calves, the soreness reminds me that they're building up. It's a 'good hurt.' My spirits are better; I'm more optimistic. Running reminds me that if I work hard, I can remain determined."

"Sounds good."

"In deciding to run, I had to accept that I'm older, I'm slow, I'll never be fast, but I can still do it. I can't be a star, but I can still gain so much every time I run. I can still make progress, even at my age."

He listened. Finally, he said, "Hmm. I hope you're right."

She continued. "You know, running a marathon is something I cannot do at home; I just told you, it's too hot there."

"Yay, California!" responded Glenn. "Of course, then I can't dive around giant coral tables in our temperate ocean water here, and you tell me that the Philippines has fantastic coral reefs for snorkeling and scuba diving."

"Oh, now you want to go to the Philippines?" she laughed.

"Well, now that you mention it...." And they both laughed.

"This is my way to accomplish something else worthwhile while I'm here."

"How long are you here for?"

"Just a few more months."

"Do you have time to accomplish such a challenge? You told me you were pretty sore after the San Francisco half marathon two weeks ago."

"But what a boost it was to my self-confidence! I could do something all these Americans did, especially young people, and it was a challenge for them, too."

"It's hard for everyone, I hear. But 13 miles—and

coming up, again, 26.2 miles! How did you decide to do **that?"**

"To support Sofie, of course. But it appeals to me as well; one year to work on a single deadline that we can both finish before the end of my tourist visa … I'm on a six-month extension now. It would raise self-esteem, for both of us."

They lingered at the lookout, leaning against the fence that apparently had been erected not long ago to discourage hikers and runners from carving an erosion-prone path down the steep south meadow of the peak. They turned around to view the Santa Cruz range to their west, dark coniferous green, and they could easily make out the individual trees spiking the top ridge. "Actually, this big hill we're on is part of the range," he said.

"The mist in the air softens the edges," Rima answered. "Maybe it's from those lakes?"

"Likely. You know, Rima, I admire your motives, and I wish I could run with you."

"Yes," she said, and squeezed his hands with both of hers.

"But I sure hope you're right, that this is good for you. I'm also worried about that right knee of yours."

"And you're one to know about knee problems, with your 'tennis knees,'"she said.

"Hey, look, we're both looking down at our knees, but they're hiding in pants!" he laughed.

"Well, I'll just find out if it's good for me in the long run. I guess I'm willing to take the risk." Then she quickly added, "I did succeed in Sacramento, you know, to qualify for Boston!"

"I'm worried that knees, and other body parts, wear out."

"Like machines?"

He looked into her eyes. "Yes, the more you use them, the faster they wear out, like my high school classmates who ran cross-country but limp now, and like my knees."

2-18. Run Across New Information
Thursday, March 6, 2008

"Night, Mom.... Yes, almost finished with homework." Tiffany looked at Sofie and rolled her eyes.

They sat at the head of Tiffany's bed with pillows behind their backs, reading lamps on the wall behind each of them, the deep bronze comforter pulled up over their laps. On top of the covers each worked on her laptop computer. At 10 p.m. on this Thursday night in March, Sofie was sleeping over again. Both girls were doing homework for the next day, and they also were responding to chats coming in from school friends. They occasionally shared a chat with the other, LOL-ing, "and stuff"-ing and OMG-ing, furiously typing a few words and hitting return to send off a response.

The girls wore plaid flannel pajama pants in pastel colors with t-shirts they had received from Gloria for Christmas. Tiffany's read "Boston Marathon" on Irish green, and on Sofie's black tee was written "Heart Breaker" with a contour of the Newton hills of that name. Their ponytail hairdos were already bedtime messy, Tiffany's blond a little frizzy, and Sofie's dark brown straight.

Tiffany searched the Net for responses to end of the chapter questions for AP US History. Tonight's chapter dealt with the changing American family.

She looked up from her computer, and then turned to her friend. The blue light reflected on Sofie's face, her eyes some 15 inches from her screen.

"Sofie, do you ever wonder about your father?"

"Not really."

"Some kids in class looked up their, um, deadbeat dads."

"Hmm." *Let's not go there*, Sofie thought. She typed a few strokes and hit "return."

Tiffany looked away from her computer to Sofie.

"Does your mom ever talk about him?"

"Nope." Sofie continued staring at her laptop. *Next topic, Tiff.*

"How about your Lola Rima?"

"Ah, yeah. She told me he used to be a runner." Sofie moved the curser, hit "return," and typed a few words.

"Oh, is that why you're a runner?" *Damn! I brought on another question!*

Sofie lifted up her laptop, and with her other hand rearranged the covers over her lap. "Oh, I don't know; maybe I got **some** good genes from him."

"I mean, when did you hear he was a runner?"

"Uh ..." and Sofie looked up from her computer and out the window. "Lola Rima told me, after we ran the Bay to Breakers."

"Never heard that before?"

"Nope."

Tiffany, silent, returned to her laptop.

Sofie looked out the window into the dark. She thought back to that afternoon last May with her grandmother, not long after she had arrived, when Sofie drove the two of them to Sigona's green grocer in Redwood City. She had asked, "Do you ever see Mr. Ayala's family, back in Manila?"

"*Oo*, now and then, like at *despedidas*, going away parties."

"Oh! How is the family?"

"Always very sad about the breakup. They miss your mom, and they always want to see photos of her and you."

"You show them?"

"Of course, why not? They're family, and they want to know!"

Sofie's lips thinned. "So what do they think of him abandoning us?"

"Well, of course, they know they heard only his side of the story. They really did love your mom. And of course he's remarried now...." After a pause, she added, "They just try to stay out of it, and I do, too."

Sofie responded. "Mom won't talk about it."

"Oh, here we are at the green grocer, *Nene*'. I'll tell you more after."

Gazing out Tiffany's window, Sofie thought, *sometime soon, I'll ask her to tell me more. Ten months ago! She won't be here much longer; her visa will be up.*

Tiffany interrupted Sofie's reflection. "Gosh, do you wonder if he still runs?"

"Dunno—haven't thought about him."

"Hey, do you think his name shows up on *Athlinks.com*?"

She's bugging me.... We're in dangerous territory ... but it's intriguing. Our psychology teacher would call this a classic "approach-avoidance dilemma"!

Sofie stared at her computer. After a long pause, she said, "Okay, I'll look." After several clicks and pauses, her eyes opened wide and she leaned toward the computer screen.

"Waddya see?" Tiffany leaned over to look.

Sofie pointed. "Looks like he entered a lot of races until around 2003. Marathons, 10Ks."

"Where?"

"I think mainly New England."

"Where's he live?""

"Mom told me 'back East'."

"Gosh, Sofie. "

Sofie exhaled a short laugh. "Don't go there, Tiffany."

"What's the matter with you? Aren't you curious?"

Sofie glared at Tiffany. "You're going too fast for me."

Tiffany looked puzzled. "Why?"

"Mm, I think he must be a creep."

"Yeah, leaving you ... But maybe he changed. Maybe he grew up."

"Hmm." *He has a new wife!*

"Hey, you could search him on *WhitePages.com*. You can learn who he lives with."

"Yeah, okay." Resigned and curious, Sofie moved the curser, hit "return," entered names, hit "return," paused, and read: "Lorna, age 40; Reed, age 16; Stephanie, age 14; Bing, age 11. Oh, Lord, Mom told me he remarried. I didn't know he had kids."

Tiffany put her hand over her mouth and quickly inhaled. "Oh my God, Sofie, they'd be your...."

"Don't say it." Sofie looked out the window. *TMI—Too much information.*

"Uh, what else can you learn about him?"

"Let's see. I'll Google him." She typed his name and entered, waited, and then browsed through the array of responses. "He's on Linkedin," and she clicked.

"What's it say?" Tiffany excitedly leaned over to look. "Oh, no photo."

"No."

Tiffany leaned back into her pillow. "Wouldn't you love to see one?"

"Yeah," Sofie responded, distracted by her reading. "Let's see, real-estate attorney. I already knew that."

Tiffany leaned toward Sofie's screen again. "Oh, look, he's a member of the B.A.A., the Boston Athletic Association!"

"Yeah, I'll look him up there." Curser, clicks, pauses, and then, "Hmm. On the legal team ... volunteers every year for the marathon. This year, captain of the volunteers at station 4, 4.1 miles, Ashland Clock Tower."

"Wow, we might even see him!"

Sofie sat back against her pillow, grabbed the sides of her laptop, and looked out the window. "Well, Tiffany, you've got me wondering."

2-19. Running Scared
Monday, March 31, 2008

Twenty days before the Boston, Rima received the letter. The first person home on this rainy, blustery afternoon, she fumbled for keys in her purse, unlocked the door, and reached into the wall mailbox for the usual *maraming basura*—a lot of junk —on her way into the house. She put down her purse and raincoat, and then casually sorted the stack into piles for Sofie, Tess, and recycle.

"Huh!" She audibly inhaled with alarm. *"Allah Akbar!"* An envelope was addressed to her from USCIS (U.S. Citizenship and Immigration Services), US Government, Washington, D.C.

Rima set it down, carefully placed a paring knife next to it, and slowly made herself a cup of her favorite Ceylon tea.

She looked at the clock—2:21—and felt relieved that she'd be alone for at least two more hours.

Slicing the white business envelope open at the counter, Rima sat down in the dining room next to the window and unfolded the letter.

Attention, Karima Masuhud Osorio:
This is a courtesy reminder that your Visitor's Visa (B-1) will expire on April 17, 2008. On October 16, 2007, you were granted a six-month extension. You are not eligible for another extension; therefore, you must depart the United States by midnight on April 17, 2008.

Overstaying your visa period is a federal felony carrying penalties up to and including jail and forceful deportation at your own expense and ineligibility to return to the United States for at least 10 years. Your overstay could lead to the charge of suspicion of terrorism, in which case, pursuant to the Terrorism Act of 2000, you could be held for investigation. During the first 92 hours, you would be disallowed the possibility to contact anyone.

There was more, but Rima folded the letter and pushed it back into its official envelope.

She drank her tea.

I didn't know they'd send a warning.
I thought the deadline was two weeks later.
Ominous.
I've seen horror stories in San Francisco's "The Philippine Star" of people overstaying their tourist visas, and others of the CIS hunting down "business marriages" in order to immigrate.
Should I tell anybody? Glenn?... Tess?... Not Sofie!
What about Gloria?

Taking her tea over to the window seat, Rima sat down next to the sleeping cat.

Glenn? He might press for immediate marriage... Too hasty, hindi tama, not wise; that would alienate his mother and his daughter.

She gently rested her hand on the back of the cat, who stirred, raised her back slightly into Rima's hand, and purred.

Tess? She'd worry that it'd cost her precious time—time to prevent a problem, time if I got caught.

What a mess I've gotten myself into!   Is this just civil disobedience?   Is it worse in this country?   Where are my standards? But several dear ones are counting on me! And I don't want to get them involved by trying to help me.

Rima gently petted the sleeping cat while looking out the window.

Sofie? I so want her to succeed. By now I'm her anting-anting, her good luck talisman. Maybe I just take the chance I get to Boston. Domestic flight, so less inspection, I read. Sofie will feel my support, and she'll start in Wave II. And even if ICE would pull me out of the race, Sofie would be way ahead of me, and she'd finish before she'd learn of my trouble.

Nope. Can't tell anybody.

She took another swallow.

Any way to run around this?... Can't pay lagay, bribe, in this country.

She looked out the window into the afternoon light,

concentrating, but not seeing.

But, some letters to the editor, say—with pseudonyms, daw, that people have overstayed for years without getting caught, and that the ICE doesn't have enough personnel anymore to track people down.

Hmm. Another swallow, and Rima again gazed out the window. She watched three little seed-eating birds hopping about on the ground. *Part of a flock returning north? Will they nest here?*

Only an extra week! That's all I need! I already decided to go to Boston. I just need a few extra days.

Another swallow and Rima looked into the live oak tree outside for more sign of birds, but saw none.

My name on the Boston registry ... ICE wouldn't hunt me down, would they? It includes my maiden name.... Would they pull me off like the race organizers did to Kathrine Switzer for being a female, way back in 1967? She chuckled nervously.

Hmm. It's scary: can I step out of my comfort zone? ... Have I faced bigger fears than this? The unknown! I was afraid I'd ruin my knee by running. The diabetes. That was scary. I started running!— That was scary. Fear of loneliness after my husband died. Maybe this isn't so bad, in comparison; they'd just deport me.... Well, maybe I wouldn't see Sofie or Tess for 10 years, or Glenn or Gloria....

Swallowing the last of her tea, Rima set the cup deliberately and quietly down on the little side table and gently stroked Kanela's head between her ears and down her back.

She's starting to show her age. She Sleeps more. The cat quietly purred.

Well, I've already decided. Sofie depends on me, and Gloria, and Tiffany. And Glenn ... he's resigned to it. And even Gloria's running club friends, Larry and Keith, expect me to be there. Tess is too busy to pay attention to my deadline. The risk is on me, not them. And besides, I want to, I have to go!

PART 3: THE BOSTON MARATHON

3-1. What Are We Made Of?
Friday, April 18, 2008

Shortly after takeoff from SFO, Sofie excitedly pulled out her new Canon camera and exclaimed "I can't believe how clearly we can see! Look at The City!" and snapped one photo after another into the blue. Tiffany, next to her and long past romantic notions about flying, brought out her iPod to thumb into her private tune, then sat back with her eyes closed, white wires of the iPod trailing down from her ears.

The older women sat in front of them, Gloria having kindly given the window seat to Rima, who gazed out, reflecting on her flight from Manila to SFO a year earlier. She wondered when she'd be crossing the Pacific again. "Very urgent that you come, *Inay ko*," Tess had pleaded back then over the phone. "Sofie's grades are way down, bad friends, drugs. She'll listen to you."

And now, just 12 months later, she was one of four runners on their way to something especially positive on this trip: an exciting new adventure with great consequences for each. She recalled reading—who was it?—PattiSue Plummer, in the 1992 Olympics, maybe, who wrote something like "Racing teaches us to challenge ourselves. It teaches us to push beyond where we thought we could go. It helps us find out what we are made of."

*What **am** I made of?* Rima mused. *And Sofie? And the others?*

Can *I measure up?* she wondered. *Well, I did qualify. In a way, my finish time in the last marathon was more important than my finish time coming up, because I don't have to qualify. And I'm pretty sure I'll finish.* She paused, then continued her thoughts, *Uh, pretty sure. I don't want to jinx myself.*

There's a difference between visualizing success and cockiness—a thin difference. She watched cars far below, on a long country road. *Where do you draw the line? Maybe careless. Maybe cockiness is carelessness. So what is careful? Preparation? I've been preparing, oh yeah!*

The plane passed over a lake, and for a while she watched the sun's reflection in it until fluffy white clouds blocked her view.

And has my preparation been enough? Hmm, I've taken this body to the outer edge of what it can do … in 10-plus months…. Maybe I could do more in another year…. But then this body would be another year older.

Now she looked out over a sea of cloud, colored white with grays and just a little late afternoon orange-pink.

After five hours in the air and a long taxi ride plus the three hours of time change, the four women arrived late in the evening at the Colonnade Hotel on Huntington Street, directly across from the Convention Center and the Expo they'd visit first thing in the morning. Hungry again, they were relieved to learn that the staff of the Brasserie Jo near the lobby could serve them a bowl of soup before they turned in.

At 11:30 p.m., surely most runners were already in beds. But as the women entered the bistro, they saw several men sitting at the bar wearing blue and yellow Boston Marathon shirts and jackets with a variety of years embroidered on the backs.

"This week's prestige uniform, maybe," said Sofie. "Vintage jackets for the more experienced."

"Girls, hear the piped-in music?" asked Gloria. "Do you think the singer is a sound-alike or the real Edith Piaf?"

"Oh, the Little Sparrow!" said Tiffany. We learned "La Vie en Rose" in French IV this year. It really sounds like her!"

The restaurant had the warm "brown café" atmosphere of a 30's Parisian brasserie, or at least that was the intention. "It's cozy here," said Rima, pointing to the painting on the wall of dashing men and elegant women, apparently pausing from a dance. Dry and warm inside, the four women looked through the full wall of glass that protected them from the cold outside to the wet black street, sparkling with reflections from headlights of cars passing by, splashing the lights.

"Well, we've arrived!" said Rima.

"I'm so nervous I'm tormented." said Tiffany.

"Hey, let's all practice deep, slow breathing," Gloria said. "It helps."

Their soups arrived, barley with carrots, onions, and green beans in a thick broth, as warm and soothing as a hot cup of milk before going to sleep.

"You know what my friend Marilu said to me last week?" Rima asked.

"Oh, is she the one with the perfect mani- and pedicures and all the rings?" asked Gloria.

"Yeah." Marilu said, "You've run two marathons already, so why are you so nervous now?"

"Oh yeah? So what did you say?" asked Sofie, who knew *Tita* Marilu and her daughter well, and dismissed them as mother and daughter princesses.

Rima put her spoon down and with her napkin patted her lips. "I thought, but didn't say, 'You have **no** idea.'"

"No!" the three agreed, with vigorous nods.

"Well?" asked Sofie.

"I said, '**Everyone** is nervous, every time. We all know that we'll get pretty sore. And **no** one is one hundred percent sure they're going to finish.'"

"Mm-hmm," they responded, waiting for more.

"**Then** she asked, 'Even the front runners?'"

The girls responded in chorus, "Of course!"

"I told her even the elites who train a hundred miles a week... And she shouted '**one hundred miles?**'"

The three listeners smiled at the buildup of this little story.

"I said, 'Yes, many of them do.' And she said, 'I can't believe **one hundred miles a week!**' So I told her, 'Keep in mind that they're after a $125,000 purse, and another 25 thousand if they break the course record.'"

Two men from the bar turned around to listen in.

"What **is** the course record?" asked Sofie.

"2:07[1] something," said Gloria. "Why, are you thinking

---

[1] Robert Cheruiyot: 2:07:14 in 2006: course record; he

of breaking it, Sofie?" she asked, to smiles all around. "Women, around 2:25..."

"Well, I **could** use the money!"

"For?"

"For college, of course."

Rima responded first. "Yay, college scholarship for the front-runner 18-year-old!"

Gloria eagerly added, "You might have a good chance at it. I looked at the other registered 18-year-old girls' qualifying times; did you? And even if you don't finish first, you might get that much with a full athletic scholarship from a college. Finishing the Boston might help. I know that you have all your applications in, but this could be added to yours, Sofie, before the schools make their final decisions."

"Thank you again for your help on my applications, Gloria. And about nervousness: well, I'm pretty nervous, too. But what else did you tell Marilu about nervousness, *Lola?*"

"I said that every runner in every marathon is running into a future we don't yet know. Everyone is worried about getting a new injury, about not finishing..."

"Or having an old injury will come back to haunt us," added Gloria.

"Or the weather..."

"Oh, the weather! I've been texting you guys about the terrible weather forecasts for this race!"

"Yeah, they've changed the forecasts a bunch of times in these last two weeks, and they're all scary," said Sofie. 'Rain, cold, headwinds....'"

Rima added, "And for me, I wonder if can I get the rehydration just right—not too much, not too little."

"When will you know if you're gonna be safe from cramps?" asked Tiffany.

"Around Mile 16. That's the big moment when our bodies change their...."

---

finished a little slower in 2007, at 2:14:13.

Tiffany interrupted, "… when we howl at the moon and hair grows all over our bodies?" and she giggled at her joke.

Gloria awkwardly tried to make up for her daughter's interruption. "Here's what we've learned from the sports physiologists: at around Mile 16 our bodies have used up the glycogen and the water stored from the couple of days before starting out—like from tonight—and our bodies make the big transition over to body fat or to the Power Gels we eat. The transition is very hard, and the body acts **real** differently than at Mile Five."

Rima continued, "Yes, that's when the cramps come. Our bodies can't replenish more than half of the water lost to sweat and urine."

"That's why Sofie's coach told us to carry water, right?" said Tiffany. "And to drink as much as we can."

Rima said "yes, if I get cramps, they're sharp enough that I'd be lucky just to walk."

Gloria turned to Tiffany. "She knows endurance. She said she presses right up to the edge."

They all diligently took spoonfuls of their soup.

"What's the edge for you, *Lola* Rima?" asked Tiffany.

"That's when I get dizzy, and my legs suddenly go weak—weak enough that I have to worry about falling."

"Wow! You work even a lot harder than I do!"

"And then I back off until I recover. I walk, maybe just 20 to 30 steps, and then I try to run again."

"Oh, is that why for some of our training runs you're a lot slower … I, I mean faster, than at other times?"

"Yeah. I'm cautious when I get dizzy. And we all learn how to endure pain."

"**That's** true," said Sofie.

Rima continued, "You know Keith, who will be running with us on Monday? From your mom's running-club? He told us about this 86-year-old woman, Helen Klein, you remember hearing about her?"

"Oh, you mean the ultra-marathoner who lives near Sacramento?" asked Tiffany. "Mom's talked about her."

"Yep. Carmichael. She said one of her mantras is 'I'll

rest this afternoon; I'll rest this afternoon.'"

Gloria responded, "That's a good way to remind ourselves that usually the pain is very temporary, and it's not doing big damage."

"Well, *I* sure hope I can finish," Tiffany brought the topic back to herself. "So how am I going to sleep on Sunday night?"

"No one can sleep the night before. But it won't matter. That's what my coach told me," said Sofie.

"That's a mantra for me," Gloria laughed. "It won't matter, it won't matter."

"Coach Ramirez said to be sure to sleep Friday and Saturday nights."

"One other thing I told Marilu, " Rima started. "I told her that I've run two marathons—it took two to finally qualify for Boston—but I've heard that everyone says that each one is very hard, as hard as the previous one. Some marathons are even harder, with more hills—and we know that downhills do lead to most of the injuries—and some have worse weather, and you maybe get more ailments, or for me, cramps. But they're **all** hard."

"I agree with you, *Lola*, that *Tita* Marilu has no idea."

Gloria raised her water glass high. "Hey, **we** do, don't we, guys? We're all in this together. Let's drink to this!" And they all raised their glasses to clink above the center of their little table. Gloria added, "And Tiffany, you're gonna make it; you can **do** it!"

"Yay!" they all said, clinking glasses again.

"I'll drink to that!" chirped Tiffany.

"Remember that quote from Hal Higdon's book, guys? From Jim Ryun?"

"Which one, *Lola*?"

"He said 'One, I learned you shouldn't ever quit. And, two'—what was it—oh! 'I learned you'll never be able to explain it to anybody.'"

"Ha!" they laughed.

Gloria said, "Is everyone finished? So we're off to bed

now," and she signaled to the waiter for the check.

"And *Dios ko*, let me sleep!" said Sofie.

3-2. Blessing of the Runners
Sunday, April 20, 2008

At nine o'clock on Sunday, the day before the marathon, the annual "blessing of the runners" was celebrated in the Old South Church. Rima coaxed her group to attend the service by joining the drop-in choir practice on Saturday, and she and Keith sang in the choir on Sunday.

The Boston Marathon would finish in front of this venerable church on Boylston Street, as it had for most of the past 112 years. In front, trees bravely blossomed in the brisk wind, bright with drops from the light rain that fell from the gray sky. Inside the church's elegant, quiet, dark polished-wood dim, wisps of the sun's light shone in through stained glass windows.

The service was held not in the main sanctuary but in the side chapel, which had a capacity of perhaps 300. The minister, Reverend Elizabeth Myer Boulton, an attractive tall, shorthaired woman in her thirties, wore a simple black robe. She announced,

"This year we celebrate the 112th year of the Boston Marathon, the oldest consecutive marathon in the US and second only to the London Marathon in longevity. It always takes place on a Monday, unique to marathons, which are usually held on Sundays. Ours is held on our Patriot's Day, a Monday holiday in mid-April for the Commonwealth of Massachusetts. The holiday has become "marathon day" in this state. We bless our runners on Sunday, the day before the race. When you leave here, you'll notice the building excitement right in front of our church, with the 5K race for children and their families, here on Boylston Street."

She asked, "How many of you have qualified to run tomorrow? Please stand." Perhaps eighty people stood, while the entire congregation avidly looked around to take in the experience.

The minister then asked, "How many hope to qualify

next year? Please join them, standing." Heads once again turned from side to side. Perhaps another fifty stood, smiling sheepishly.

The minister asked her third question: "How many of you are supporting someone who's running?" And of course, with that, the rest of the congregation smiled and stood.

The minister invited all to sit, and then said, "Five hundred thousand of us will be spectators tomorrow, and 20 thousand will be runners. This is a happening!"

Rima felt growing excitement among the congregation in the chapel, noting a contrast to the hushed reverence she had experienced in religious services she had attended in the Philippines, both in her village Muslim mosque on Sakol Island and the Catholic church where she was married in Manila. With a brief flash, she recalled the excitement in Stanford University's Memorial Church where she had sung in the *Messiah*, and had met Glenn.

The choir here, including Rima and Keith, stood and assembled for their anthem, *We Are Going*.

> We are going.
> Heaven knows where we are going,
> But we'll know we're there.
> And we'll get there,
> Heaven knows how we will get there,
> But we know we will.
>
> It will be hard we know,
> And the road will be muddy and rough,
> But we'll get there,
> Heaven knows how we will get there,
> But we know we will.
>
> Wo-ya-ya (wo-ya-ya)
> Wo-ya-ya (wo-ya-ya)
> Wo-ya-ya (wo-ya-ya)

Wo-ya-ya-ya (wo-ya-ya)
Wo-ya-ya (wo-ya-ya)

The 20 choir members, most of them drop-in volunteers visiting Boston, then retired to the pews of their companions.

The minister delivered a short sermon about how those who had departed before were there in spirit, supporting everyone to do well. "We are not alone."

Filing out of the chapel less than an hour later, Sofie whispered to the others, **"I am the one sending a message to our dearly departed. I am thinking of them,** and I am doing this in honor of **them,** my *lolo*, my departed elders."

Rima responded, "Maybe we can have back and forth communication."

Gloria said, "Maybe Fred Lebow is communicating with us. Remember him?"

"Who is he, again?" asked Tiffany.

"He was the founder of the New York Marathon, and the man who first allowed women to join marathons ... in, uh, 1971."

"What would he say?"

"He said, "In marathon running, everyone is a winner; everyone is a champion."

"What did he mean, Mom?" asked Tiffany.

"I think he meant that no one is a loser if they finish."

"Hmm, those who don't get injuries," said Tiffany.

Gloria ignored her daughter's remark. "Think of the difference: for team sports like soccer, spectators cheer inside a stadium for maybe two hours, for just one of two teams, and for just 11 soccer players."

"And, I guess you mean, half of them will lose," said Tiffany.

Gloria continued. "Yes. But marathons are quite different: the runners are out on the street, where 10 times as many spectators cheer for much longer, as long as five or six hours, and for maybe 25,000 runners, all of them winners."

"Hmm," the girls said, and they looked at one another, impressed and inspired.

Rima mused, "Marathoners run to all the people."

3-3. Let's Roll!
Monday, April 21, 2008

The four women—for the two teenagers, at age 18 now, were almost women—performed their morning rituals of dressing and preparation, having laid out their clothes and gear the night before. Having learned that the hotel wouldn't serve breakfast this early, they made their instant oatmeal with hot almond milk heated in their room's coffee pot, and they ate it covered with blueberries, almond slices and fresh banana circles. They carefully choreographed individual time in the bathroom. At 6:20, and five minutes early, they agreed to head downstairs to board one of the five buses waiting in front of the hotel. Outside in the morning chill they saw other runners moving their legs and feet to avoid the cold, and the four overheard quiet, excited talk of "No rain—forecast is for 59 degrees at noon—tail wind of seven mph!" This sounded much, much better than what had been forecast a few days earlier.

Gloria quietly said, "Another exciting adventure together, girls." She added, "Let's huddle for warmth," and they put their arms around one another.

They climbed into the second bus, relieved to feel the warmth from the bus's heater, and took the first empty seats, halfway back. An organizer came on board to announce that this would be one of the gear check buses, so they could just leave their stuff in this bus—but only in the official bag with their bib numbers on it. More good news: this bus would stay parked outside of the high school in Hopkinton, the start point, so the runners could stay in it until the last minute.

"Oh, goodie! We get to stay warm," Tiffany said, rubbing her gloved hands together vigorously. The others nodded in agreement.

Rima looked out the window on the bus's slow, one-hour journey westward to Hopkington. She watched the sky slowly light up and reflected that in a few hours they'd be passing near here, coming back by foot all this distance. Four months earlier, in December, the 26-mile bus ride had also seemed so overwhelmingly far, for the Cal International in Sacramento's point-to point marathon

She reflected, *these are our last quiet, passive moments. We've been waiting so long for this—and now, almost, finally!* She observed that leaves on broad-leaf trees were just starting to open. Mostly, the branches and trunks were still bare, black in the early morning shadows, but showing promise of spring.

We'll have to stand in the Porta-Potty line at least once while waiting.... A three-hour wait! I'm glad we didn't eat too much last night and we had just the right breakfast this morning. I'll eat a banana in about, hmm ... an hour. I'll drink about 10 ounces of water before the start, and then I'll have to refill my water bottle somewhere before starting....

She turned to her seatmate. "Gloria, sure we have enough clothes? Or maybe too many? We came prepared for a blizzard!"

"We're fine. We'll be able to send our extras in the gear check bag."

Tiffany, sitting across the aisle with Sofie, overheard her mother. "So our jackets will ride back to Boston in this bus; they have it easy!" She chuckled.

Looking back out the window, Rima went back to her thoughts. *My body? The usual stiffness on rising, but none of us has any special problems starting out. Leg cramps? Avoided them, lately. Maybe I've finally learned the system for this body. Or it'll let me know by Mile 16....*

The bus turned off the freeway; Rima noticed the Hopkinton exit sign. *My attitude? I know I'll finish. Fortitude is part of my core. I think I can manage the rehydration ... avoid leg cramps. My dear Sofie? She starts thirty minutes before us. I know she'll finish well. Gloria and Tiffany....*

Gloria's voice broke into her thoughts. "There's the high school, ahead of us. Our parking place, our launching pad."

Rima continued her quiet reflection. *First Sofie, and then what about the three of us? We'll start out together. And then, Gloria and Tiffany will stay together. I'll be running ahead solo, same as Sofie, as usual, most of my 45,000 steps. Larry and Keith said they wanted to stay with me, even though I'm a little slower. Gotta find them by cell phone, here in Hopkinton.*

Solo, but the BAA organizers don't want to see any white wires coming out of anyone's ears, a safety matter, and we never use them anyway. I'd miss a lot: when we're training, the birds, later the buzzing insects on the trails, and here, snippets of conversations, and all the spectators!—Really a half million spectators? How crowded will the course be? Let's see: for 26.2 miles, that's … times 5,280 feet per mile.. that's… 138,000-plus linear feet, the whole course. Then, spread 500,000 people along those feet. That's … over three and a half people per foot, the whole way! No way!—Well half that, half on each side of the course… Even so, the spectators will be two-three deep, the whole course!

She again visualized her start. She recalled that the BAA had sent out directives on rehydrating, refueling, running in hot weather, running in cold, and on pacing. "The first half mile is a 150-foot drop in altitude, so hold yourself back," they wrote, "or you'll hit the wall." (Sofie's coach had told her, "Go out fast, die like a pig.") The BAA's directive continued the advice. "Don't let the excitement carry you too fast, or you'll never get over Heartbreak Hill."

The girls had scoffed at the name Heartbreak Hill when they looked at the course elevation contour that the BAA had sent in advance: just 150 feet in a little less than a mile, "and we've been training in Woodside and San Francisco." Rima recalled, but the veterans told us that it's the position on the course—miles 19 to 20—and the steep downhill afterward that make this, and the three Newton hills before it, "hills you'll notice." Actually, the Newton Hills would start just after mile 15.

Theirs was one of the first buses to pull into the high school parking lot at around 7:30 a.m., but right behind them were dozens and dozens of other buses. Most of the runners needed to leave their buses so the drivers could return to Boston for another load. People slowly climbed out, already bundled up against the cold, to stand in Porta-Potty lines, to look for the coffee table, to mill around, to find friends, to huddle together.

The driver repeated his promise over his loudspeaker: "You can stay in the bus if you want. I'll stay here until the start." Again he got cheers, loud whistles, and applause. The four women lingered for a while, observing their fellow runners outside. "It's much harder for them, waiting out there," Sofie observed. Outside, runners hunched their shoulders in thick jackets and warm-up pants that they would later surely roll into gear-check bags before heading for the start line. Tucking their hands into their armpits, they stood with their friends in tight groups, puffing out steam as they chatted. After half an hour, the four noticed that their bus was still half full of runners, waiting and chatting. A woman re-entered the bus, telling her seat companion in the front seat, "They've got portable flushers over there—that side—with basins and soap. The companion responded "You sure they're not urinals with deodorant cakes?"—to widespread laughter. The first woman, who turned out to be Lois, an ophthalmologist from Tampa, said, "You got me. I owe you one," to more laughter.

Gloria looked at her watch. "Nine-thirty. We're too far away to hear the announcer and the gun for the wheelchair start."

"The start times, again?" asked Tiffany.

"Nine-thirty for the wheelchairs, because they're faster than the runners. Nine thirty-two is the elite women's start; 10:00 for the elite men and the Wave One start, including our Sofie. And we'll start at 10:30." They took off their jackets and warm-up pants, put them into their plastic bags, and looked for the place to deposit them behind the bus driver. Then they put on their Goodwill jackets and black trash bag "suits."

Sofie had qualified at 3 hours, 15 minutes—19 minutes faster than the cutoff of 3:34 for the first wave of 14,000 runners. "So let's roll!" Gloria announced. They slowly climbed down from the bus.

Out in the open now, the air felt a little less unfriendly, a little less cold than they had expected. Sofie said, "I can't believe we're finally here!"

Gloria agreed. "We've prepared months and months for this, and now our wait is almost over!"

"What an honor, to be included in such an elite crowd," said Rima.

Gloria added, "When we meet again we'll be Boston Marathon finishers!" The others smiled, each with a question in her eyes. Rima thought, *how could I deserve that title?* Sofie thought, *Well, at least a champion for my high school, not more!* Tiffany appeared doubtful that she could really finish.

"But the suspense! It's hard to endure. And I know we're going to feel so different, very soon." They all nodded vigorously in agreement.

They stretched. Right IT band, then the left. Achilles tendons, calf muscles, hamstrings. They lightly held each other's shoulders to stretch the right quads, and then, shifting hands and feet, the left quads.

"I'm so afraid," shivered Tiffany.

"Everyone here is afraid," responded Gloria. "We're all afraid we might not do our best, or that injuries might stop us. But everyone who has qualified for the Boston knows that they can endure."

Tiffany started, "But...."

Gloria interrupted, "We can, we can go to the very outer edge of fatigue."

Tiffany began: "But..."

Gloria interrupted again. "We know that we'll feel better as soon as we finish." She turned to her daughter. "Say this, Tiff, 'I'll rest this afternoon.'"

Tiffany withheld her usual eye-rolling. She squeezed her eyes shut and repeated, "I'll rest this afternoon, I'll rest this afternoon."

"Group hug!" said Gloria. They did, and they wished all a great experience. "New start line, new adventure!" And then Sofie trotted off ahead of them for her Wave One start.

3-4. Start Out Slowly
Monday, April 21, 2008

The others watched from the sideline as Sofie started out with Wave One at ten o'clock. Ahead of her were other fast runners, and in front of them ran the invited elite men. The elite women had started 28 minutes earlier; they were competing for part of the $500,000 purse. Gloria had inquired in advance and learned that the organizers had provided no special start for elite 18-year-olds vying for the college scholarships, so Sofie wouldn't be identifying her competitors on the course. Sofie's *lola*, Aunt Gloria, Tiffany, and Larry and Keith from their running club would start in Wave Two at 10:30.

Sofie took stock of herself. *Am I focused on the race ahead? Well, not entirely. Plenty of time to identify **him**.... Will I really see my father? Just say "hello," and I'll be gone long before the others pass by his clock station, at Mile Four.*

She and the other Wave One runners did the slow, several-minute shuffle to the start mat, then crossed over it, hearing the "ping, ping!" of their time chips, fastened to their shoes, being recorded. Sofie noted the time, 10:08, as she punched her Garmin watch to start her own record of her distance, pace, and time elapsed. Immediately the crowd thinned out as the runners' gaits shifted to an easy lope. The road sloped slightly downward, and Sofie was comforted by the sight of the now-familiar-appearing liquid flow of runners ahead of her. Her eyes focused first on the overall smooth fluidity she had joined, and then she noticed individual heads, many of them covered with blue or black caps, bobbing up like shallow creek water rippling over stones in its bed.

Still cold from the wait in her corral before the start, Sofie shivered, but was relieved that she had finally started the race and would soon warm up. She tossed her black trash bag to the side, but kept on her white waterproof windbreaker for another few minutes before tying it around her waist. Under it, her white tank top carried her identification. On the front of her shirt she had pinned her official rice-paper bib with her number, and above it, her name. Gloria had said, "Wear your name. You'll hear it five hundred thousand times! The crowd will encourage you." So Rima had machine-embroidered each of their names onto a small rectangle of cloth—Sofie, Rima, Tiffany, Gloria—in four-inch high letters twice and then had sewn them onto the front and back of their shirts. Sofie had also agreed with her *lola* to wear the Philippine flag, and Rima had carefully hand-stitched to the back of her own and Sofie's white shirts the royal-blue, red, and white tricolor with three yellow stars and the sun on the white. Rima had told her that the three yellow stars represent the three major islands – Luzon, Bisayas, and Mindanao – and the eight rays of the sun represent the eight provinces that revolted against Spain.

Sofie reined herself in to a slow start, to withstand her inclination to whoosh down that first hill like so many of the others on both sides of her. She thought of the big challenge coming up soon, at Mile Four. *Now remember, Sofie, be positive*, and as she exhaled apprehensively, she repeated aloud, to herself, *"Positive, positive … and just wait to discover what will happen. Just discover."*

At 10:31, Sofie could just make out the Mile Four event clock appearing now and then on the right side of the road between the runners in front of her. *No one's at the clock! The volunteer list had shown that he was responsible for that clock. Why isn't he there? He's still missing, all my life!* Sofie exhaled heavily and her shoulders slumped with disappointment. She hadn't realized how much she had been counting on seeing this man. *But, hey, steady rhythm!* She looked down at her feet, and they were still moving along, still trustworthy, seemingly independent.

Just around the next curve, Sofie saw the Ashland Clock Tower and evidence of the first water stop at Mile 4.1. A short distance ahead of the water tables, Sofie saw a lineup of maybe 20 pale-blue Porta-Potties, and in front each were lined up some 10 impatient runners. Runners ahead of her slowed down and moved to the sides of the road. Tables lined both sides, each covered with cups filled with water or Gatorade. Runners and volunteers crowded the tables in front, and volunteers worked vigorously behind them to keep up with the demand. Sofie carefully scanned the volunteers at each of the tables.

Teenagers, perhaps all from the local high school here in Ashland, stood in front of the tables to hand out cups of water at the first few tables and Gatorade at the last few. Some thirty young people on each side of the road were reaching out to deliver the liquid. At this early point in the race, the runners were still clustered together and the cups were quickly taken, so the young volunteers worked fast. They pivoted to pick up more cups, then quickly turned back to more approaching runners, who gave slight nods of the head or held out hands to indicate which volunteer they would approach.

Behind each table, older volunteers, maybe local teachers, poured liquid from gallon plastic bottles into paper cups. They filled them only halfway so that runners could drink without spilling them. The pourers' dance looked similar to that of the cup givers out front: pivot to pour, turn to the table, and then pivot back again. All appeared challenged to maintain the fast rhythm: the pourers spilled some liquid as they quickly placed cups on the tables; the high schoolers in front picked up two or four cups, sometimes spilling them onto their clothes as they reached out toward the runners. The runners, who slowed only slightly to veer to the side of the course, grabbed one or two cups and then immediately sped back onto the road, drinking as they ran. They sometimes spilled some of the precious liquid down their chins and onto their shirts.

As Sofie moved toward the tables, she saw one man pouring Gatorade who looked Asian, the best candidate for a Filipino. He was shorter than the other men and appeared to be not much taller than she was. As she moved closer, she looked around all the tables.

The most likely one. Is this the man who is supposed to be my father? But no one wore nametags. This man wore a "Boston Marathon 1995" aqua-blue shirt, slightly faded, so he must have run it. *No one would dare wear a Boston Marathon shirt unless they'd earned it.* Among the 70 or 80 people handing out drinks and the 20 or 30 pourers behind the tables, *he must be the one.*

She doubted her plan. *I don't have time for this. Gotta run, gotta run!* She noticed plenty of empty cups strewn on the ground, evidence that many runners had already passed by, drunk, and thrown their cups down, some still partially filled with Gatorade. Runners just ahead of her ignored the cups, but their feet crushed them or kicked them into movement to clatter away. With each step, the runners' shoes made the slapping noise of a handclap in their contact with the pavement, because it was already sticky with spilled Gatorade. Clatter, clatter, and slap, slap, joined into a chorus pitched just a little higher than applause at an outdoor amphitheater.

She neared the table. *Slim, slight body, arms have smooth light brown skin... I can't see his eyes with that cap's bill shading his face ... yep, black straight hair under the cap.*

She accepted a cup from a high schooler, took a quick swig, and then turned her eyes back to peer at this man. *I can just make out Asian prominent cheekbones.... He must be at least in his forties, because the diamond cheek lines from his nose to the outside corners of his mouth are noticeable, even though he's not smiling. He's too busy pouring, looking at the cups on the table, not following his cups to the high schoolers' hands or faces, not to the runners taking them.*

She stopped at the end of his table, out of the way of her fellow runners. "Mr. Ayala?"

"Yep, you're doing fine, young lady."

"Mr. Alec Ayala?"

"Yes I am. And may I know your name?—Oh, I see on your shirt: Sofie."

"Sofie Ayala".

After a long pause, he inhaled, and then said, "Oh, *Dios*

ko!"

They looked intently at one another. He saw a very fit, young, Filipina-American, dressed in white tank top and shorts.

Sofie could now see his eyes in the shadow under his cap. At first they had looked enthusiastically committed to this event, supportive of the thirsty runners. *Yep, almond-shaped lids, eyes as dark brown as his hair, and, oh, familiar!* from the wedding photos she had tucked away on the bookshelf in her bedroom. Her mother had told her to take them, said she didn't want them in her own room. Now, suddenly, his lids opened wide with astonishment. She saw disbelief, his search to comprehend, and.... *What is it? Wonder? Fear? Joy? Delight? Even a glimpse of compassion?*

"How'd you know?" He took a step toward Sofie, and reached out his two hands.

She backed up, and turned toward the road: "My finish time," letting him know she had to continue. "Can't stop."

"*Siempre.* He paused, then blurted out, "Perhaps we might meet for a short time *lang,* only, after the finish?"

"Where?" She was still stepping backward, heading toward the throng.

"How about your hotel lobby?"

"Um, no, another place." *What would Lola say?* She reversed direction and with very short, quick steps returned closer in order to hear him.

"Mmm, How about the Starbuck's at the Marriott Copley? A lot of finishers will be there."

"On Huntington Street?"

"Yes. What's your expected finish time?"

"At 12:53 this afternoon, plus ... the eight minutes to cross the start mat, so ... 1:01 o'clock. Two hours, fifty-three minutes."

"Wow, that'd be under seven-minute miles; wow!"

Sofie felt a flurry of mixed emotions, and was anxious to continue running. She looked toward the runners passing by.

He added, "I'll be finished with my water and clock post before then. I'll try to see you finish. *Mabuhay, iha* [goodbye, daughter]!"

She gave a quick wave, and turning toward Boston, trotted out to the street. *Oh my God! What have I just done?*

He called after her, "Uh, three o'clock, Marriott Copley Starbucks, okay?" Then, seeing the flag on her back, he added, "Oh! *Pilipina ka!*"

Now back in the run, she waved her hand over her head in agreement.

By herself again, she shivered, and then shook out her arms and hands, shocked by the realization of her success in finding him.

Oh, Dios ko, what have I done? She mumbled over and over as she stumbled back into the crowd.

He looked so ... happy, then so ... overwhelmed, so vulnerable, so ... happy. He didn't have a photo on his LinkedIn so I couldn't see what he looks like until now. He's so thin below his cheeks. He talked in falsetto, 'under seven minute miles, wow!' Happy."

She ran; she was back on the road, but she pondered the experience. *What did he see? At least he didn't deny me! And what's with the Tagalog?—'Mabuhay, iha!' Kinda corny! Does he think I've been back in the Philippines all these years?*

She ran; she felt thoroughly warmed up by now. *Maybe I'm going a little too fast. I'd better slow down and save energy for the later miles... Marriott Copley Hotel lobby.*

Gotta focus, gotta focus.... Dios ko, don't let this get me off focus. Why did I introduce this interruption in my focus? And what an interruption! Why did I see him? And Nanay would so disapprove! And what about Lola? I'm relieved she didn't come along and see me talking with him. Lola supported her daughter when they divorced ... and she sure does support me ... running ... and by not telling Mom everything she knows about me... Raoul, weed, and all...

Why did I do it? Oh, why did I do it? Oh, Sofie, you're so stupid! This became her new mantra as she moved along toward Mile Five.

3-5. Run, Rima, Run!
Monday, April 21, 2008

At 10:20, the remaining three women crowded into one of the corrals and waited for the Wave Two gun at 10:30. Their California friends Larry and Keith saw them and pushed their way through the crowd to wait together. The five hugged and then called "see you after the finish!" They all heard the start gun and then shuffled for a long time, 12 minutes, they noticed, before they crossed the start mat.

"So much excitement in the air, it's hard to start out slowly," Rima said. To keep her pace down, she looked at her Garmin's pace-tracker now and then. The three, now five, had agreed on a slow, ten-and-a-half-minute mile pace for that first couple of downhill miles. They ran together, side by side.

After just a few minutes, they peeled off their black trash sacks and Goodwill jackets and threw them to the side, where spectators caught them. And then Rima, Larry, and Keith went ahead of Gloria and Tiffany.

So many spectators!—They've already been shouting encouragement for … must be more than an hour already, thought Rima. *Even so, they sound like they've finally gotten a glimpse of me, with my name front and back, as if I'm their dear auntie!* She was to hear her name, enthusiastically shouted, thousands and thousands of times, "Rima, go Rima! You can do it!"

At Mile One and their first water stop, Rima pulled over to the right for water, handed to her by a 10-year-old girl. Rima's feet, and those of all the runners traveling with her, scuffled through empty paper cups, tossed down by those ahead of them. *Porta-Potties, I don't need them now and I'm happy to pass them by, especially with those long lines, 20 runners deep!*

The spectators—the kids! She ran along the right side to meet dozens of children's hands for high fives. After awhile she stayed on the right side. *Those sweet children have been waiting so long, they deserve to be acknowledged!*

She overheard conversations. "I hate the sticky pavement at these Gatorade stops, don't you?" a woman runner asked her companion.

Some 25,000 runners and a half million spectators, but almost all were new to her. *Same as the other races: new people became companions with the same goal, a successful finish.*

So many charities! Runners wore names of organizations or honorees on their shirts. "This is for Mom;" "In memory of Jason, 2002-2006"; "Liver Foundation."

But then at Mile Two, before coming into the town of Ashland, she heard her name called quite differently from two men who stepped out from the spectators on the left side to approach her. "Number 21511, you're Rima Masuhud?" Not only were their voices ominous; they looked startlingly out of place in their business suits and shiny leather shoes. Their faces were flushed pink, but not from exertion, and both had light brown hair cut short in Marine butch style

Should I answer? But before she could sort out her thoughts, they tried to grab her. One on each side reached to put one arm around her back and grab her other arm, to move her off the course.

Startled, and already in flight mode, she struggled to escape by reaching out for Larry, who was still running at her right side. Larry and Keith reacted astoundingly quickly. Keith quickly linked his right arm into Rima's left elbow and whispered, "Let's go!" while Larry firmly linked his left into her right arm. The three tugged against the two bulky men and leaned forward into the course. Suddenly free from their drag, the three picked up their speed to nine minutes per mile, knowing that the "suits" wouldn't be able to keep up that pace for long.

The two men heaved their big bodies with all that clothing into a heavy running gait, but they couldn't keep it up. Gloria looked back to see them veering off to the side of the road. They each had a Bluetooth at their ears, and the taller one looked like he was talking on the phone.

"Oh my God!" said Tiffany, when she and Gloria

caught up. "Now what?"

"They might try this again," said Gloria.

"Well, Rima, we told you we'd stay with you," said Larry.

"But your finish time… !" protested Rima.

"Never mind that," said Larry. "You're gonna finish."

3-6. Hold Your Head Up High!
Monday, April 21, 2008

Rima needed to release nervous energy. *I'll think of Sofie, ahead of me. I'll think of my dear deceased Paolo, mother, father, others who have gone on before me. Light feet, Rima, sprint at the finish!*

She silently sang the song she had first heard as a child in the movie *Carousel*, the aria, *You'll Never Walk Alone*. She had been taken, a full day trip by outrigger canoe and then bus, into the City of Zamboanga to see the movie, which starred Shirley Jones.

When you walk through a storm
Hold your head up high
And don't be afraid of the dark

At the end of the storm
Is a golden sky
And the sweet silver song of the lark

Walk on through the wind
Walk on through the rain
Though your dreams be tossed and blown

Walk on, walk on with hope in your heart
And you'll never walk alone
You'll never walk alone.

"I'll just go on ahead for awhile; you guys will surely catch up with me before long."

"Well, okay, but.... They probably won't come back now," called Larry.

Now running solo, she overheard other conversations: "I still feel like I'm floating above the pavement." "Where will your brother meet you after the finish?"

Occasionally she exchanged words with a fellow

runner: "May I pass through?" and "That's okay" to a runner's "sorry" at accidentally bumping into her arm after he had let his elbow swing out.

At Mile 4.1, at Ashland's clock tower, Rima stopped to fill her fuel belt water bottle and to pick up another cup of Gatorade. She didn't know that she had just passed her former son-in-law among the dozens of volunteers handing out water, nor did he know to look for her, busy as he was with his clock monitoring and re-hydration tasks … and reflecting on his extraordinary experience a half hour earlier.

Rima ran back into the moving crowd; she felt fine. *Oh, I've finally arrived! I can run on my own energy, all the way to Boston, Boylston Street.… Breathing fine—Two steps inhale, one step exhale, comfortable, just the right pace, around a 9.5-minute mile.* She continued silently singing, *Walk on through the wind, Walk on through the rain.…*

Rima played with numbers throughout the entire experience. She counted her steps to the next tree on the right. She noted distance and time and with these she calculated her pace, over and over again. *Mile Six: two more tenths and then 20 miles to go.… Let's see*—and she looked at her watch—*Fifty-seven minutes: good; just right pace.… Mile Seven—more than one-fourth finished.*

She passed a purple-shirted TNT woman runner at about Mile 12. Ahead she heard happily shouting women. *Must be the Wellesley students, already?*

At Mile 12.5, she could make out the cheers of the Wellesley College women ahead. *Ah yes, I heard they hold up "kiss me" signs.* Rounding a curve, through the trees she saw hundreds of college women leaning over temporary metal barricades that lined the course, barricades to keep the spectators away from the runners. "Kiss me, I'm from Connecticut"; "Kiss me, I should be doing my homework"; and "Kiss me, I'm from the Philippines." With that one, tears spilled out of her eyes and her breath exhalations filled with sobs. She blubbered for the next half mile, and at the same time she laughed at herself, smiling as the tears streamed down her face. *Guess I'm pretty fragile, otherwise how do I explain this? I'm so emotional!*

Her sobs subsided and Rima noticed that her fingers had become puffy, a familiar sign of over-hydration, and so she decided to take only a couple of sips of Gatorade and water for the next few miles. She had been taking two-fisted drinks at each water station, only a mile apart.

At Mile 13.1, *the "Half Marathon" sign! So far, the body is working well.... I'll get the finger puffiness down. But hey, where are Larry and Keith?* When she slowed for water, she looked behind her, but didn't see them. *They're usually faster than I am.*

At about Mile 13.5, Rima's right knee complained, outside by the IT.. Band. *Maybe I can just run through it, and it'll calm down.* She reached into her fuel belt for a salt capsule, swallowed it, and then followed with water from her bottle.

Spectators expected to have interaction with the runners, and frequently she complied. So many children! They appeared delighted to read her name. They called to her, and held up their hands for a "high five." And so many college students! Many times she came upon a group that had noticed her name, and then they'd pick up the chant from their neighbors as she passed by, "Rima! Rima! Go Rima!"

She saw just one barefoot runner, at about Mile 14, whom she passed. Then at about Mile 16 she passed a young couple wearing Vibram Five Fingers, minimalist shoes, and she guessed that they had sore feet by now, otherwise, how could she be passing them? *Maybe they didn't train enough in them.*

By mile 16, her fingers were back to normal and Rima evaluated her progress. *No increase of the burn on the knee; probably my patellar tendon, not IT band; but so far, so good.*

She saw the first of the Newton Hills ahead of her. *I've come to the hills. Oh-oh, we're here! Allah Akbar!* The crowd was thick on each side, shouting "You can do it, Rima, run!" *Dios mio, they don't want me to walk these hills …. Gotta comply by running up them. I'll push harder. I'll try to run on their encouragement. Can I hold out? … 10.2 miles to go; I'll be moving down to single digits before long.*

Into her head came another song, this one a parody of *Old Black Joe.* She smiled at her response to the crowd:

I'm running, I'm running,
For my head is bended low,
I hear those gentle voices calling,
"Run, Ri… ma."

She sang it silently to herself, over and over as she struggled upward.

Oh, the hills. Gloria said Easterners don't know about real hills—they're only 200 feet total, according to the course contour…. Why, it's 270 feet just up to the Golden Gate Bridge. I can do that with no trouble. I'm finally to the last hard part, then I'll coast downhill to finish…. Will the knee hold out? If it holds out, I can do it, and in good time.

Once Tiffany had asked them all, toward the end of a long training run, "Hey, guys, are we having fun yet?" And now, Rima answered that question for herself. *Oo! Am I having fun! … Good mantra … Having fun!*

At the Mile 19 marker, with two more miles to climb, she looked again at her watch, *Two oh two p.m.. Hmm, Sofie must have passed by here…. Let's see, maybe more than two hours ago. I wonder how she's doing? … Long ago finished, surely…. I wonder where Larry and Keith are.* She looked back, she scanned the faces of the runners following her, but she didn't see either of the men, hadn't seen them for many miles now.

Rima saw the Mile 20 marker ahead and thought, *Three behind me; only the fourth Heartbreak Hill to go, then downhill. Hey, that's a 10K; I can do that! …But my body is very different after twenty miles…* She looked up and heard the crowd encouraging her to keep running, and ... she suddenly got such a sharp pain in her right knee that she slowed to a limp, limp, limp. She reached into her fuel belt for her little knee strap and leaned over to strap it below her right knee. She straightened up to resume running, but she had to keep limping, and she tried to ignore the crowd's encouragement to run up the hill. *One more mile up, then a 250-foot elevation drop in three miles, then a flat two miles to the finish.... The uphill's hard, but downhill will have more impact. Most injuries happen on the downhill. Will my leg loosen up? Or even hold out?*

PART 4: AFTER THE MARATHON

4-1. In The Long Run:
Monday, April 21, 2008

Sofie sang silently to herself throughout the last half, her steps doing double time to the rhythm of the song:

> I used to hurry a lot, I used to worry a lot,
> I used to stay out till the break of day.
> Oh, that didn't get it,
> It was high time I quit it.
> I just couldn't carry on that way.
> Oh, I did some damage, I know it's true,
> Didn't know I was so lonely, till I found you.
> You can go the distance,
> We'll find out, in the long run.
> In the long run.

Approaching the finish, Sofie heard an announcer calling out names and of some of the finishers along with their cities—or was it states?

We're coming in too many at once to name us all, maybe. I've gotta step up the pace for a strong finish, and she leaned into quicker, longer steps, her arms pumping more vigorously, her eyes looking straight ahead for the big overhead finish arch.

Bleachers!—Still so many spectators! The clock... Far ahead, she saw the numbers of elapsed time shift to 2:59:00, 2:59:01... *Gotta keep up this pace...* Her feet touched the finish mat beneath the hours-elapsed clock at 3:01:15. No announcement of her finish. No family or friend to meet her, but she hadn't expected anyone. She was just a little disappointed.

Let's see, subtract eight minutes to cross the start line, so 2:53 plus. My PR!

She thought of the award. *No one approached me to*

*congratulate me; surely there must have been a faster 18-year-old
woman ahead of me, who would have won that scholarship. Well, I
didn't really expect it; I saw that another registered 18-year-old
woman ran her previous marathon in 2:40! I'll look on the computer
back in the hotel room.*

She slowed her run to a walk and looked at her watch
to see the daytime clock at 1:09:24. She stopped her trip
counter on her wrist and then dropped her gait down to a
walk behind several finishers ahead of her. Four volunteers
put finisher's medals around the runners' necks. "You're
not gonna hug me?" she asked the volunteer who had
dozens of medals hanging from her forearm. "Of course,
dearie!" from the pleasantly surprised older woman—
maybe her *lola*'s age.

Beyond the hug, Sofie saw the Old South Church,
where they and other runners had received their blessing
the day before, and she suddenly felt overwhelmed with
gratitude. *Finished! Did it! So much was at stake. I can rest,
Coach will be so happy,... And Lola too. Hey, I qualified for next
year!* The thoughts tumbled out, along with tears, which
she brushed off her cheeks with the back of one hand, and
then the other, just as she had brushed the sweat off her
face so many times during the last hours while running.

Sofie turned to look for an exit, and saw ahead of her
that the next full city block along Boylston was lined with
tables on both sides. The first few of these were topped
with black opaque goody bags lettered with "Boston
Marathon 2008." She picked up one and opened it to see a
neat array of snacks: a Power Bar, Famous Amos cookies,
and pretzels in wrappers. The next set of tables held 16-
ounce bottles of Poland Spring water, Gatorade
Endurance Formula, bananas cut in half, and bagels cut in
half. *Twenty-five-thousand runners, so lots of tables,* she thought.
No exit yet—metal barriers behind the tables, volunteer monitors...

The enclosed route for runner-finishers continued
another block, past Clarendon Street. Just before that
street, Sofie was handed the familiar silver Mylar sheet

blanket, and she was helped to get it around her shoulders. She knew from her previous marathons to tie the top corners together in front to make a cape, so that she could use her hands to gather more goodies and to eat while walking.

Approaching the next cross street, Berkeley, Sofie saw her exit to the right. But first she continued on Boylston to the gear check buses, where she picked up her bag containing the pants and jacket she had stored just before the start, all those hours and miles ago. Again, tears rolled down her cheeks—these clearly of relief—and she wiped them away. Back to the exit on Berkeley Street, she felt grateful to pass by the medical tent on her left, and she reveled in the quiet excitement and afternoon sun among other finishers and their supporters, all walking— *sauntering!*—to their cars, hotels, and the MBTA Green line.

Walking into a little breeze, Sofie noticed that she was finally getting chilly from slowing down and from her sweat-damp clothes, but she didn't want to stop to fish her jacket out of the gear bag. *Ten more minutes of walking, I have my key card in my shorts pocket; the lobby will be warm, and I'll be up the elevator and into the quiet of our room. Hard to wait.*

This turned out to be a victory walk; she heard "congratulations!" over and over again from people on the street, spectators, shoppers, and even other runners. She smiled with pride and called "to you too!" to the other silver-draped finishers, and "thanks!" to the others.

This is the only time, these few minutes. Enjoy it while it lasts. Next time I leave the hotel, I'll have on street clothes, no Mylar blanket, no running shoes, no shorts. Maybe I'll wear the medal when we go out later, but just for today, tonight. It would be tacky after today.... She noticed that she felt proud, not a bit shy, because she really had met a big challenge. *I wasn't a top finisher, of course, but I can endure a lot. I put my all into it, maybe as much as the elites. I didn't quite risk my life, but it's along the same trail, just around the bend.*

The little green spot in the door lock lighted up when she inserted her key card, and Sofie stepped into her refuge. The door whooshed to a quiet close behind her as she turned to deposit her goody bag, water bottle, and Mylar blanket on her designated part of the table top, relieved to contemplate her solitude.

But, "Hey, Gloria and Tiffany!" Both were stretched out on their king-sized bed, in street clothes, hair wet and wrapped in white hotel towels. Tiffany held a fashion magazine in one hand and with the other hand an ice bag on her right thigh; Gloria, with both hands, held the massage "Stick" to her own right shin.

"Oh, Why?..."

Tiffany giggled, sheepishly, "We took a taxi from Wellesley." Gloria added, "I decided to keep her company; she got an IT band problem." They both hurriedly sat up on their bed. "So sorry we didn't see you finish, Sofie," said Gloria.

"Yeah, I needed the ice.... What was your time?" Tiffany hurried over to her laptop by the window to check on the real-time progress.

"The finish clock said 3:01 hours and.. something."

"Oh, yes, here it is; chip time 2:53:15—so you qualified to come back here next year!"

"Yay-ay-ay!" they both called and grabbed Sofie into a hug. Tiffany returned to her laptop. "But you came in Number Two ... ohhhh." She paused, then added, "Missed the scholarship. Ohhh."

Gloria leaned over to the computer. What was the time of Number One?" Tiffany searched. "Here it is: 2:51:51 chip time, Shannon Beardsley, Bethesda, Maryland.... Oh, I'm sorry, Sofie."

"I couldn't possibly have gone faster.... Well, if a mountain lion had chased me, maybe I could have taken off one minute, but no more. *The stop to see Mr. Ayala? Just let it be.*

"Hmm. How about next year? Is there a winning purse for the following three years of full scholarship ride?" asked Tiffany.

"I don't think so," responded Sofie.

"No, just the full four-year one," said Gloria.

"Hey, second place in your age group, you'll certainly

be invited back next year," Tiffany offered.

"Oh, that'd be good.... But hey, let's see about the guys ... and how is my *lola* doing out there?" Tiffany entered "Karima Masuhud Osorio" into the search box and waited for the array of her mat crossings, one entry for each 5K along the route, and an added one for the half, at 21 plus kilometers or 13.1 miles. All three hovered over Tiffany's computer display. "She finished the half at 12:43, and it shows 2:01 hours and at a nine-minute 16 second pace. Faster than usual!"

"Just what she had hoped for," said Gloria.

"But look here, at the 30K mat," warned Tiffany, "She's was at 9:53 minutes per mile. So she slowed down a little."

"That'd be... 1:51 p.m.. Hey, that was just ... three minutes ago," said Sofie. "Isn't this amazing? We're up here in the hotel, and we can watch her real-time progress, down there?"

"And look, they show her projected finish at 3:03 p.m." said Gloria.

"You know, I'm gonna go catch her finish," said Sofie, grabbing her key card and jacket. "And hey, I met someone on the course I said I'd meet again at the Marriott Copley Place Hotel at three o'clock for a half hour. See you all after."

She was out the door before they could think to ask anything.

4-2. Kalma Te, Kalma Te
Monday, April 21, 2008

Rima turned the corner on Boylston Street and picked up her pace, her elbows pumping her to the finish. *My knee calmed down, and there's still a little spring in my legs.* Crowds on both sides cheered her on—her and a few other four-and-a-half-hour finishers, and she saw the finish clock showing "3:03:57." *Four hours, 33 minutes, minus 12 minutes to start; uh, my brain's foggy … four hours 21 minutes.* She raised both arms high in victory, and knew that she had qualified—just barely—for next year. *But I don't think I'll be here next year.*

She and her fellow finishers slowed to a stroll, passing the table-stations on both sides of their narrow walkway down the middle of Boylston, cordoned off from spectators by temporary metal barriers. First, a finisher's medal was put around her neck by a woman about her own age—with a big smile and "congratulations!" At the next station, a Mylar blanket was put around her shoulders.

Continuing along the chute-like course, Rima saw a table with water bottles, and probably the bananas and packaged food would be near, and after that, the gear check.

As she walked with the others toward the water bottles, two men in warm-up suits approached her. *Are they volunteers handing out more stuff?… But no smiles. Hmm… There's a camera around one guy's neck…. Reporters?* They placed themselves in front of her and stopped. She needed to keep moving or she'd get cramps in her legs. *Hey, these guys are blocking me.*

She couldn't quite think clearly. *News reporters with that camera? But they're wearing sweat pants and very clean white Reebok shoes—new shoes. Not runners… Ooh! The same men! wearing dark suits back then,* who had come after her at Mile Two, what seemed like ages ago.

Oh-oh, where are Larry, Keith, … Gloria, when I need them? She stopped her forward movement, but continued pacing her legs, and now she brought her knees up higher to continue pumping the lactic acid out.

The shorter one asked "Ms. Masuhud?" Both men

pulled badges out of their pockets and held them out to her. *Kind of hard to read their demeanor, kind of hard to see,* still wiping salty sweat off her face, still pouring down into her eyes, she hadn't yet answered when the shorter man asked, "Ms. Rima Masuhud?"

She stepped back. She wiped her closed eyes with the "elbows" of her index fingers, and looked at the men again, this time more attentively. "Yes, what do you want?" Her mind whirled. *How do they know my name?—Probably from my bib number? It's public information, posted on the BAA site.*

The same man said "USCIS officers—United States Citizenship and Immigration Services. While tying it up, he said, "here's your gear check bag. We picked it up for you." He held her bag out for her. *They allowed that? Hey, he looked inside my bag! You have to show your bib to pick up—oh, the badges... .* She calmly took it from him.

"Please come with us to our office."

Oh, Dios mio! she whispered to herself. And then, *kalma te, kalma te,* calm yourself. She glanced behind her, hoping to see Larry and Keith. She respectfully asked, "May I please decline?"

By now a few of the fellow finishers stood nearby, marching in place to keep their legs moving, to listen in, and they appeared to be ready to support her. The short CIS man said, "Sorry, but we won't detain you long. Our office is in South Boston."

Rima asked if they could pass by the tables with water bottles and bananas on their way. The men reluctantly agreed.

They led her to a silver Chevrolet Impala and opened the back door for her. Already getting stiff from the run, she softly exclaimed, "ohh!" and carefully lowered herself onto the seat. *Oh, Dios, this is a prisoner compartment! I'll get stiff, sitting here.* The two men looked at one another and rolled their eyes. The tall man drove, and the shorter sat in the passenger seat, twisting sideways so that he could watch Rima.

She moaned "ohh." The short man squinted his eyes at

her, but he seemed relieved when she said, "Sorry, a cramp. I must move my legs." And then she stretched them out, a difficult move in the back seat. While rotating both feet in circles, she pressed with her fingers into the cramp, and it slowly released. She kept moving her feet throughout the ride to their office, while the short man looked worried.

As they moved through the heavy post-race traffic, Rima thought of something she had heard in American movies. "May I please make a call?"

"After we get to the office," was the gruff response from the front seat.

Rima remained silent, but she quietly and continually pumped her feet on the car's floor, toes to heels to toes. Several times she lifted up her feet to stretch out her whole legs, and she noticed the short man watching her, warily.

The car pulled into a staff parking lot. The men got out and motioned to her to get out as well. As soon as Rima climbed out of the car, she stretched her legs: her calves, Achilles, adductors, the IT bands, her quads. *Gotta get the lactic acid out of my legs.... They'll have me sit in there.* The men both rolled their eyes and turned away, apparently figuring she was just delaying.

The building was not lighted. *No guard on duty, holiday,* she noticed. The men opened a side door and turned on lights. They led her into a little conference room, seated her, got her another bottle of water, and asked her to sit in an easy chair. *Softening me up,* she thought.

"I'm Mr. Billings," the short man said, and then complimented her on her finish of The Boston.

Oh brother! thought Rima. "And this is Mr. Duggan." She nodded to each, but didn't offer her hand, nor did they.

Rima tried to prepare her response to the question she expected, why she had overstayed her tourist visa by four days. Instead she was surprised by the first question: "What were your **other** reasons for coming to Boston, Ms.

Masuhud?"

"She blinked her eyes, and then said, "What? Uh, can I please make my phone call now?"

Mr. Billings curtly responded, "In a few minutes. Please answer."

Another blink, a look to the side and then to him, and she said, "Well, I wanted to come to the marathon with my granddaughter.... And I haven't yet learned her finish time; do you know how she did?" They sat silently, glaring at her. She added, "And I wanted to come with our friends as well. We're all staying together ... in the Colonnade Hotel.... Oh, you probably already know that ..."

The men looked at her with stony faces, clearly not wanting her to know what they thought of her response.

"What else?" Mr. Billings asked, very gruffly.

Rima returned to her silent mantra, *kalma te, kalma te.* She recalled her little running group's way of reducing their excessive nervousness before the marathon ... *was it just this **morning?*** It seemed like much longer ago. They all had said, "take deep, slow breaths," and they said they could even feel their heartbeats slow down. So she tried it again, and she felt a little better. She finally answered, "Well, I had already planned to go to your San Francisco office first thing this next Thursday morning. We're scheduled to fly back to San Francisco on Wednesday."

The other man, Mr. Duggan, asked, "Why Wednesday and not Tuesday?"

Rima responded, "We were advised to wait a day after running the marathon before getting on a plane...."

"Why is that, Ms. Masuhud? And **who** advised you?" And he glared at her.

She stammered, "Uh ... in order to avoid getting an embolism in our legs or lungs; the altitude in the plane is more dangerous than at ground level. That's doctors' and race directors' strong advice."

"Well, Ms. Masuhud. We'll see about that." He appeared to disbelieve her.

They followed these initial questions with dozens over the next hour and a half, about her childhood, about her

Muslim heritage, about why six percent of all Filipinos were Muslims, why almost all live in the south, about her relatives down there, and they told that now her relatives are being watched as well. They asked her about a certain nephew there, how Al Qaeda had now infiltrated the southern Philippines, what she knew about that certain nephew's association with Al Qaeda, about her recent visit down to Zamboanga, about whether she attended a mosque in California, and about her application for immigration to the U.S. Several of the questions were repeated later, and she recognized the men were testing her for consistency. *They don't have to keep repeating their questions. I've heard that it's harder to remember what you said if you're lying, but it's not hard for me to keep repeating the same answers, because I'm telling the whole truth.*

She moved her legs now and then, and twice she asked if she could stand and walk back and forth. They reluctantly agreed, but each time soon said "Enough. Please sit down." All three appeared to grow fatigued with the questioning. Then the phone rang.

The three appeared to be startled. Mr. Billings answered, he turned away, and he talked too softly for Rima to hear. Mr. Duggan continued with the questioning, making it hard for Rima to eavesdrop. Mr. Billings asked a few questions into the phone and he said "mm-hmm" several times, and then, "All right, but she'll have to have a CIS hold." He hung up.

The three sat in stunned silence for a moment, and then the two men whispered together for a couple of minutes. Next, Mr. Billings told her that she could now make her telephone call, and she could be picked up. She immediately pulled her cell phone out of her fuel belt and called Gloria, and then turned back to the men to ask the street address of the building

4-3. The Rundown
Monday, April 21, 2008

Sofie felt torn with dilemma. *No way to call him; no time to see Lola finish.* With great frustration at having to choose between these two important people in her life, she went directly to the hotel, arriving ten minutes after the hour named by Mr. Ayala.

She started on her third decaf coffee with cream and sugar, along with her water with no ice, before she gathered the courage to ask Mr. Ayala the big question. Actually, he made it easy for her.

They sat in Starbucks, just up the street from her hotel. Her face was still flushed from the run, and her hair, still damp from running, was pulled back in a low ballerina bun. Sofie wore her new "Boston Marathon" shirt, and over it, her finisher's medal on its yellow and blue ribbon. Under the table she continually moved her legs and feet in recovery, but her upper body, what Mr. Ayala could see from across the table, was quiet, apparently calm, and coasting on success.

He had expressed his delight in learning that she loved running, like he, and they had shared their special reasons. Sofie said she had started running to escape bad influences at school; her father had started running, he dared to divulge to her, in order to escape his guilt about abandoning his pregnant wife, Sofie's mother.

"So why **did** you leave her, then?" She poured more cream into her coffee, and then looked up intently into his eyes.

He still wore his "Boston Marathon 1995" shirt that she had seen him in at the water stop. His short salt-and-pepper hair was full and perky; he had used silver-rimmed reading glasses when he read the menu, but now rested them on the table. *Is that a Rolex on his wrist?* Sofie wondered. *Head high, shoulders back but relaxed, straight back … like our coach says, "posture of success."*

"I loved her. I was jealous, thought her former boyfriend..."

"Hmm?"

"She told me she was two months late, had just gone for a test, and was excited to report she was pregnant."

"Oh, I was conceived in Manila, then."

"The U.S. Embassy took another two months to grant her visa after I came here. I didn't know...."

"Two months."

"I didn't believe her... I couldn't take a regular job on my student visa; I was afraid I'd lose my visa, my fellowship, and I had to start at the university. And she would work in California for a few months, so we had expected to be apart for awhile even after she would get to the U.S."

He looked down to flick a crumb off of the white tablecloth. His fingers absently searched for more crumbs.

Sofie's eyes remained on him. "Why didn't you believe her? And how were you going to get together, anyway? I never could figure this out because she told me a long time ago that she came to a job at Sequoia Hospital in Redwood City, California, where she still works. And you had been accepted to Tufts in Boston."

"I felt I couldn't support three...." With both fists, he gently pounded the table, and then brought up his eyes to look into hers. "Oh, Sofie, my whole adult life, I've tried to make up for abandoning your mom and you."

Sofie remained silent. They continued searching into each other's eyes, eyes the same shade of dark brown, same almond shape, startlingly familiar to each of them, these new eyes.

"From my family back home, I heard the baby was a daughter.... You've been on my mind every day. Oh, and now I am sitting here with you, and you've grown up!"

"Why, then?"

"She closed me out because I left her in California."

"And accused her of infidelity, right? Why didn't you just keep trying?" Sofie had moved her hands to the edge of the table and into "push-off" position; she squinted slightly as she continued her steady gaze.

"Your mom was very insulted and very stubborn…"

Sofie softened her interrogation and leaned back into her chair. "Still is."

"Does she know you found me?"

"No, but *Lola* is here."

Alec quickly leaned back into his chair. "Oh, Rima!" He looked away for awhile." I always had great respect for her." He turned to face Sofie again. "Do you know that she introduced us, back in college, at Ateneo de Manila University?"

"No."

"You know what she told me back then? She said she knew how to read people's characters well."

"Hmm, maybe **she's** been feeling guilty all along as well. Maybe that explains more.…"

"About what?" Alec leaned forward again and put his elbows onto the table, forearms and hands folded between them.

"About her coming to the U.S. to take care of me, even joining in on running".

He opened his eyes a little wider. "Oh, running! And does she know you came to meet me?"

"No. She doesn't know you're here."

They each sipped their coffees.

He said, "I'll get back to the why."

"Yes." She didn't move; even her feet and legs remained still.

"I had been accepted to law school at Tufts here in Boston; you knew that part. Tess - your mother - had a friend, Sally, in California, who was also a nurse. It was Sally who helped your mother to get that job at Sequoia Hospital, and they were the ones who got her work visa for her."

"Oh, yeah, *Tita* Sally! But how were you going to manage that?"

"Before I left the Philippines, she said that after getting the visa, first she would take that job and then immediately start looking for a job in Boston."

"But?"

"When the visa came through and when she arrived in the U.S., I flew to San Francisco to meet her. I had to borrow the money for airfare for the two of us."

"And?"

"We were so happy to meet there in San Francisco, so excited! But when she told me she was pregnant.... I had already been here two months. I calculated, I worried. We argued. I suggested an abortion to settle it." His hands flopped back onto the table.

She took a long inhalation. "Lord."

"She refused. I left, she started her job; we telephoned."

"Emailed?"

"We had no computers yet. And even calls cost a lot back then."

"No offer of hope?" Sofie leaned one elbow onto the table and gazed out the huge window next to the table.

"I pleaded. In October she sent divorce papers. She didn't waste time. She didn't even want my name on the birth certificate, *daw.*"

Sofie moved her fingers vertically over her lips and inhaled. "But my name is Ayala."

"You told me that earlier today, on the race. I was very surprised!" he gasped. "My brother back home sent me a very damning letter; he said there was no former boyfriend in those two months, and how could I have accused her?" He paused. "So I sent her a huge apology."

"And?"

"No answer." He sighed and looked down at the table, placing his hands on it.

Another big inhalation, and then Sofie asked, "Then what?"

"I got a student job on the campus assisting a professor so that I could send money, but she sent back the envelope unopened."

Sofie exhaled. "Only one?" She looked out the window.

He followed her gaze out the window. "I sent several more; all were returned."

She looked at him. "So you lost hope." She waited.

His gaze remained out the window. "Later, I met a fellow student, a woman. I decided to treat **her** right."

Sofie looked out the window again and inhaled shallowly. "What does she know?"

"I told her I had married in the Philippines and then divorced after arriving here in Boston."

"And?"

He continued looking out the window. "I didn't tell her about the pregnancy."

Sofie looked at him again, eyelids narrowing slightly. "When **did** you tell her?"

He inhaled, exhaled, then quietly said, "I didn't."

After a long moment, Sofie looked again into his eyes. "Aren't you doing her a disservice, then?"

"Every day I'm doing my best to keep her happy. And the children."

"*Dios ko*. Hey, Mr. Ayala, tell me about your good traits. You do have some?" Sofie lightly slapped the table with her right hand, and then put it into her lap.

He looked back at her. "I've never been able to get out of this mangrove swamp He looked toward the window. "Every idea seems to be self-serving." He leaned back in his chair.

"Or, self-protecting?"

"How can I ever.... Uh, I've saved a college fund for you."

Sofie pulled her cell phone up from her lap. "Please excuse me; this is the fourth time my girlfriend has called. She came to Boston with us." She punched a button and put her phone up to her ear.

"Hi, Tiffany," then she paused. Her expression of annoyance turned to worry. She turned away from him and lightly slapped her second hand against her cheek.

"Shall I go look for her?" She listened.

"Your mom already called the BAA?"

"You looked for her progress online?" She listened.

"She did finish? At what time?" She paused.

"But that's almost two hours ago! It's, uh, 5:15 now. And the hotel is so close to the finish," She listened.

"She's already called the police?" She paused. "She's talking with them now? Oh! Call me right back, Tiffany."

Sofie punched "end call," put her phone into her purse, and jumped up. "My *lola* is missing. I gotta go."

"Oh! May we meet tomorrow afternoon?"

"Uh… okay. Gotta go."

4-4. Stiff Legs
Monday, April 21, 2008

Ooh, stiff legs! Can't run! Sofie headed for the hotel as fast as she could manage.. A chilly headwind had developed while she had sat with *"this Mr. Ayala. Can he really be my father?"* She quickly pulled on her new yellow "Boston Marathon" warm-up jacket.

Could a person who did such a bad thing, a long time ago, become a good person? She quickly crossed a side street; a car turning right off Huntington patiently waited for her. *So he didn't just disappear; ang nanay ko refused **him**!*

Moving toward the red light at a second quiet side street, she looked both ways, saw no car or policeman, and quickly started to run the red.... *Nope, can't run!* She slowed to an awkward crab-like scurry. *But it's a very bad sign that he didn't tell his new wife.* A short downhill now to the Colonnade Hotel and she quickened her pace to a race walk. *I can't think about him now.* She rushed through the hotel lobby, up the elevator, and along the dark corridor to the room.

Gloria and Tiffany had already put in a missing person report to the police and to the BAA. The three of them worried and considered their next move. Gloria had been on the phone with her family's attorney in California, and now they waited for him to call back with advice.

All the while, the three women walked around the room, putting their legs up into the air and stretching. Occasionally one sat in a chair with her legs curled up, and then gave a little shout when her leg cramped from unreleased lactic acid buildup. "Our bodies continue their natural functions for the physical crisis; they haven't taken time out for emotional crisis management!" smiled Sofie weakly.

They waited.

Gloria's phone rang.

"Rima!"

"Yes, of **course** we'll come, right now! We'll get a taxi downstairs...."

Gloria continued. "Are you all right?"

"Can you wait there?"

"There are no taxis there?"

"They say it's not so far? What's the address? She took the hotel notepad and pen that Tiffany had grabbed and excitedly reached toward her.

"We're leaving right now. Can't wait to see you."

She hung up, and then said, "Let's go!"

They rushed to the elevator.

4-5. Deep, Slow Breaths
Monday, April 21, 2008

The three women jumped out of the taxi as Rima came into the late afternoon dusk out of the CIS building. They grabbed her and opened the taxi door for her.

"We're so grateful we have you back!" said Sofie.

"Yes, so happy, all of us," added Gloria.

Rima quietly but stiffly climbed into the back seat. Tiffany handed her a bottle of water, and Sofie put a banana and a small bag of pretzels into her lap; she had noticed that her grandmother clutched a big manila envelope along with her gear check bag.

"Oh, *salamat! [thank you]* I'm so thirsty and hungry."

"You're welcome," Tiffany said. They all laughed, relieving their nervousness a bit, for even Gloria and Tiffany knew the Tagalog word for "thank you" by now.

After they settled in, with Gloria in the front with the driver and the other three in the back, the driver started the taxi.

Sofie said, "You must need to rest. We can wait to hear everything." She noticed her *lola's* salt and pepper hair was dry now, but her temples were crusted with salt, and apparently she had only finger-combed her hair. Of course she still wore her running clothes and shoes.

She might still be damp from the marathon, thought Sofie.

"I'm okay, *Nene*," thanks to being with my dear ones again." Rima closed her eyes tightly and pulled Sofie's toward her to press Sofie's cheek against her own. Sofie responded with a soft squeeze of her grandmother's hand.

After the cab was under way, Rima said, "I can tell you now." She paused. "I worked hard to remain very calm. Like before the start of the marathon, remember? We all said, take deep slow breaths? So that is what I did."

They respectfully and incredulously listened; they restrained themselves to few questions.

"At first I thought they might be news reporters, but then I saw that they were the same guys who came after me at Mile Two."

"Oh, what was **that?**" asked Sofie.

"I'll tell you shortly."

"They confronted me right after the finish, showed me their badges, and put me in their car. They worried each time I stretched my legs...."

Sofie said, "I don't know how you could manage it, *Lola*, sitting still right after the finish. They always tell us to keep walking for a half hour, hmm."

Tiffany quickly added, "And you **have** to stretch or you get big cramps, right?"

Rima continued. "I did get some cramps. And, of course, getting out of the car—I was very stiff already." She hesitated, and then looked at the others. "You three have been stretching, surely?"

"And we walked a lot!" said Gloria. "But Rima, why did they pick you up?"

"Well, uhh, I have to tell you now. Last month I got a letter reminding me that my tourist visa deadline to leave the US would be ...... last Thursday."

"*O-o-o*-h!" said Sofie. "You didn't tell us. Mama either? Or Glenn?"

"Well, no, because I decided to come with you guys to run the Boston."

"So was that what this capture was all about, overstaying?" asked Sofie.

"That's what I figured, but...."

"Go on," said Gloria.

"They asked *maraming* more questions: about my childhood in the Muslim part of the Philippines, about the application for immigration your *ina* had filled out for me, Sofie... For more than two hours."

"Yeah, Mom is hoping she'll come live with us," Sofie said to Gloria and Tiffany. "But the process takes so long, we don't talk much about it."

Gloria opened her eyes wide to acknowledge this new information, but she wanted to know more about today's ordeal. "By then we were all panicked about you. We couldn't find you."

"Oh, I knew you'd be worried about me. I felt so sorry

to cause you to worry. They wouldn't let me call." She paused, "And then, you won't believe what happened next."

"Oh, tell us!" said Tiffany.

"Well, the phone rang. Mr. Billings answered. I heard him say, 'Okay, we'll let her go, but she'll have to have a CIS hold,' and when he hung up and the two whispered together for a couple of minutes. They finally told me I could make my call. I called you, and here you are."

"Wow, who was it on the phone with Mr. Billings? And what is a CIS Hold? Do they hold you in... ? Sounds ominous," said Tiffany.

"I don't know. I'll read the information sheet they put in this envelope for me," and she lifted it up. "Something about CIS holding the papers about my immigration."

"And what do you have to do next?" asked Gloria.

"Yes, and who was it who called?" asked Tiffany.

Gloria interrupted, "I talked for some time with my attorney in California, but he hasn't called back yet. He said he'd call around to find you, to the marathon organizers maybe, and call me back. Oh! By the way, I'd better inform him of your whereabouts." She reached into her purse for her phone.

"Hey, Rima, could it be your Glenn who called there?" asked Tiffany.

Rima responded, "You know, I haven't had the chance to call him at all yet! How would he know anything? He probably followed my marathon progress on his computer, but those agents grabbed me after the finish, so my race updates wouldn't hint of a problem."

"Maybe it's just some bureaucratic thing," said Gloria.

Sofie was silent. She didn't know, but she suspected. She had rushed out from her meeting with her father saying, "My lola is missing; gotta go!" *I know he's an attorney, but in real estate...*

Who else knew her *lola* was missing? Of course, the police and the BAA, Gloria had put in the calls to both, reporting a missing person.

And what did CIS Hold mean? *Can Lola even get on the*

plane on Wednesday morning?

Rima sighed, "Mainly, now I can't wait to sit in a hot bathtub. Never mind the ice-cube bath, guys. Five hours after the finish is far too late for that! My clothes have been wet and cold all this time. Did you all take ice baths? Bet you didn't. *Brr!* I'm so hungry—I just grabbed a banana and a water bottle on the way to their car; I'll be extra sore tomorrow."

Gloria looked back from the front seat. "At least you're safe with us, for now."

Rima responded, "And now can we finally talk about the race? How did you all do?"

4-6. See That Path?
Tuesday, April 22, 2008

"We don't want to be sitting ducks here in the hotel for the ICE," Gloria said early the next morning. "Let's go to Walden Pond."

"Yippee," Sofie said; and Tiffany added, "Yay, Henry David Thoreau!"

They winced and laughed about their sore legs when they climbed into Gloria's rental car. After a quiet, sunny 25-mile drive out to Concord—"No car following us," said Tiffany—they parked and entered the path on the east side of the lake. They saw an elderly couple walking toward the water's edge, but apparently no other human visitors this early Tuesday morning.

"It's really the same lake as when **he** lived here?" asked Tiffany, looking around.

Rima couldn't tell if Tiffany was disappointed or in wonder after having read Thoreau's writing of 160 years earlier.

Sofie guessed that Tiffany was disappointed. "We can easily walk around it, just a mile and a half; remember, Tiff?"

"Oh yeah, I'd forgotten it was so small ... especially for being so important."

"It's so peaceful and serene," Rima quietly said. "Look at how beautiful it is with the woods all around. We might be seeing it just the same as in Thoreau's time, so long ago."

"The water is so calm, it's a glass window," said Sofie. "You can look down to the bottom here at the shore."

"See that path?" Gloria pointed toward the south side. "Let's take it. We can look for ducks." She and Tiffany set out under dappled sunlight on the soft, slightly damp earth.

Sofie walked slowly and so Rima stayed back with her. *Gotta talk alone with Lola.*

After awhile, Gloria and Tiffany looked back for them,

and Gloria quietly said to her daughter, "They're in deep discussion; let's stay discretely ahead, okay?"

Behind them fifty paces by now, Sofie thought, *good, we're alone.* She and Rima contentedly walked under new-leafing beech, hickory, and eastern oak trees in silence for a short while.

"I can't believe we're really Boston Marathon finishers, *Lola!*" She smiled gleefully into her grandmother's eyes, and grabbed her hands to squeeze them. "We can't say this in front of Gloria or Tiffany, can we?"

"You're right; I'm so sorry they didn't finish. But for us, it's hard for me to believe as well."

Again, they walked in silence for a short while.

"Who would've thought … but you, of course, my *mahal*, dear, we knew **you'd** do well!"

"Well, I couldn't have done it without you, *Lola*. I mean, Mom was right to send for you to come to California. I wouldn't have gotten away from Raoul, late nights, bad grades, no cross-country coaching, if you hadn't come."

"Well, **you** changed **my** life, too; you got me into running. I had thought my old body with all its ailments could only head downhill. I'm in much better shape now—not counting the soreness—and besides, I got to share these experiences with you."

"You're my good luck, *Lola*." They squeezed hands again and walked under the partial shade of a hickory tree, its branches still mostly bare, but promising green with tiny leaf buds almost ready to open.

I can't tell her yet. Too scary!

"Hey, *Nene'*, we'll always be Boston Marathon finishers, both of us, won't we! I get to share the big experience with you, even with our age difference."

"Yep, not so many grandmother-granddaughter finishers! And I feel so **different** today, don't you?"

"Yes, relief, first of all…"

"Oh, yeah!" Sofie closed her eyes, smiled, and nodded.

Rima continued. "And for all of us, a whole year of hard   running,   failures   and   injuries,   nervous anticipation...."

Sofie added, "sore legs... until, suddenly, it's over! We finished!"

"But not like a popped balloon, not an explosive finish.... Maybe a slow whoosh, all the energy spread out behind us over those long miles. Maybe the whole year of nervousness was with us until the finish."

"Yeah, I was too tired to jump for joy, but I suddenly realized, 'hey, I just crossed the **finish** line! I **did** it!'"

"*Dios mio*, I'm grateful for both of us, *Nene'*. I bet our realization will keep growing."

"Yeah.... Finishing, I feel like I can do anything now, how about you, *Lola*?"

"Hmm, yes, anything! But not to*day!*" They both laughed long and hard.

Rima added, "I'll hang on to that thought. Maybe I can face a couple of old challenges."

"Like your knees and your diabetes, hmm. And maybe *I* can face going off into the unknown, off to college, even far away."

They walked in silence for a short time, now in the shadier west side of the pond, under conifers.

Gotta tell her. Sofie looked into her grandmother's eyes and asked, "Runners tend to be good people, don't you think?"

"That's my experience so far. What are you thinking of?"

"Well, for one thing, we help each other."

"Yes. But, hey, you were competing for a serious prize, that scholarship!"

"Well, I can handle that a faster 18-year-old girl signed up and ran. But, I mean for us non-elites, we help our fellow runners more than we compete against them, right?"

"*Siempre.*"

They moved into single file through tree roots exposed in the path.

Side by side again, Sofie continued. "You know, in cross-country at school, anybody can be on the team. But since most of the kids at school don't want to work real hard, they don't go out for cross-country. The ones who do go out sure love it."

"You know how to work hard, and I'm so proud of you. And your coach says you have the potential to become an elite."

"Well, aside from that," Sofie laughed, "I hear from the kids on the football and basketball teams that they have to prove to the coach that they can be starters, and that means others have to sit on the bench."

"This is one reason I've come to love organized runs."

"Yeah, but *Lola*, we do help one another, right?"

"We sure do. I wouldn't have done the Boston yesterday without all your help, and Gloria's and even Tiffany's."

"Yeah. And another thing about runners: they're—we're—pretty honest."

"What are you thinking of?"

"Well, like how we don't show off with fancy clothing.... And we all work hard, we can take pain, we know how to endure, we stand on our own efforts.... Hey, *Lola*, that reminds me of Thoreau's '*Self-Reliance*'!"

"Yes, I think you're right, *Nene'*. We got to the finish yesterday by our own hard work."

They walked in quiet for a while. Soon they saw Gloria and Tiffany not far ahead of them on the path. Sofie thought, *not much more time alone. Gotta bring it up.*

But Rima continued the "hard work" topic. "Sofie, have you noticed, the runners we know who dropped out this last year?"

"Yeah…"

"… Some said it was just too hard, getting up in the dark, running hard, enduring pain…"

"Yeah, most of the girls at school say they don't want to get sweaty."

"By the way, how's your soreness from yesterday?"

"Not bad. How about you?"

"Also not bad."

"But I wonder about tomorrow; second day might be worse!"

"Yep, me too," said Rima. "We all know by now, if the

soreness doesn't come until the second day after, then it's going to be a lot worse."

"You're right. I wonder why?"

Rima said, "I don't know, but if you really overdo, you're likely to feel more sore on the second day after. Just weak in the muscles, first day."

"Yeah, for me too!"

Rima happily continued their topic. "Back to why we **like** running: We do love being out in nature, hmm..

"Oh yeah. Birds singing in the early morning, feet on real earth.... I bet that Thoreau probably walked around this lake many times.

Sofie stepped ahead into another single-file section of the path, pushed aside a beech tree branch, and held it for her grandmother to pass by.

"*Lola*, I want to tell you about someone I met on the course yesterday."

"Oh, I heard you went to meet someone after you finished. You're wondering about his or her character?" *A young man?* Rima wondered.

"Yes." Sofie stopped and turned to her grandmother. In response, Rima stopped as well. Sofie reached for her grandmother's hands. "*Lola*, I have something very big to tell you."

Rima's mind raced, guessing, wondering. *Good, bad? Can't tell yet. Bigger than just meeting an 'exciting guy'? What could it be? Will I like this? I'm a little scared!*

"*Oo, mahal, ituloy mo* [continue]," she said. Standing under the shade of a huge old beech tree, the grandmother and granddaughter continued to look into one another's eyes.

Sofie spoke quietly and slowly, "I met Alec Ayala yesterday."

4-7. Runners: Good People, Right?
Tuesday, April 22, 2008

Rima, whose mouth had fallen wide open, was inclined to pull her hands out of Sofie's grasp and move them up to cover her mouth. Instead, she inhaled quickly and deeply as she lightly squeezed Sofie's hands. They searched each other's eyes, both wondering what the other was thinking. Finally, Rima quietly said, "Tell me about it, *Nene*."

Sofie inhaled deeply and paused. "I already knew from you that he was a runner. I think that helped me decide to meet him. As you know, *Inay* never talked about him much at all. She didn't answer my questions."

"Yes, he ran the Boston, years ago."

Sofie looked away and then quickly back to her grandmother. "How'd you know that?"

"His family told my family back in Manila. It was only a few years after the divorce."

"Yeah. In 1995, he told me, and again in 2002."

"*Sige, Nene*."

"So about a month ago, Tiffany and I were having fun doing searches on our computers, and she talked me into looking him up."

"Oh, the modern technology."

"And so I learned on *LinkedIn* that nowadays he volunteers at the Boston. And the B.A.A. website even showed where he'd be, so yesterday I looked for him there."

"Oh, then I must have passed him as well!"

"Yeah, at Mile Four, the second water station, Ashland Clock Tower."

"So you stopped there? You mustn't have stayed long to chat; your finish time was pretty good."

"No, we agreed to meet afterward for coffee."

"Oh, *Dios mio*! All these years, I've wondered when you'd ever meet him and what it would be like."

"I was scared, believe me. But he was nice. So I agreed to meet him after the finish. But over coffee, while we were talking, Tiffany called to say you were missing."

Rima was silent. She took Sofie's arm so the two of them could resume walking. "Hey, Sofie, do you think— he's an attorney now, I heard from his family—do you think he was the one who called the ICE?"

"*Lola*, this is another reason I've wanted to tell you right away. After Tiffany called, I told him that you were missing, and then I left for our hotel. I'm wondering if he might have had some attorney's way of getting information."

"Hmm. Now what? ... We'll go back to California tomorrow, *Allah Akbar*. What about your *nanay*, do you suppose?"

"Yeah, *Lola*, can you help me figure out how to tell her? And **what** to tell her?"

"Of course, *Nene'*, we'll put our heads together."

"But Lola, I have a bigger question to ask you."

"*Oo, mahal?*"

"Do you think a person who has done something very bad in the past can become a good person?"

"Are you talking about Mr. Ayala?"

"You know. But, he abandoned my pregnant mom. And me, of course. Now, he wants to meet again

"And do you?"

"I'm very mixed up."

"Of course. I would feel mixed up too. In fact, I do now. I cried myself to sleep about this man for a long, long time.

"I mean, my mom would just think he's self-serving by helping you last night."

"Hmm, probably so."

"And he told me he's been saving for my college. But, oh, *Lola*, I didn't look him up in order to get money from him." She hugged her grandmother and pressed her forehead into the older woman's shoulder. Rima returned the hug.

Sofie stepped back, looked into Rima's eyes, and said, "And get this, Lola. He never told his new family about me. His wife probably doesn't know about any college fund for me. I'm disgusted, the more I think about it."

They continued walking.

"He told me that he wanted to become a better person, so he has tried very hard to be good to his family, and that's why he never told them about me. And, besides, my mom had refused to let him see me or even send anything to me, he said."

"*Nene'*, I think that's true."

"Oh my God, *Lola!* Maybe he didn't just simply abandon us!"

"Maybe he felt that she gave him no choice. He did visit his family in Manila a few times over the years, and he would have seen the photos of you that I had given to them."

"You did?"

"Yes, why not? They asked, and they know you're family."

"I don't know anything about that family."

"Hmm. Maybe you will, some day."

"So, *Lola*, do you think he could be a good man now? I mean, do you think I could trust him? What do you think of him?"

"I haven't seen him in 19 years. I did hear about him from time to time, from my family. His family said he's become a good family man and a successful lawyer."

"Good for his **second** family. Do you think I should give him a chance, *Lola?*

"Hmm. You know, *Nene'*, it may be very different, the way that Americans might think about him.

"How do you mean, *Lola?* How different? You mean that I should think like an American?

"I don't know. Americans confuse me. I hear Americans saying, 'It's gracious to forgive and forget.' Even, 'It's Christian. A person repents, takes 'the way of the Lord,' and we're to honor the new character. On the other hand, I see politicians campaigning here, like back home, and they dig up dirt from the distant past about the opposing party, and sometimes that soils, even buries, the opposition's campaign."

"I don't think Americans forgive and forget. The girls in school remember stuff forever. In our psychology class, our teacher talked about early childhood experiences and how they can shape a person's character, lifelong, like, even sibling order."

"Well, in my experience, Filipinos know just a little better how to forgive and forget. Though I'm not sure about your mom."

"Yeah, she's still angry. But how do Filipinos learn to forgive and forget?"

"I think of it like the Sulu Sea. Usually the sea is tranquil, with little waves lap-lapping against the white coral sand at the shore. But sometimes we have storms, big storms—even typhoons, once in awhile—down in Zamboanga, with 150 kilometers-per-hour winds. And dark gray, very angry clouds and torrents of rain, even hail. Lightning, thunder, oh, you have to hold your fingers in your ears when you run for cover."

Sofie opened her eyes wide. "Ooh! That's scary, but exciting!"

"But then, the next day, the Sulu Sea can be completely tranquil again. There's no sign out on the water of yesterday's turbulence, no big waves crashing or climbing up high on the beach, threatening our *bahay kubo*—our little nipa hut. Instead, the sea is calm, glassy even. Maybe some broken coral pieces at the shore. So would you think can you trust the sea, go out on it in your little double outrigger canoe and little paddle?"

"I don't know. Weren't you afraid to?"

"Well, fishermen know to be vigilant about the future. The experience of the typhoon teaches us that when the wind changes, we must be extra cautious about the weather, and sometimes even head for land. But if we pay close attention, then we can trust the sea.

"So can I trust Mr. Ayala? Maybe just pay close attention? Or could he be just another of those creepy deadbeat dads I've read about?"

"Read about?'

"Yeah, I've done some searches. Anyway, I've heard some divorced dads just want to prove that it was all the mom's fault, and then they compete for the kid's affection."

"Hmm. "

"And, oh! Helping **you!** – that is, if that call came from him or a colleague. Might he just be ingratiating himself? Maybe to spite my mom?"

"Hmm. It's difficult to know.... It takes awhile to learn about a person."

Sofie paused. "I can't stop thinking about the worst of all, that he never told his second family about me. I asked him; he told me that."

Rima said, "Oh, so maybe that's why he never took them to the Philippines to meet his family. Oh, *sayang* [sorry], *Nene'*. But you know, your mother never took **you** to the Philippines either, and his family told me they're very sad they've never met you."

"I never knew that."

"I couldn't tell you. I couldn't convince your mother."

"Oh, I didn't know all this."

They looked up at a squirrel scampering along an overhead branch.

"*Lola*. What was he like back then?"

"Oh, your *lolo* and I thought Tess had made a good selection."

"My *lolo* was still alive?"

"Oh yes, and he approved of him as well.... He was good looking, easy to talk with, a good listener. Good plans for the future, very respectful of Tess..."

"Wow, I never heard this."

"Ambitious, unpretentious, good family...."

"Why didn't ... ?"

Rima resumed. "He asked our permission to marry her,

and later asked our permission to take her to the US. Getting a visa was a problem for her, but everyone in the Philippines knows about problems getting U.S. visas. In Manila it's easy to see the long, long lines in front of the US Embassy, and we know people who have waited there for days and days. So it was no surprise that she might have to wait three or four months before following him. So she came back from UP [University of the Philippines] to live with us. There was no way she was dating someone else. She got her visa in just two months, and she left immediately. But it wasn't until two months after her departure that we learned about her pregnancy and his suspicion about who the father was. Mail was very slow, telephoning very difficult, and no one sent a telegram. Even his family told him there was no other man, but he was already in Boston; he had left her behind. So she filed for divorce right away."

"Oh, *Lola!*"

"Both families supported her; everyone was very angry at Alec. But then his brother went to the US and came back to tell that Alec was suspicious of her former boyfriend. The former boyfriend had made some contacts, and your mom had talked on the phone with him. So Alec did have some reason to be suspicious. A little reason. But she never met with the former boyfriend, just told him on the phone that she was going to live in the US."

"Couldn't they have talked this out?"

"We didn't know why he didn't give her the benefit of the doubt. Back then, there was no DNA testing."

They walked in silence for a few moments.

Sofie said, "So now I'm trying to decide if I will accept his offer to see him this afternoon, after we return to Boston."

They walked a few steps in silence, and then Rima carefully said, "My dear Sofie…"

"… Oh, of **course**, Lola! You knew him a long time ago! Oh, **please**! Will you go with me?"

"*Siempre*, my dear Sofie. I'll always protect you. And I **also** want to see if he is to be trusted. You're my *dahil sa iyo* [raison d'être]."

Their very slow stroll had finally brought them around to a little beach on the southwest side of Walden Pond, and they saw Gloria and Tiffany walking briskly toward them. Tiffany excitedly called, "We found the foundation of Thoreau's house up there under the trees!" She pointed.

"How do you know it's his?"

"It has a bronze plaque and everything; come on!"

4-8. Let's Walk
Tuesday, April 22, 2008

Rima and Sofie emerged from the Arlington Station of the MBTA green line and headed for the George Washington statue in the public garden. In the late afternoon sunshine, they saw Alec Ayala waiting for Sofie.

He saw Sofie, smiled, and took a step toward her. Then he noticed that she had a companion. He stopped to observe her. The women approached, and all looked intently at one another.

He reached for Sofie's hand with both of his, closed his eyes for a moment, and gently said, "Hello, Sofie."

He turned to Rima, and quietly said, *"Kumusta ang aking biyenan?"* [Formal hello, mother-in-law]."

Rima responded, *"Kumusta, rin ang ama ng aking apo?"* [Informal hello, father of my grandchild.]

He smiled. "Oh, you look the same. Maybe some gray hair."

She responded, "You as well."

He worked to maintain his composure. "Sofie told me that you came to the U.S. to help her out.... And you both ran yesterday. Congratulations on running the Boston Marathon!"

Rima had had time to prepare herself with dignity. "We're both very honored to have had the experience. And you've run the Boston as well, and you volunteer now."

He worked to stay with the friendly flow. "Uh, I saw pictures of Sofie that you took to my family in Manila over the years."

"Yes, your *nanay* asked me."

He inhaled and pulled his shoulders back. "Let's walk," and he gestured toward the walkway into the park. The three walked abreast, and then Sofie, in the middle, sank back a step so that they could all look at one another now and then as they walked and talked.

"Oh, the trees are in full bloom," said Sofie.

Rima turned to Alec. "Beautiful pink colors. What kind of trees are they?"

"Crabapple and cherry. We'll walk over to the Boston Common next, and you'll see even more."

Sofie pulled out her little Canon camera for photos.

"Here, let me take one with you and your *lola*," said Alec, and then he asked a passerby to take one of the three together, standing near a tree filled with pink flowers and the pond behind them.

"How are your family in the Philippines, *Nanay*?" asked Alec.

"Gone, husband too."

"Oh, *talaga* [really]. My parents are gone too."

"Yes, I know; I'm sorry. But you still have *maraming* family there. Your brothers and sister, they're doing all right?"

"Yes, but everyone is having a hard time with the peso losing value. How about the others in your family?"

"They're all in Zamboanga del Sur. Maybe I'll go down there when I return."

"Uh, about returning, *Nanay*; Last night I had called my friend, an immigration attorney, who called down to the CIS office. I wondered if they were suspicious of your Muslim family surname. I hope you don't find me ingratiating to you or your daughter or your granddaughter. I knew you would need help."

"No, actually, I must thank you. I hadn't expected to make trouble for others." She looked around at the other people strolling in the park, and then back to Sofie and Alec. "Don't look now, but see those two men in business jackets way back there? Those are the men who interrogated me last night at the CIS. Mr. Billings and Mr. Duggan."

Alec waited for Sofie to glance back, and then he took his turn and noticed that the men had stopped to admire a flowering tree.

"Oh, *Dios ko*, I'd have thought...."

"What's a CIS Hold, Alec? Mr. Billings told the

telephone caller last night that I'd have to have one."

"Well, so far as I know, it means that any prior proceedings you would have had with the CIS, U.S. Department of Citizenship and Immigration Services, or the D.H.S., Department of Homeland Security, would be 'on hold,' that is, stopped. It shouldn't mean they will holding **you.** Did you have a prior proceedings?"

"Well, my daughter—Tess, of course—applied for a Green Card for me. She called it an I-485."

"So probably that is what is on hold now. Sofie told me on the telephone that you're an overstay?—That's what they call a legal immigrant who stays beyond the length of the visa. Why'd you take the risk?"

"I was hoping that the bureaucracy would be too overloaded to notice. I didn't think about that my Muslim name would, maybe, flag me on a computer search. I'm overstaying by just..." and she counted, "Thursday, Friday... just eight days."

"Do you have your ticket already for return to the Philippines?"

"Yes, for Friday, three days from now."

"Well, the U.S. I-94 tourist visa stamp in your passport will automatically show 'expired,' but you won't have to show your passport here at Logan; you can just show another photo I.D."

"But at S.F.O.. on Friday?"

"Of course you'll have to show it there. But they're likely to just let you board, because it'll be only eight days' overstay, and you'll be voluntarily departing. Probably you'll be safe."

"May I ask your opinion about something else? I had thought I must go to the CIS office in San Francisco to explain myself. I intend to go on Thursday and stand in line."

Alec looked concerned. "*Hindi ko alam* [I don't know]. It may be risky."

"But I don't want to get in any more trouble than I have already caused by overstaying. And I don't want

'Deported' stamped in my passport, or to be held in custody, like Mr. Billings threatened me last night."

"I'd have to ask legal counsel." He laughed at that, and asked, "Would you mind if I ask my friend for you?"

"I guess I don't mind. I didn't have the opportunity to ask last night. Those men just told me I could go. And by the way, now must I always have followers? They seem threatening." She pointed behind her with her thumb.

"I'm guessing that the D.H.S. is asking them to keep a watch on an older woman with a Muslim name with birthplace in a Muslim area. It's a good thing you're not carrying a big bag or wearing a great big overcoat!" He laughed, and then quickly apologized, "Oh, sorry, it's not a joke. My immigration attorney friend didn't say anything about "a tail" when he called me back last night. I'll call to ask him right now." He moved toward a park bench and pulled out his cell phone.

Sofie, in the meantime, had discovered the bronze ducks modeled from the famous 1930's story *Make Way for Ducklings*. They walked near. "*Inay* used to read that story to me many times because I liked it so much," said Sofie, dreamily.

"What did you especially like about it, Sofie?"

"The mother focused all of her attention on taking care of her little ducklings. And even when the father said he needed to fly up the river a ways to see about things there, the mother looked and looked to find the best place for her nest. And then she took care of her babies by herself."

"Oh, you're right, Sofie. They managed, didn't they. But she didn't know enough about cars, and she took her ducklings onto the street to cross over into the park and a policeman had to help them."

"That's true, but she was able to find help. And mostly, she was self-reliant. Like Henry David Thoreau. Oh, *Lola*, I'm so happy we went out to Walden Pond today, aren't you?" She grabbed her grandmother's hand into a strong squeeze.

Rima smiled and squeezed Sofie's hands in response.

"You know, *Lola*, just once I was teased by other girls

for having a single mom. We had a holiday sing at school, and the parents were invited to our performance. Some girl, Anita, I think, asked if my dad would be coming, and then her friend, Sherri, said, "No, she doesn't have a dad," and they laughed.

"Oh, dear. What did you do?" asked Rima.

"I told them, 'You know, some dads are **dead.** And you know, we can manage just fine on our own, thank you!' And they stopped their teasing."

"Oh, my dear *Nene'*, you know how to survive," She squeezed Sofie's hands again.

Alec returned. "My friend thinks you'll be all right, and said to be sure to call him if you have any trouble. Here's his cell number. He said to just try to forget these guys on your tail, and don't bother to go to the San Francisco branch office. You'll probably be able to get on both planes, he says, with no trouble."

4-9. Thoughts Run Through Her Head
Tuesday, April 22, 2008

Sofie couldn't sleep. She quietly climbed out of the king-sized bed she shared with her grandmother in their luxurious hotel room and onto the window seat. She pulled her knees up to her chest for warmth and looked out the window, up at the cloud-covered sky, and then down at the city lights. She saw one walker down there, ant-sized, and then another.

Did I do the right thing, looking him up?

He looks good. Kinda cool. He was kind to me, fascinated, seemed genuine.

Is he trustworthy; will we meet again?

He didn't rush me, didn't give phony excuses.

He was honest about something very big, that he hadn't told his family about me! I wonder how he said it, when he did tell them; what he said about me. And did they gasp with shock?

He said his family "is adjusting." What does his wife think of him now? What are they all like? If I ever meet them, what if I don't like them?

But is it true he sent many letters to Mom, and she returned them, unopened?

She never told me It'd be hard telling me now, having kept that news from me, all these years. She kept me away from him and him away from me!

But Lola knew? Why didn't she tell me? Mainly, we only talked on Skype across the Pacific....But she's been here now for a year! Of course she didn't know I was going to see him, and I suppose she thought it wasn't her place to divulge....

Mom will kill me for finding him.

They never talked about him.

I wonder what Lola is thinking by now. She seems to have forgiven him for abandoning Mom and me.

But how shall we approach Mom? I'm glad to have Lola's help.

He helped Lola; he found someone to call the ICE for her. Is he just trying to get in good with her? Maybe he had a better reason.

Today, they seemed to have appreciated one another, and it looks like they did in the past too.

I didn't look for him in order to put his mind at ease, about how I have turned out or about the past; I just wanted to step out of my comfort zone to take a look at him...I'm not sure how I turned out, or who I'm going to be.

She saw another walker far below, huddled against the cold, hurrying. She shivered.

He runs! I'm astounded.

What will my running future be? His?

He's offering online training to both of us, Lola and me. Should we take him up on it?

He asked about college: East Coast?

Can anything good come out of this?

Should I give him the benefit of the doubt? Runners are good people, right? Or am I just biased toward my sport?

She got a terry cloth bathrobe out of the closet, put it on with another shiver, and then carried her laptop to the window seat. She pulled her legs up, turned sideways against a pillow on the wall, and turned on the computer. Blue-white glow lighted her face.

Checking her email, Sofie saw a new message from "AAyala."

"Sofie, may we stay in contact?

"I hold good hopes that your *lola* will be all right. To offer legal help was the least I could do for her. I always admired her; she was a gracious, wise woman back then, and of course, she is now as well.

"Sofie, you are so important to me, and I am grateful that you had the courage to look me up. All these years I've wondered about you. I saw the photos of you as a child that your *lola* had given to my family in the Philippines, and I've carried those images with me in my mind and heart daily. These last many years, I didn't want to disturb your mother's need for distance. But now....

"My family here is adjusting well to my big news about you, even my wife. They all want to meet you. I know it's too late for your trip now, but....

"You'll graduate from high school in two months. What are your college plans? Might you come to the East Coast? You'll be getting your letters from your university applications in just a couple of weeks, isn't that right? I told you yesterday that I have a college fund for you. You may be reluctant to accept it now, but I want you to know that it's always here for you.

"Your mother... Maybe you haven't yet told her about our meeting. I hope and pray for you that she'll accept your news well. In the future, I would like to have contact with her if she would allow.... She'll need time to adjust.

"Your mother and I were both very stubborn people. I hope you are taking after your wise grandmother.

"You run! I'm astounded. You looked very strong when you ran back to the course at Mile Four. And you had such a good finish time!

"I have so much to learn about you, and you may want to learn more about me. No rush; but I want you to know that from now on, I'll always be here for you.

"Yours,

"Your father, Alec Ayala"

Sofie clicked "sleep" on her laptop, closed it, and held the warmth to her chest; then she looked out the window again.

Rima had felt Sofie slip out of the bed. She wondered what Sofie was doing, and then she saw her on the window seat, silhouetted by the city lights far below and the blue-white light of her computer screen.

Rima's thoughts as well coursed through recent events, to the past, and to the future.

Now what!

How are we going to tell Tess?

Should I have pressed Tess long ago to tell Sofie about the letters?"

And now Alec has told his family about Sofie. Oh, Dios mio, ang mga toong nagdurusa. [those suffering people] This is big news in that household, too.

4-10. Gonna Fly Now
Wednesday, April 23, 2008

"Wow, this plane looks like a victory party!" Tiffany said as they shuffled down the aisle toward their seats.

Gloria had coerced Sofie and Rima to wear their bright sky blue Boston Marathon shirts and big pewter finisher's medals with the Boston unicorn and the yellow and blue satin ribbon. Gloria had insisted that they accept her gift of Boston Marathon jackets as well. She had bought one for each of the four at the expo, two days before the race. She and Tiffany, having not finished the race, now refrained from wearing theirs. Several others on the flight wore the same celebration gear, and they quietly acknowledged one another with a "we're members of the same exclusive club" nod.

Tiffany and Sofie sat in seats D and F, on the shady side of the American Airlines flight back to San Francisco. They were delighted that Seat E had remained vacant, so halfway back to San Francisco, Tiffany scooted closer to Sofie and rested her elbows on Sofie's armrest to look down below at, by now, the vast wilderness of the American West. The two older women sat just behind them, and the last time Tiffany looked back, they appeared to be fast asleep.

The young women thought they'd go to sleep as well; they even talked about putting their legs up on the food tray of Seat E. Instead, they whispered about their experiences in Boston and pondered the future.

"You came so close to first place in our age group, Sofie!"

"Yeah...."

"I'm so sorry you didn't get that scholarship. What're you going to do now?"

"Well, you know, your mom got me to apply to colleges with big cross-country and track programs."

"Yeah, she talked with the college counselor at my high school, and she looked online. She said that you could get a scholarship. And results will come in just a couple more weeks, right? I can't wait!"

"Well, you know, my grades really dropped last year, **ex-**boyfriend Raoul and all; and I didn't take any AP classes, not even any other real hard classes. My junior year was a mess."

"But your SAT scores were high; Mom said those would get you into a CSU or maybe even a UC, even if only by testing in."

"Yeah. The main thing is, my college counselor said that the colleges that would consider me for an athletic scholarship will add this marathon to my application, even just two weeks before the acceptances come out. Hope he's right; I need the help."

"Oh, I hope, I **hope,** Sofie. Maybe we'll both get into a great university back east. The kids in my school think the East Coast is more prestigious."

"Yeah, of course I'll need a full scholarship.... Uh, Mr. Ayala said he had saved a college fund for me, but I don't want to accept it ... at least not this year."

"Oh, that's a hard one, Sofie But why not? If that were my only way to pay for college; I don't know.... Hey, Sofie, you could take his money and run; he's a creep, right?"

Sofie looked out the window and then back to Tiffany. "Do you think I should ever forgive him?" Sofie didn't tell her about the letters he'd sent and she had just learned about because she hadn't yet processed the information. *If it's true about many returned letters, then my mother deceived me as well, not telling me that he tried and tried. And he was gracious to me in his talk about her. I'll just have to think about my mom later."*

"I couldn't forgive him." Tiffany leaned back in her own seat, adjusted her folded-up jacket behind her head to form a pillow, and turned to focus better on Sofie.

"But it'd make such a difference to me about my family. I'd even have two sisters and a brother. God! My feelings are all mixed up."

"You know, Sofie, I read in *Parade Magazine* a few

Sundays ago that there are **so many** deadbeat dads, maybe 60 percent of all divorces with kids at home involve a disappearing dad, without any contact."

"Is that enough to never forgive him?"

"A lot of our friends must have deadbeat dads, but I don't know of any. Do you?"

"No, I kind of thought I was the only one."

"But Sofie, think of it, and here's what we learned in our economics class last week. Half of marriages end in divorce in this country. So that leaves half of kids living with one parent. And—this is what the text said—60 percent of divorced fathers disappear from their kids' lives. So that leaves, uuh … one half times 60 percent is … uhh… 30, yeah, maybe 30 percent of our friends who don't have contact with their dads."

"Why don't we know about any of those kids, then?"

"Maybe because some of our friends' dads are step-dads."

"Yeah, maybe.… Well, I know of some other single moms … kids at my high school.…"

A flight attendant stopped her cart alongside their seats. She held out a package of peanuts to each girl and offered drinks. After she trundled her cart to the seats ahead of them, Tiffany resumed the topic.

"There sure aren't many single moms in our little Atherton."

"Nope; couldn't be. Single parents don't have as much money, so it'd be hard to afford Atherton."

"So maybe that's why, at least in our oasis."

Sofie leaned away from Tiffany to look outside for a while at fluffy white clouds, which slowly receded behind them. She noticed that the clouds' shadows moved a little faster far below on the landscape. Only occasionally did she see any sign that a human had touched the terrain, an occasional narrow road winding through hills. *No people! Are these the Badlands of the American West that I've heard about?*

Tiffany broke the silence. "How did you get the courage to see him, in the first place? After we found him on LinkedIn, I mean. He had just **disappeared?** I never thought of these things before. I never thought of you living what I had been learning about in class. He left your pregnant mom, just as she arrived in this country? And we saw on his LinkedIn profile last month that he has a new family. Did they know about you? Or even about your mom?"

"Well, both my parents probably knew a lot about each other, after they split, on the *radjo balagung*."

"What's that?"

"The 'bamboo radio,' that's what they call fast traveling gossip in the southern Philippines. And now I hear that everyone there has a cell phone, even a lot of smart phones."

"You told me most people there are poor!"

"Yep. But in the Philippines, India, China, everywhere, people are getting smart phones, even if they don't have electricity in their houses—and no one has electricity out on Sakol Island, where my *lola's* relatives live. They charge them with little solar panels or when they go into the city."

"Wow. Hmm. Sofie, do you think you'll ever learn what really happened with your parents?"

"I don't know. But maybe I **will** meet my half brother and sisters sometime.

"Oh, that'd be scary too! ... But take me with you."

They felt movement behind Tiffany's seat, and both girls turned left to see Rima standing in the aisle beside them.

"Oh, I hope we didn't wake you up, *Lola*," said Sofie.

"No, but please forgive me for dropping in, is that how you say it?"

"Eavesdropping.... Here, sit with us!" Tiffany scooted into the middle seat so that Rima could sit with them.

Rima fastened her seat belt, and then looked up to say, "I know some of the truth."

"Oh, *Lola* Rima," Tiffany said, for she had been "adopted" into fictive kinship by Sofie's grandmother. "Don't you think he's the same stinker as he was when he walked out on Sofie's mom when she was pregnant?"

Rima slowly inhaled, pulled her new Boston Marathon Finisher jacket off of her shoulders and arms, exhaled, and slowly looked up at both of them. "We Filipinos usually know how to forgive. He was young; he's more mature now."

Tiffany persisted. "But we know his real character, right, *Lola* Rima?"

Rima paused again, and then said, quietly and slowly, "I think he's trying his best to make up for something terrible, something the whole world thinks is damnable. He didn't know how to make up, and maybe he thought the only way he could have any self-respect would be to do better with the next family. And he'd keep the past all to himself."

"Well, it sounds like **they're** doing fine. They sure have a nice address!"

Sofie added apologetically, "Uh, *Lola*, we looked on Google Street View at his house.... Two stories, entrance with huge pillars, a big garden in front."

Tiffany rushed in. "Hey, maybe that's why he didn't send any money or even contact Sofie after he remarried."

Rima was quiet for a moment, and then said, "Hmm." *This is becoming too private.*

Sofie, who was getting uncomfortable about Tiffany's attack, decided to defend him. "Hey, Tiffany, remember— you're the one who urged me to look him up in the first place. And now you're only dissing him. This is my chance to have a father, my only chance. No one gets to choose their father. And by the way, you **have** one, so what would you know about it?" She threw her arms and head down onto her tray, sobbing.

Rima needed to soften the tension. "Well, dears," she said, "I think his actions these last two days show that he wants, maybe even long ago wanted, to make up, but had no idea how."

Tiffany hadn't softened; she wanted to defend her friend against a bad guy, so she interrupted, "Of course. How **could** he make up?" She triumphantly sat up straight in her seat, though she rose only a tiny bit, strapped in as she was, and dramatically crossed her arms across her chest.

Rima carefully continued. "That is, **until....**"

"Until?" asked Sofie.

"Until you took the first step to meet him, Sofie."

Tiffany was indignant by now. "Maybe he's buying your favor, Rima. Wasn't **he** the one to get that attorney for you, to get you out of that mess in Boston?"

Rima paused. *I don't want to get angry at this innocent, privileged young girl. She forgot to show me respect with "Lola." For 18 years I've resented that man who falsely accused my daughter of infidelity and didn't believe her, and I've resented my daughter for being so stubborn, not allowing any real communication, any financial support, even... But I try to take the high road, the path of dignity.*

She responded. "I didn't have a choice; I was simply told "you are released for now. You may return to your hotel."

Tiffany wasn't subdued. "We don't even know if he was completely successful. At least we didn't see anyone following you to the airport. But didn't you say you still have to appear at the CIS office in San Francisco?"

"I'm not sure now. I had planned to go, but that's for the ordinary exit permit, not because I'm a suspect for terrorism, as I was informed on Monday night."

"You **were?** Do you have to get permission to leave?" asked Sofie.

"Remember, I overstayed my tourist visa extension in order to come to Boston."

"Oh," Sofie cried. "Does Mom know? Weren't you keeping track? Wasn't it on our kitchen calendar?"

"Most of all, I didn't want to disrupt **your** preparation for the marathon, Sofie. Or yours, Tiffany, or your mom's. Or my own, I guess."

Tiffany asked, "*Lola* Rima, did running the Boston mean that much to you?"

Rima looked at Tiffany and decided not to answer. Instead, she said, "I was not allowed a second extension of my tourist visa; no one is. And the marathon was just four days after my deadline. And I investigated and I figured they wouldn't notice."

"How?" asked Sofie.

"I read in the *Philippine Times Bay Area* newspaper about all the overstaying tourists."

The girls looked at her with wonder, silent, waiting.

Rima continued. "I didn't know they had me on a list as a Muslim just because of my birthplace and my Muslim name, and that overstaying would pull my name up into scrutiny."

"Oh, *Lola,* I hope you don't get into more trouble," said Sofie. "You're safe, so far, right? You were able to get on this flight with us, and today we didn't see those men who were following you yesterday in the park…"

Rima responded. "And thinking about avoiding trouble, have you thought more, dear Sofie, about telling your mom about contacting your father?"

Sofie looked down to her lap and brushed off imaginary crumbs. "I thought about her from the beginning, from when I saw him on LinkedIn. I've been thinking about not telling her. I'm 18 now. That makes me an adult, right? Legally independent here in the US, right? So maybe I don't have to tell her everything."

"Think about it, *Nene'*, dear."

Sofie took a deep breath and looked from her grandmother to Tiffany and back to her grandmother. She put her hand over her mouth. "Oh, yeah, he helped **you** get released. She'll have to know…. Oh, *Lola,* she'll see us both as traitors!"

4-11. Take the High Road
Wednesday, April 23, 2008

Tiffany gasped, "Oh My God!" and pointed ahead to a group of screaming teenagers who held up big signs. "You the ONE, Sofie!" and "You Make M-A PROUD!" and "Nobody gonna catch her NOW!"

Around 10:30 p.m., the four returning runners trundled their suitcases behind them along the long corridor of SFO airport toward the exit. Sofie saw her mother standing beside the students, smiling expectantly and happy to make eye contact.

The two groups in Arrivals converged. The Menlo-Atherton High School students clustered around Sofie, all trying to hug her, some girls on the perimeter of the cluster still excitedly squealing their congratulations. Stanley emerged from the crowd of family and friends to meet Gloria and Tiffany. They distractedly greeted him, and both signaled for him to wait as they searched for Rima and Sofie. Finally making eye contact across the din, they sent messages with their eyes and hand waves: "I care for you; I'm reluctant to leave you!"

Glenn came out of the crowd to greet Rima with a big hug. Tess moved in and waited her turn to give her mother and her daughter a group hug and a "congratulations!" After a quick discussion, they agreed that Rima would ride with Glenn and that Sofie would ride with Tess.

Rima noticed a man in the crowd who kept his eye on her—*for how long now?*—but on her notice of him, he stepped back into the crowd and was gone. *Oh-oh... But maybe he was just looking for his family. Maybe I'm mistaken.*

Sofie apologized to her cheering fans, "Hey, guys; you're all out late. We all gotta go home!" During that moment, Rima turned for another hug with Tess and whispered into her ear, "Be gentle with her; she's fragile." Tess pulled back to look into her mother's eyes, surprised, questioning, but recognized that this wasn't the place for an explanation. Instead, before separating in the parking garage, Tess grabbed her mother and her daughter for another big hug, saying, "Oh, my two Boston Marathon finishers."

Just the two, Tess and Sofie, were finally in Tess's car. Tess exited the parking garage and turned onto Freeway 101 South. She patted her daughter's thigh and said, "I'm so proud of you."

Sofie patted her mother's hand, and murmured "hmm." She was a little annoyed. *She's proud? Did I do this to make her proud?*

Tess continued, "I watched your progress on the B.A.A. live stream of the marathon. I saw every mat you crossed." Sofie scowled, annoyed at her mother's attempt to show her attentiveness. She recalled that her mother had hardly even heard of the Boston Marathon when Coach Ramirez had first told Tess that he wanted Sofie to be their high school's first finisher ever. *Now that I'm a so-called success, she pays attention to me*, she grumbled to herself.

"And thank you so much for your call right after the finish. All my colleagues at the hospital were rooting for you … and Steve as well."

"I didn't come in first; I didn't get the college scholarship."

"No … but you were still fast. Gloria said that your finish will enhance your college applications, so you'll have a better chance for scholarships."

"Yeah."

They rode in silence for a few minutes.

"But *Nene'*, you're so quiet. You must be pooped."

"Mom, don't get mad at me."

"What, *aking mahal?*"

"I decided to find Mr. Ayala. I met him."

Tess jerked the car into the rightmost lane, then drove slowly and deliberately.

A few moments passed. Sofie felt overwhelmed by her mother's reaction. She noticed the firm grip on the steering wheel, the muscles clenched in her jaw. Sofie braced herself for some kind of blow; she didn't know what. *Like Lola says, take the high road*, she reminded herself.

Finally, Tess quietly said, "And?"

Sofie was relieved to see her mother shift into her "I'm strong, I can take anything" gear—just as Sofie had. *I've learned fierce independence from her.* She replied, "He was friendly. Very surprised, of course."

Tess quietly said, "I bet." *Oh-oh, cynical. Probably thinks he dumped on her. I'll try to put her at ease.* "Oh, Mom, he didn't say anything bad about you, not at all. He just asked kindly about you, how you're doing."

"Hmmpf."

She's still clenching her jaw; she's afraid to believe me. Sofie added, "You know what else, Mom? He apologized to me."

"What kind of apology?"

"He kept saying, 'I'm sorry, I'm so sorry. I'm sorry for all those years." Sofie felt her chest tighten and her eyes well up with tears; she felt close to panic that she'd break into to an uncontrollable cloudburst as she had in the airplane just an hour earlier.

Tess's hands continued to squeeze the steering wheel. At the next exit—their exit—she turned off, and then pulled over to the side of the road. When she turned to look at Sofie, her eyes as well were brimming.

"So that's why your eyes have been red," she said, with an apologetic, embarrassed smile.

"Oh, Mom, I don't know what to do," and she grabbed her mother's hand. The two clutched the other's hand and stifled sobbing sounds. They looked into the other's eyes and then away. Sofie squeezed her eyes shut and felt the wet spill over onto her cheeks. She reached down into her purse for a tissue, found two, and offered one to her mother.

"What do you mean, *Nene*?" Tess asked, worriedly.

What does she think I mean? Like I'd want to go live with him and his family or something? I gotta reassure her in a hurry. She responded, "I mean, should I see him again?"

"Oh!" said Tess, apparently relieved.

They stayed at the side of the freeway turnoff,

headlights on. *We can't let this rare opportunity to really talk pass us by.* Sofie said, "I mean, can I trust him? All my life, he's been the creep who abandoned you."

"Hmmpf."

Why doesn't she tell me what she's thinking? But I'm not going to confront her about unopened letters. Wait to see if she'll tell me. Sofie couldn't stand to wait for more. "But, but … you know what he told me, Mom?"

"What?"

"He said I look somewhat like him and his sister, and especially like his Mary Beth, who's eleven now. They call her Bing."

Tess started up the car and drove the few city streets to their house. They arrived before Rima and Glenn, and they stayed in the car in the driveway.

Tess crossed her arms, looked toward her daughter, and said, "So **now** what?"

It's now or never. We've opened up this far, and Lola and Glenn will come any minute. "Mom, it's been **hard** not having a father. Oh, I mean,"… and she reached for her mother's hand, "You've done everything for me, you've worked so hard, and you've tried to stay up with what's going on in school."

"Well.…"

Sofie wanted to finish this important thought, so she interrupted. "You brought *Lola* over to help me.… Your Steve is very nice, good for you, nice to me, but.…"

Tess looked straight ahead, not at her daughter, and remained silent.

Sofie continued. "I've always wondered what our lives would have been like."

Tess's lips pressed together.

Sofie added, "I even heard of the Marin Study in my social studies class last year; you know about it? It showed that children raised with just one parent achieve less."

Tess finally responded by protesting, "I've always reminded you that you are a Masuhud Osorio, family of your *lola* and your *lolo*, and you will make the whole family proud."

Sofie continued on without acknowledging her mother's statement. "And I always felt sad for **you:** abandoned by that creep when he learned you were pregnant. How could he have? Didn't the family back home in Manila tell him?"

They both looked ahead toward their house, absorbing the topic they had needed to share all these years.

Sofie said, "And now, he wouldn't even need a DNA test!" she turned to her mother, smiling, wiping tears off of her cheeks, and squeezed her mother's hands, hoping for humor in response.

"*Nene'*, I told you long ago that anyone who thought I had lied, who accused me of being with an old boyfriend, a man who didn't believe me, could only be trouble in the future. That's why I refused further contact."

"All these years?"

Tess turned with an angry frown to Sofie, who worried, *I can't tell her more; she's closed off listening. Oh, what should I say?*

Glenn pulled his car into the driveway behind them; headlights interrupted their focus in the dark. He jumped out to open the door for Rima and then to collect her bag from the trunk. At that, the moment passed, and Tess and Sofie climbed out of the car and got their bags from the trunk. Tess positioned her key for the front door, and they all entered the house. Glenn stepped forward and said, "I'll leave you to rest up." He gave each of the three a short hug and then he left.

Sofie trundled her suitcase into her bedroom.

In these few moments since Rima had arrived, Tess had started a slow burn. Seeing her in the driveway, she started wondering about her mother's possible role in that meeting in Boston. She had waited, and now they had their privacy. "So, *Inay*, did you meet him too?"

"Yes, I did," Rima responded with a steady look into her daughter's angry eyes.

They turned away from one another and went about their settling-in tasks. Tess retreated to her bedroom, and Rima followed Sofie into the room and bed they shared. They whispered.

"Oh my God, *Lola*. She's mad ... I told her that Mr. Ayala didn't say anything bad and that he apologized several times."

"Did you tell her about the ICE?"

"No."

"About Alec Ayala's offer of a scholarship for you?"

"No."

Rima continued. "In her current frame of mind, she's likely to figure he's trying to buy our favor."

"I don't know for sure he's not. Do you?"

"Not my favor; I'm not sure about yours."

"His unopened, returned letters?"

"No, and she didn't say anything about them, either."

They looked into each other's eyes, and then Sofie said,

"Oh, *Lola*, how can we help my mom accept?" They hugged, and turned themselves into bed. They whispered more, and Rima said, "Better go to sleep, *Nene'*, for school in the morning."

Sofie whispered back, "You know, *Lola*, those kids would never understand how we Filipinos sleep in the same bed or even how much we talk together across generations about what's really on our minds. Tiffany thinks it's weird." They stifled their giggles, and before long, they slept.

4-12. I Can Coast Now!
Thursday, April 24, 2008

"We have a half hour, tops, before we're at your home," he said. "Tell me everything." Glenn drove at just the speed limit in order to maximize his time alone with Rima.

Now, with his comforting companionship in the quiet warmth of his car in the dark, and with only light traffic moving southward on 101, Rima suddenly felt tired, like this place was a foyer to her bed.

"Hmm, your car is much quieter than the plane. I'm getting sleepy."

Glenn reached for Rima's hand on her lap. "Still sore?"

"Mm, it was hard to sit still in the plane for so long, and it's still hard to walk down stairs, but I'm okay. Sofie says she isn't real sore. Mainly I'm **so** grateful we could do it. We've experienced a very big happening." Rima stretched her knees out straight, and resting her heels on the car's carpet, discretely stretched her feet up and down, into flexion, then extension, and back again.

"I'm so **proud** of you!" He squeezed her hand. "Oh! I watched your progress on the B.A.A. live monitor on my computer. And thank you for—**finally**—calling me... Sure took you awhile, though." He smiled but kept his eyes on the road ahead.

"Well, uh, I was pretty tired. I'll give you the details later."

"Please do; I was so happy to hear your voice."

"Same with me, **your** voice, that is." They smiled; they squeezed hands.

She inhaled deeply. "This has been such a surprise in my life."

"Hmm?"

"I mean, just 12 months ago, I came to California to help my Tess take care of her, I mean our Sofie. I had no idea of ever running. Then, for both of us, to take on such a big goal was daunting. Exciting. It colors the whole

picture.... Oh, Glenn, I hope you don't feel jealous." She
turned to him and smiled teasingly.

"Of course not, my dear.... Well, maybe a little jealous.
I wanted to join you in Boston, cheer you on. I've
wondered whether it's really good for you. You might get
hurt. Maybe I worried too much. Maybe I've been
suspicious about your priorities. But I've admired you as
well, going out in the early cold and dark to run, week after
week, and of course starting such vigorous exercise later in
life."

She turned toward him, pulling her knees up onto the
seat, legs turned sideways, carefully avoiding touching her
socked feet to the seat. "You know, Glenn, it feels **so
good** to have succeeded. Working a whole year on that
goal, wondering if I could really do it—if this old body
could really do it."

"You've sure proven you could succeed."

"Yes, you're right, aren't you.... And the others: Sofie,
so powerful; she was able to leave a bad path behind her.
She brought her grades up, she got her college applications
in, and she seems to have left that boyfriend. And of
course she consistently trained all these months for the big
event. We've shared a goal across our generations. And we
met others, especially Gloria and Tiffany."

"They're good friends by now, aren't they."

"Yes, even more so after sharing this big experience."

"And you conquered those ailments!"

"After a couple of weeks I noticed I started feeling
more springy the rest of the day. Life became simpler, and
I became a little less anxious about my dear ones'
problems."

"So maybe this is why you appeared so calm to me
back when we first met, in December. You were already
running for ... six-seven months by then. 'Graceful and
quiet as a cat,' I thought back then, and I still do."

"Oh yes, a cat—what a compliment!" She leaned
toward him to brush a quick kiss onto his cheek.

"I'm so proud of Sofie," she said. "She showed her

strength. She has strength to conquer setbacks. She can also take on other challenges, like going to college and going far away. Sorry Gloria and Tiffany didn't finish. We already knew that determination is crucial, determination to build strength as well as to cross the finish line. But I guess Gloria showed solidarity with her daughter by dropping out with her, rather than just criticizing her.

"How did you convince yourself you could do it?"

"Success in finishing all the training runs was crucial. Umm, hoping for success? Visualizing success? Maybe having faith based on past achievements? Not being afraid to suffer pain to achieve a big goal? ... I knew that pain would stop shortly after I would finish."

"And did it? Does it?"

"Well, by last July, with the shorter runs twice a week, I experienced very little pain. The hardest part was getting up early, but comradeship at the trailhead meant a lot. I didn't want to let the others down."

"How about pain from the longer runs?"

"I had more difficulty during and soreness after. But I could also notice I was building strength. The first 12-mile run, I was so sore! But two weeks later, when I ran the 14-miler, at 12 miles, I felt okay."

She looked toward him for a while, admiring his fine profile, his competent driving. "Part of the value is meditation. Like, I try to be more aware of myself, not stand in my own way."

"How do you mean?"

"Well, take sweat. I used to say, before starting this running, that I couldn't exercise, especially in the mornings, because then I'd have to shower, calm down from sweating, and change clothes. It's messy, takes too much time."

"True. So?"

"So starting out last May, I noticed that after running, the sweat still shining on my skin didn't smell—no nervous smell, no smell of chopping onions the night before. Like my running had cleaned out my system. And I thought, 'people go into a sauna for this. Why not running?' And I talked with myself. I asked, 'Rima, do you really want to avoid all exercise just for fear of **sweat?**'"

"Ha! I hadn't thought of it like that. Maybe I stand in my own way, too."

"But you used to play tennis!"

"Yeah, in the afternoons. I changed into, and then out of, tennis clothes. I guess I got out of the habit of routinely dealing with sweat. It seems like too much trouble now, and I can avoid it by remaining sedentary."

She let him ponder this self-discovery, and then said, "About how I feel after the big marathon, I haven't yet absorbed all of the body work—the rehabilitation—or all the thinking. I don't yet know what it all means to me."

"I suppose it'll take awhile to all sink in."

"Yep, but in the meantime, I can coast for awhile on my success. She looked intently at his face, profiled because his eyes were on the road. "Glenn, I love to run because I **can!**"

He said, "At first I didn't know you could do it. You sure showed me!"

She said, "The challenge has been important to me. Amby Burfoot, an editor of *Runner's World,* paraphrased Don Quixote, something like, 'We all need to pursue some noble and difficult-to-attain goals, or what's life for?'"

He smiled and reached for her hand again.

She continued. "I do wonder how this will play out over time. I don't know just what it will mean to me. I'm wondering; the future looks unknown, but bright. Around that bend, I see myself running. I think it's become part of who I am: now, I'm a runner."

He had turned on the seat warmer of his Acura TLs. She felt calm. *Today's air travel's over, car travel's almost over.* Bed was nigh. Her chilly fingers gradually warmed, her toes as well. A vision of her bed came into her head; she smiled. *I'm sleepy—sweet misery, so tired and sore. So grateful that Glenn is the driver, alert.*

Glenn spoke again. "I'm so happy for you."

"Thank you! Now, maybe I could consider another big goal, even a goal other than running."

"Like moving to California? And by the way, have you been thinking about my offer, I mean, my proposal?"

"Of course, my dear man!"

"Any progress on your decision-making, my dear?" He turned to her for a quick smile before turning back to the road ahead.

"I've been thinking a lot about it. Also, I still feel very, very complimented by your proposal."

"Well, then?"

"I still need time to think. Can you manage that? You're not offended? Not insulted?" She laughed, teasingly.

"No, of course, my dear, I hear from you that you need time.

"Yes: I see two main obstacles: I wouldn't want you to suffer if your family disapproved, and I wouldn't want marriage to be seen as a way to avoid deportation." She put her feet back down onto the floor. *Also, he's said nothing yet about his mother loosening up. He probably hasn't yet found a way to placate her, if he would marry a "person of color," as they call us here. That'd doom this relationship.*

"My dear, I hope I can reassure you. But about your visa deadline: what day is that, again?"

"Friday is my departure date".

"So soon. We have a lot to talk about."

She answered, "Yeah." *Oh, Dios ko, no time for this topic now!* And then she quickly added, "Oh, we're here already. Will you come in?"

4-13. Get Used to Success
Thursday, April 24, 2008

Rima got up early to start a new big day. *Three dear people to see, and one tomorrow.*

She immediately noticed the two sky-blue Boston finisher's shirts that she and Sofie, before retiring, had draped over the bedroom's easy chair to admire.

Gently shaking Sofie awake, with a big smile, Rima held up Sofie's shirt. "Hey, Sofie, look what we get to wear today."

Sofie brought her face up out of her pillow to look in her grandmother's direction. "Uh ... too bright, don't you think?" she mumbled.

"You earned this shirt, Sofie; don't be afraid of success."

Sofie turned over to face Rima. "I feel kind of like a show-off in it."

"If you **act** triumphant—with appropriate modesty at school, of course—you'll **feel** triumphant before long."

"I've heard that from you before, *Lola.* 'Pretend you're confident, and you'll become confident.'"

"Well, does it work?"

"Maybe. Sort of. I guess it worked on the marathons."

"And you've done well each time. Better get used to success, *aking mahal.* I'll wear mine today, too, see?" She held up her shirt and made a full circle spin, fingertips holding onto the tips of her new shirt's shoulder seams.

Sofie looked out the window and then climbed out of bed. "*Salamat, Lola,*" and she gave her grandmother a long hug. "For everything."

"Now," continued Rima, "your mom told us last night that a student reporter and photographer want to interview you for your school newspaper, so take your medal in your backpack." She paused, and then added, "Wearing the medal all day **would** be showing off!" They laughed and hugged again. Sofie broke away, passed through the kitchen, grabbed three *pan de sal* rolls, took an energy drink out of the fridge, and was off.

Next, thought Rima, as she prepared little plates of *pan de sal* and fresh strawberries for herself and for Tess. *She must have gone to the barrio bakery for us yesterday.* Tess rushed in from her bedroom carrying her purse and jacket on one arm and fixing earrings into her lobes. "Oh, *Inay,* I'm so proud of you and Sofie, and I'm **so** grateful for all the help you've given her." She approached her mother to give a quick Philippine kiss before going out the door to work.

"*Anak ko,* we need a short talk."

"Uh, uh … okay," Tess said, and reluctantly sat down in front of the plate of food and the cup of Ceylon tea that Rima had prepared for her. She struggled to shift gears and calm down from her outward-bound morning rush. She picked up her teacup and inhaled the aroma of the tea. *Uh-oh, this is serious. I'm going to be late for work,* she thought.

"*Inay,* remember how other kids coming to visit us noticed our special tea?"

"Oh, yes, and I saved this tea for today, *Iha.*" *She's nervous, wondering why I called her here, so she's delaying my big topic.*

Wrists on the table, they looked at one another expectantly.

Rima started. "Our Sofie is safe now."

"Oh, *Inay,* when I think of last year, she was having so much trouble, boyfriend, pot, diving grades, and I was **so** grateful you agreed to come."

"Well, she has matured a lot."

"Thanks to **you,** *Inay.*"

"I can't take so much credit. Give credit to her high school coach for getting her into distance running. She's fast, and she's passionate about running. With running, she pulled herself out of that relationship and the substances, and she's conquered big challenges."

"You know that I didn't like it at first; I thought it'd get her off her homework. But you, *Inay,* you helped convince me that running could help, not hinder, her schooling. And you joined, yourself! I worried about you as well, especially when you first started."

"Running has helped me, too."

"I know you **like** running, and…" Tess seemed resigned to staying seated by now. "Please remind me how else it has helped you."

"Well, you'll remember that when I came here a year ago, I was worried about my health: my knees, the pre-diabetes, the downhill with age. I feel more capable now, I have more courage. And most of all, I have valued running with your dear daughter, our Sofie."

"I'm so proud of both of you." But Tess looked unsettled.

She's wondering if this was my reason for stopping her from going to work. I've got to come out with it, now. She waited for a return gaze from Tess.

"You must already know that I knew all these 18 years," She paused, and then continued, "that Alec tried many times back then to stay in contact with you, and later with Sofie."

"I figured you knew. There aren't any secrets back in Manila. And, besides, you told me you had given photos of little Sofie to his family."

"*Anak ko*, I haven't interfered all these years. But today, Sofie deserves to hear from you that her father had tried and tried to contact her."

"Why today?"

"Because of my leaving tomorrow."

"Oh, I see. Of course, you want me to tell her before you leave." Tess jumped up to put her arms around her mother's shoulders. "Oh, *Inay*! I haven't been paying attention to the calendar. And we're still waiting on the application for your green card. Oh, I don't want you to leave. You're such an important part of our little family, and you've helped Sofie—and me—so much!"

Rima pushed her to arm's length, looked for her eyes

again, and said, "So do you have the courage to tell her?"

4-14. Recovery Run
Thursday, April 24, 2008

"Don't get me an immigration attorney, Gloria, I'm going back to Zamboanga." Rima spoke quietly and deliberately after a sip of her too-hot coffee. The Sumatra blend at Peet's Coffee Shop on University Avenue in Palo Alto reminded Rima, just a little, of her tasty Basilan Island coffee back in the Southern Philippines. Now in dry clothes—Gloria in her blue jeans and white button-down shirt, and Rima in her usual dark-green velour warm-up suit, they met for Rima's third important talk of the day.

The two women had just finished their first recovery run, a slow five miler in Edgewood Park. Rima had told her the story about Mr. Ayala.

Gloria cried, "Oh, no! You can't leave now! You won't let the ICE defeat you, will you?"

"Well, I do have good reasons for going home."

"Oh, I don't want to miss you. Hey, you've become my best friend! You might be penalized five **years** for overstaying! An attorney could help you And besides, your daughter wants you to stay, and of course your Glenn.

"*Dios mio*, Gloria, Glenn doesn't know yet. I'm seeing him tomorrow.... Hey, my *minamahal* [dear] best friend also, are you up to hearing all about it, even my mixed feelings?"

"Of course I'll listen, dear." They laughed and reached for their coffees, carefully testing for heat before sipping.

Rima leaned back into her chair and gazed out the window at the passing pedestrians.

"Let's see." With her right index finger, she touched her left pinky finger. "I came to California to help Sofie.... And then you came into our lives; and Gloria, how can I thank you enough for all your help?"

"It's very easy to help you two!"

"I mean, it's all a new system to me, college in this

country. It's in large part thanks to you that she's on track to go to a good college. Thank you **so much** for helping her with her applications."

"Well, she couldn't have done it without her grandmother, and she knows it, especially getting the Boston Marathon onto her applications. Hey, the Boston—let's drink to the Boston!" They clinked their ceramic mugs together with a laugh and put them to their lips.

They watched an Australian Shepherd tied to the lamp post in front of Peet's door, standing in alert position, ears forward, eyes bright and watching for movement of the door. Its mouth was open in a doggie smile and the tip of its tongue was hanging out.

"So my purpose for coming to this country is accomplished, and I'm very grateful. The Lord loans us our children, and even our grandchildren, for only about 18 years. Sofie's on her own path now."

"And may she continue to thrive," said Gloria.

"Next," and Rima held up her right hand and touched the left ring finger, "my daughter. She's going to be an empty nester in a few months, and she has her Steve— they get along pretty well—so she's going to be all right."

"What did Tess think about Sofie meeting her father? Did she blow up?"

"No, she handled it well. She and I had a good talk this morning, and of course she's got a lot to think about—about Sofie, and about her former husband—but I think she'll work it out."

Rima looked out the window again. *I'm not going into the details with her. Oh, I hope Tess will do the right thing. Oh, why did I wait all these years? Sofie should have known about her father her whole young life, that he had tried to communicate with her. Why was I so afraid of confronting my daughter? But I didn't want to meddle.*

"But Tess wants you to stay here, right?"

Rima shifted back to the conversation. "Well, she did apply for a green card for me, but she doesn't really need me now. She wants me to move here, but you know that she is always too busy."

"Mm-hmm." Gloria watched Rima, and waited for more.

Rima then added, "You know, I don't want to, as you Americans say, hitch my wagon to her star."

"How do you mean?"

"Well, if we were in the Philippines, a widowed Filipina would move in with her child and family. Filipinos say their social security is their children and old people are not 'left to live alone.' But here, that doesn't work."

Gloria interjected, "Yeah, you're all so family oriented! It's shameful here. They say our distance from our senior parents nowadays comes from our pioneer heritage, moving westward and leaving our elders behind for good." Gloria took a sip of her coffee and then continued. "The other day I read an article in the paper about research that a lot of grandparents become disappointed after they move close to their adult children."

"Oh, why?"

"They move to be with the children and maybe grandchildren; but then their children get jobs elsewhere and move. Or they get divorced, or remarried, or otherwise hooked up. Young people are so transient here. And so the grandparent either is left behind or has to move again."

"Oh, you know, then, that it's very different in the Philippines. Extended families tend to live together there."

Gloria added, "I'm guessing depression is a factor for a lot of older people moving to be with their children, as if now we have only our children and grandchildren to live for."

"That's in the Philippines, too."

"Especially the widows I know here; they lose their optimism, their own plans for the future."

Rima agreed, "Yeah, you've gotta have your own plans in this country, and maybe even in the Philippines. Me, I've been a widow for so long, I've learned to take care of myself. I'm not even sure I want to remarry."

"Aha!" laughed Gloria. "About remarriage!"

"I'll come to that topic," smiled Rima. But first," and she held up her fingers and touched her pinkie and then her ring finger, "Sofie, Tess...."

"Next?" asked Gloria.

"Yes, next, reasons to go home. I'll go to Manila, of course, but down to Zamboanga as well, to see my younger sisters, and all my cousins, that is, the ones still living, and their children..."

"Some are gone?"

"Yeah, they die too soon back there. Even the fishermen, who can hold their breath for three minutes and more in the underwater corrals. They herd schools of tuna between two long fences offshore that narrow down to an arrowhead near the shore. Then, with a fence "gate," they quickly close the fish into an arrowhead-shaped enclosure, and then spear them. The men die too soon."

"Why?"

"They say, too much exercise. My people say their labor kills them."

"I don't understand," said Gloria.

"Yes, I'm wondering as well. Here, we hear that **lack** of exercise kills. I want to learn more about this. I want to talk with people."

"But, hey, Rima, are you going to be **allowed** to go? What about those guys who you said keep following you? It was probably those ICE men again who we saw walking at Edgewood, right?"

"Probably. But Alec told me not worry about them. And back to Alec—that is, my former son-in-law..." She pointed to her left index finger.

"Oh, yes, him. Well, he did help you get away from the ICE, didn't you say? For awhile, anyway."

"He told me they'll follow me to make sure I don't have a bomb to plant, and then they'll want to make sure that I really get on that plane tomorrow."

"Tomorrow **already?** So you're not going up to the ICE office in San Francisco?"

"No, remember, Alec said to stay away from that office, in case someone there would decide to detain me to keep a watch on me."

"Oh, Lord. So, tomorrow night?"

"Yeah, the PAL flight leaves at midnight."

"And how about Alec?"

"Well, we'll just find out if he and Sofie continue to communicate. I think; I **think** that he can be trusted. And now, I think Tess will remain calm." They drank, their coffees now half gone.

Then silence fell as they watched a young man dressed in bicycle gear—padded black shorts, Shimano shoes with clips that clicked on the floor, wearing a multi-colored, multi-advertisement shirt—who held the door open for his maybe four-year-old daughter to exit. He balanced a little box holding two hot drinks in his other hand. His daughter jumped into a chair next to an outdoor table. Rima noticed their bicycles and their helmets padlocked together in the bike rack near the smiling dog.

"So how about your Glenn, my dear?" asked Gloria, as she placed her elbows onto the table, her hands under her chin, her eyes in steady contact with Rima's.

"Yeah, hmm. Well, And I need time to think. I'd have to leave my teaching position and my homeland. And my going back to the Philippines will give him time to think about us. I don't want him to "rescue" me from my tourist visa overstay by marrying. I also need good will from his mother and his children."

"**That** might be too much to hope for. On the other hand, it's not nearly as tense as the Montague and Capulet families, in *Romeo and Juliet,* you know, who gave much stiffer resistance; surely you and Glenn can overcome **his** family's doubts!" Gloria laughed.

"Well, let's see what happens. I wouldn't call this the romance of the centuries. But," Rima blushed, "if I **would** return, especially with this CIS hold on the immigration visa that Tess sent in for me, I'd better return with a fiancée visa. Of course I'm hoping not to get a five-year penalty for overstaying."

"Do you know the requirements for that kind of visa?" asked Gloria.

"Well, I actually looked it up. Six months to set it up, and on arrival, must marry within 30 days."

"Oh, goodie, I'll help!"

"Oh, thank you, Gloria. If, if! I haven't decided yet."

Their coffee was almost gone by now.

Rima held up her fingers again, and with her right pointer, touched her left fingers, saying, "Sofie, Tess—and Alec—ICE and Philippines, Glenn." She held her pointer finger on her right thumb.

"What **does** work is running: the training, the events, and most of all, running with friends." She reached for Gloria's hand to squeeze it.

"Yes," smiled Gloria. "Yay, California!"

"Yeah, it's harder to run in Zamboanga or Manila. There, I'd have to start out well before dawn, and the timing is awkward."

"Because of the heat?"

"Yeah, immediately when the sun comes up, it's too hot and humid. And it's harder to be 'weird' there, because that's how I'd be seen, with all the pressure of the relatives. They think a respected older woman like me shouldn't be getting sweaty or running in the dark when it's cooler. And it's also scary when the *multu* are out."

"*Multu?*"

"Ghosts. It's a Sanskrit word."

"Sanskrit? That's Indian, isn't it?"

"Sanskrit. Oh, I'll explain another day."

Gloria sat back and looked at Rima from another perspective. "So, running is high in your thinking."

"Yes, who would have ever thought that my new... hobby? pastime? ... would emerge as a most optimistic focus in these later years of my life?"

"You know? Maybe by now for me as well."

"You've showed me the way," Rima continued, "so now I'm focusing on something I'm not especially good at. Hey, how did that happen?"

"But you qualified for the Boston Marathon, and then finished it, and in just one year."

"I'm still in the back of the pack."

"You'll win more. Mainly you'll have fun, and you'll be healthy."

"As you know, when I started running, I had one big goal: to get Sofie back on track in high school, and the path took her to Boston."

"And you got yourself there in the process!"

"Right."

"And now what?"

"You know, that big goal is finished—achieved—but I still want to run." Rima tipped her cup high to drain the last drop of coffee.

"Hey, you're deciding for running! And I hear you, on your reasons to return to the Philippines. I sure hope you'll come back soon! Hey, let's go. We'll have a quiet dinner at my house."

They stood up, grabbed their jackets and car keys, dropped their cups and napkins into the trash, and left the coffee shop.

4-15. Runs in the Family
Thursday, April 24, 2008

"You won't believe what I just did," Sofie said, as she tossed her backpack into the trunk of Tiffany's BMW 328i convertible.

"What?" Tiffany impatiently waited for Sofie to climb into the passenger's seat, and they zoomed off for the Dish.

"I just said another 'goodbye' to Raoul—I mean, **really** goodbye, like I'm really so over him."

"Oh my God! I thought you'd already completely dumped him. Where? When?"

Sofie knew that Tiffany loved all matters related to romance. "Right back there, in the parking lot, at his car, with all his friends."

"Oh my God, in front of everyone? Was he mad? Humiliated?"

"No, he went over and put his arm around two girls who were leaning on his car. But you know, at noon, they had all cheered for me at the rally."

"That was big of him."

"Yeah. But this afternoon they were all pretty mellow. Puffing, inhaling herb."

"Well, goodbye, Raoul, goodbye high school! ... Hey, have you gotten any, you know, acceptances yet?"

"Nope, of course, my dear Tiff, I'd call you right away! But I can't wait. How about you, have you heard any?"

"No, no one at school either. So what's your biggest hope?"

"Oh, I think Oregon. You know, Steve Prefontaine, Nike shoes started there. Maybe I can play with the big kids."

"Oh, I hope you get in there, Sofie."

"Tiffany, your mom has helped me so much. And she just sent an update about the Boston to all my applications, didn't she."

"Yeah, she says your success on the Boston will punch up your apps."

"And, you know, I'm a hard one to help, because, you know, my grades went down last year."

The stoplight turned green, and Tiffany zoomed out ahead of the car in the next lane.

"Remind me of who you're waiting to hear from, again?"

"Well, your mom advised me to apply to several, and not just in California. Let's see: Florida State is ranked number three for women's cross-country, and Princeton is high, but I'll never get in there."

"Yeah, but you know, I kinda hope you get into Princeton, because it's the only university we both applied to. Wouldn't it be out of this world to go there together?"

"The only other ones on the east coast are Villanova and Georgetown. On the west coast, the very top ranked is Washington, so I applied there, and Oregon is number two. Then, Stanford is number 12, but I'll never get in there either. Boy, everyone in my school applied to at least 12 schools; same at yours?"

"Oh yeah. And where else?"

"The others are in the middle of the country: Minnesota is sixth in cross-country, Michigan is eighth, Wisconsin is tenth. And yours again, Tiff?

"I'm waiting for 12.

"If you get in to Princeton, Tiff, you gonna try out for cross-country?"

"You know, I don't think I want to run anymore."

"Oh, Tiff, you can't drop out."

"Well, you know, I don't want to be a full-time jock. And besides, I'm not good enough. And it just doesn't do for me what it seems to do for you."

"I was afraid of this."

"I have to confess to you, I didn't put "cross-country" on my apps. And, as you know, I haven't been a starter on my soccer team, so I didn't put down any sport."

"You had already decided that way back in January, when you sent in your applications?"

"Yeah."

"Oh, Tiff, you've been such a good running buddy."

"Yeah, you too. But we're probably going to be leaving each other anyway, going off into the big world."

"Yeah, yikes!" They both squealed "eeee!" into the wind of the open top.

Tiffany parked. With no one nearby, they changed their clothes in the car and walked over the San Francisquito Creek bridge and through the gate to the Stanford University protected hill to head up to the Dish.

Tiffany said, "Oh, I can't wait to hear, the suspense is killing me! How about you?"

"Yeah," Sofie said, dreamily, for she was thinking about her big transitions ahead. She shook herself into politeness. "How about you—I mean, besides Princeton? Where are you most hoping for?"

"Well, you know that I have a legacy from Mom at Wellesley and from Dad at Stanford, but those places are real long shots."

"Do you want to leave California?"

"It's exciting, but scary. Aren't you scared?"

"Yeah, I guess we'll never see all our high school classmates together again."

"And we'll know a lot more in just a week."

They started running. "Oh, I'm still sore! How about you, Tiff?"

"Not too bad, but I did just 13 miles in Boston, you know."

"Well, let's just walk, okay?"

So they passed the eucalyptus grove and walked up the first steep hill, the first of four hills on this loop above the university campus. Some 10 heifers grazed on the spring grass in the afternoon sun, and, while chewing their cud, they lazily looked around at the two young women.

"So my *lola* is going back to the Philippines tomorrow

night. We'll take her to the airport."

"Oh, I bet you're gonna really miss her."

"Yeah. She told me this morning that one way or the other she has to leave the country in order to enter with another visa."

"So, is she coming back?"

"She didn't tell me everything."

"That Glenn friend of hers seems like a nice guy, and it looks like he's really fallen for her."

They looked up into the huge radar dish on their right as they turned left to the three-mile loop on the hilltop. "Do you notice, you hardly ever see birds up there on the dish?"

"Yeah, maybe they don't like its electric hum."

"Oh, look, there's a pretty clear view today. Look way over there! You can see Lick Observatory up on Mt. Hamilton." She pointed to the east. They both admired the panoramic view of the Stanford University campus in the foreground, and the peninsula and the bay.

"Yeah, today we can see the tall buildings in San Francisco over there," Tiffany pointed to the north, "and even Oakland." She pointed to the northeast. She paused, and then said "Uh, Sofie, I have something else to say to you."

"Sure."

"I'm **so** sorry I was so critical about your father. I didn't even meet him, you know."

"No, you didn't."

"And I was so naive. I mean, I didn't even **think** about how it might have been for you all these years, not knowing him."

"Yeah, that's all right."

"Or even what it's been like to not have a dad."

"Yeah."

"I mean, I get mad at my dad sometimes. He doesn't even much like that Mom runs—says it's not dignified. But at least he's always around. And besides, you haven't had a dad's income."

"Yeah, we've managed, though."

"Well, I mean, your mom has taken good care of you, being a nurse and all." Tiffany stopped and turned to Sofie, who politely returned her gaze. "Oh, Sofie, can you ever forgive me for being so dumb? I guess I never really thought what it'd be like; you always seemed to be managing fine."

"Sure, Tiff. How could you know?" Sofie kneeled down to tie a tight double bow in her shoelace. She stood up and said, "Of course I forgive you, dummy." She held Tiffany's shoulder and gave a pretend blow with the other hand, in a fist. They laughed.

"So, what are you gonna do now? Are you gonna see him again?"

"I'm sure I will.... I'm trying to decide what to do. He didn't seem like as bad a guy as I had thought...."

"How will you know?"

"Well, I guess only time will tell.... You know I don't believe in love at first sight." They laughed again.

Sofie added, "But I am astounded that he's a runner."

"Yeah, how'd **that** happen?"

"What do you mean?"

"That you're both runners. I mean, it must be nature, not nurture. Or did you ever hear before that he was a runner? Maybe it was planted in your brain at an early age?"

"I can't remember ever hearing that. I can ask my mom or my grandmother, if they ever told me. But I don't think so."

They ascended the second hill of the course. Down a side track they saw the two smaller radar dishes, both silent. *Are they still functioning?* wondered Sofie. The two continued walking on their loop while admiring the bay, the university, and now to their south, even the city of San Jose.

"What does it mean to you, Sofie, that your father is a runner?"

"Well, I wonder if it's more than a coincidence that I love running."

"Sure, you were born to run!"

"Maybe. But maybe more important than that, it means something good about his character, maybe same as with other athletes."

"Like, he's an early riser?" Tiffany laughed at her joke.

"Well, probably for him, running helps him like running has helped **me.** Maybe even **you.** We've talked about this before, right, Tiff? Yeah, getting up early to run, and...."

"Working very hard. Very hard," said Tiffany.

"And keeping at it, day after day, month after month."

Tiffany took her turn. "Trying to overcome pain, sickness, setbacks...."

"Visualizing success. That's a real important one. And completing action toward a goal."

Tiffany added, "And you told me that he's been training other, younger people."

"And, don't forget, runners are mostly unpretentious."

Tiffany laughed and said, "Yeah, it's all out there: very little clothing." They laughed together.

They carefully walked over cattle crossing bars on their way back down to Tiffany's car.

"Now, I have to wonder what I've thought all these years."

"You mean about **him?"**

"I mean about both parents. I'll leave mom in four months, and now I'm wondering about her, now that I've seen him. I've always felt pretty sorry for her. Guess I'm wondering about both of them now."

A soft breeze caressed their bare arms and dried their perspiration. In the broad meadows now on each side of their track, ground squirrels sat in front of their burrows and watched the two young women. Small white butterflies appeared to playfully chase one another.

"Sofie, I shouldn't have said what I said on the plane last night. I guess I've been mad at him ever since you and I got to know each other."

"Yeah ... me too, but now, the timing is hard."

"How do you mean?"

"I mean, *Lola* is leaving tomorrow, just when I'll be leaving home soon myself, and I'm wondering about my mom, why she and he couldn't work it out.... But he still abandoned her when she was new to this country and pregnant. I don't know if I can ever get over that."

4-16. He Ran Out on You
Thursday, April 24, 2008

Sofie was pleasantly surprised to see her mother's car in the driveway. "Hi, Mom ... hey, you're cooking! Smells good!" She tossed her backpack into her room and returned to the kitchen. "Want some help with the vegetables? And where's *Lola*?" She grabbed an energy drink out of the refrigerator and sat down on a bar stool at the counter. Her mother placed a knife, cutting board, and green beans before her.

"Sure. Plenty of vegetables for our *bihon* [thin "Chinese" rice noodles] tonight. It's just the two of us; your *lola* left a note that she's over at Gloria's and so she won't be back for dinner."

"So if you have to, you still know how to cook," laughed Sofie. "I thought you forgot how, after *Lola* arrived."

Tess laughed, and said, "I came home early to hear all about your day and to talk with you, *Nene*."

"Great," responded Sofie, who was well under way with her trimming of the green beans, on the diagonal, four centimeters long, just the way her mother liked them.

"So tell me about your day." Tess carried the pot of noodles to the sink and held the lid to the tilted pan in order to drain the water.

"Oh, Mom, they treated me like a returning hero!"

"Oh. I wish I had been there." Smiling, Tess gazed at Sofie.

"I kind of liked it, but I was kind of embarrassed, too."

"Glare of the spotlight, hmm."

"You won't believe it, Mom. They had a pep rally for me at noon in the quad—cheerleaders, student newspaper cameras, and an interview with a microphone. It lasted only about five minutes."

"Wow," said Tess, and beamed at her daughter.

"You know, even Raoul and his friends cheered for me,

and you know that I kind of dumped him after I started training for Boston."

"Hmm," frowned Tess. "He's still in school? So what did they ask in the interview?"

"Well, first, they told me that the coach—the **coach**— Coach Ramirez, on marathon day had a monitor set up in the quad. And so when the kids showed up for school early Monday morning, they were showing my live progress on the screen every five kilometers, and I was already an hour into the marathon. And they saw the TV coverage of the front runners."

"This was a **very** big deal for your high school, then," said Tess, her eyes wide with wonder. "I guess I hadn't realized."

"Yeah, and then they told me that my finish in Boston came during the ten o'clock class break, and a **lot** of students went out to the quad. And Coach told them that the teachers would let them come late into their next classes."

"Oh, so what did they ask in the interview at lunchtime, *aking mahal?*" Tess checked on her pot of rice, steaming on the stove. She cut up an onion and two garlic cloves, put coconut oil into the pan, and added the onion and garlic to sauté and caramelize. She looked lovingly at her daughter.

Sofie responded, "Let's see. They asked, 'How was the marathon? Was it hard?' and, 'How many other high school kids ran?' I told them just six in total. And 'How many runners in all?' I told them 25,000. And 'Did you get to meet the winners?' I told them that I had heard that the elite runners were treated like royalty, and that the rest of us didn't even see them."

"This is fun! When will it be in the school newspaper?"

"Tomorrow. Oh yeah, they asked if I am going to continue to run in college and how I got into running?"

"So what did you say?"

Sofie finished trimming the beans and started on the carrots. She chopped them into four-centimeter lengths also, and then turned them 90 degrees and brought the blade down horizontally with both hands onto each length several times to make very thin sticks.

"I told them, 'Sure, I love running now, and I want to run for a college varsity cross-country team.'"

"Oh, I hope you get into your very favorite college," Tess said, and gave her shoulders a squeeze from behind. "But what did you do after school? You had a few hours."

Sofie put down her knife and turned to look at her mother. "Now don't get mad, Mom. I agreed to meet Raoul after school, out in the parking lot with his friends."

"Oh, no." grumbled Tess. "You didn't get stoned on the school grounds!"

"Well, I didn't, Mom. They invited me to 'El Tulense' for a taco and an *horchata* [cinnamon-rice milk drink], but I told them I was already booked."

"Booked into what?" Tess snorted.

Sofie ignored her sarcasm. "Tiffany picked me up out on Middlefield Road, and we drove up to the Dish for our first recovery run."

"Oh, **that's** healthier! But I thought you said Tiffany didn't finish the marathon."

"She didn't, but she still ran the first half, and she still did all that training."

"The Dish! The view is so beautiful from up there, isn't it! And not just of the Stanford campus; I bet you could see all around because it's so clear today."

"Yep, it was good. But we walk-ran slowly. It took more than an hour, the five-and-a-half miles.... And you know, Mom, Tiffany says she doesn't want to run in college. She didn't put it on her college apps."

"Oh, too bad. Is her mother real disappointed?"

"I think she's known for awhile. She read the applications before Tiffany sent them off."

"Hmm." Tess had started the sauce for the *bihon* with soy, vegetable broth, and a *kamoteng kahoy* [tapioca] thickener, and let it simmer while she continued to beam at her daughter.

Sofie stopped her carrot-stick cutting. *God, she's paying attention to me today! I like it, but does she care for me only when I'm successful?* She turned toward her mom again. "And you know what else, Mom?"

"What, *Nene*? asked Tess, absent-mindedly stirring her sauce with a wooden spoon.

"You know what?" she repeated. "I told them that I met my father there, and that he was a volunteer on the course, and that he had run the Boston in the past."

Tess was quiet for a moment and then said, slowly and carefully, "I've been thinking since you told me last night. You have the right to see your dad."

"So you're okay with this now? I know we've both had a night's sleep...."

Tess turned to her daughter, her eyelids red and filled with tears. "Yes, I've been thinking."

"Oh, *Inay*!" Sofie stood up to put her arms around her mother.

"Oh, can you ever forgive me, *Nene*? Can I ever forgive myself? I thought I was acting in your best interest, but now I see I just closed off the topic from myself **and** from you."

"But *Inay*, you told me he thought he wasn't the father—my father. He insulted you."

"Yes, I did tell you that. I felt he so insulted my integrity, so how could **he** be a person of integrity? I needed to protect myself from him, and that meant that I needed to protect **you** from him as well."

She searched for a Kleenex. Sofie grabbed two from

the bathroom, and they both tried to dry their eyes and
cheeks.

Tess continued. "Maybe it was all a mistake.... I
pushed it all out of my head; I thought I could be both
parents to you. I tried."

Sofie put her arms around her mother's shoulders.
"You've done your best, Mom."

"All these years that I've had to work hard at the
hospital to support you, I've been unavailable to you.
Maybe I've been unavailable emotionally because I had to
keep up the solid front of a single mom."

She chopped an onion and two garlic cloves, tasted,
and then sprinkled salt, while adding, "Mostly I didn't even
have a boyfriend all those years; besides, in general, men
are put off by a woman with a child."

"Oh, *Inay,* but now you have Steve in your life. And
hey, are you making soup for tomorrow, too? That's your
second cutting of onions!"

They both laughed, and they hugged again.

"I even thought maybe Steve could be a substitute
father for you, but ... the step-relationship rarely works
out well."

"No, but he's nice to me," Sofie offered.

Tess kept talking while Sofie softly patted her back.

"I hadn't been thinking of **your** right to see your
father."

Sofie sniffled, found a Kleenex, and progressed to
audible sobbing. Tess squeezed her arms tighter around
Sofie's shoulders. She was quiet again, and then she said,
"I never took you to the Philippines because I couldn't
figure out how could we sneak in and see **my** family and
out again without seeing **his** family? And of course there's
the cost: the airfare, the *pasalubong.*"

"Sofie, I've deprived you of your father. All these years,
I thought **he** deprived you of a father. Today, I see that I
was the one."

Sofie pushed her mother to arm's length in order to
look into her eyes. "But *Inay,* you told me that he
abandoned you, that you never had further contact from
him. He ran out on you, right?"

Tess looked away, then back to her daughter's eyes, and then away again as she pushed Sofie's arms down to her sides. Again she looked away, out the window, and then back to her daughter. "Sofie, I have something to tell you."

She remained silent, looking at Sofie. "Yes, *Inay*?" Sofie finally asked.

"He sent several letters, and I sent them all back, unopened. He even sent several after you were born."

I'm not going to let her know he told me. He didn't know he was ratting on her. Sofie's eyes and mouth opened wide, and then she closed them again.

"Wh … why…?" she asked, her voice breaking. She turned away from her mother and looked out the window at the dimming daylight, and then turned to put her arms and head down on the counter. *She got it out; she **did** have the courage to tell me!*

Tess let Sofie have her time alone and went about finishing preparation of their dinner. She steamed the beans and carrots for a couple of minutes. She tossed the *bihon* noodles into the soy-onion-garlic sauce, which bubbled quietly and thickly, and then she added the beans and carrots. After a short wait, she spooned steaming rice into two deep plates, filled them with the stir-fry vegetables, and placed the plates on the dining table.

"*Halika dito,* come here, *Nene',*" she said softly, and sat down. Sofie slowly stood up, mopped her face with a Kleenex, brought two glasses of water to the table, and sat down.

They ate in silence for a short while.

"I've been stubborn. Your *lola* told me that, years ago."

Sofie quickly looked up with surprise. "Did she know back then?"

Tess interrupted her. "I don't know what all she's known, but I think she's been silent all these years because she felt it's my business, not hers. Probably it's been very hard for her to keep quiet. I've been stubborn, too stubborn to have listened to her, and she's wise enough to know that. Too stubborn for my own good, and for yours."

They both ate in silence, using their flatware in the Philippine way, with the fork for pushing and the spoon for lifting.

Tess said, "Maybe I've been kind of stubborn about your running as well, or at least disinterested. At first I thought it would take your mind off your studies, and you were already distracted by that, that..."

"Well, you know that my grades have gone up this year."

Tess smiled. "Yep. But now I see that it might even have enhanced your chances of getting a good scholarship, maybe even get accepted into a major college. These American colleges are so different for me, with their interest in athletics."

Sofie added, "Maybe running has helped me get away from Raoul as well. I know you'd be happy about **that!**"

"Hmmpf! **and** his self medication!"

Sofie turned away and rolled her eyes to herself. *Would she ever believe that "that stuff" never did me any harm? I'll just keep my lip buttoned. It helped me run—at least train—in the beginning. Couldn't take it across the border to Portland; saw I didn't need it there; maybe not anymore.*

"Sofie, on a bright note, you conquered a major challenge, finishing the Boston! Your whole school is delighted with you. So are your mother, and your *lola*, and your friends."

"Mmm-hmm," Sofie smiled.

"And next week or the following, you'll get responses from colleges and scholarships, and you'll be off to college in …" she held up a finger for each month she named, starting with her little finger, "… May, June, July, August: four months."

"Oh my God, four months! But, uh, first I have to graduate. Oh, too much, *Inay!*"

"Have you thought about what you'd like for your graduation present, *anak ko?*"

"Uh … uh … to graduate?" And they both laughed. "Uh, were you thinking of something?"

"Well, you know that your *lola* will be returning to the Philippines."

"Yes. Oh, did she tell you about the ICE?"

"Yes. If the CIS let her, she'll leave tomorrow night for Manila."

"Yes. I'll miss her, terribly."

"Me, too…. Well, I was wondering if you'd like to follow her there for the summer, to Manila and even down to Zamboanga, after you graduate. You could visit your father's family as well, in Manila. In order to run down there in the tropics, the two of you would have to get up well before dawn, but you'd have each other as companions."

Sofie looked up toward the ceiling, put her fingertips on her mouth, and then broke into a big smile and grabbed her   mother   for   another   long   hug.

4-17. They Ran Her Down, Again
Friday, April 25, 2008

"SFO departure hall at night, *Inay*, is like a long, slow-mo bad dream with no end."

Tess helped Rima load her suitcase and cardboard box onto a trolley, and the three entered the great, somewhat dimly lighted, hall.

"Oh my God, look at the lines! And what enormous suitcases and boxes," said Sofie.

"*Siempre*, everyone taking lots of *pasalubong* home, like I have," said Rima.

They had arrived at seven o'clock for the nine p.m. PAL flight; so many flights across the Pacific would depart between nine and one a.m. Little children waited long past their California bedtimes with their families, a few of them crying or impatiently running around. The bulk of the people would have to wait, just wait. The three women joined one of the long lines, and within a few minutes, several other families stood behind them.

An hour later, when it was finally her turn, Rima was told by the PAL ground attendant that one of her bags was too heavy. She motioned to Rima to put her bags on the floor in order to rearrange them. The three women found space to hunker down and work down by the feet of all those other waiting people.

"This is the heaviest," whispered Rima, and she picked up a dense package of three wine bottles wrapped in plastic and clothes, all tied tightly with twine. Out of the smaller of the two bags she pulled clothes, and she worked to replace them with the wine package. Sofie quietly said, "And this is heavy; what is it?" looking into a plastic bag holding small electronic items and wires. "Oh, your travel clock, and let's see, your California cell phone and some ear buds." She handed the bag to Rima, who quickly tucked it in near the wine bottle package.

At a loud, deep "Ms. Masuhud?" the three women looked up along two pairs of dark suited legs to two men looking down at Rima, each holding out his CIS badges at her. "Please come with us." They waited impatiently for her to stand up, and one took her arm and led her away. The other man said, "You, too, Miss," to Sofie.

Oh, Dios mio, what now? thought Rima. *Well, we'll just patiently endure this, too. I sure hope they don't cause me to miss the flight.... Sofie's probably more scared than I am, poor dear.*

Tess looked after them with a concerned expression, then back down at the bags. She hunkered down again to complete the rearrangement, closed the bags, and then stood up, bags next to her legs, and waited.

A moment later, two airport attendants, Bluetooth devices at their ears, rushed in with a luggage cart and a beagle on a leash. Four guards ordered the others in line to stand aside. The dog sniffed the bags. The attendants and the guards hurried the cart and the dog outside, the dog continuing to sniff as he trotted along beside the bags.

In the meantime, Rima and Sofie were taken to a small room. "So what do you have in your bags, Ms. Masuhud?" demanded one.

"Masushud Osorio are my surnames, sir," Rima said.

"Just answer, please."

"Three bottles of Napa wines for my relatives in Manila," she answered.

"Hmm. What else?"

"Clothes only."

"Anything to declare to us?"

"Nothing. Oh, I will declare the wines in Manila, and maybe I must pay import duty."

"You would do well to inform us immediately of anything else ... **or**..." he said dramatically, "we can just wait to hear from the guards."

They waited. Just a couple of minutes later, one of the guards knocked on the door, and then after a short period of quiet talking, a CIS official quietly but impatiently said, "You are both allowed to go. Your bags are being delivered back to the head of the line."

What do those looks mean? Rima wondered. The two CIS men had glanced at one another after freeing Rima and Sofie. *Boredom? Defeat? No, I know!—Humiliation. Humiliation for the airport guards, that they had caused a false alarm. Hah!* She and Sofie rushed back to the front of the PAL line where Tess still stood, receiving Rima's two huge bags from the guards.

They hugged, they gave Filipino kisses, they cried, and they wiped their tears. They smiled over their promises that Sofie would be on this same flight in just nine weeks.

Finally in the air, Rima looked out the window into the night. Leaning against the little window to see back toward California, she saw the moon, now in its last quarter phase, just rising above a few sparse San Mateo coast lights receding into the dark.

She settled herself in for sleep. But she couldn't sleep. Experiences of these last few days ran into her head: the Boston, the ICE, her last talks with her dear friend Gloria, with her daughter, her granddaughter, and especially with her Glenn. *Oh, oh, did I do the right thing?*

4-18. Beyond the Blue Horizon
Friday, April 25, 2008

Glenn, so far away now, but just a few hours ago…

Glenn parked his car near Mavericks, north of Half Moon Bay and the site of world championship surfing contests in February. The previous night's fog was finally burning off, retreating back to the ocean, and allowing the late morning sun to shine on their backs. He and Rima walked alongside the still water of the harbor with its myriad small fishing boats, which were protected by a breakwater. The bay was a favorite place for dogs to chase tennis balls thrown out by their humans. The trail led them just a quarter mile along an earthen path above the sandy shore, and they approached the open ocean. Out here only a few sharp rocks jutted out of the waves near the shore, rocks that enhanced the danger of the Mavericks surfing competition.

Glenn and Rima shuffled through the soft sand toward the shore. They breathed deeply to inhale ocean smells, they saw seagulls, they saw kelp strewn on shore with its tiny hovering flies. With a somewhat low tide, they easily selected a dry stretch of sand near the cliff, above and away from the rocky, seaweed-strewn shore. Glenn had brought a space blanket from his car, and Rima spread a tablecloth over it; they had happily grown accustomed to this teamwork. He placed her picnic basket to the backside of the ground cover, and with an expectant smile, asked, "What do you have in here?"

Rima knelt down on the ground cover and opened the basket for Glenn to see. "I brought a Filipino picnic for you. Let's see." She pointed out *"bihon* noodles with tiny slices of carrot, parsley, sautéed and onions, and here are *lumpia*. Tess had all of these fixings for us on our return from Boston, and, I think, to prepare me for tonight's flight to Manila. And these are *lanzones* in their thin yellow-gray skins, very easy to peel. And in this container we have mango cubes and banana circles. And you can choose a drink; this thermos holds hot Ceylon tea, and in these little cartons the coconut water is cold." She closed the basket and they sat in front of the little nest they had made together. "I love to smell this ocean," she said. "It smells quite different from our Philippine seas."

"How?"

"Well, the seaweed, the birds, the fish, and even these shells," and she picked up one from the sand, "they're different. Temperate, I guess, not tropical."

"Oh, Rima, you really are going, aren't you?"

"Yes, and I wanted to share the food with you."

He grabbed both of her hands in his. "It's very hard to let you go."

"It's very hard to leave you. I'll miss you terribly." She moved up onto her knees and faced him.

"Will you come back and marry me?"

She squeezed his hands and continued to look into his eyes. "I can't answer right now."

He looked away from her, out to the ocean and to the fog bank, now far off shore. "You're going beyond that wide blue horizon."

"Glenn, dear Glenn, will you wait for me, for a little while *lang* [only]?"

"Tell me, how long must I wait?"

"Oh, the timing is already part of the structure. "

"How do you mean?"

"I mean, to change my visa, even if I come back to marry you," *Marry—shocking; I said the word!* "I would have to leave this country in order to come back with the new visa. "

"That could be just for a day to Vancouver, couldn't it?"

"Not coming from the Philippines—too many have disappeared here—and especially because I've overstayed my tourist visa by a week. It would take six months to get any new visa. And that's if they don't penalize me for overstaying these few days."

"Six months!" He looked out toward the ocean again, and then back to her.

"Of course I'll wait for you." He squeezed her hands again. "And what will you do during all that time, my dear?" he said as he pulled her toward him, his arms around her shoulders.

"Oh, a lot. I have to think about leaving behind my home country. That'd mean retiring early. I'll visit relatives and friends in Manila and down in Zamboanga. I'll think about my way of life there, and how it would change by coming here and marrying."

He smiled lovingly. "Your family must be very proud of you."

"Yeah, I've been a success story in Zamboanga, I'm embarrassed to say. I became a schoolteacher, and I went to Manila, even California. But now in my twilight years, I've become a runner. I run even though I'm slow. They'll be wondering 'what's happening with her?' And I'm even wondering, myself."

"You're very brave." He smiled, admiringly.

She smiled back. "Oh, and I want to see how hard it is to run in Manila and in Zamboanga; your temperate climate is surely much better for running."

"Oh, so **running** will bring you back," he teased.

She smiled. "I want to give you time to think as well."

"I already know, my dear. I want you to come back to me." He pulled her toward him again.

She resisted. "About your fam—." She thought, *Finally, I'm bringing up the biggest problem.*

He interrupted her. "About my family. You know that my mother has been ... distant. But she's been loosening up."

"Oh?" Rima looked at him with an inquiring smile.

"Do you know that she used live tracking to follow the four of you on the Boston?" She was rooting for all of you."

"No!"

"True! And we had a long talk while you were in Boston. I told her about my feelings for you and that I had asked you to marry me. You know what she said?"

"No, what?" Rima was surprised that he had gone this far. *I was worried that he wasn't this brave.*

"She said, 'I've been noticing how cheerful and lighthearted you've been, how caring of me, your old mother! And I figured it's because you love that woman.' And then you know what she said?"

'What did she say, Glenn?"

"She said, 'You have my full blessing. I think she brings out the best in you. I'm happy for you, and I'll do my best to understand her different ways.'"

"How brave, how very honest of her to acknowledge that she's had difficulty accepting me."

"I thought so. And my children, they're fine. They like you, they both told me."

"Well, they may be relieved to know that I'm going tonight and that you didn't rush into something to rescue me from my tourist visa problem...." She looked around the beach, and then back to Glenn. "You know, I wouldn't be able to stand tense relations with your family. I'm very relieved to hear your report.... And we'll learn if their blessings hold over these months." *I can't sob over this. Bite your cheek, Rima, be tough!*

"I think their blessings will hold up. And I know about my own feelings; I know I've found the love of my life." He pulled her toward him; they hugged, kissed, and hugged again. Rima rested her face in the nape of his neck.

Soon she pulled back to look into his eyes. "My reasons to return here are very strong, of course."

"Tell me."

"You, of course. And my daughter. Even with her Steve, she may be lonely as a new empty nester, with Sofie going off to college."

"Oh, and of course you'll miss **her**."

"I sure will. But we'll be in touch and we'll probably meet at a marathon now and then."

"The running..."

"And the running. California weather is better for running. I hadn't known that running would become such a big part of my life...." She suddenly turned to face him again. "Can you handle that?"

"Of course I can; I'll be your best support. Oh, I was

kind of nervous at first, but I see that happy glow on your face each time you return from a run. I see that it makes you happy, and I suppose it does help keep you healthy."

"This has been quite a year for me. I felt a big hollow in my life the day after the Boston. Then the goal was met. You know that Anais Nin poem?"

"No, which one?"

The dream was always
Running ahead.
To catch up, to live
For a moment
In unison with it,
That was the miracle."

-Anais Nin, *Quotes*

"But then what? The dream was finished."

"Finished?"

"But then I figured out, I want to keep running."

"You know what, Rima? I know you'll come back to me!"

"Oh, this wind is chilly; hold me close." She snuggled closer to him.

Glenn opened his jacket, and said "Come inside here" and wrapped it around her back. He softly said, "Let's warm up at my house."

Rima giggled. They kissed, and then a longer kiss. "Can you get me home by four?"

GLOSSARY

Words are English unless otherwise indicated.

Tag.= Tagalog, one of the official national languages in the Philippines, now officially called Pilipino. One of the larger of the Austronesian Family of languages. The language family, before the European global conquests, was spread across the earth's surface—about 1/3 of the globe—more than any other language family , from Easter Island in the East to Madagascar in the West, and from South China in the North to New Zealand in the South.)

(Austr = Austronesian language family)

< : Comes from the language following this symbol.)

… … … … … … ….

Aking mahal: my dear <Tag.

Ako rin: same here < Tag.

Allah Akbar: God is great <Arabic

Ama: father <Tag.

Ampalaya: bitter cucumber < Tag.

Anak: child. **Anak ko**: my child. term of reference or address: any child, one's offspring, or address to a young(er) person < Tag.

Ang nanay ko: my mother < Tag.

Anting-anting: Good luck talisman < Engl., Tag.

AP: Advanced Placement: advanced "college level" high school course.

Apo: grandchild < Tag.

Apong baba'e: granddaughter < Tag.

Aray!: Oh my! < Tag.

Avenidas: Senior Center of Palo Alto, California

B.A.A.: Boston Athletic Association

Bagoong: fermented fish paste < Tag.

Bahay kubo: nipa (nipa palm thatch-roofed) hut <Tag.

Bakasnen: Leavings < Austr.

Balikbayan: the return home trip <Tag.

Bandit: non-registered runner of an organized event.

Bantay: chaperone < Tag.

Barrio: neighborhood < Tag. < Spanish

Basura: garbage, trash < Spanish

Bayan kong Pilipinas: my dear Philippines < Tag.

Binalaki: tomboy < Tag.

Bituin: star(s) < Tag.

Biyenang: mother-in-law. Formal. <Tag.

Bihon: thin "Chinese" rice noodles

Bisayan: Central islands of the Philippines. Person from the Bisayan islands.

Bok choy, cf. pechay: leafy green vegetable < Tag. (Cantonese?)

Boondocks: rural areas. Engl, < Tag.

BQ: Boston Qualifier. A marathon finishing time fast enough to qualify for the Boston Marathon.

Buck's: The famous restaurant in Woodside, California. Its owner, Jamis MacNiven, declares that more high tech businesses have been started at Buck's tables than anywhere else in the US.

Calamansi: tiny lime-like citrus, size of a cherry < Tag.

Cassis: black currant < French

Ceylon tea: A red tea grown and processed in Sri Lanka. Its desirability in the Southern Philippines comes from its association with traveling to Mecca on the Hadj, the religious ritual hegira to the seat of Islam in Saudi Arabia. Rima served it to her husband and daughter in Tess's early years in Manila, and Tess knew it to be unusual, drinking "Muslim" tea in the Christian environment of Manila. Muslims live mainly in the southern islands of the Philippines. Those who make the Hadj to Mecca in Saudi Arabia, usually by ship, pass by Sri Lanka and buy the tea there. On return home, after the big adventure, they give some packages of tea as gifts.

Chirimoya: a tropical fruit. Cf. guayabano. < Spanish

CIM: California International Marathon, held first Sunday in December, Folsom to Sacramento

CIS: (US) Customs and Integration Services. (See ICE,

INS)
CSU: California State University
Cytomax, Gatorade: two of many brands of energy drinks
Dahil sa iyo: raison d'être, most important purpose in life. < Tag.
Damo: marijuana < Tag.
Daw: allegedly, tag word, <Tag.
Despidita: Going-away party < Tag. < Spanish
DHS: (US) Department of Homeland Security
Difunto esposo: deceased husband < Spanish
Dios mio: My God, mild expletive. Cf. dios ko.< Tag. <Spanish
Dish, The: A hill on the west side of Stanford University in California, on which is positioned a giant radio telescope and several smaller ones. A 5-mile loop walking trail and a 360o vista surrounded by the university on the east side, by residential property on the north and south, and the Freeway 280 on the west side, make it a relatively natural oasis in the Peninsula's suburbia.
Dis: criticize, speak disrespectfully to or about someone, or to disparage someone/thing. < Am. Engl.
DNF: "Did Not Finish"
Double Dipsea: a 13.7 mile, hilly Marin County annual race
DSE Runners: Dolphin South Enders, San Francisco's oldest and largest running club, founded in 1964.
Duenya: chaperone Tag. < Spanish. Cf. Kasama, the one who accompanies, < Tag.
Ganja: marijuana. < Hindi
Garmin: sport watch brand with GPS capability
GPA: Grade Point Average
GU: sweet syrup in a 100-calorie wrapper. Cf. Power Gel
Guacamole: mashed avocado with garlic, salt, and chili Engl. < Spanish < Mexican Spanish
Guayabano: a tropical fruit. Cf. chirimoya < Spanish
Habagat: name of a prevailing west wind in the

Philippines, characterized by hot and humid weather.
< Austr. < Arabic

Hadj: formal religious visit to Mecca, the aspiration of every Muslim. < Arabic

Halika dito: come here! <Tag.

Hindi: no, not. Hindi ba? No? Hindi ko alam: I don't know. Hindi tamo: not wise <Tag, Sp.

Horchata: a Mexican cinnamon and rice milk drink

ICE: Immigration and Customs Enforcement (Cf. CIS, USCIS, INS) Most common currently used acronym for the federal agency and its agents.

Iha: daughter <Tag. < Spanish 'hija'

Imam: Muslim priest < Arabic

Ina, inahan, inay: mother Cf. nanay <Tag.

INS: U.S Immigration and Naturalization Services, former name of CIS

Inhaling, puffing: smoking marijuana

IT band: Iliotibial band of the leg.

Ituloy mo: continue < Tag.

Ka: you, singular. <Tag.

Kagalang-galang balo: venerable widow < Tag.

Kalma te: calm yourself <Tag. <Spanish

Kami: < Tag. We, not you. Cf. kita.

Kamoteng kahoy: tapioca < Tag.

Kamusta: Hello, How are you < Tag., < Sp.

Kanela: cinnamon < Spanish

Kang kong: swamp spinach, a leafy green vegetable < Austr.

Kasama: chaperone Cf. Duenya < Span.

Kita: you, plural < Tag.

Ko: I, my, mine <Tag.

Kolayet: lantern < Austr. (lampara in Tag. < Span.)

Korget: dynamite paste < English Colgate toothpaste

Kumusta: How are you? <Tag <Spanish

Kumpit: large motorized fishing boat < Bisayan

Kuting: cat < Tag.

Lagay: bribe < Tag.

Lang: only, just. De-emphasis marker. <Tag.

Lanzone: small lichee-like appearing tropical fruit. < Tag. smooth white translucent sections inside an easily peeled shell, each section wrapped around a large smooth seed. Looks kind of like a potato. Taste is more sweet and sour than lichee, without the mellowness of the lichee taste.

Lentes: reading glasses < Tag< Spanish

LLSA: Leukemia and Lymphoma Society of America, major promoter and trainer of marathoners, especially first-timers, since ca. 1988. Cf. TNT; formerly LSA.

Lola: grandmother <Tag.

Lolo: grandfather < Tag.

Lumpia: thin "pancake" of rice flower, wrapped around vegetables and possibly meat. < Tag. Frequently eaten with a thick soy dipping sauce.

Mabuhay: greeting (hello, goodbye). Formal. (<Tag.)

Macapuno: young fresh coconut meat < Tag.

Magkalma ka: calm down < Tag., Span.

Mahal: dear < Tag.

Maligaya: happy < Tag.

Malikot: restless < Tag.

Maraming: much, many, a lot of <Tag.

Masjid: mosque < Arabic.

Maverick's surfing competition: this almost-annual competition takes place, usually in February, when the waves grow to some of the tallest in the world, peaking at a height of eighty feet.

Mem Chu: Memorial Church, Stanford University. Called so by students since its dedication in 1903

Mestizo: mixed, person of more than one race. < Span.

Metate: stone grinding mortar < Spanish

Mga /manga/: approximately < Tag.

Milikano: American < Tag. < Spanish < English

Minamahal: dear, beloved. Cf. mahal. < Tag

Multu: ghost < Tag < Sanskrit

Naku! Aha! < Tag.

Nanay: mom < Tag.

Nene': young girl. Frequently used as address, term of endearment. < Tag.

Ng: /nang/, possessive marker <Tag.

Nipa: a palm tree < Tag. <Latin Nypa fruticans. The only palm which adapts to the mangrove swamp biome. Its leaves are widely used, e.g., for roofing of traditional houses. Its trunk grows horizontally, underground, and only the branches and leaves rise above the ground.

Nobyo: boyfriend, fiancé < Spanish 'novio'

Ohlone: California Bay Area tribes of Native Americans.

Oo: yes (pronounced like "oh oh") < Tag cf. oho (yes, by younger, respectfully, to elder)

P.A.: Parent Alert (computer texting acronym)

Pan de sal: "salt bread" < Tag. < Spanish

Pasalubong: gifts to family and friends on return from a trip. < Tag. The total price of these typically exceeds the airfare cost.

Pechay, cf. bok choy. Leafy green vegetable <Tag. < Cantonese

Philippine kiss: closed lips next to the recipient's cheek, near the recipient's ear; strong, audible inhalation

Pilipina: Female Filipina. < Tag. < Spanish -a. Pilipino: male Filipino.

Pinoy: Filipino, -a < Tag.

Porta-Potty: portable toilet (™ > generic).

Power Gel: sweet syrup in a 100-calorie wrapper. Cf. Gu.

PR: Personal Record.

Queen Wilhelmina Windmill: one of two Dutch-gifted windmills in Golden Gate Park, San Francisco.

Radjo balagung: bamboo radio, slang for fast travel of gossip. < Yakan, a southern Philippines language

Rin: also < Tag.

Sakol Island: A small inhabited island to the SE of Zamboanga City, Philippines. At the tip of Mindanao Island, 600 miles to the south of Manila.

Salamat: thank you (<Tag. < Arabic)

Sasakyan traffic: plenty of traffic < Tag.

Sayang: sorry <Tag.

Siempre: of course, surely < Tag <Spanish "always"

Sige: continue (< Tag. <Spanish sigue

Sus: Jesus, as mild expletive <Tag. <Spanish

Susmaryahosep: Jesus, Maria, and Joseph (y todos los santos) (and all the saints). Mild expletive. <Tag. <Spanish

Talaga: really < Tag.

Tama: wise < Tag.

Tapus na: finished; I did it. < Tag.

TGIF: "Thank God it's Friday"

TIA's: Transient Ischemic Attacks: tiny strokes.

Tita: aunt <Tag.< Span. 'tia'

Title 9: Federal law requiring public school funding for sports be divided equally for boys' and girls' sports

Tito: uncle < Tag. < Span. 'tio'

TMI: Too much information (computer texting acronym)

TNT: "Team in Training," the endurance-event organization of the LLSA. Their "password," on seeing another runner wearing their iconic purple shirt, is "Go, team!"

Tong: payoff money in mahjong gambling < Tag. < Fukien Chinese 'Chinese Secret Society"

Toong nagdurusa: suffering people < Tag. And Span.

Totoo: certainly, surely < Tag.

Tupara: eye goggles for underwater, sometimes homemade, of coconut husk and recycled glass. < Austr. Cf. 'antipara' in Tag.

UC: University of California

UP: University of the Philippines, Manila

USCIS: United States Citizenship and Immigration Services. Cf. ICE

VO2 Max: The maximum amount of oxygen that one's body can process in a given period of time (and then maintain, over an endurance event).

Wala' iyo: I don't know <Tag.

Zamboanga: A city and province in the Philippine Islands, 600 miles to the south of Manila. One of three

main cities for Muslims in the Philippines, who comprise
seven percent of the nation's population.

REFERENCES:

Athlinks.com: runner's individual records, sorted by chronology, distance, pace, and placement

BAA: Boston Athletic Association: organizer of the Boston Marathon

Dr. Walter Bortz: Stanford University and Hospital M.D., author of many books on health, including *Dare to be 100*.

Rev. Elizabeth Myer Boulton, reverend of Old South Church, Boston

Buck's Restaurant. Celebrated restaurant in Woodside, California, owned by Jamis MacNiven.

Amby Burfoot: editor at large of *Runners' World*. Author of many seminal articles, including 2011 qualification ratings for the Boston Marathon. Quoted Don Quixote: "We all need to pursue…" in his book *The Runner's Guide to the Meaning of Life,* 2007.

ChiRunning, by Danny Dreyer, 2004. Simon & Schuster, NY.

T. Colin Campbell, 2005 *The China Study*. BenBella Books. From the China-Cornell-Oxford Project. Oxford U. Press.

Jim Furman > Jen Furman: transgender Marin County front runner featured in *Runners' World*.

Hal Higdon, *The Gigantic Book of Running Quotations*. Skyhorse Publishing, NY, 2008. Quote by Jim Ryun, p. 110.

Helen Klein, (ultra) marathoner who lives in Carmichael, California. World's record holder, F85, marathon, in 2008.

Fred Lebow: Founder of the New York Marathon, in 1970. The next year, he allowed women to officially register, a year before women could register in the Boston Marathon.

LinkedIn: communication website

Little Brown Brother, by Leon Wolff, 1961. Doubleday, New York.

LLSA, LSA: Leukemia and Lymphoma Society of

America. Trains people, mainly newcomers, to run marathons, since 1988. (Cf. TNT.)

Make Way for Ducklings by Robert McCloskey, Viking Press, NY, 1941.

Marathonguide.com, John Elliott, founder.

Marin Independent Journal: newspaper, San Rafael, CA.

Anais Nin: *The Quotable Anais Nin.* Collected and compiled by Paul Herron. Sky Blue Press, 2014.

Philippine Star, San Francisco newspaper, in English and Tagalog

PattiSue Plummer, U.S. Olympic runner in 1988 and 1992. Born in 1962, she now teaches at Gunn High School in Palo Alto, California.

Steve Prefontaine: Univ. Oregon, who competed in the 1972 Berlin Olympics, and died at age 24.

Psalm 121:1 "I lift mine eyes..." Holy Bible, King James version.

Romeo and Juliet by William Shakespeare, 1597.

Runners' World: world's leading running magazine, founded in 1966, now owned by Rodale Pres. Amby Burfoot was editor from 1980's until 2003; now edited by David Willey.

Running Times: Magazine for serious runners, Jonathan Beverly, editor; Rodale Press.

Joan Benoit Samuelson: winner of the first Olympics women's marathon, 1984, Los Angeles, CA.

George Sheehan, *Personal Best*, 1989, Rodale Press.

Sports Speed, by George Dintimian, Bob Ward, and Tom Tellez, forward by Leroy Burrel, 1977. Human Kinetics Press, Champaign, Ill. 61825.

Kathrine Switzer, first registered woman to run the Boston Marathon, in 1967. She registered with "K.V." – like she signed her college essays. With initials only, organizers didn't know she was a female. The race director passed by her, saw her long hair down her back, from his bus, ca. Mile 2. He jumped out, grabbed her to pull her off the course. Her (male) friends – fellow runners – pulled her back on. She completed the course, the first registered female runner to finish. Five years later, in 1972, the B.A.A. finally allowed women to register.

Henry David Thoreau: *Walden*, 1854.

TNT: "Team in Training," the sports training branch of the Leukemia and Lymphoma Society, founded in 1988.

Whitepages.com: national record by telephone number. In 2007-8 mostly free; now usually for fee.

SONGS:

(In order of appearance):

For All We Know, 1934. Music by J. Fred Coots, lyrics by Sam M. Lewis.

Bahay Kubo, Tagalog Folk Song.

Summer Nights, from the musical comedy *Grease,* 1971, film 1978.

Blowin' In The Wind, by Bob Dylan, 1963.

Today We're Younger Than We Ever Gonna Be, by Regina Spektor.

Messiah: Oratorio By George Frideric Handel, 1741

La Vie En Rose, written and sung by Edith Piaf, 1945.

We Are Going, Old South Church, Boston. 2010(?) Composer Unknown.

You'll Never Walk Alone, from the musical *Carousel,* 1947, by Rogers & Hammerstein.

Old Black Joe, by Stephen Foster, 1853.

In The Long Run, by the Eagles, 1980. Songwriters Don Henley And Glenn Frey.

Beyond The Blue Horizon, by Leo Robin and Richard A. Whiting, 1942.

LIST OF CHARACTERS

- Karima (Rima) Masuhud Osorio, 59, on a tourist visa from the Philippines to Redwood City, California.

- Teresa (Tess) Osorio Ayala, Rima's daughter. 39, naturalized American citizen, RN at Sequoia Hospital in Redwood City, divorced before Sofie's birth.

- Sofie Ayala, Tess's daughter, 17, junior at Menlo-Atherton High School. Plays on a CYSA recreational soccer team and is on the M-A track and cross-country teams.

- Alec Ayala, 40, ex-husband of Tess. Attorney in real estate in Boston.

- Gloria Kent, 54, distance runner for many years, lives in Atherton, CA with her family.

- Tiffany Kent, 17, junior at Menlo School, a private high school. Plays on her school soccer team and on a CYSA recreational soccer team,

- Stanley Kent, 56, Gloria's husband and father of their son and Tiffany, their daughter.

Fellow runners: Larry, Keith, Leonard, Nancy, Julie, others
High school coach: Coach Ramirez
Sofie's boyfriend: Raoul
Tess's boyfriend: Steve
Rima's deceased husband: Paolo Osorio
Rima's deceased uncle: Samad

ABOUT THE AUTHOR:

Carol Hodson Pechler started distance running at age 59. She says, "I ran away from the abyss of 60," after noticing her standing leg shaking in the morning as she stood to put the other leg into her pants. She wondered if such an old body could still build muscles, one accustomed to sitting at a desk writing university lesson plans and academic articles.

A friend invited her to take a short run. Then, later, becoming a distance runner herself, she came to believe that "any couch potato can become a marathon finisher." She investigated expert reports about running, but wondered, "where's the advice for seniors?" The lack of information stimulated her to write this novel about an older woman, a woman who accidently discovers the world of distance running, and how entering this world affects her life.

Carol Pechler, Ph.D.

www.ingramcontent.com/pod-product-compliance
Lightning Source LLC
Chambersburg PA
CBHW030552260626
47157CB00006B/2280